U0091894

Tourism English
Marketing

旅遊營銷英語

王向寧 主編

崧燁文化

目 錄

Part III

References 參考書目

前言

本教材以營銷知識為構架、以旅遊知識為引證和案例、以英語語言為表達方式、以學習運用英語表達營銷知識為目的,試圖透過基礎與專業相結合、知識與技能相結合的途徑,力圖全面提高學生旅遊英語綜合運用能力,為順利閱讀和理解專業原著打下紮實的基礎。

學生在學習本課程之前應已完成基礎階段的英語學習,具備了一定的聽、說、讀、寫、譯的能力,同時對旅遊和營銷專業的基礎知識有一定的瞭解和掌握。

本教材分為三大部分,由旅遊營銷基礎知識逐步過渡到具體旅遊業要素的營銷,共有33課,可供一學年常規教學使用。需要說明的是,本教材不同於系統的營銷著作,它的每篇課文獨立成章。教師在組織教學時,可根據學生的具體情況有所側重,課時分配也可因校而異,建議每課用2～4課時完成。

本教材在課文材料的選擇上力求注重典型性和代表性,突出介紹中國國內外旅遊營銷發展的現狀和趨勢。但由於篇幅所限,而且近年來旅遊營銷發展變化迅速,各課內容不可能面面俱到,教師在授課過程中可以補充一些最新的資料給學生,以期跟上時代的發展變化。

本教材在編寫過程中,參閱了大量的旅遊管理專業和營銷專業的著作和教材(詳見參考文獻),由於選材廣泛,書中沒有一一註明出處,希望得到原作者的支持和諒解,並接受我們誠摯的謝意!

本書由王向寧副教授擔任主編,具體分工如下:

第1、2、3、20、31、32、33課由王向寧編寫;

第6、9、10、13、26、27課由徐明宇編寫；

第4、22、23、24、25課由韓鴿編寫；

第7、12、15、28、29課由陸萍編寫；

第11、14、16、17、30課由程維編寫；

第8、18、21課由王元歌編寫；

第5、19課由馬振濤編寫。

目前，關於旅遊營銷方面的專業英語教材尚不多見，此次編寫是編者對此領域的初步嘗試，因此還望廣大讀者和業內專家多就本教材的編排模式及內容的不足回饋意見，我們定將透過修訂來不斷完善本教材。

編者

Part I

Lesson 1 Marketing and Marketing Mix 營銷與營銷組合

導讀：

市場營銷的職能是識別消費者的需求和慾望，確定企業最能滿足其需求的目標市場，並設計出與這些市場相適應的產品、服務及相應的計劃。可以說，營銷在我們周圍無處不在，任何行業和個人都需要懂得一些營銷知識，而營銷組合又是營銷知識中最為重要的概念之一。本文將首先介紹營銷概念，然後詳細闡述傳統意義上的營銷組合四要素，即4P，同時論述它們在旅遊行業中的運用。此外，本文還將介紹旅遊行業中特殊的4P延伸組合。

What Is Marketing

Marketing is perhaps one of the most overused and least understood terms. The most important concern is that everyone involved needs to be quite clear that marketing is an approach, not just a concept. There are many definitions of marketing, but Lyndsey Taylor's acronym sums up the key characteristics and messages that genuine marketing should concern:

◆ Meeting customer needs;

◆ Attracting new customers;

◆ Reacting to market trends;

◆ Keeping up with competitors;

◆ Encouraging customer loyalty;

◆ Targeting specific customers;

◆ Identifying market opportunities;

◆ Noting customer feedback, getting it right every time.

Traditional Marketing Mix

One of the most basic concepts in marketing is the marketing mix, defined as the elements an organization controls that can be used to satisfy or communicate with customers.(註1) The traditional marketing mix is composed of the four Ps:

◆ Product — design, quality, range, brand name, features;

◆ Price — price list, discounts, commissions, surcharges, extra;

◆ Place (distribution) — distribution channels, methods of distribution, coverage location;

◆ Promotion — advertising, sales promotion, salesmanship, publicity.

These elements appear as core decision variables in any marketing plan. The consideration given to each element will vary from one event to another, but on each occasion all four elements need to be balanced. Balance cannot be achieved if any one of them is ignored.

Marketing Mix in Tourism Industry

Tourism industry belongs to service industry, and services marketing is different from goods marketing.

Product

The product is what is actually delivered to the consumer, and will be composed of both tangible and intangible elements. For example, the consumer will be buying the use of a room in a hotel as part of their package, and this will include various facilities including a bed (whose comfort is all-important), a bathroom, perhaps a balcony or terrace, coffee-making equipment, etc. The guest may also choose to eat in the hotel's restaurant, so food is another key tangible component of this experience. However, there are intangible elements in each hotel which add to the satisfaction of the experience(註2) — the hotel room may include a sea view (an intangible asset that is seen as such a bonus that a higher price is usually charged for this(註3)), the ambience of the public rooms may meet a guest's individual needs for status-building or relaxation, or the room may be decorated in a way which enhances their satisfaction. The professional manner in which the front of house staff(註4) deal with the incoming guest, and the service received from waiters in the restaurant, are intangible benefits which are every bit as important as the rooms and food.

Price

Price refers to the amount of money eventually paid for the product or service by the consumer. In tourism, price is often variable and negotiable with the consumer seeking to obtain best value for money between a range of competitive products on offer(註5). Product and price are inextricably interconnected, together representing the bundle of benefits that the consumer purchases. From the standpoint of the producers, price is the figure at which they are prepared to make the product available to the consumer, taking into account cost, market conditions and other factors such as sales targets(註6).

Place

Place is a controversial variable in considering the tourism product. In general marketing theory it represents the point of sale, i.e. the place where the product can be inspected and purchased, and the means by which it is delivered to the consumer. In tourism, however, place is often defined in terms of the channels of distribution of the product(註7). Traditionally, tourism products would be purchased through travel agents or through the outlets of travel organizations, but in recent years the advent of new forms of delivery system, particularly in the use of computer technology, has vastly expanded the choice in delivery systems for tourists.

Promotion

Promotion is concerned with the techniques by which products and their prices are communicated to the marketplace. This includes advertising, sales promotion techniques, public relations activities, direct selling and the use of more recent forms of reaching the customer through ICT (information and communications technology). Of course, there are overlaps in these concepts, given that both place and promotion involve communicating and delivering messages about products to the consumer(註8), but perhaps if we accept that the former refers to the process by which the product is presented, and the latter to the techniques of persuasion to buy the product, the distinction between these concepts will be clearer(註9).

Four Extended Ps in Tourism Marketing

In addition to the four Ps mentioned above, some people argue that a further four Ps should be added to the original list. They are:

◆ People,

◆ Process,

◆ Physical evidence,

◆ Productivity and quality.

People

Tourism is a service product, and employees are therefore an integral part of that service — whether we speak of the travel agent selling the package behind the counter, the resort representative aiding customers in their chosen resort, the air cabin crew caring for their passengers en route to the destination, front of house staff in the hotel where the customers are staying, or the local guide interpreting sites on excursions at the destination. Arguably, no other service depends as much for its satisfaction on the quality of personal service provided by so many different human participants in the package(註10).

The interrelationships between fellow tourists are also crucial for the success of travel experience. Similarly, tourists come into contact, to a greater or lesser extent, with members of the host community, and these local interrelations form another key element of the experience. These interrelations may be limited to commercial contacts with shopkeepers, guides, restaurant and bar staff, etc., as is often the case with mass-market package tours (especially of the all-inclusive variety), but independent travelers may enjoy more personal contacts with locals, through conversations on public transport, in bars, caf　s and the like.

Process

Some experts hold that process is actually the service delivery process which focuses on the various encounters between the tourists and representatives of the travel organizations, and in particular the "critical incidents" in such encounters which ensure satisfaction. The ability of employees to turn round a negative experience by appropriate handling, and to deal with complaints as they arise, is crucial in such encounters(註11). Tourists find themselves in unfamiliar situations where they will need help more frequently than is likely to be the case on their home grounds(註12), and the ability of staff to step in and ease this process is immensely important for overall satisfaction.

To illustrate this, one might consider the uncertainty about whether or not to tip in foreign settings, the problems facing the confused tourist at a congested airport or what is the required protocol for purchasing a ticket on a foreign bus or underground railway(註13) (often a surprisingly complex process for foreigners, involving canceling the ticket in a machine when boarding the vehicle, within a given period of time, etc.). The clarity with which this information is imparted and the help given to resolve this complexity by locals will be a significant factor in the overall satisfaction level of the tourist.

Physical Evidence

Physical evidence involves all of the cues received by the tourist experiencing their flight, package or other service, based on sight, sound, smell, touch and taste. One might cite elements of the package embracing the design of buildings, the taste of a meal, the sound of taped music in a hotel lift — all without doubt elements of the product but ones which it is difficult to quantify to customers in advance(註14). All are nevertheless features subtly designed by the marketing team to enhance the experience of their customers.

Productivity and Quality

Productivity and quality are considered by some marketing theorists as important elements in which inputs are transformed into outputs that are valued by customers, and successfully meet their needs, wants and expectations. Identifying this as a separate issue reinforces the importance of monitoring costs to find ways in which products can be delivered to customers more cheaply, without reducing the quality that customers rightly expect from the product(註15).

Vocabulary 內文詞彙

marketing mix　　　　　　　營銷組合

approach　　　　　　　　　方式，手段

acronym	只取首字母的縮寫詞
service industry	服務行業
tangible	有形的
intangible	無形的
balcony	陽臺
terrace	露臺，陽臺
coffee-making equipment	製作咖啡的設備
ambience	周圍環境，氣氛
status	身分，地位
enhance	提高，增強
variable	可變的，易變的
negotiable	可透過談判解決的，可商量的
inextricably	不可避免地，無法擺脫地
controversial	爭論的，爭議的
point of sale	銷售點，零售點
travel agent	旅行社，旅遊代理商
outlet	門市部，銷售點

advent	出現，到來
physical evidence	有形展示
integral	構成整體所需要的，不可或缺的
en route	在……途中
excursion	遠足，遊覽，短程旅行
host	接待地，主辦方
mass-market	大眾市場
inclusive	包含的，包括的
step in	走進，插手幫助
ease	減弱，減輕
impart	給予，傳授
satisfaction level	滿意程度
productivity	生產力
transform	轉換，改變
reinforce	加強，增加

Notes to the Text 內文註釋

1.One of the most basic concepts in marketing is the marketing mix, defined as the

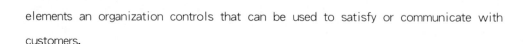

elements an organization controls that can be used to satisfy or communicate with customers.

營銷學中最基本的概念之一就是營銷組合，它被定義為企業可以控制的、能夠用來滿足顧客需求或與顧客溝通的多種元素（組合）。

2.However, there are intangible elements in each hotel which add to the satisfaction of the experience.

然而，每一家飯店也都有很多無形的因素，這些因素可以增加顧客的滿意程度。

3.an intangible asset that is seen as such a bonus that a higher price is usually charged for this：這是一種無形的資產，它經常被看做是一種獨特的優勢，因此這樣的客房的房價定得就（比普通客房）高。

4.the front of house staff：一線人員，前台服務人員。

5.In tourism, price is often variable and negotiable with the consumer seeking to obtain best value for money between a range of competitive products on offer.

在旅遊業中，顧客要在眾多有競爭力的產品中挑選出最物有所值的產品，因此產品的價格經常是變動的、可以協商的。

6.price is the figure at which they are prepared to make the product available to the consumer, taking into account cost, market conditions and other factors such as sales targets：價格是生產者準備將產品讓與消費者時的價錢，確定價格時要考慮成本、市場狀況和銷售目標等因素。

7.In tourism, however, place is often defined in terms of the channels of distribution of the product.

在旅遊領域中，地點通常指產品銷售管道。

8.there are overlaps in these concepts, given that both place and promotion involve communicating and delivering messages about products to the consumer：由於管道和促銷都涉及與顧客溝通和向顧客傳遞產品資訊這兩個方面，所以它們之間在概念上有交叉。given：鑑於，考慮到。

9.but perhaps if we accept that the former refers to the process by which the product is presented, and the latter to the techniques of persuasion to buy the product, the distinction between these concepts will be clearer：但是，如果我們理解為前者指的是展示產品的過程、後者指的是勸說顧客購買的技巧的話，這兩個概念之間的區別就清晰了。

10.Arguably, no other service depends as much for its satisfaction on the quality of personal service provided by so many different human participants in the package.

可以説，沒有任何其他服務會像包價旅遊服務這樣，滿意度如此取決於人的服務品質，而且這種服務是由數量如此眾多的不同人群提供的。

11.The ability of employees to turn round a negative experience by appropriate handling, and to deal with complaints as they arise, is crucial in such encounters.

員工透過恰當的方式來扭轉不利情況，以及處理顧客投訴的能力，在這些交往中是很關鍵的。

12.Tourists find themselves in unfamiliar situations where they will need help more frequently than is likely to be the case on their home grounds.

旅遊者在身處陌生環境時，要比在其本國環境中需要更多的幫助。

13.To illustrate this, one might consider the uncertainty about whether or not to tip in foreign settings, the problems facing the confused tourist at a congested airport or what is the required protocol for purchasing a ticket on a foreign bus or underground railway.

要説明這個問題，我們可以想像一下如下情形：在國外時拿不準應不應該給小費，一個困惑的遊客在擁擠的機場會碰到的問題，或者在國外的汽車或地鐵上有關購票的一系列問題。

14.One might cite elements of the package embracing the design of buildings, the taste of a meal, the sound of taped music in a hotel lift — all without doubt elements of the product but ones which it is difficult to quantify to customers in advance.

旅遊者可能會提到旅遊過程中所經歷的很多因素，如建築物的設計、飯菜的口味、飯店電梯裡播放的音樂等。毫無疑問，這些都是產品的組成部分，但事先卻很難透過量化將它們介紹給顧客。

15.Identifying this as a separate issue reinforces the importance of monitoring costs to find ways in which products can be delivered to customers more cheaply, without reducing the quality that customers rightly expect from the product.

把這一點單獨提出來，可以提醒企業重視透過控制成本，去尋找如何以更低的價格把產品提供給顧客，而不是降低顧客所期望的產品品質。

Useful Words and Expressions 實用詞彙和表達方式

| 交易營銷 | transaction marketing |
| 關係營銷 | relationship marketing |

無差異性營銷 undifferentiated marketing

差異性營銷 differentiated marketing

集中式營銷 concentrated marketing

目錄市場營銷 catalog marketing

直接市場營銷 direct marketing

一體化直接營銷 integrated direct marketing

人員推銷 personal selling

電話市場營銷 telemarketing

電視市場營銷 television marketing

創新式市場營銷 innovative marketing

直接營銷管道 direct marketing channel

非直接營銷管道 indirect marketing channel

傳統分銷管道 conventional distribution channel

水平營銷系統 horizontal marketing system

垂直營銷系統 vertical marketing system

混合營銷系統 hybrid marketing channel

互動式市場營銷 interactive marketing

營銷管理	marketing management
營銷觀念	marketing concept
營銷中間機構	marketing intermediary
營銷環境	marketing environment
顧客滿意度	customer satisfaction
競爭優勢	competitive advantage
市場擴展	market development
市場滲透	market penetration
市場定位	market positioning
子市場	market segment
市場細分	market segmentation
目標市場選擇	market targeting
消費者市場	consumer market
政府市場	government market
國際市場	international market
市場領導者	market leader
市場挑戰者	market challenger

市場跟隨者	market follower
市場填補者	market nicher

Exercises 練習題

Discussion Questions 思考題

1.What is marketing?

2.What is marketing mix?

3.How do you understand the marketing mix in tourism industry?

4.What is the extended marketing mix?

5.How can the element of "physical evidence" in tourism be explained?

Sentence Translation 單句翻譯練習

1.中國發展旅遊業的道路是先發展國際旅遊（international tourism），後發展國內旅遊（domestic tourism），先發展入境旅遊（inbound tourism），後發展出境旅遊（outbound tourism）。

2.飯店產品的核心和本質（core and nature）是服務，它包括服務項目、服務品質、服務設施以及服務環境。

3.旅遊服務是透過一次旅遊活動提供所需要的各種產品與服務的組合（combination）。

4.旅遊業主要由旅館業、飲食業、交通運輸業、旅行社業與遊覽娛樂業組成。

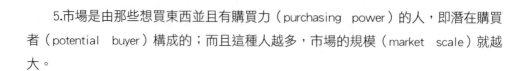

5.市場是由那些想買東西並且有購買力（purchasing power）的人，即潛在購買者（potential buyer）構成的；而且這種人越多，市場的規模（market scale）就越大。

6.有些市場營銷手段對提高市場份額（market share）很有效，卻不一定能增加收益。

7.一些學者把服務業市場營銷組合修改和擴充為七個要素，即產品、定價、地點和管道、促銷、人員（people）、有形展示（physical evidence）和過程（process）。

8.促銷組合是指企業根據需要，對廣告、促銷活動（sales promotion）、宣傳與人員推銷（personal selling）方式進行適當選擇和編配。

Passage Translation 段落翻譯練習

A market consists of individuals and organizations who are interested and willing to buy a particular product to obtain benefits that will satisfy a specific need or want, and who have the resources (time, money) to engage in such a transaction. There are markets sufficiently homogeneous that a company can practice undifferentiated marketing in them. That is, the company attempts to market a single line of products using a single marketing program. But because different people have different needs, wants, and resources, the entire population of a society is seldom a viable market for a single product or service. Also, people or organizations often seek different benefits to satisfy different needs and wants from the same type of product (e.g., one car buyer may seek social status and prestige while someone else wants economical basic transportation).

The total market for a given product category thus is often fragmented into several distinct market segments. Each segment contains people who are relatively homogeneous in their needs, their wants, and the product benefits they seek. Also, each segment seeks a different set of benefits from the same product category.

Lesson 2 The Nature of Tourism Services 旅遊服務的性質特點

導讀：

　　旅遊業是一個以出售勞務為特徵、憑藉固定場所的有形設施向旅遊者提供無形服務的服務性行業。它透過旅行社、飯店、交通、遊覽、娛樂等各方面人員熱情周到的服務，向旅遊者提供吃、住、行、遊、購、娛等方面的綜合服務。本文將在此基礎上詳細闡述旅遊產品和旅遊服務的特色。

　　Most industry produces either products or services; however, tourism industry is very different and unusual. It simultaneously produces both products and services. When a person walks into a travel agent's office to buy a tour — product — he is also buying many services. The travel agent will plan the itinerary for him, make his hotel and transport arrangement and handle his meals.

　　Tourism services differ from those of goods in many aspects. There are 6 main factors to be considered:

◆ Intangibility,

◆ Perishability,

◆ Parity,

◆ Inseparability,

◆ Complementarity,

◆ Heterogeneity,

Intangibility

The products of most industries are tangible. They can be seen, touched, and sometimes even smelled and tasted. For instance, when one buys a car, he can choose whatever color and make he likes(註1); he can examine it carefully and drive it for a distance as a test.

Tourism products, too, have some tangible components. There are spaces available at a specified time, such as a seat on a plane, train or bus, a room or bed in a hotel, a table in a restaurant. There are also goods that can be touched and used, such as meals, drinks, local products in a souvenir shop. On the other hand, there are intangible aspects in tourism products. Take an inclusive tour for example. An inclusive tour is a travel package that offers both transportations and accommodations, and often entertainment as well. For the greater part, an inclusive tour cannot be seen or touched. It cannot be inspected by prospective purchasers before they buy, as can a washing machine.

Since tourism products cannot be inspected or sampled in advance of their purchase, an element of risk is involved on the part of the purchaser(註2). This is a critically important aspect of the transaction. From one perspective, this makes marketing efforts much easier; none of the usual problems of physical distribution is encountered(註3), and there is no question of storing the product in warehouses prior to its delivery to the customer. For another, intangible products have many drawbacks. The fact that travel agents, for example, do not have to purchase their products before they sell them to their clients reduces their commitment to the sale and their loyalty to particular brands(註4). In place of a distribution system, the travel industry must deal with a reservation system, which is simply a method of matching demand with supply.

It has often been said that selling holidays is "selling dreams", and this is true to a great extent. When a tourist buys a tour abroad, he is more than buying an aircraft seat, a hotel room and opportunity to sit on a sunny beach; he is also buying the temporary use of a strange environment, novel geographical features — old towns, tropical landscape plus the culture and heritage of the region and other intangible benefits such as service, atmosphere and hospitality. The planning and anticipation of the holiday may be as much a part of its enjoyment as is the trip itself(註5), and the later recalling of the experience and the reviewing of slides or photos are an added bonus(註6). Tangible objects such as seats on an airplane, beds in a hotel room and food in a restaurant are used to create the experiences, but these are not what the customer is after(註7). Instead, the customer seeks for the intangible benefits — pleasure, relaxation, convenience, and excitement — that the experience can yield(註8).

Tourism marketers must attempt to overcome the drawbacks posed by an intangible product of tourism service. There are a number of imaginative ways in which this has been achieved in practice.

◆ First, take advantage of the advances in technology. The development of videocassettes, which produce a more faithful and more favorable image of the holiday product than can be obtained from a holiday brochure, will allow tourists to take a moving picture of their destination home with them to play back on their screens. And interactive television will take one step further in imparting an in-depth picture of a destination to the holidaymakers of the future.

◆ Second, introduce the idea of low-price "trial tour" to a destination(註9). Sometimes the fare charged will be refunded against the later purchase of a holiday(註10). In 1990s, the British company Airtours experimented with low-price short flights to help prospective passengers overcome their fear of flying.

Perishability

Tourism product is highly perishable. If the television set in the showroom is not sold today, it can be sold tomorrow, if necessary, at a reduced price. Or it can be stored and offered at a later date(註11). However, because the consumption of the services and their production occur simultaneously, tourism products have no inventory. An airline has a specific number of seats to sell on each of its flights. A hotel has a specific number of rooms available for each night of the week. If an airline seat or hotel room is not sold today, then the opportunity to sell is lost and gone forever.

This fact is of great importance for marketing, particularly when determining pricing. The heavy discounts on rooms sold after 6 pm and the "standby" fares offered by airlines to fill empty seats(註12) reflect this need to offload products before their sale potential is lost. The problem is compounded by the fact that the travel industry suffers from time-variable demand(註13). Often, holiday demand is concentrated in peak summer months such as July and August, and short trips are more likely to be taken at weekends than weekdays. Business travelers wish to fly at convenient time to them, whereas airports and airlines prefer to offer a balanced service around the clock to maximize the use of their resources.

This puts pressure on hospitality businesses to operate at as high a level of capacity as possible, hence great efforts are made here. One idea is to make proper pricing strategies that can help spread demand by offering substantial reductions during periods of low demand.(註14)

Parity

Some tourism products possess parity, which means that competing companies offer the same basic products.

A flight on one airline is very much like a flight on another. All airlines use similar equipment. In fact, they may fly airplanes manufactured by the same company.

Government regulations require all pilots to meet the same training standards. Even the food served on airlines is similar, very often having been prepared in the same airport kitchen. With standardization and chain or group management, hotels are becoming more and more similar. A tourist who stays with the Sheraton hotels may go through similar check-in procedures, have similar rooms, eat similar meals, use similar recreational facilities. As a matter of fact, if there is no dramatic change in external environment, he may not realize that he has been to different places.

The fact that so many qualities are the same is both an advantage and a problem for marketing efforts. Of course, parity is not a problem when the tourism product is unique. Therefore, many destinations and attractions, for instance, try to emphasize their built-in appeal that is different and remarkable(註15). Places such as Hawaii, the Eiffel Tower and the Statue of Liberty offer experiences that cannot be duplicated, and possess everlasting attraction for tourists all over the world.

Inseparability

Tourism services are highly personalized, and the product is the outcome of the performance of the seller. If we see, for example, an advertisement for a particular brand of TV set that we want to buy and the price is highly competitive, we are likely to visit the shop. If we find that the salesperson selling the television is unkempt and lacking interest, this alone is likely to dissuade us from making the purchase. However, transpose the same scenario to a restaurant or a hotel, our reaction will be very different. Whatever the quality of the food, however attractive the d cor, service is so much an integral part of the product that it would be unlikely for tourists to be prepared to purchase from such a poor representative. The travel agent who sells holiday, the airline cabin staff who cater to tourists' needs en route, the resort representative who greets us on arrival, the hotel's front office receptionist — all are elements in the product we are purchasing, and their social skills in dealing with tourists are an essential part of the product. It is for this reason that training becomes

so vital for the successful marketing of travel and tourism.

Complementarity

The purchase of one tourism product sets up a chain reaction of tourism purchases. As a result, what affects one product affects another, sometimes for better and sometimes for worse. If an airline that flies skiers to a resort changes its route or goes out of business, the ski resort's business will suffer. If fewer skiers are coming to the ski resort, there will be fewer customers for nearby restaurants and shops. The fortunes of these businesses are linked even though they may be separately owned(註16).

Due to this complementarity of tourism products, more and more tourism companies are working together on joint-marketing efforts in order to get a bigger share of the market. A fly/cruise package is a good example. In such a package, an airline, a cruise company and a travel operator join hands in designing a total travel product. In this way, both airlines and cruise company may have more clients; and the travel operators, by persuading local hotels, restaurants and facilities into giving better rates, may put together a package that will attract more tourists and make more profit of course.

Heterogeneity

Although there is parity between tourism products, they can not be exactly the same. In the first place, tourism is not a homogeneous product and it tends to vary in standard and quality over time. A holiday taken in a week of continuous rainfall is a very different product from one taken in glorious sunshine.

In the second place, heterogeneity tends to arise where service is involved. A consumer buying tourism is buying a range of services provided by individuals. Service is the experience for the guest and the performance of the server. The guest and server are both a part of the transaction. This personal element makes service quality control very difficult.

The server's behavior is, in effect, a part of the product. Since servers are not the same every day or for every guest, there is a necessary variability in this product that would not be encountered in a manufactured product. A guest who is not feeling well or takes a dislike to a member of staff may have a bad experience in spite of all efforts to please.

While good quality control procedures can help to reduce extreme variations in performance, they cannot overcome the human problems inherent in the performance of tourism services.

Vocabulary 內文詞彙

simultaneously	同時地
travel agent	旅行代理商，旅行社
itinerary	旅行計劃，行程
intangibility	無形性
perishability	易變質性
parity	相似，類似
inseparability	不可分性
complementarity	互補性

heterogeneity	多樣性
transaction	交易
warehouse	倉庫
inclusive tour / package tour	包價旅遊
accommodation	膳宿，住宿
prospective	潛在的，未來的
prior to	在……之前
drawback	缺點，弊端
distribution system	分銷系統
reservation system	預訂系統
novel	新奇的，新穎的
landscape	風景，景色
heritage	遺產，古蹟
brochure	宣傳冊，小冊子
impart	給予，帶來
holidaymaker	度假者
short flight	短程飛行

showroom	陳列室，展覽室
inventory	庫存
around the clock	日夜不停地，整天地
standardization	標準化
chain management	連鎖經營、管理
group management	集團化經營、管理
recreational facility	娛樂設施
external environment	外部環境
unkempt	不修邊幅的，不整潔的
dissuade from	勸（某人）不要做某事
transpose	使換位置
scenario	情景，事態，局面
cater to	滿足……需要，悉心照料
en route	在……途中
chain reaction	連鎖反應
out of business	破產
ski resort	滑雪勝地

joint-marketing	聯合營銷
cruise	巡遊，乘船旅行
rate	價格，定價
server	服務員，侍者
service quality	服務品質
inherent	內在的，固有的
tourism services	旅遊服務

Notes to the Text 內文註釋

1.he can choose whatever color and make he likes：他可以選擇自己喜歡的任何一種顏色和型號。

2.Since tourism products cannot be inspected or sampled in advance of their purchase, an element of risk is involved on the part of the purchaser.

由於在購買旅遊產品之前不能事先檢查或試用，所以對消費者來說就存在一定的冒險因素。

3.none of the usual problems of physical distribution is encountered：不存在實物分銷中的各種常見問題。

4.reduces their commitment to the sale and their loyalty to particular brands：減少了他們對特定品牌的責任感和忠誠度。

5.The planning and anticipation of the holiday may be as much a part of its enjoyment as is the trip itself：對度假的計劃和期待也許與旅行本身一樣給他們帶來快樂。

6.the later recalling of the experience and the reviewing of slides or photos are an added bonus：事後對旅遊經歷的回憶以及欣賞當時所拍攝的幻燈片或照片又增添了一番新的樂趣。

7.be after：對……追求。

8.the customer seeks for the intangible benefits — pleasure, relaxation, convenience, and excitement — that the experience can yield：顧客尋求的是無形的收益——如快樂、放鬆、便利和興奮——這些都是旅遊活動所能帶來的益處。

9.Second, introduce the idea of low-price "trial tour" to a destination.

第二，引進一種到目的地進行低價的「體驗式旅遊」的概念。

10.Sometimes the fare charged will be refunded against the later purchase of a holiday.

有時，收取的費用將在顧客後續的旅遊度假費用中退還。

11.Or it can be stored and offered at a later date.

或者可以將其儲存起來，以後再拿出來銷售。

12.The heavy discounts on rooms sold after 6 pm and the "standby" fares offered by airlines to fill empty seats：下午6點以後對房價打很大的折扣，以及航空公司為減少空位所提供的「餘票價」機票。

13.The problem is compounded by the fact that the travel industry suffers from time-variable demand.

這個問題由於旅遊業容易受到季節需求因素影響而變得更為複雜。

14.One idea is to make proper pricing strategies that can help spread demand by offering substantial reductions during periods of low demand.

一種做法是制定合適的定價策略，在需求較低的時候透過提供實在的折扣來擴大需求。

15.try to emphasize their built-in appeal which is different and remarkable：努力強調自己內在的與眾不同的、不平凡的吸引力。

16.The fortunes of these businesses are linked even though they may be separately owned.

儘管這些旅遊企業可能屬於不同的所有者，但是他們的命運是相互關聯的。

Useful Words and Expressions 實用詞彙和表達方式

旅遊散客	independent traveler
旅遊團隊	tour group
觀光旅遊	sightseeing tour
度假旅遊	vacation tour
專項旅遊	specific tour
會議旅遊	convention tour

獎勵旅遊	incentive travel
度假區	holiday resort
特種旅遊	special interest tour
遊覽地	place of sightseeing
餘暇	leisure time
修學旅遊，教育旅遊	study tour
入境旅遊	inbound tourism
出境旅遊	outbound tourism
過境旅遊者	transit traveler
境內旅遊	internal tourism
國內旅遊	domestic tourism
洲際旅遊	intercontinental travel
旅遊勝地	tourist attraction
包價旅遊	package tour
帶薪假日	paid holiday
大眾旅遊	mass tourism
包機旅遊	charter tour

旅遊經營商	tourist operator
國際旅遊者	international tourist
國際短程遊覽者	international excursionist
單程旅行	one-way trip
商務旅遊者，差旅旅遊者，公務旅遊者	business traveler
娛樂型旅遊者，消遣型旅遊者	pleasure traveler
旅行代理商，旅行社	travel agent
海濱度假地	seaside resort
度假地	destination resort
旅遊勝地	tourist resort

Exercises 練習題

Discussion Questions 思考題

1.In what way is the tourism industry different from other industries?

2.What elements of tourism services are tangible?

3.How do you understand the parity of tourism services?

4.In what sense are tourism products complementary?

5.How do you understand the heterogeneity of tourism services?

Sentence Translation 單句翻譯練習

1.旅行業在國民經濟（national economy）中的重要性可以透過其產值占國民收入（national revenue）的比例來衡量。

2.世界旅遊組織（World Tourism Organization）是當今旅遊業中最能夠得到廣泛承認的組織，該組織的總部設在西班牙馬德里。

3.餘暇（leisure）時間的增多，再加上收入水準（income level）的提高，人們要求去國內外旅遊的需求越來越多。

4.對於那些對異國文化（foreign cultures）感興趣的旅遊者來說，地理位置和是否有文化活動及其發生地點都將影響他們對旅遊目的地（tourist destination）的選擇。

5.透過旅遊，人們可以在世界各地交朋友、尋找和其他人的共同點，可以傳播期盼世界和平的願望。

6.隨著賓館、餐廳及其他旅遊者所需要的設施的建立，秀麗的鄉村風光被破壞了。

7.粗心大意的旅遊者在野餐地點等處亂扔廢物，在古蹟上亂刻亂畫造成視覺汙染（visual pollution）。

8.會議及獎勵旅遊（incentive travel）是近十多年來世界上發展迅速的旅遊產品之一，深受各國旅遊行政主管部門（tourism administration）和旅行社的青睞（appeal to）。

Passage Translation 段落翻譯練習

Tourism businesses are categorized by some people as direct providers, support services, and developmental organizations.

The first category, direct providers, includes businesses typically associated with travel, such as airlines, hotels, ground transportations, travel agencies, restaurants and retail shops. These businesses provide services, activities, and products that are consumed or purchased directly by the tourists. They tend to reflect those sectors of the tourism industry that are visible to the tourists.

Below the surface of direct providers lie a large variety of businesses lending support to direct providers. These support services include specialized services, such as tour organizers, travel and trade publications, hotel management firms, and travel research firms, and basic supplies and services, such as contract laundry and contract food service.

The third category, development organizations, is distinct from the first two in that it includes planners, government agencies, financial institutions, real estate developers, and educational and vocational training institutions. These organizations deal with tourism development, which tends to be more complex and broader in scope than production of everyday travel services, and involves sensitive issues regarding the environment, people, and culture of an area.

Lesson 3 Product Mix & Product Life Cycle 產品組合和產品生命週期

導讀:

擁有數個產品系列的公司都有產品組合的問題,經營旅遊業務的機構和公司也不例外。通常,一個公司的產品組合包含四個方面,即廣度、長度、深度和相配度。對產品組合因素的瞭解和分析可以幫助企業制定良好的營銷策略。同時，任何產品都有自己的生命週期，營銷人員只有充分掌握產品及產品組合的這一特性，才能在激烈的市場競爭中立於不敗之地。

Product Mix

Few companies produce a single product. Companies are therefore faced with making marketing decisions on the mix of products which they propose to offer to their customers. The product mix comprises the range of different product lines the company produces (the product width), together with the number of variants offered within each product line (the product depth). A white goods manufacturer, for example, will have to decide on the range of products it will manufacture (washing machines, dryers, dishwashers, vacuum cleaners, toasters, irons, etc.) as well as what options will be made available in each product — different motors, designs, capacity, colors and so on. Such decisions have implications for the whole marketing mix. Different products may be targeted at different market segments, for example, requiring different advertising and promotional strategies. Some products may be marketed in an intensely competitive environment, with consequent implications for pricing and profit margins. Some, because of technical complexity or other factors, will need exceptional sales back up, while others may be suitable for self-selection, affecting distribution strategies(註1).

In the manufacturing process, a critical factor is to what extent existing resources such as machinery and skilled labor can be used in making diverse products. If a machine has spare capacity and can be used in the manufacture of a new product line, this may make all the difference as to whether it will prove profitable for the company to make the new line.(註2) For each product line, the manger must be knowledgeable about the market: who is buying the product and why, how competitive it is against those of rival organizations(註3), what market share the product enjoys, the level of sales achieved, and the contribution it makes to overall revenue and profits. Such knowledge will enable further decisions to be made about new products: should existing products be strengthened or extended, should some options be withdrawn, should new product lines be introduced and should such products be consistent with the existing product range, or would it be better for the company to diversify into entirely new lines?

Just as with any other industry, most sectors of the travel and tourism business must also decide their product width and depth. A large mass market operator, to take one example, has to make a number of critical marketing decisions.

Although at first glance one might be inclined to think that a tour operating program is a single product line, in fact the nature of package holidays makes each distinct in its appeal to different market segments, satisfying different needs(註4). Large-scale operators have in the past tended to organize their products into separate divisions, under separate product managers, producing separate brochures, and often operating their range of holidays under different brand names, although the trend recently has been to reduce this diversification to bring products into line under a single brand(註5), but as we have seen, this has not always been successful. The Thomas Cook range, for example, includes Thomas Cook as the leading brand for principal products, with JMC brand restricted to families and young adults, Sunset as the budget brand(註6) and smaller-scale subdivisions such as Club 18-30, Nielsen and Style retaining their own brands. Within each of these programmers, decisions must be made on product depth: what holiday length to offer (3, 7, 10 or 14 days)? From which airports to operate? To which destinations and airports? How will the price of each product be determined in order to achieve the overall target profitability for the company?

Product lines may be "stretched" to encompass new market segments. Such decisions might be taken if the current market is experiencing slow growth, or the company finds itself increasingly under attack from the competition. A company at the bottom end of the market may find profits squeezed, and attempt to reposition its products further up the market to allow a greater margin of profit(註7); or a company which has focused on the upper end of the market may choose to widen its appeal by reaching a larger market, capitalizing on its reputation for quality in the top-market field. Such policies carry the inherent danger that the public image of the company and its markets may become confused, causing it to lose its niche and original marketing strengths. Some shipping companies, for example, in their attempt to widen their appeal to reach new mass markets for cruising, downgraded the product, thereby losing the confidence of their loyal, original customers(註8). It is interesting to note that this lesson has been learned and the experience acted upon — Carnival, now the world's biggest cruise operator, has been careful to retain the multiple brand names of the companies it has absorbed, which apart from the Carnival brand itself includes subsidiaries like Cunard, Holland America, Seabourn, Princess and Windstar, each with its own distinct target market.

Product Life Cycle

A product is much more than a combination of raw materials. It is actually a bundle of satisfactions and benefits for the consumer. Product planning must therefore be approached from the consumer's point of view. Creating the right product is not easy; because consumer needs, want, and desires are constantly changing. On the other hand, all products exhibit characteristic life cycles as follows (although the exact duration of a product's life cycle(註9) can never be forecast):

◆ Introduction,

◆ Growth,

◆ Maturity,

◆ Saturation,

◆ Decline.

Because of the rapidly changing consumer lifestyles and technological changes, the life cycle for products and services has become shorter, but the product life cycle remains a useful concept for strategic planning. Each stage of the product life cycle has certain marketing equipment.

The introductory phase of the product's life cycle requires high promotional expenditures and visibility. The most productive time to advertise a product or service is when it is new.(註10) Operations in this period are characterized by high cost, relatively low sales volume, and an advertising program aimed at stimulating primary demand(註11); in this stage of the life cycle, there will be a high percentage of failures.

In the growth period, the product or service is being accepted by consumers. Market acceptance means that both sales and profits rise at a rapid rate, frequently making the market attractive to competitors. Promotional expenditures remain high, but the promotional emphasis is on selective buying motives by trade name rather than on primary motives to try the product.(註12) During the growth stage, the number of outlets handling the product or service usually increases. More competitors enter the marketplace, but economies of scale are realized and prices may decline some.(註13)

The mature product is well established in the marketplace. Sales may still be increasing but at a much slower rate; they are leveling off. At this stage of the product's life cycle, many outlets are selling the product or service, and they are very competitive, especially with respect to price, and firms are trying to determine ways to hold on to their share of the market. The ski resort is an excellent example of a mature product. After years of spectacular growth, sales are now leveling off, and the resorts are looking for ways to hold market share and diversify.

In the saturation stage, sales volume reaches its peak; the product or service has penetrated the marketplace to the greatest degree possible. Mass production and new technology have lowered the price to make it available to almost everyone.(註14)

Many products stay at the saturation stage for years. However, for most products, obsolescence sets in, and new products are introduced to replace old ones. In the decline stage, demand obviously drops, advertising expenditures are lower, and there is usually a smaller number of competitors. While it is possible for a product to do very well in this stage of product life cycle, there is not a great deal of comfort in getting a larger share of a declining market. Hot spring resorts are a good example of a tourist product in the decline stage. These facilities, at their peak in the 1920s, are no longer the consumer's idea of an "in"(註15) place to go.

The theoretical model holds true for all products, including tourism. A destination will gradually become known to tourists, who are initially attracted in small numbers. As it becomes more popular, and is exploited by other carriers and tour operators, sales will rise rapidly, perhaps attracting a different market. The uniqueness of the resort is lost, and it becomes another mass market destination, appealing to a more down market holidaymaker. The expansion of hotels and other facilities at the resort may lead to a surplus of supply over demand, while the despoliation of the resort may make it less attractive to the holiday market, who will move on elsewhere. Eventually, the resort may decline to a point where tourism is no longer significant and other industries may be encouraged into the region, or the local authority decides to take action to improve the appeal of the destination again.

The Lessons of the Product Life Cycle for the Tourism Marketer

As we have seen, the growth, maturity and decline of products take place over widely varying timescales, so it is unwise to use the concept of the product life cycle to make detailed forecasts for a product or product mix. There is no way of telling from a sales graph when introduction will become growth, when growth will flatten out into maturity, or when maturity will begin to decline.(註16)

Nevertheless, awareness of the characteristic shape of the product life cycle will protect managers against the myopia which assumes that their wonderful product will be successful for all the time. They will begin to develop new products to add to their product range and in time will replace the current best-selling brand. And because they know that new product may have a slow introduction stage and take time to grow into their full sales potential, they will introduce new products while the current ones are still at the top of the curve rather than wait until they show signs of decline. Otherwise there may be a period where the old product's sales have slumped but the new product has not yet taken off.(註17)

All managers need to monitor market trends for signs that their competitors are introducing new improved features or that their customers are becoming bored with the existing features. They should regard their business as a collection of assets — physical, financial and human — to be used in whatever way best satisfies their customers profitably.(註18) At leisure complexes like park or entertainment center, the buildings are fundamentally just shells, spaces for leisure activities to take place. (註19) If the existing activities no longer attract people, they could be replaced with, for example, virtual reality games.

However, it would be equally wrong to assume that declining sales will inevitably continue. Ten-pin bowling was first introduced into Britain in 1960. By 1964, there were 150 centers. This growth in interest was short-lived and by the end of 1967 only 50 centers were left. Only one new center opened in the next 20 years. Then in 1988 a new cycle of growth, a new wave of popularity began. This can be attributed to several factors:

◆ A new market: a new generation of bowlers;

◆ An improved image: better facilities, more to do while waiting to bowl;

◆ Technological improvements: new electronic scoreboards;

◆ Changing fashions: a new vogue for American style in leisure.

Vocabulary 內文詞彙

product mix	產品組合
product life cycle	產品生命週期
product line	產品系列，產品種類
product width	產品廣度
variant	變量
product depth	產品深度
white goods manufacturer	家用電器生產商
market segment	細分市場
profit margin	利潤率
complexity	複雜的事物，複雜性
market share	市場份額
mass market	大眾市場

brand name	品牌名稱
leading brand	領先品牌，著名品牌
stretch	伸展，延伸
encompass	包括，包含
capitalize	變成資本
top-market	高端市場
inherent	固有的，內在的
marketing strength	營銷優勢
subsidiary	附屬的、次要的，子公司
visibility	可見度，曝光度
level off	變平，穩定
with respect to	關於，至於
hold on to	堅持，保持
spectacular	驚人的，突出的
saturation	飽和
sales volume	銷售量
penetrate	滲透

mass production	大規模生產，成批生產
obsolescence	過時，淘汰
hot spring	溫泉
down market	低檔市場
surplus	過剩，剩餘
despoliation	掠奪，剝奪
myopia	目光短淺，缺乏深謀遠慮
slump	衰退
virtual reality game	虛擬遊戲
ten-pin	（美）（十柱戲的）柱子
bowling	保齡球
scoreboards	記分板
vogue	時尚，流行

Notes to the Text 內文註釋

1.Some, because of technical complexity or other factors, will need exceptional sales back up, while others may be suitable for self-selection, affecting distribution strategies.

有些產品由於技術上的複雜性或其他一些因素將需要特別的銷售支援，而有些產品則可能適合自選，這些情況都會對分銷策略產生影響。

2.If a machine has spare capacity and can be used in the manufacture of a new product line, this may make all the difference as to whether it will prove profitable for the company to make the new line.

如果機器還有額外的生產能力，能夠用來生產一種新的產品系列，那麼它將對企業是否能夠靠新產品贏利產生重大影響。make all the difference：產生很大影響，起重要作用。

3.how competitive it is against those of rival organizations：與競爭對手企業的產品相比，它有多大的競爭力。

4.in fact the nature of package holidays makes each distinct in its appeal to different market segments, satisfying different needs：實際上，包價旅遊的本質決定了每一個包價旅遊產品對不同細分市場的吸引力是不同的，它們滿足的是不同的需求。

5.although the trend recently has been to reduce this diversification to bring products into line under a single brand：雖然目前的趨勢是減少這種多樣性，把產品歸屬於一個單一品牌名下。

6.with JMC brand restricted to families and young adults, Sunset as the budget brand：JMC品牌針對的是家庭和年輕人市場，Sunset品牌針對的則是比較經濟的大眾市場。

7.A company at the bottom end of the market may find profits squeezed, and attempt to reposition its products further up the market to allow a greater margin of profit：產品針對最低端市場的企業或許發現自己幾乎沒有利潤可得，於是它就會力圖重新定位自己的產品，讓其針對高端市場以期獲得更多的利潤。margin   of profit：邊際利潤，餘利。

8.downgraded the product, thereby losing the confidence of their loyal, original customers：降低了產品品質，因而失去了原有忠實顧客的信任。

9.duration of a product's life cycle：一個產品週期的長度。

10.The most productive time to advertise a product or service is when it is new.

宣傳產品或服務最有效的時間是當產品新上市時。

11.Operations in this period are characterized by high cost, relatively low sales volume, and an advertising program aimed at stimulating primary demand.

這階段的特點是成本較高、銷售量較低，廣告活動的目的是刺激市場的基本需求。

12.but the promotional emphasis is on selective buying motives by trade name rather than on primary motives to try the product：但是，促銷的重點是針對商品名稱的選擇性購買動機，而不是以嘗試產品為目的的初級動機。trade name：商品名稱，指商品在市場上已經被顧客熟知，但不一定是註冊商標的名稱。

13.More competitors enter the marketplace, but economies of scale are realized and prices may decline some.

雖然有更多的競爭對手進入了市場，但是規模經濟已經實現，產品價格也可以降低一些了。

14.Mass production and new technology have lowered the price to make it available to almost everybody.

批量生產和新技術的運用降低了產品的價格，幾乎讓人人都可以買得起。

15.in：指時尚的，熱門的。

16.when growth will flatten out into maturity, or when maturity will begin to decline：成長期何時將趨於平淡走入成熟期，或者成熟期何時將開始步入下降期。

17.Otherwise there may be a period where the old product's sales have slumped but the new product has not yet taken off.

否則就可能會出現這樣一個時期，即舊產品的銷售量已經大幅下降，但是新產品還沒有進入市場。

18.They should regard their business as a collection of assets — physical, financial and human — to be used in whatever way best satisfies their customers profitably.

他們應該把企業看做是多種資產的組合體——既有物質資產，也有資金和人員資產——應該千方百計地用這些資產來最大限度地滿足顧客的需求並帶來利潤。

19.At leisure complexes like park or entertainment center, the buildings are fundamentally just shells, spaces for leisure activities to take place.

在公園、娛樂中心這樣的綜合娛樂設施裡，樓房只是最基本的外殼，只是進行娛樂活動的場所而已。

★★★★

Useful Words and Expressions 實用詞彙和表達方式

產品延伸	line extension
品牌延伸	brand extension

產品開發	product development
輔助產品	augmented product
消費品	consumer product
產品設計	product design
產品系列	product line
多品牌策略	multi-branding
產品調整	product adaptation
測試新產品	testing new product
產品演變	product evolution
產品特徵	product feature
產品定位	product positioning
產品範圍	product scope
產品規格	product specifications
產品類型	product type
產品用途	product usage
市場研究	market research
細分市場	market segment

市場細分	market segmentation
市場份額	market share
目標市場選擇	market targeting
市場開拓能力	marketability
市場進入戰略	market-entry strategies
營銷行動計劃	marketing action plan

Exercises 練習題

Discussion Questions 思考題

1.How do you understand the concept of product mix?

2.What is product's depth?

3.What are the four stages of a product life cycle?

4.What marketing tactics should be taken at different stages of a product life cycle?

5.Why should marketers keep an eye on the market trend all the time?

Sentence Translation 單句翻譯練習

1.中國的旅行社按照經營業務範圍（business　range），分成國際旅行社和國內旅行社。國內旅行社的經營範圍僅限於國內旅遊業務。

2.國際旅行社的經營範圍包括入境旅遊業務、出境旅遊業務、國內旅遊業務。

3.國內旅遊的發展不僅為入境國際旅遊奠定了基礎，同時也為本國或本地區的出境國際旅遊創造了條件。

4.航空客運主要分為定期航班（scheduled flight）服務和包機（chartered flight）服務兩種。

5.旅遊城市內的兩點往返式旅遊路線（route），即住地與景點的單線連接，很容易使旅遊者感到乏味，景點必須透過宣傳擴大知名度來吸引客源。

6.旅遊業是當今投資見效（return on investment）最快的經濟行業之一，這一特點在各旅遊地的建設初期表現得尤為突出。

7.向國際與會者（international meeting attendee）介紹會議設施情況時，需要給他們提供充分詳盡的資訊，這樣他們的疑問才會減至最少。提供資訊可分為入境（entry）、當地資訊、交通、住宿（lodging）、貨幣和其他六大類。

8.定量調查（quantitative survey）和定性調查（qualitative survey）是營銷工作中最常用的兩種基本調查方法。

Passage Translation 段落翻譯練習

Quality is a measure of how well a product performs and how long it will perform. It is common sense that if quality is too low, buyers will not repurchase. But quality that is too high, more than what buyers require for their uses, will also hurt sales: buyers may not be willing to pay the higher price it commands. The marketing manager must decide how much quality, for the cost, each particular product needs.

The average quality of a product from unit to unit is important, but so is consistency in quality. Buyers want uniformity as they buy units over time. And within any product they expect every element or part to perform equally well and equally long. This requires manufacturers to have tight quality control. It usually raises production costs, but the fact is that buyers will accept just so much variation and no more.

Lesson 4 Service Design and Positioning 服務的設計與定位

導讀：

　　根據最近的一項調查，製造、服務和消費新產品中只有56%在五年後仍然還在市場上。失敗的原因有很多：產品沒有獨特的優點，需求不足，對新產品有不切實際的目標，新服務與企業其他服務不一致，沒有花必要的時間去研究和開發新服務，等等。一個好的服務設想常常由於設計和規劃上的缺陷而導致失敗。本篇文章將首先介紹新服務開發的注意事項、新服務的類型、新服務開發的各個階段，然後闡述服務定位的概念和操作步驟。

New Service Development

Research suggests that products that are designed and introduced by following the steps in a structured planning framework have a greater likelihood of ultimate success than those not developed within a framework. The fact that services are intangible makes it even more imperative for a new service development system to have four basic characteristics:

◆ It must be objective, not subjective;

◆ It must be precise, not vague;

◆ It must be fact driven, not opinion driven;

◆ It must be methodological, not philosophical.

Since service products are produced and consumed simultaneously and often involve interaction between employees and consumers, it is critical that the new service development process involve both employees and customers. Employees are often services, or at least perform or deliver the service, therefore their involvement in choosing which services to develop and how these services should be designed and implemented can increase the likelihood of new service success, because the information they glean from their daily interaction with customers can be very helpful in identifying customer requirements for which new services can be offered. As active participators in service delivery, customers too should be involved in the service design process. They can not only provide input on their own needs, but also help design the service concept and the delivery process, particularly in cases where the customer personally carries out part of the service process.

When we talk about the new service design process, it must be noted that not all new services are "new" to the same degree. The types of new service options can run the gamut from major innovations to minor style changes(註1), as described in the following:

◆ Major innovations are new services for markets as yet undefined(註2). Federal Express's introduction of nationwide, overnight small-package delivery service is one of the examples(註3).

◆ Start-up businesses consist of new services for a market that is already served by existing products that meet the same generic needs, such as ATMs for bank transactions, door-to-door airport shuttle services(註4) that compete with traditional taxi and limousine services.

◆ New services for the currently served market represent attempts to offer existing customers of the organization a service not previously available from the company. Examples include Barnes and Noble(註5) offering coffee service, a health club offering nutrition classes, and airlines offering FAX and phone service during flights.

◆ Service line extensions refer to augmentations of the existing service line(註6), such as a restaurant adding new menu items, a law firm adding additional legal services, and a university adding new courses or degrees.

◆ Service improvements represent the most common type of service innovation. Changes in features of the existing services (e.g. extended hours of service), or augmentations such as added amenities in a hotel room fall into this category(註7).

◆ Style changes represent the most modest service innovations, though often highly visible, and can have significant impact on customer perceptions, emotions and attitudes. Examples include changing the color scheme of a restaurant and revising the logo for an organization.

The actual steps to be followed in the new service development can be applied to any of the types of new services just described (in some ways to the new manufactured products). Due to inherent characteristics of services, the development process for new services requires unique and complex adaptations.

Business Strategy Review and New Service Strategy Development

Since the new service strategy and specific new service ideas must fit in with the general objective of the organization, the first step in new service development is to review the overall strategic vision and mission of an organization(註8).

By defining a new service strategy (in terms of markets, types of services, time horizon(註9) for development, profit criteria, or other relevant factors), the organization will be in better position to identify possible directions for growth and begin generating specific ideas.

Idea Generation

Many methods can be used for searching out new service ideas. Brainstorming, solicitation of ideas from customers and employees through suggestion boxes, learning about competitors' offerings are some of the most common approaches. The multiple ideas generated can be screened through the new service strategy mentioned in the preceding step, and combined into a few solid concepts(註10). Finally the selected concepts can be refined into a finished form.

Concept Development and Evaluation

Once an idea is regarded as fit with the overall strategy and new service strategy, it is ready for initial development. Due to the inherent service characteristics, defining and describing an intangible service in concrete terms are difficult. It is therefore important that agreement be reached on exactly what the concept is. After clearly defining the concept, it is important to produce a description of the service with its features and characteristics, and then the new service concept would be evaluated by asking employees and customers whether they understand the idea of the proposed service and whether they feel it satisfies an unmet need.

Business Analysis

This step is to determine the feasibility and potential profit implications of the service concept, including demand analysis, revenue projections(註11), cost analysis, and operational feasibility.

Service Development and Testing

This stage involves all stakeholders in the new service: customers, contact employees, and functional representatives from marketing, operations, and human resources. During this phase, the concept is refined to the point where a detailed service blueprint representing the implementation plan for the service can be produced. Afterwards, the blueprint is translated by each party involved in rendering the service into specific implementation plans for its part of the service delivery process(註12).

Market Testing

There are alternative ways of testing the response to the new service. The new service might be offered to employees of the organization and their families to assess their responses. Or the organization might test it in less realistic contexts by presenting customers with hypothetical service.

Commercialization

At this stage, the service goes live and is introduced to the market, with the purpose of building and maintaining acceptance of the new service among service delivery personnel, and carrying out monitoring of all aspects of the service.

Post-introduction Evaluation

At this point, the information gathered during commercialization of the service can be reviewed and changes made to the various aspects of the delivery process on the basis of actual market response to the offering.

Service Positioning

A service offering's positioning is the way in which it is viewed, in relation to competing offerings, by consumers. The service positioning lies ultimately in the mind of the consumer: it refers to how the market perceives the organization, rather than how the organization perceives itself. Whether or not an organization or a particular offering of an organization is successfully positioned depends on whether it has established and maintains a distinctive and desirable place for itself in the consumer's mind relative to competing organizations or offerings(註13).

The positioning task requires three key steps:

◆ Identifying a set of possible competitive advantages upon which to build a position, such as price, superior accommodation, speedy journey times, highly motivated and professional staff.

◆ Prioritizing these advantages so as to select the right competitive advantages. For example, a static and price sensitive market will prefer a positioning strategy which highlights value for money(註14).

◆ Effectively communicating and delivering the chosen position to a carefully selected target market.

A company can differentiate itself from competitors by bundling competitive advantages. It gains competitive advantage by offering consumers lower prices than competitors for similar products or by providing more benefits that justify higher prices. To the extent that it can do better than its competitors, the company has achieved a competitive advantage.

Not every company faces an abundance of opportunities for gaining a competitive advantage. Some companies can identify only minor advantages, which are often easily copied and therefore highly perishable. These companies must continue to identify new potential advantages and introduce them one by one to keep competitors off balance(註15). Few or perhaps no companies can achieve a major permanent advantage, but instead gain smaller advantages that help them build their market share over time.

The purpose of planned positioning is to create a differentiation in the customer's mind which distinguishes the company's services from other competitive services. But not all differences are meaningful and can make good differentiators. It is therefore important to select distinguishing characteristics which satisfy the following criteria:

Importance: The difference is highly valued to a sufficiently large market;

Distinctiveness: Competitors do not offer the difference, or the company can offer it in a more distinctive way;

Communicability: It is possible to communicate the difference in a simple and strong way;

Superiority: The difference is not easily copied by competitors;

Affordability: The target customers will be able to pay for the difference;

Profitability: The company will achieve additional profits as a result of introducing the difference.

Companies normally develop a memorable statement to communicate their desired position. La Quinta's(註16) "Just Right Over Night" catches the attention of travelers coming in by car and needing overnight accommodation, but not needing a full-service hotel(註17). Avis Auto Rental(註18) originally positioned itself with a statement and strong supportive program to convince the customer, "We're only No.2 so we try harder." This also positioned Avis with number one company, Hertz, and away from Budget, Dollar, National, and Thrifty.

After choosing positioning characteristics and a positioning statement, a company must communicate their position to targeted customers. All of a company's marketing mix efforts must support its positioning strategy. Thus, if a company decides to build service superiority, it must hire service-oriented employees, provide training programs, reward employees for providing good service, and develop sales and advertising messages to broadcast its service superiority.

Positioning involves both launching new brands into the marketplace and repositioning old brands. Because of the intangibility and other features associated with services, companies find the differentiation of services more difficult and complex. The key to successful positioning strategy is to promote the feature which the company is best at and which exactly matches customer expectations and needs.

Vocabulary 內文詞彙

methodological	方法的，方法論的
philosophical	哲學上的，研究哲學的，富於哲理性的
glean	蒐集
innovation	革新，創新，新發明
generic	普通的，非專利的
limousine	豪華大客車
augmentation	擴大，增大，加強
amenities	便利設施
logo	標誌

solicitation	徵求，徵集
stakeholder	利益共享者
prioritize	按重點先後排列
differentiate	使不同，構成差別
static	靜態的
perishable	易損壞的
likelihood	可能性
imperative	必要的，緊急的
screen	篩選

Notes to the Text 內文註釋

1.run the gamut from major innovations to minor style changes：涉及從大的革新到小的樣式變化的全部範圍。

2.Major innovations are new service for markets as yet undefined.

大的革新指的是為尚未確定的市場設計的新服務。

3.Federal Express's introduction of nationwide, overnight small-package delivery service is one of the examples.

聯邦快遞推行全國範圍連夜快遞小包裹服務就是其中一個例子。

4.door-to-door airport shuttle services：全程機場往返班車服務。

5.Barnes and Noble：邦諾書店（美國連鎖書店集團）。

6.Service line extensions refer to augmentations of the existing service line.

服務產品延伸指的是在現有服務產品基礎上增加的服務。

7.fall into this category：屬於這個範疇。

8.review the overall strategic vision and mission of an organization：回顧公司總體的戰略目標和使命。

9.time horizon：時間範圍。

10.The multiple ideas generated can be screened through the new service strategy mentioned in the preceding step, and combined into a few solid concepts.

產生的多種想法經過上述步驟中提到的新服務戰略的甄別，結合成幾個完整的設想。

11.revenue projection：收入估測。

12.the blueprint is translated by each party involved in rendering the service into specific implementation plans for its part of the service delivery process：參與提供服務的每一方把規劃轉化成具體的實施計劃，作為其服務傳遞過程的一部分。

13.whether it has established and maintains a distinctive and desirable place for itself in the consumer's mind relative to competing organizations or offerings：是否在消費者心中建立並保持較之於競爭企業或競爭產品更獨特的、更具吸引力的地位。

14.a positioning strategy which highlights value for money：強調物有所值的定位

戰略。

15.keep competitors off balance：使競爭者望塵莫及。

16.La Quinta：拉昆塔旅館及套房酒店，是美國的一個飯店品牌。

17.a full-service hotel：提供全面服務的飯店。

18.Avis　　Auto　　Rental：安維斯汽車租賃公司，它與赫茲（Hertz）、巴吉特（Budget）都是美國非常著名的連鎖租車公司，遍布美國各地。

Useful Words and Expressions 實用詞彙和表達方式

旅遊服務品質	service quality in tourism
旅遊服務規範	service specification in tourism
旅遊服務品質標準	standards of service quality in tourism
旅遊服務品質評定	evaluation of service quality in tourism
旅遊服務品質認證	validation of service quality in tourism
旅遊安全管理	management of tourism safety
旅遊投訴管理	handling of tourist complaint
旅遊投訴理賠	settlement of tourist complaint
旅遊定點餐館	designated tourist restaurant

旅遊定點商店	designated tourist shop
旅遊團隊餐	meals for tour group
旅遊小冊子	tour brochure
最低旅遊價格	minimum tour price
旅遊接待國	receiving country
旅遊業務	tour operation
旅遊路線	tour route
團隊包價旅遊	group inclusive tour
散客旅遊代理商	retail travel agent
旅遊代號編碼	tour code number
旅遊黃金週	golden week for tourism

Exercises 練習題

Discussion Questions 思考題

1.Assume the service company you are working with wants to grow by adding new services. Describe the process you might use to introduce a new service to the target market.

2.What steps in the new service development process do you think are the most difficult? Why?

3.Choose a service in your neighborhood or on your campus which is not satisfactory. Redesign the service or change it in some way.

4.What is service positioning? Describe an example of a service which you believe is clearly positioned.

5.What roles do product attributes and perceptions of attributes play in the positioning of a product?

Sentence Translation 單句翻譯練習

1.旅遊開發被認為是造成環境惡化（environmental degradation）的主要原因，幾乎世界上每一個國家都有這樣的例子，如西班牙沿海地區由於過度地建設旅遊住所（overbuilding of the tourist accommodation）造成水汙染，印度的泰姬瑪哈陵由於大批遊客的頻繁參觀而日漸破損（wear and tear）。

2.保護、美化（enhancement）和改善人類環境的各個組成部分是協調發展旅遊業（harmonious development of tourism）的最根本的條件之一。同樣，合理地管理旅遊業能大大促進對物質環境（physical environment）和文化遺產（cultural heritage）的保護和開發，也有利於提高生活品質。

3.旅遊被普遍認為是「乾淨的產業」（clean industry），但旅遊開發也帶來空氣汙染，如果一個地區旅遊者使用的車輛和為旅遊者提供的車輛過多（excessive vehicular traffic used by and for tourists），就會造成空氣汙染。

4.如果度假區（resorts）和飯店的固體廢物（solid waste）得不到適當的處理，就會引發蟲害（vermin）、疾病、汙染等環境衛生問題，也會使度假區失去吸引力。

5.旅遊企業應該為有不同需求的遊客提供多元化（diversified）、特色化的旅遊產品選擇，最大限度地滿足不同細分市場（market segments）的需求。

6.政府在扶持旅遊發展上起了很大的作用，如提供通訊、衛生、警事服務等大眾服務（general services），以及為建築項目提供土地、機場、培訓設施等。

7.旅遊業促進歷史古蹟（historic sites）的保護，並為其提供資金。如果沒有旅遊業，這些古蹟的狀況就可能會惡化（deteriorate）或消失。

8.旅遊發展可以帶來有益的社會文化影響（sociocultural impacts）。相互交流觀念、文化和認識會大大有利於消除（dispel）無知和誤解。

Passage Translation 段落翻譯練習

The development of new tourism offerings tends to be stimulated by both proactive and reactive strategies, although much of the growth in the market relates to imitation and repositioning of tourism offerings. Very little could be classified as concepts or innovations entirely new to the market. Those organizations which do have a proactive strategy tend to have a real commitment and resource base to plan a succession of new products or offerings. This is very much the case in the visitor attractions sector where updating and addition is commonplace. In some respects the stress on new product development is a misnomer.In reality, very few new products or services are actually new to the world; they mainly constitute modifications to existing products or service offerings, or a repackaging of core brands, such as Sheraton Hotels' Body Clock Cuisine which is designed to help long haul travelers adjust to new time frames and to combat fatigue.

Lesson 5 Pricing the Product 產品定價

導讀：

價格代表願意購買產品的顧客和希望賣出產品的生產者之間進行自願交換的條

件。在旅遊營銷組合中，價格是唯一能產生收入的因素，同時也是最為活躍的因素。定價問題是許多旅遊企業所面臨的主要問題。本篇文章在介紹價格與定價含義的基礎上，重點介紹了定價的幾個目標和旅遊產品常用的一些定價方法，並指出了這些定價方法的優點與缺點。

Pricing Concepts

"How much is it?" This question is repeated many times a day in stores around the world. It shows that the consumers and companies will buy lots of things if the price is right. One can design the finest products in the world, but if the price is perceived too high, the effort may be for nothing. Pricing decisions, therefore, should be completely integrated with product decisions(註1), for price is part of the product offer, just as the package and the brand are.

Price is one way in which a seller can differentiate his offer from those of competitors(註2). Pricing may thus be considered part of the product differentiation function in marketing. But pricing is also a part of the valuation function. Since the price at which the consumer purchases a product involves his evaluation of the satisfaction it will yield(註3), it can be said that the total sales of a company represents the sum of the satisfactions, as measured in dollars and cents, which it has delivered to its customers.

Pricing objectives

The beginning point in setting prices is the establishment of pricing objectives. These objectives must be consistent with the company's overall purpose or mission(註4). They must also be consistent with the decision the company has made as to what it wants to accomplish with the product or service(註5), given a selected target market and positioning strategy. There are numerous pricing objectives companies may pursue. We will introduce five of them.

Profit

Some companies set profit maximization as their goal. Profit maximization means that the company develops a marketing plan to enable management to achieve the greatest profit per unit sold(註6). Demand and cost estimates associated with different output and price alternatives are determined, and a price is chosen that will enable the company to maximize current profits.

A goal of profit maximization does not necessarily lead to high prices(註7), although some people believe such to be the case. Companies attempting to maximize current profits may charge relatively low prices if good substitutes are being offered by competitors and demand is elastic. The low price may lead to market expansion, which, in turn, leads to lower costs, greater revenues, and hence greater profits(註8).

Companies often pursue an objective of earning a satisfactory profit rather than attempting to maximize profits(註9). Earning a satisfactory profit means achieving a target rate of return. Profit maximization is often a short-term strategy that requires the company to minimize investment in equipment, research and development, and developing human resources skills so as to increase the level of corporate earnings. Earning a satisfactory profits is often perceived as being more socially responsible(註10). Also, it may be easier to implement a satisfactory profit goal. Companies often do not have all the information needed to determine at what price profit will actually be maximized.

Return on Investment

Management may seek a target rate of return on internally generated and borrowed funds, since the assets of a business can be provided by the owners or through external sources of capital. Leverage occurs when management uses debt to acquire assets worth more than the amount of capital invested by the owners. Leverage allows a company to limit owners' investments in the assets of the company and to borrow the remainder of the needed funds. Profits are earned, however, on the entire amount of funds invested.

A variety of factors influence the choice of a target rate of return on investment. The current and impending competitive picture is a factor, for example. If a company wishes to discourage competitors from entering a market, it may set a low target return goal. A high target return goal may be set if there is little threat of impending competition. Little threat exists for example, when management is able to secure patent protection for a unique process. In certain situations a company may set a high return on investment goal to encourage competitors to enter a market. Such an approach might be followed for antitrust reasons or to encourage market expansion(註11).

Market Share

The purpose of a market share objective is to take market from competitors or to hold an existing share. Management in such situations expects to sacrifice short-run profits in return for an acceptable level of market share(註12). Once the company obtains an acceptable market share, prices can be raised and profits return to normal levels. As observed, "The chance to grab market share which should pay off later can outweigh the pain of short-term sacrifice for the companies involved(註13)."

Cash Flow

A company may set price to recover cash as rapidly as possible(註14). Such an objective may be especially relevant when introducing a new product.An early cash recovery objective does not necessarily mean that the company should set a high rather than a low price on its products. The specific price that will result in the largest cash flow may be high or low(註15), depending on such variables as price elasticity of demand and whether economies of scale can be achieved. Constant unit costs and low elasticity of demand suggest that cash flow will be maximized through a high price; falling unit costs and high elasticity of demand are conditions that indicate the company can maximize cash flow by setting a low price on its offering.

Survival

A company faced with overcapacity, an adverse cash flow situation, and related problems may set survival as its short-term pricing objective. Such an objective leads to price reductions, often to the point where only variable costs are being covered. Large cash rebate programs are often used. In the recent past, Chrysler Corporation changed its pricing strategy and used large rebates in an effort to survive in the market place, until better economic times prevailed and the company was in a less precarious financial situation(註16). The special price incentives were necessary to induce consumers to purchase vehicles from a manufacturer whose future was in doubt.

Pricing Methods

There is no single method used by all tourism suppliers to price their products. Suppliers may use a number of methods, each with their pros and cons, to establish prices(註17).

Intuitive method

The intuitive method requires no real knowledge of the business (costs, profits, prices competition, the market). The operator just assumes that the prices established are the right ones. This method has no advantages. Its main disadvantage is that the prices charged are unrelated to profits. If they are too high, they might drive away customers, thus reducing profit. If too low, they are depriving the business of profits that it could make(註18).

Rule of Thumb Method

Rule of thumb method, such as that a restaurant should price its menu items at 2.5 times food cost to achieve a 40 percent cost of sales, may have had validity at one time, but should not be relied on in today's highly competitive environment because they pay no attention to the marketplace (competition, offering value for money, and so forth).

Trial and Error Method

With the trial and error method, prices are changed up and down to see what effect they have on sales and profits. When profit is apparently maximized, prices are established at that level. However, this method ignores the existence of many other factors (such as general economic conditions and the competition) that affect sales and profits apart from prices, and what appears to be the optimum pricing level may be affected by these other factors(註19). This method can also be confusing to customers during the price testing period.

Price-Cutting Method

Price cutting occurs when prices are reduced below those of the competition. This can be a risky method if it ignores costs, because if variable costs are higher than prices, profits will be eroded. To use this method, demand must be elastic. In other words, the reduction in prices must be more than compensated for by selling additional products(註20). If the extra business gained is simply taken away from competitors, because total market demand is inelastic, the competitors will be forced to reduce their prices and a price war will result. This method should not be confused with price discounting, which is done with a full knowledge of fixed and variable costs.

High-Price Method

Another method is to deliberately charge more than competitors do and to use product differentiation (emphasizing such factors as quality) that many customers equate with price. If this strategy is not used carefully, however, it can encourage product substitution as customers move elsewhere realizing that price and quality are not synonymous.

Competitive Method

Competitive pricing means matching prices of the competition and then differentiation in such areas as location, atmosphere, and other non-price factors. When there is one dominant business in the market that generally takes the lead in establishing prices, with its close competitors matching increases and decreases, this method is then referred to as the follow-the-leader method. Competitive pricing tends to ensure there is no price cutting and resulting reduction in profits. In other words, there is market price stability. This may be a useful method in the short run. However, if competitive pricing is used without knowledge of the differences (in such matters as product and costs) between one business and another, this method can be risky.

To sum up, pricing is a marketing tool that can be effectively used to improve profitability. The dilemma is often a matter of finding the balance between prices and profits.In other words, prices should only be established after considering the effect they have on profits. There is no one method of establishing prices for all tourism products. Each company will have somewhat different long-run pricing strategies related to its overall objectives and will adopt appropriate short-run pricing tactics depending on its market situation. Over the long run, price is determined in the marketplace as a result of supply and demand. When prices are established to compete in that marketplace, they must be set with the company's overall long-term financial objectives in mind. A clearly thought out pricing strategy will stem from the objective or objectives of the business, as well as recognize that these objectives may change over the long run.

Vocabulary 內文詞彙

differentiation	區別，分化
elastic	有彈性的
elasticity	彈性
implement	執行，使生效
leverage	槓桿，槓桿作用
patent	專利
antitrust	反托拉斯的
rebate	折扣，回扣
incentive	刺激，誘因
precarious	危險的，不穩定的
overcapacity	生產能力過剩
pros and cons	贊成票和反對票，長處與短處
intuitive	直覺的
optimum	最優的，最佳的
compensate	補償

validity	正確性，有效性
erode	腐蝕
synonymous	同義的
dilemma	困境，窘境
economy of scale	規模經濟
variable costs	可變成本
profit maximization	利潤最大化
trial and error method	嘗試法
intuitive method	直觀法

Notes to the Text 內文註釋

1.Pricing decisions, therefore, should be completely integrated with product decisions.

因此，定價決策應當與產品決策緊密地結合在一起。

2.Price is one way in which a seller can differentiate his offer from those of competitors.

價格是銷售者得以將其產品同競爭者相區分的一種方式。

3.the price at which the consumer purchases a product involves his evaluation of the satisfaction it will yield：消費者購買產品的價格體現出他對產品的滿意度。

4.be consistent with the company's overall purpose or mission：與該公司的整體目標或任務一致。

5.the decision the company has made as to what it wants to accomplish with the product or service：公司所做的關於產品與服務目標的決定。

6.Profit maximization means that the company develops a marketing plan to enable management to achieve the greatest profit per unit sold.

利潤最大化意為公司透過制定營銷計劃以使公司的管理取得最大的單位銷售利潤。

7.A goal of profit maximization does not necessarily lead to high prices.

利潤最大化的目標並不一定非要提高價格。

8.The low price may lead to market expansion, which, in turn, leads to lower costs, greater revenues, and hence greater profits.

低價可能擴大市場，反過來使成本降低，收入增加，因此帶來更大的利潤。

9.Companies often pursue an objective of earning a satisfactory profit rather than attempting to maximize profits.

公司經常追求令人滿意的利潤而非無限擴大的利潤。

10.Earning a satisfactory profits is often perceived as being more socially responsible.

獲取滿意的利潤通常被理解為承擔更多的社會責任。

11.Such an approach might be followed for antitrust reasons or to encourage market expansion.

如果出於反托拉斯或鼓勵市場擴展的目的，可以採用這種方式。follow a approach：採用某個方法；antitrust：反托拉斯的。

12.sacrifice short-run profits in return for an acceptable level of market share：犧牲短期利益以獲得可接受的市場份額。short-run 意為「短期的」；相對應的是「long-run」（長期的）。

13.The chance to grab market share which should pay off later can outweigh the pain of short-term sacrifice for the companies involved.

其中grab market share為「攫取市場份額」；pay off 意為「贏利」；outweigh 意為「超……價值」；short-term sacrifice意為「短期的犧牲」。整句意為：攫取市場份額雖說會冒一定風險，但也會帶來利潤；對公司而言，冒這種風險在價值上遠遠超出其短期犧牲所需付出的代價。

14.A company may set price to recover cash as rapidly as possible.

公司定價的目的是盡快地回籠資金。

15.The specific price that will result in the largest cash flow may be high or low.

帶來最大資金流動的具體價格可高可低。result in意為「造成、導致、帶來」。

16.until better economic times prevailed and the company was in a less precarious financial situation：直到經濟局勢有所好轉，公司的財政狀況略微脫離困境。prevail：盛行、流行；precarious：危險的。

17.Suppliers may use a number of methods, each with their pros and cons, to establish prices.

供應商可以使用多種方法來確定價格，每一種方法都有其優點與缺點。pros and cons：長處與短處。

18.If too low, they are depriving the business of profits that it could make.

如果價格過低，就會減少公司本可以獲得的利潤。deprive...of...是固定搭配，意為「從……剝奪……」。

19.what appears to be the optimum pricing level may be affected by these other factors：表面上最佳的定價水平可能會受到這些其他因素的影響。

20.In other words, the reduction in prices must be more than compensated for by selling additional products.

換句話說，價格的下降必須透過出售更多的產品來得以充分地補償。

Useful Words and Expressions 實用詞彙和表達方式

加成定價法	markup pricing
認知價值定價法	perceived-value pricing
轉移定價法	transfer pricing
定價範圍	price range
定價談判	price talk
指示性價格	indicative price

炒高價格	ramping
現貨價格	spot price
場外價格	street price
門檻價格	threshold price
定價目錄	priced catalogue
定價成本	pricing cost
定價政策	pricing policy
價格標籤，標價條	price tag
市價表	price current (p.c.)

Exercises 練習題

Discussion Questions 思考題

1.Describe the functions of pricing.

2.If a company's major goal is to maximize profits, why not set the product's price to achieve the desired profit?

3.Why a cash flow objective may or may not lead to a high price being set for a new product?

4.Describe the competitive method of establishing product prices, and state its main disadvantages.

5.What are the main disadvantages of trial-and-error method?

Sentence Translation 單句翻譯練習

1.旅遊價格對旅遊需求（tourist demand）的作用是顯而易見的。

2.要想吸引更多的顧客，旅遊產品的價格必須反映（reflect）旅遊產品的品質。

3.企業經營的目的就是最大限度地獲取利潤（maximum profit）。

4.通貨膨脹（inflation）程度和匯率水平對旅遊價格的高低有著直接的聯繫。

5.旅遊需求的產生和變化不僅由價格因素（factor）決定，而且還受到旅遊者收入和閒暇時間等因素的影響。

6.無論採用何種定價方法，旅遊企業必須分析產品成本、市場需求和競爭狀況。

7.我們要根據定價目標選擇適當的定價方法和定價形式，並注意保持價格的相對穩定（stability）。

8.價格的基礎是價值，價值量的大小決定（determine）價格的高低。

Passage Translation 段落翻譯練習

A new pricing policy that breaks away from the all inclusive package system to a more flexible system are the key features of the new tourism master plan which, tourism officials say, will help spread the season through the year and benefit the industry and tourists alike. The master plan recommends an incentive on the royalty during the low season months to spread the season and extended tourists stays for better regional spread that would lead to rural development. The new policy will maintain the image of exclusivity which Bhutan already has because tourists will be able to come for a quick and inexpensive visit, said one of the experts from Austria, Dr.Martin Uitz, working with the Department of Tourism who helped develop the master plan. For example tourists visiting Bhutan will be required to pay a minimum tariff of US 700 royalty for seven days while the package price on the other hand will be liberal, said Dr.Martin Uitz, who added that the tourism royalty payable to the government should be increased because it had not changed in the past 15 years. At present from the US 200 that tourists pay US 65 goes to the government as royalty.

Lesson 6 Marketing Control 營銷管理

導讀：

營銷控制是市場營銷中的一個非常重要的監督環節，在旅遊市場營銷中也占有非常獨特的地位。本篇文章透過對效率控制、戰略控制、品質控制、預算控制、贏利性控制五個概念具體內涵的介紹，幫助讀者深刻認識到它們的價值和意義。

Controlling is the management function which checks to see if what is supposed to happen is happening, or going to happen. This is a crucial part of management because it is necessary for things to happen, not just someone promises they will. In any business system certain inputs into the business, such as labor, money and enterprise together create a process which is designed to produce an end-product for consumers(註1). This end-product is the organization's output. A system can be defined as an input, a process and an output, and the objective of good management is to ensure that the input and process is subject to constant monitoring to ensure that the output is the right product, at the right price, in the right place at the right time, a classical definition of good marketing practice(註2).

The key word is monitoring, the process which is designed to provide feedback on the effectiveness and efficiency of the system, to control it, and where necessary to change it. The monitoring procedures are designed to control the marketing system. It is widely accepted that planning is an essential part of the marketing process, but the plan will be only as good as the control to which it is subjective(註3). Plans are not carved on tablets of stone; they have to be adjusted constantly in the light of changing circumstances, as the company reacts to market forces. Planning and controlling are equally crucial to successful marketing. In the planning states of an event, control systems must be established to ensure that objectives are accomplished within the prescribed timescale. That is to say they are born at the same time, and should always be considered at the same time.

One thing that must be made clear is that controlling does not mean manipulating or to apply to the individual, rather to systems and resources(註4). Effective control is to do with: planning what you are aiming to do; measuring what has been done; comparing achievements to the blueprint; and taking action to correct anything that is not as it should be.

Marketing is carried out in an organization in three stages:

◆Pre-action: at this stage, activities associated with planning for action have to be undertaken. This includes the development of an information system, and a program of planned market research. Marketing objectives are established, and strategies devised to achieve objectives. Forecasts are drawn up based on the strategies to be implemented(註5).

◆ Action: at this stage, the marketing plan is implemented. This brings into play the coordinating role of the marketing manager, who must ensure that the channels of action are integrated within the department, so that promotional activities serve a common aim(註6). The coordinator must also make certain that where other departments are contributing to the marketing plan, these commitments are met, and in time. Day-today activities undertaken as part of plan will be regularly reviewed and adjusted as necessary(註7).

Post action: at the final stage, the marketing manager has the responsibility of reviewing the plan in its entirety, both to see whether targets are being achieved and to see if ways can be found to further improve the performance of the department.

Five different forms of control can be identified in a control system: performance control, quality control, financial control, efficiency control and strategic control.

Performance Control

This is designed to make sure the organization meets its set targets. The normal targets identified in the marketing plan will include issues such as:

Turnover,

Profitability,

Market share,

Return on investment(註8),

Quality,

Consumer attitudes.

The extent to which these targets are being met can be monitored on a daily or weekly basis, and control is therefore dependent upon a regular flow of information which will indicate performance variance coming to those responsible for corrective action(註9). These members of staff must ascertain why the deviance is occurring and whether action can be taken to bring it back into line with forecasts.

Actual identification is a largely mechanical process, but correcting it calls for management skills, both in interpreting data and in the suitable deployment of resources(註10). Here the manager must distinguish between controllable factors, and those outside the control of the business which will require readjustment of the forecast or the marketing plan.

Quality Control

Measuring quality and ensuring that quality is maintained is a relatively simple matter in the production of durable goods; these can be inspected, rejected if below standard, and some tolerance agreed for the proportion falling below standard. Maintaining quality control over a product such as tourism, is far less straightforward. Uncontrollable factors such as whether exert a considerable influence over the perceived quality of a tourism service.

Tour operators pay close attention to the requirement that their products live up to their description in their brochure, because this is required under law. Increasingly, they are establishing acceptable tolerances for levels of complaints, as this is a measure of quality control(註11). This can be easily measured, since complaints can be measured through letters of complaint received by the company, or complaints made to the resort representative, which can be easily recorded. The correct operation of a monitoring system means that complaints are fed back in the form of corrective actions that prevent complaints in the future. Thus, as well as counting overall numbers of complaints, even just one complaint could mean, for instance, a change implemented in copy for the next edition of the brochure. The use of questionnaires is less effective in monitoring complaints, as most questionnaires used require only that clients list their levels of satisfaction or dissatisfaction with the product; there is insufficient information to take action to correct a situation if a high level of complaints is registered(註12). One needs to know exactly what is wrong with the service, and what action is needed to correct the situation. Suggestion boxes can provide a good picture of consumer dissatisfaction, as can debriefing of staff such as resort representatives at the end of a season(註13).

Financial Control

It is not only the financial controller who will be concerned that departments keep within their budgets. While the budget itself is designed to exercise an automatic control over the operations of the business, the marketing department must constantly check that sales promotion and other expenses remain within the agreed limits. However, too tight control can lead to missed marketing opportunities. The marketing plan must not become a strait-jacket.

The use of ratios to determine marketing mix expenditure is a common means of judging performance, but can be misleading if it is based on what the average company in the industry is achieving(註14). While it is common to determine that a fixed proportion of turnover be allocated to promotion, it should be made clear that spend will need to vary according to the established objectives of the marketing plan. In a time of falling sales, more often than not the control mechanisms go into operation to cut promotional spend where it might be more appropriate to increase it to generate more sales(註15).

Changing circumstances can also result in a particular product carrying too high a proportion of the company's overheads. Let's say that fuel prices have been increased. This could lead to a disproportionately large fall in long-haul tour booking, which will require some readjustment to the allocation of overheads to those programs.

Efficiency Control

If performance control has indicated a weakness in some aspects of the organization's marketing, analysis will be needed to determine whether the marketing activities or the structure of the department needs to be changed in some way to make the marketing more efficient. Even if marketing targets are being met, sheer pressures of competition between principals or between retailers require that ways be constantly sought to reduce costs without impairing efficiency. This means constant re-evaluation of the marketing mix. All means of measuring success must be taken into account, not merely levels of turnover.

Reviewing the organizational structure of the department might mean considering whether sales should be separated from marketing and given its own head; or whether the department has grown to a point where it is worth introducing a marketing controller to co-ordinate activities in the department(註16). Should the marketing function become increasingly centralized, as has happened in some large hotel chains, or should they be more decentralized, as other chains have done? Does the administrative structure facilitate the marketing function, or does it hinder it? Above all, is the quality of the staff up to the standard required?

The last question is a crucial one for the travel and tourism industry. In most sectors of the industry, the belief remains that profit levels do not allow better salaries to be paid, and therefore better staff cannot be recruited. However, performance standards do vary between companies, and different management styles are a major contribution to these variations. Are staff being properly trained in marketing techniques? Are they adequately motivated? What does the manager know about levels of satisfaction among the staff? How is the staff managed — by sanctions, rewards, or simplest of all but surprisingly rare, by thanking them for a job well done? Frequent examples can be shown of small companies in travel where the manager seldom meets or greets the staff, but nevertheless expects them to give of their best for the company. Measures of staff turnover and levels of staff satisfaction are important methods of judging the efficiency of the organization with respect to staff. It is not sufficient simply to count the proportion of staff leaving the company; managers must know for what reasons the staff are leaving.

Even with a good workforce and organization, the communications mix must be monitored constantly to compare the relative performance of different promotional tactics and seek ways of making these more cost-effective.

Strategic Control

From time to time it becomes necessary to look at the total process by which strategic marketing is undertaken in the company, in order to judge whether the organization is taking advantage of the marketing opportunities open to it. This will require senior staff from outside the department to consider the extent of market orientation of the department and of the company as a whole, how well organized it is to spot opportunities when they occur and exploit them, and how well the organization plans its strategies. No travel business today can afford to rest on its laurels; markets change rapidly, and complacency over present occupancy level, load factors or bookings can quickly change to concern as new challenges emerge to face the company.

Management will want to review the effectiveness of its internal, as well as its external, communications. Do the staff share common objectives, and are they working towards a common aim? How well do other departments co-operate with the marketing staff to meet their needs? These are important questions which relate to the operating efficiency of the company as a whole. Where there are divisions of the company on separate sites, or staff are employed far from head office, communications can easily suffer. One of the most common management problems in tour operating is the failure to establish common aims between the head office staff and staff in the field such as area managers and resort representatives. Head office staff making field visits may not even take the time to meet their field representatives; yet it is the resort representative who is closest to the company's clients, knows their problems and can best offer suggestions for the improvement of services.

If a serious weakness is found in some aspect of the organization's marketing, a full marketing audit may be commissioned. This generally means bringing in outside consultants to undertake a systematic investigation into every aspect of the company's marketing operation.

Vocabulary 內文詞彙

manipulate	操縱，把持
prescribe	命令，規定
exert	運用（力量、技巧等）
incur	招惹
comprehensive	全面的，詳盡的，廣泛的
flexible	靈活的，有彈性的
implement	實施
accountable	有責任的
priorities	優先考慮的事情
turnover	銷售量，營業額
deviance	異常，偏離
strait-jacket	阻礙自由發展之物
allocate to	撥出，留下

overhead	企業一般管理費用
impair	損害，削弱
co-ordinate	協調
decentralize	分散，疏散
recruit	招募（某人）為新成員
sanction	批准，認可；制裁，處罰
orientation	位置或方向
laurel	月桂樹；桂冠

Notes to the Text 內文註釋

1.That is to say those certain inputs into the business, such as labor, money and enterprise together create a process which is designed to produce an end-product for consumers.

也就是說，諸如勞動力、資金和計劃等一些針對公司經營的輸入，必然產生一個旨在為消費者提供終端產品的過程。

2.A system can be defined as an input, a process and an output, and the objective of good management is to ensure that the input and process is subject to constant monitoring to ensure that the output is the right product, at the right price, in the right place at the tight time, a classical definition of good marketing practice.

這個系統可以解釋為輸入—處理—輸出的組合，優秀管理的目標就在於讓輸入過程和處理過程接受持續性的監督，確保以恰當的價格、合適的時機和地點輸出恰當的產品；這也是良好市場營銷行為的經典模式。

3.It is widely accepted that planning is an essential part of the marketing process, but the plan will be only as good as the control to which it is subjective.

無疑，計劃是市場營銷過程中非常重要的環節，但是計劃只有在監督下才能產生良好的效果。

4.One thing that must be made clear that controlling does not mean manipulating or to apply to the individual, rather to systems and resources.

必須明確一點，控制並不意味著操縱，也不意味著控制某個人，而是對系統或資源的控制。

5.Marketing objectives are established, and strategies devised to achieve objectives. Forecasts are drawn up based on the strategies to be implemented.

建立了市場營銷目標，並確定了達到目標的策略。通常在打算實施的策略基礎之上擬定預測方案。

6.This brings into play the coordinating role of the marketing manager, who must ensure that the channels of action are integrated within the department, so that promotional activities serve a common aim.

市場營銷經理的協調職責在此派上用場，他必須保證部門內部各個行動小組通力合作，這樣所有促銷行動才能服從於同一個目標。

7.Day-to-day activities undertaken as part of plan will be regularly reviewed and adjusted as necessary.

作為計劃一部分所進行的日常活動會受到定期的檢查並在必要時做出調整。

8.return on investment：投資回收。

9.The extent to which these targets are being met can be monitored on a daily or weekly basis, and control is therefore dependent upon a regular flow of information which will indicate performance variance coming to those responsible for corrective action.

對這些目標的實現情況可以每天或每週進行一次檢查，因此對經營狀況的掌控，依靠的是那些負責調控的人員定期收到的能夠反映經營動態的資訊流。

10.Actual identification is a largely mechanical process, but correcting it calls for management skills, both in interpreting data and in the suitable deployment of resources.

在很大程度上，實際上的認定過程是一種機械的過程，但要糾正它卻需要數據分析和資源合理分配方面的管理技巧。

11.Increasingly, they are establishing acceptable tolerances for levels of complaints, as this is a measure of quality control.

越來越多的經營者都規定出哪些程度的不滿投訴是可以容忍的，因為這是品質控制的一種措施。

12.The use of questionnaires is less effective in monitoring complaints, as most questionnaires used require only that clients list their levels of satisfaction or dissatisfaction with the product; there is insufficient information to take action to correct a situation if a high level of complaints is registered.

調查問卷的使用在投訴監督效力上日見減弱，原因在於大多數的調查問卷只要求客戶將對產品的滿意度和不滿意度陳列出來；對於不滿程度較高的投訴，調查問卷不能為採取改進措施提供足夠的資訊。

13.Suggestion boxes can provide a good picture of consumer dissatisfaction, as can debriefing of staff such as resort representatives at the end of a season.

意見箱能夠很好地反映出顧客有什麼不滿，其效果就像每個旅遊旺季結束後聽取景區代表的意見一樣。

14.The use of ratios to determine marketing mix expenditure is a common means of judging performance, but can be misleading if it is based on what the average company in the industry is achieving.

使用比例來決定市場營銷組合的花費是一種常見的業績評價方式，但是如果所用比例建立在本行業普通公司的業績基礎上，就可能產生誤導。

15.In a time of falling sales, more often than not the control mechanisms go into operation to cut promotional spend where it might be more appropriate to increase it to generate more sales.

在銷售滑坡的情況下，控制機制通常會削減促銷支出，而實際上更明智的做法卻是增加此項支出來促進銷售。

16.Reviewing the organizational structure of the department might mean considering whether sales should be separated form marketing and given its own head; or whether the department has grown to a point where it is worth introducing a marketing controller to co-ordinate activities in the department.

重新審核部門的結構意味著要考慮銷售是否可以從營銷中分離出來成立單獨的部門，或者該部門是否已經發展到值得任命一位營銷專員來統一協調各方面業務的地步。

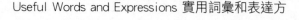

Useful Words and Expressions 實用詞彙和表達方

式

分銷成本	distribution cost
無彈性需求	inelastic demand
機會成本	opportunity cost
溢價品牌	premium brand
邊際利益	profit margin
拉動戰術	pull strategy
價格彈性	price elasticity
投資回報率（ROI）	return on investment
銷售預測	sales forecasting
細分變量	segmentation variable
獨特的銷售建議，賣點	unique selling proposition (USP)
個人購買力	individual purchasing power
市場潛在需求量	market potential
銷售潛力	sales potential
營銷體系	marketing system
行情	market conditions

市場容量　　　　　　　　　　　　capacity of the market

Exercises 練習題

Discussion Questions 思考題

1.What is the general function of marketing control?

2.What factors should be considered in terms of the performance control?

3.Is quality control in other industry different from that in tourism industry?

4.There is in the travel industry a misunderstanding concerning the staff training. What is it?

5.How can it be judged whether the organization is taking advantage of the marketing opportunities open to it?

Sentence Translation 單句翻譯練習

1.實施營銷控制的最根本原因在於營銷計劃與實施過程中遇到的現實情況並非總是保持一致。

2.營銷管理控制職能能否得到充分的發揮取決於如下三點：目標和標準是否明確，資訊來源是否及時可靠，組織結構是否完整清晰。

3.戰略控制是更高層次的控制，市場營銷是變化很快的領域，企業必須注意定期對其整個市場營銷活動進行檢查、評價。

4.促銷（sales promotion）指激發買主購買和試用產品（trial product）的興趣。

5.旅遊市場營銷是透過分析、計劃、執行、回饋和控制這樣一個過程來以旅遊消費需求為導向，協調各種旅遊經濟活動，從而實現提供有效產品和服務，使遊客滿意，使企業獲利的經濟和社會目標。

Passage Translation 段落翻譯練習

The state plays an important part in controlling and supervising tourism, as well as helping to facilitate it. This is necessary to restrain undesirable growth, to maintain quality standards, to match supply and demand and to protect tourists against industrial malpractice or failure. A government can act to restrain tourism in a number of ways, whether through central directives or through local authority control. Refusal of planning permission is an obvious example of the exercise of control over tourism development. However, this is seldom totally effective, since if an area is a major attraction for tourists, the authorities will be unlikely to dissuade them from visiting the district simply by, say, refusing planning permission for new hotels; the result may be that overnight visitors are replaced by excursionists, or that private bed and breakfast accommodation moves in to fill the gap left by the lack of hotel beds.

Lesson 7 SWOT Analysis SWOT分析法

導讀：

SWOT分析法又稱為態勢分析法，它是一種能夠較客觀而準確地分析和研究一個企業或組織現實情況的方法。SWOT分析法常常被用於制定集團發展戰略和分析競爭對手情況，在戰略分析中，它是最常用的方法之一。本篇文章著重圍繞SWOT分析法在企業制定市場營銷戰略過程中的運用問題進行了具體說明。

What Is SWOT Analysis

SWOT analysis is a basic, straightforward model that provides direction and serves as a basis for the development of strategic marketing plans. It is the first stage of planning and helps marketers to focus on key issues.

SWOT stands for strengths, weaknesses, opportunities, and threats. SWOT analysis accomplishes its role by assessing an organization's strengths (what an organization can do) and weaknesses (what an organization cannot do) in addition to opportunities (potential favorable conditions for an organization) and threats (potential unfavorable conditions for an organization).

SWOT analysis' value is often underestimated despite the simplicity in creation.The role of SWOT analysis is to take the information from the environmental analysis and separate it into internal issues (strengths and weaknesses) and external issues (opportunities and threats). Once this is completed, SWOT analysis determines if the information indicates something that will assist the firm in accomplishing its objectives (a strength or an opportunity), or if it indicates an obstacle that must be overcome or minimized to achieve desired results (a weakness or threat).

What makes SWOT particularly powerful is that, with a little thought, it can help you uncover opportunities that you are well placed to take advantage of(註1). And by understanding the weaknesses of your business, you can manage and eliminate threats that would otherwise catch you unawares(註2).

More than this, by looking at yourself and your competitors using the SWOT framework, you can start to craft a strategy that helps you distinguish yourself from your competitors, so that you can compete successfully in your market.

Elements of SWOT Analysis

Strengths

Relative to market needs and competitors'characteristics, a manager must begin to think in terms of what the organization can do well and where it may have deficiencies(註3). Strengths and weaknesses exist internally within an organization, or in key relationships between the organization and its customers. SWOT analysis must be customer-focused to gain maximum benefit; a strength is really meaningful only when it is useful in satisfying the needs of a customer. At this point, the strength becomes a capability.

When writing down strengths, it is imperative that they be considered from both the view of the firm as well as from the customers that are dealt with. These strengths should be realistic and not modest. A well-developed listing of strengths should be able to answer a couple of questions.

◆ What advantages does your company have?

◆ What do you do better than anyone else?

◆ What unique or lowest-cost resources do you have access to?

◆ What do people in your market see as your strengths?

In looking at your strengths, think about them in relation to your competitors — for example, if all your competitors provide high quality products, then a high quality production process is not a strength in the market; it is a necessity.

Weaknesses

A customer-focused SWOT may also uncover an organization's potential weaknesses. Although some weaknesses may be harmless, those that relate to specific customer needs should be minimized if at all possible. In addition, a focus on an organization's strengths in advertising in promotion is important to increase awareness in areas that an organization excels in(註4). This method not only evokes a positive response within the minds of the consumer, but pushes the weaknesses further from the decision making process(註5).

Weaknesses should also be considered from an internal and external viewpoint. It is important that listing of an organization's weaknesses is truthful so that they may be overcome as quickly as possible. Delaying the discovery of weaknesses that already exist within a company will only further hurt the firm. A well-developed listing of weaknesses should be able to answer a few questions.

◆ What could you improve?

◆ What should you avoid?

◆ What are people in your market likely to see as weaknesses?

The role of the internal portion of SWOT is to determine where resources are available or lacking so that strengths and weaknesses can be identified. From this, the marketing manager can then develop marketing strategies that match these strengths with opportunities and thereby create new capabilities, which will then be part of subsequent SWOT analysis. At the same time, the manager can develop strategies to overcome the organization's weaknesses, or find ways to minimize the negative effects of these weaknesses.

Opportunities and Threats

Managers who are caught up in developing strengths and capabilities may ignore the external environment(註6). A mistake of this magnitude could lead to an efficient organization that is no longer effective when changes in the external environment prohibit the firm's ability to deliver value to its targeted customer segments. These changes can occur in the rate of overall market growth and in the competitive, economic, political, legal, technological, or sociocultural environments.

Changes in the Political/Legal Environment.

Regulatory actions by government agencies often restrict the activities of companies in affected industries(註7). The American Disabilities Act of 1990 placed restrictions on the way firms construct their places of business and design jobs. Companies with significant investment facilities that did not comply with the law viewed its implementation as a major threat(註8). On the other hand, companies that market products designed to assist disabled shoppers and employees saw the act as a key opportunity.

Lawsuits against the tobacco industry have led to dramatic changes in the way cigarette companies market their products. Today, companies such as Phillip Morris are airing advertisements illustrating the negative effects of their products. As can be seen, it is important to identify political/legal threats and opportunities in order to keep an edge on the market.

Changes in the Sociocultural Environment.

Social and cultural influences cause changes in attitudes, beliefs, norms, customs, and lifestyles. An organization's ability to foresee changes in these areas can prove beneficial while failure to react to these changes can be devastating. For example, the sales of Mexican-food products have increased at an annual rate of approximately 12 percent. The trend went unnoticed by major food producers for a long time. However, Heinz Company recognized the existence of a viable opportunity and responded by introducing two versions of salsa-style ketchup. Although Heinz's strategy was sound, its salsa ketchup eventually failed due to poor distribution during the implementation phase.

Product modifications are often used to take advantage of market opportunities. However, these changes can also create potential new competitive threats. Failure to re-evaluate and realign the threats and opportunities in the sociocultural environment can hurt an organization.

Changes in the Competitive Environment.

One of the largest trends in the U.S.economy in recent years has been the rapid decline in the number of small, independently owned retail businesses. Small mom-and-pop supermarkets and locally owned bookstores are fading away quickly and will soon be extinct. Likewise, many locally owned restaurants around the country are experiencing difficulties due to the growth of large, national restaurant chains. The most recent businesses to face extinction are neighborhood hardware stores, which have lost customers to retail giants such as Home Depot and Lowes. Although they cannot be competitive with pricing, hardware retailers such as Ace Hardware and True Value expect to survive by offering outstanding service and convenient locations.

Changes in the Internal Organizational Environment.

Various elements within an organization's internal environment can also have an impact on marketing activities. Changes in the structuring of departments, lines of authority, top management, or internal political climate can all create internal weaknesses that must be considered during the SWOT analysis as well as in the development of the marketing plan(註9).

Take McDonald's case for example. McDonald's has recently been feeling increased competitive pressure from Wendy's and Burger King. In order to increase market share, McDonald's created new marketing campaigns and new sandwiches. However, McDonald's failed to get the cooperation of all its franchisees. When store sales began to fall, individual franchisees started to band together to gain power to protect their investments. The increased power of the franchisees forced McDonald's to pull several advertisement campaigns due to lack of support. Prior to this McDonald's was used to getting their way with franchisees(註10). Now, the shift in power from McDonald's to its franchisees has created an internal weakness that the company must address as it develops and implements new marketing strategies. Again, it is necessary to emphasize the importance of evaluating specific opportunities and threats within your company.

The decision to put any individual item under either the opportunity or threat column will depend on the nature of the current strengths and weaknesses of the organization. What is seen as a threat now can be transferred into an opportunity by changing the organization itself in a way which allows this transformation(註11). For example, if a zoo decided to invest in improvements to give it a reputation for conservation work and looking after the welfare of its animals, it could possibly overcome the potential threat caused by the rise of public dislike of the idea of zoos(註12). It would be seen as a market leader and could sell itself as a new kind of "post-zoo" animal attraction. It could even exploit new technology such as virtual reality to take the idea further, perhaps by replacing animals altogether.

Conclusion

It is not simply enough to identify the strengths, weaknesses, opportunities, and threats of a company. In applying the SWOT analysis it is necessary to minimize or avoid both weaknesses and threats. Weaknesses should be looked at in order to convert them into strengths. Likewise, threats should be converted into opportunities. Lastly, strengths and opportunities should be matched to optimize the potential of a company. Applying SWOT in this fashion can obtain leverage for a company.

As can be seen, SWOT analysis can be extremely beneficial to those who objectively analyze their company. The marketing manager should have a rough outline of potential marketing activities that can be used to take advantage of capabilities and convert weaknesses and threats. However, at this stage, there will likely be many potential directions for the managers to pursue. Due to the limited resources that most companies have, it is difficult to accomplish everything at once. The manager must prioritize all marketing activities and develop specific goals and objectives for the marketing plan.

Vocabulary 內文詞彙

straightforward	簡單的，易懂的
underestimate	低估，看輕
minimize	將……減到最小
eliminate	排除，消除
unawares	冷不防地，出其不意地
deficiency	缺乏，不足
imperative	必要的，必須的
excel	優秀，勝過他人
evoke	引起，博得
magnitude	巨大，重要性
to air advertisements	大做廣告
keep an edge on	在……上保持優勢
norm	標準，規範

devastating	破壞性很大的，毀滅性的
viable	切實可行的
version	種類
product modifications	產品調整
realign	重新排列
retail businesses	零售企業
extinct	消失，不復存在
depot	倉庫，庫房
ace	第一流的，傑出的
franchisee	有產品經銷特許權的人或團體
transfer	改變，轉變
exploit	運用，利用
virtual reality	虛擬現實
optimize	使……最優化
leverage	槓桿作用
prioritize	把……區分優先次序

Notes to the Text 內文註釋

1.What makes SWOT particularly powerful is that, with a little thought, it can help you uncover opportunities that you are well placed to take advantage of.

SWOT之所以成為一種尤為有力的分析方法，是因為你稍加思考，就可以在它的幫助下發現你在所處境況中恰好可以利用的機會。

2.you can manage and eliminate threats that would otherwise catch you unawares：你就可以應對威脅，消除威脅，否則這些威脅會出其不意地降臨。

3.Relative to market needs and competitors' characteristics, a manager must begin to think in terms of what the organization can do well and where it may have deficiencies.

在考慮有關市場需求和競爭者特點的問題時，管理者必須首先從企業做得好的方面和存在的不足之處入手。

4.In addition, a focus on an organization's strengths in advertising in promotion is important to increase awareness in areas that an organization excels in.

此外，在促銷廣告中強調企業的優勢也很重要，這樣可以增強顧客對企業優勢的瞭解。

5.This method not only evokes a positive response within the minds of the consumer, but pushes the weaknesses further from the decision making process.

這個方法不僅可以在顧客心目中引起一種積極的反響，而且會讓企業在決策制定過程中更好地避開自身的劣勢。

6.Managers who are caught up in developing strengths and capabilities may ignore the external environment.

那些埋頭於提升自身優勢和潛能的經理們可能會忽略外部的環境因素。

7.Regulatory actions by government agencies often restrict the activities of companies in affected industries.

政府機構的規範措施往往會限制受其影響的行業中的公司的經營活動。

8.Companies with significant investment facilities that did not comply with the law viewed its implementation as a major threat.

那些擁有與該項法律要求不符的重大投資設備的公司，把該法律的實施視為一項很大的威脅。

9.Changes in the structuring of departments, lines of authority, top management, or internal political climate can all create internal weaknesses that must be considered during the SWOT analysis as well as in the development of the marketing plan.

在部門的構建、上下級關係、最高管理層或者內部政治氣候等方面的變化都會在企業內部造成劣勢，這些劣勢在制定營銷計劃和進行SWOT分析時都必須考慮在內。

10.Prior to this McDonald's was used to getting their way with franchisees.

在此之前，麥當勞習慣於讓其特許經銷商服從自己的意志行事。

11.What is seen as a threat now can be transferred into an opportunity by changing the organization itself in a way which allows this transformation.

現在被視為威脅的東西可以透過企業組織對自身的調整而轉變為機遇。當然，企業的調整方式要容許這種轉變才可以。

12.For example, if a zoo decided to invest in improvements to give it a reputation for conservation work and looking after the welfare of its animals, it could possibly overcome the potential threat caused by the rise of public dislike of the idea of zoos.

比如，如果一家動物園決定投資改善動物的生活條件，以期提高自己保護動物的聲譽的話，它就有可能克服公眾對動物園反感不斷增加所引發的潛在威脅。

★ ★ ★ ★

Useful Words and Expressions 實用詞彙和表達方式

旅遊總體規劃	master plan for tourism
規劃項目	planned project
規劃模式	planning model
整體開發戰略	integrated development strategy
集中開發戰略	concentrated development strategy
分散開發戰略	dispensed development strategy
科學管理戰略	scientific management strategy
文化致勝戰略	cultural-prevailing strategy
以人為本戰略	human-oriented strategy
旅遊總量	amount of travel
旅遊流向	tourist flow

旅遊交通強度	intensity of tourist traffic
輔助吸引物	secondary attraction
旅遊資源儲量	inventory of tourist resources
派生需求	derived demand
你死我活的競爭	cut-throat competition
明顯勸誘性資訊	overt inducing information
隱蔽勸誘性資訊	covert inducing information
隨機抽樣	random sampling
零售點	retail outlet
重新定位，調整定位	repositioning
重新，再次購買	repeat purchasing
再上市	relaunch
參照群體	reference group
傳銷，金字塔式銷售	pyramid selling
定位試銷	placement test

Exercises 練習題

Discussion Questions 思考題

1.How do you understand the role and value of SWOT Analysis in the development of marketing plans?

2.What is meant by considering both strengths and weaknesses from an internal and external viewpoint?

3.How do changes in the socio-cultural environment influence an organization's ability to deliver value to its customers?

4.What lesson(s) can we draw from what happened to McDonald's?

5.Why is it not enough to simply identify the strengths, weaknesses, opportunities, and threats of a company?

Sentence Translation 單句翻譯練習

1.營銷戰略是企業戰略的重點，因為企業戰略的實質是企業外部環境、企業內部實力（capabilities）與企業目標三者的動態平衡（dynamic equilibrium）。

2.隨著互聯網的發展，從有形市場（tangible markets）轉向網路市場使企業的目標市場、顧客關係、企業組織（business structures）及營銷手段等發生了變化，企業既面臨著（confront）新的挑戰，也面臨著無限的（infinite）市場機遇。

3.事實上，企業內外部環境分析及企業優劣勢分析，即所謂的SWOT分析，是企業進行戰略選擇的基礎，一般情況下，企業內外部情況不太可能發生突變。

4.優勢和劣勢是景點內部問題（internal issues）。它指的是景點在某個時間，即規劃開始時的狀況，以及景點是否能夠對這方面因素加以控制或發揮很大的影響力。

5.在所規劃的年限（span）中，作為SWOT分析基礎的企業內外部情況都會發生變化。因此，應該根據變化對戰略進行不斷的修改（modify）。

6.與其他行業有所不同的是，由於旅遊經營與相關的其他國家有著緊密聯繫（closely related），所以旅遊經營商（tour operators）的某些決策同樣會對其他國家產生直接的影響。

7.各種各樣的外部因素可能會對旅遊經營產生影響。一些外部因素可能會影響旅遊的價格，一些會影響旅遊市場，而另外一些則可能決定宣傳（publicize）或不宣傳哪些國家。

8.雖然旅遊經營商顯然可以在一定程度上控制其價格，但是他們無法控制的因素也可能迫使他們提價，而提價則有可能會影響一些旅遊項目的銷路（sales）。

Passage Translation 段落翻譯練習

The marketing strategy, or mix, should be viewed as a package of offerings designed to attract and serve the customer or visitor. Recreation and tourism businesses and communities should develop the internal marketing mix for different target markets as well as the external marketing mix, which includes product/service, price, place/location, and promotion.

As stated, marketing services such as recreation and tourism differ from marketing tangible products. Recreation and tourism businesses must direct as much attention in marketing to customers on site as they do to attracting them.In this respect, internal marketing is important because dissatisfied customers can effectively cancel out an otherwise effective marketing strategy. The success of internal marketing is dependent on creating an atmosphere in which employees desire to give good service and sell the business/community to visitors. To create such an atmosphere requires the following four important elements: hospitality and guest relations, quality control, personal selling and employee morale.

Lesson 8 Market Research Tool—Survey and Questionnaire
市場調研工具：調查與問卷

導讀：

市場調研是系統地設計、收集、分析並報告與企業或公司面臨的特定市場營銷狀況有關的數據和調查結果。營銷經理經常會為了特定的問題或目的進行市場調研。在旅遊業中，營銷者可能需要對遊客的偏好、動機、滿意度、旅行中的支出、廣告的效果等進行調研，以此來開拓新的市場。本篇文章圍繞市場調研中兩種最常用的方法——調查和問卷展開，詳細介紹了如何進行調查以及如何設計有效的問卷。

There is a wide range of tools in marketing research available to tourism marketers and marketing researchers. Among them, the most frequently used tools are survey and questionnaire.

Surveys

Survey is the most popular marketing research method in tourism industry because it is flexible and easy to use. Tourism marketers undertake surveys to find out about their customers, their attitudes, motivations, likes and dislikes. For example, what characteristics do customers share, why do they wish to buy a particular holiday package or visit a certain type of attraction, what they think about the levels of service of this travel agents, and so on.

Identifying the Objectives

Because surveys are so expensive to conduct in terms of time and money, tourism marketers need to be sure that a survey is necessary before they begin. They also need to be sure that they know the main purpose of the survey. Examples of goals for tourism surveys might be:

◆ An airline wishing to know what its image is with business travelers;

◆ A hotel chain testing the reaction to a room rate increase;

◆ A cruise line wishing to know why 95 percent of the population has never taken a cruise;

◆ A restaurant wishing to know what items customers like to have on menus;

◆ A tour wholesaler testing the acceptability of new packages to be offered in shoulder travel seasons(註1).

Types of Survey

After identifying the objectives, tourism marketers can choose from the following ways to collect survey:

Mail survey is the most common form of survey. It involves sending out one copy of the survey. If no response is received, then a reminder postcard is sent to the respondent(註2). Or sometimes a second copy of the survey may be mailed to the respondent. It works best when a comprehensive list of visitors' names and addresses are available so that a random sample can be drawn from this list(註3). Mail surveys also work well when targeting a specific geographic or interest group where lists of total populations exist.

The cost of mail survey is relatively low, and its coverage can be of a wide geographical area. The respondents can complete the questionnaire anonymously and at their convenience(註4). The major problem of mail survey is the relatively low response rate despite organizers offering prizes or monetary or nonmonetary incentives(註5). It is not unusual to achieve a response rate of less than 10 percent.

Personal interview can be conducted in the office, home, hotels, airport, or at any given tourism destination. It is often difficult to refuse to give answers in a personal interview. Therefore, there is generally a high response rate of personal interviews.

In personal interviews, the interviewer can adjust to each particular situation, like explaining a question that appears to puzzle the person being interviewed. They can also gather far more complete information by getting clues from the respondent's behavior and "body language" or by probing further(註6). And the interviewers can show or demonstrate more things. Let's assume we are a hotel company considering a video-based checkout system. The most effective way would be personal interview. We could show the description to some of our current guests and ask them for their reactions. The disadvantages of personal interview are cost and interviewer bias.

Telephone survey is more flexible than mail survey, since the interviewers can reword questions for greater clarification and skip questions that are not applicable(註7). Information can be gathered quickly and inexpensively. However, many people use answering machines and caller ID to screen their calls and refuse to pick up the phone if someone they do not know is on the line. The response rates of it have lowered drastically in the last few years.

Exit Survey seeks tourists' feedback and it is becoming more common in hotels, at visitor attractions and among transport operators. Most of the major tour operators issue package holiday travelers with a questionnaire on the flight home. On the plane the customer has time to reflect and time to fill in a fairly lengthy form. Thus, a mass of data is collected on a continuous basis about the travel(註8), destination resort, hotels, apartments and hostels visited by the customer.

Diary survey is the way of issuing a diary to the tourist before he or she travels or begins a holiday. The diarist is expected to record places visited, activities undertaken and the amount of spend per day(註9).

Now, with the advances in technology, the use of FAX, E-mail, and Internet surveys are on the rise. These are other options that may be considered.

Sources of Error in Surveys

There are some problems in collecting accurate data in the case of survey.

Although tourists may be able to provide a fairly accurate total expenditure amount, day-to-day expenditures for food, drink, souvenirs, and similar items may not be easy to recall accurately, particularly for an extended trip(註10). Travel expenditures may also be spread out over a wide geographical area embracing several states or provinces. Again, this confuses recall.

Failing to select a random sample can result in high levels of coverage error and biased results. In visitor surveys, one common problem is caused by surveying visitors during only a portion of the year and then estimating annual totals from these surveys(註11).

Questionnaire

A questionnaire consists of a set of questions presented to respondents for their answers. Because of its flexibility, the questionnaire is by far the most effective way used to collect data.In preparing a questionnaire, the professional tourism marketers and marketing researchers should carefully design the questions and their form, wording, and sequence.

The Design of Questions

A questionnaire usually requests three key levels of response:

◆ Identification — name, address and telephone;

◆ Classification — socio-economic group, lifestyle, frequent or infrequent traveler;

◆ Subject data — core information being gathered.

Questions requiring the same level of response should be grouped together.

A common error in designing questions is including questions that cannot, would not, or need not be answered and omitting questions that should be answered. Questions that are merely interesting should be dropped because they may exhaust the respondent's patience(註12).

The Form of Questions

The forms of questions asked can influence the response. Most questionnaires comprise mainly closed-end questions where the respondent is given a limited choice of possible answers to tick, usually dichotomous （yes or no response） or multiple choices(註13). For example,

In arranging this trip, did you personally phone American Airline?

☐ Yes

☐ No

With whom are you traveling on this flight?

☐ No one

☐ Spouse

☐ Spouse and children

☐ Children only

☐ Business associates/friends/relatives

☐ An organized tour group

At the end of the questionnaire, there might be one or two open-ended questions where a more free flow comment is expected. Open-end questions reveal more because they do not constrain respondents' answer. For example,

What do you think we should be concentrating on most to improve our operation?

What could this restaurant have done to improve your dining experience today?

Scaling is of vital importance to closed-end questions when considering response rates. It allows a gradation of opinion to be expressed regarding certain aspects(註14). When designing closed-end questions, the designer should use the technique of scaling to ensure that the questions cover a full range of possible options, so that they need only check off one option and do not have to write out their selection. For example,

☐ Excellent

☐ Very Good

☐ Satisfactory

☐ Poor

☐ Very Poor

Options like "undecided", "don't know", "other" or "none" should be included in some questions, which allow respondents to at least provide some answer.

The Wording and Sequence of Questions

The questionnaire designer should exercise care in the wording and sequencing of questions. The questionnaire has to be easy to understand and complete, and should also be visually attractive if higher response rates are to be encouraged. Therefore, the questions need to be formulated with clarity, using unambiguous language, avoiding bias and redundant questions (i.e. a question that asks basically the same thing as another question).

The questionnaire should start with fairly simple and interesting questions. For example, tourists often enjoy talking about where they have been and where else they are going on this trip. The most important questions should come soon after a few warm-up questions so that they are less likely to be affected by respondent fatigue. Difficult or personal questions should be asked toward the end of questionnaire so that respondents do not become defensive early(註15). Finally, the questions should flow in a logical order.

Some Guidelines for Designing Effective Questionnaire

Avoid technical terms or jargon that may not be significant to respondents (e.g. check average, occupied room nights, covers).

◆ Keep questions, and questionnaires short and simple. Keep in mind that people's willingness to respond will be affected by how many pages they see in the questionnaire.

◆ Avoid embarrassing personal questions (e.g. income level, age). If personal questions are used, place them at the end of the questionnaire.

◆Date the questionnaire and provide instructions on how the respondent should answer each questions.

Vocabulary 內文詞彙

survey	調查
questionnaire	問卷
holiday package	假日套裝行程
attraction	旅遊勝地
cruise line	遊輪公司
tour wholesaler	組團旅行社
shoulder travel season	旅遊平季，次旺季
mail survey	郵寄調查
reminder postcard	提醒卡片
respondent	被調查者，回答者
respondent rate	回應率
comprehensive	全面的，綜合的

random sample	隨機樣本
coverage	覆蓋率
anonymously	匿名地
incentive	激勵措施，激勵
personal interview	面訪，個人訪談
probe	探查，查究
interviewer bias	調查者偏誤，訪者偏誤
telephone survey	電話調查
caller ID	來電顯示
drastically	激烈地，劇烈地，大幅度地
exit survey	返程時調查
tour operator	旅遊經營商
transport operator	運輸經營商
resort	度假地，遊覽勝地
diary survey	日記本調查
Internet survey	網路調查
souvenir	紀念品

extended trip	延伸旅行，增加景區或遊覽地
wording	措辭
identification	身分證明
classification	類別
subject data	主體資料
closed-end questions	封閉式問題，選擇題
dichotomous	二分法的
open-ended questions	開放式問題，問答題
scaling	度量標準，量表
gradation	分級，層級
fatigue	疲乏，勞累

Notes to the Text 內文註釋

1.A tour wholesaler testing the acceptability of new packages to be offered in shoulder travel seasons.

組團旅行社在旅遊平季測試旅遊者對即將推出的新套裝行程的認可度。

2.If no response is received, then a reminder postcard is sent to the respondent.

如果沒有收到回覆，可寄給被調查者一張提醒卡片。

3.a random sample can be drawn from this list：可以從這份名單中隨機抽取樣本。

4.The respondents can complete the questionnaire anonymously and at their convenience.

被調查者可以在他們方便的時候匿名填寫問卷。

5.despite organizers offering prizes or monetary or nonmonetary incentives：儘管組織者會提供獎品、獎金或實物獎勵。

6.getting clues from the respondent's behavior and "body language" or by probing further：透過觀察被調查者的行為和「身體語言」或透過進一步的詢問得到一些線索。

7.since the interviewers can reword questions for greater clarification and skip questions that are not applicable：因為調查者可以改變問題的措辭使問題更加清晰，並且可以跳過一些不適用的問題。

8.a mass of data is collected on a continuous basis about the travel：可以連續地收集大量有關旅行的資料。

9.The diarist is expected to record places visited, activities undertaken and the amount of spend per day.

要求接受日記本調查者記錄他們參觀的地點，參與的活動以及每天的支出。

10.Although tourists may be able to provide a fairly accurate total expenditure amount, day-to-day expenditures for food, drink, souvenirs, and similar items may not be easy to recall accurately, particularly for an extended trip.

儘管遊客或許能夠提供一份相當精確的有關總支出的記錄，但是他們，尤其是那些參加延伸旅行的遊客，很難準確地回憶起每天在食物、飲料、紀念品或其他一些類似項目上的花銷。

　　11.by surveying visitors during only a portion of the year and then estimating annual totals from these surveys：僅對一年中某個時段的參觀者進行調查，然後根據這些調查來估計全年的總體情況。

　　12.Questions that are merely interesting should be dropped because they may exhaust the respondent's patience.

　　應該放棄那些僅僅是有趣的問題，因為這些問題可能會讓被調查者失去耐心。

　　13.closed-end questions where the respondent is given a limited choice of possible answers to tick, usually dichotomous (yes or no response) or multiple choices：封閉式問題給出一些有限的可能性答案供被調查者選擇，通常都給出兩個選項（回答「是」或「否」）或多個選項。

　　14.It allows a gradation of opinion to be expressed regarding certain aspects.

　　度量法使被調查者能夠在某些方面表達出有一定層次區別的意見。

　　15.Difficult or personal questions should be asked toward the end of questionnaire so that respondents do not become defensive early.

　　難度大的問題或私人問題應該出現在問卷的最後，以免被調查者一開始就對問卷產生戒備心理。

★ ★ ★ ★

Useful Words and Expressions 實用詞彙和表達方式

觀察法	observational research
專題討論法	focus group research
試驗法	experimental research
約定訪談	arranged interview
實地調查	field survey
帶薪假期	paid holiday
專門經辦商務旅行的代理商	business travel agent
全包旅行團	inclusive tour
小包價旅行	mini-package tour
旅遊方式	mode of tourism
可選擇的旅遊	optional tour
一日遊	one-day tour/day trip/day excursion
旅遊客源國	origin country
旅遊目的地國	destination country
區域旅遊	regional tour
觀光旅行，遊覽	sightseeing tour
特殊興趣旅遊	special-interest tour

考察／修學旅遊	study tour
文化旅遊	cultural tour
教育旅遊	educational tour
民俗風情遊	folklore tour
市區遊覽	city tour
獵奇旅遊	exotic and unusual holidays
自行車越野旅行	cross-country bicycling
個體包價旅遊	independent inclusive tour
價格全包旅遊	all-inclusive package tour
旅遊中多次停留的散客旅遊	multi-stopover independent tour
過境旅遊	transit traveler
國內長途旅遊	long-haul domestic travel

Exercises 練習題

Discussion Questions 思考題

1.What are the main ways to collect survey?

2.What is the major problem of mail survey?

3.Compared with mail survey, what are the advantages of personal interview?

4.What are the advantages and disadvantages of telephone survey?

5.In preparing a questionnaire, what are the problems the professional tourism marketers and marketing researchers should pay attention to?

Sentence Translation 單句翻譯練習

1.政府的旅遊機構會提供一些對於預測遊客的總需求（demand）、評估（evaluate）經濟和政策對旅遊的影響非常重要的數據。

2.由於遊客的流動性（mobility）很大，一旦遊客離開遊覽地就很難再和他們取得聯繫。

3.例如，連鎖旅店會聘請諮詢公司（counseling firm）進行可行性研究（feasibility study），以決定是否應該在某地建立一個新的連鎖旅店。

4.可以透過住宿登記（guest registration）卡片來獲得遊客的資訊，如果包括國際遊客的話，也可以透過過境（border-crossing）記錄來獲得遊客的資訊。

5.像假日酒店（Holiday Inn）這樣的連鎖旅店能夠在全球經營的原因就是它們能夠滿足遊客的住宿需求，為遊客提供和在本國一樣的住宿標準。

6.在進行了全國範圍的調查之後，該旅行社增強了對其週末遊套裝行程（weekend package）的重視。

7.到某個目的地旅遊的願望或動機受人們的消費心態（psychographics）和社會經濟因素的影響，其中包括到目的地的成本和時間，居住國（country of residence）和目的地國（country of destination）的文化差異等。

8.如果透過問卷調查航空公司發現遊客對自己的評價（rating）相對於其他競爭者來說下滑了，那麼它就會採取措施來提高自己的服務水準。

Passage Translation 段落翻譯練習

Let us take the example of a survey of visitors to a seaside resort by means of a street interview. An interviewer could be assigned to stand on a particular street corner and question every nth person who passed by. This convenience sample will have a number of inherent biases. Many visitors to the resort not passing these points will have no opportunity for selection, and the flow of visitors will be greater at certain times of the day and certain days of the week than at others. It is also possible that other biases will emerge. Passers-by with more time on their hands will be more likely to stop to answer questions than those who are busy, and there is a strong temptation for interviewers to approach those who look friendly, or are from the same age group, sex or social background. Ethnic minorities might be ignored, and people who cannot speak sufficient English to be interviewed will be rejected. By the use of good interviewer training, and by supporting the survey with other forms of research such as hotel occupancy surveys and car park observation, bias will be reduced, if never entirely eliminated.

Part II

Lesson 21 Experiential Marketing　體驗式營銷

Lesson 9 Understanding Decision-making Process 瞭解顧客決策過程

導讀：

　　雖然人類有著不同的種族、膚色和文化背景，但是從心理學的角度看，人們具有共同的身體需求和精神需求。本篇文章透過對決定購買旅遊產品過程中的問題認知、資訊搜尋、選擇評估和影響因素的介紹，幫助市場營銷人員理解消費者心理需求和消費者旅遊動機，以及由此產生的購買行為。

　　Marketing's main aim may be described as improving the profit and sales of a firm. It will not do so if the executives are ignorant of what marketing is as well as what the techniques can and cannot do. The management must not only explore various techniques to make the products known, but also cater the products to mass tastes.

　　How and why does a consumer decide to buy a tourist product, or what is the process whereby people reach a decision to buy a particular holiday? The first thing to study in solving the problem is the consumer decision-making process. Understanding how and why your customers make their choice of leisure services or products, or being clearly aware of each stage of marketing strategy in relation to the consumer decision in the consumer decision-making process is central to effective marketing(註1). The consumer decision-making process involves five stages — problem recognition, information search, evaluation of alternatives, choice at point of sale and evaluation of post-purchase experience, which will not be concerned in this text.

　　Problem Recognition

The consumer must be aware that he needs a holiday. Since all purchases and activities are motivated by fundamental human needs, it is the marketer's task to recognize and help consumers recognize their needs, and then to motivate consumers to act to satisfy their needs. Marketing can persuade consumers to try some new ways of meeting their needs, but it can not essentially create the needs. Therefore, understanding the needs of consumers is fundamentally crucial to successful marketing(註2).

People's needs for leisure change with age and their stage in the family life cycle. At different ages, people have different preoccupations which manifest themselves in interests which are channeled into various leisure activities(註3). Any particular activity has different meanings for different kinds of people in relation to the interests they are pursuing.

The tourist products, unlike a television, a car or a dress, which just meets a single personal demand, represent either an escape from daily reality, or a means of self-fulfillment. In fact, tourism can offer more than this; it does highlight one particular characteristic of the product which differentiates it from many other purchases. Essentially tourism is not a purchase of the physical product, but a means by which the holidaymaker acquires experiences and fulfills dreams.

Some of the psychological motivations may initiate the type of holiday chosen. Whatever type of holiday is selected may in fact be a statement about our self-identity; a statement about a set of priorities felt at the time of decision making. Motivational research in the 1950s attempted to understand consumer behavior in terms of hidden psychological motives:

◆ For escape,

◆ For relaxation,

◆ For play,

◆ For sexual opportunity,

◆ For educational opportunity,

◆ For self-fulfillment,

◆ For wish fulfillment,

◆ For shopping.

Information Search

Once the consumer decides to have a holiday, he will begin to look for information on what is available. The company should know where customers normally look for information on their type of holiday, and make sure that their brand appears there. The consumer will then choose from the many products the travel agency put on sale. While the company may have hundreds of products available, the consumer is unlikely to look at more than half a dozen. People make their choices from a very limited set of alternatives. As the customer gathers information, only a few will exactly meet their requirements. The company should know where their brand stands in relation to these choices.

The product the tourist actually chooses will be the one that he believes will best satisfy his needs. This may not be the best quality product or even the most suitable product for him. The decision is not made by a rational comparison of all the facts available. It is the result of a very subjective processing of the information to which the consumer has been exposed(註4) as following:

◆ Exposure — The consumer must be exposed to information, usually through advertising or by seeing the product on display;

◆ Attention — The consumer is likely to be exposed to anything from 500 to 2000 promotional messages a day, so whether he pays any attention to this particular one will depend on how well it stands out and whether it appears relevant;

◆ Comprehension — Even if the consumer pays attention, he may not understand the message in the way the advertiser intended;

◆ Acceptance — The consumer may not accept what it is saying because it conflicts with his previous experiences or attitudes;

◆ Retention — The message needs to be memorable or it will be forgotten when the consumer comes to make his choice.

There is a believing that the mind is always trying to make new images and information fit into what it knows already, which helps to explain why people are selective in their attention, why advertising meanings can be distorted to fit their preconceptions, and why they remember some messages better than others(註5).

Effective advertising often starts with a familiar situation or phrase and changes it slightly. This element of surprise means that it is more likely to be ignored than something either completely unfamiliar or completely predictable(註6). Another advertising approach is to show an unfamiliar product in a situation which evokes a pleasant emotional response. The third form of learning is by experience. In this case, our experience of the product creates a set of positive or negative associations which influence subsequent decisions.

Evaluation of Alternatives

Then, the customer evaluates the alternatives and makes a choice by checking the features of the holiday against a mental list of attributes, and his choice will depend on the relative value of each attribute to him, and how well they provide the key attributes(註7). For example, he may want a quiet location, close to the beach, with baby-sitting service and a children's club, in a certain price range. Actually, the customer's choice will depend on the relative value of each attribute to him, and how well he believes the particular brand provides that attribute. The company can carry out research asking potential customers to rank in importance the attributes they expect from a holiday(註8), and to rate different companies according to how well they provide the key attributes. The company then has the choice of changing the attributes of the brand or of trying to change consumer perceptions and attributes(註9).

Choice at Point of Sale

Having made his choice, the consumer returns to the travel agent to book it. It is by no means certain that he will come out with the holiday he intends to book(註10). The company needs to know how likely it is that the customer's decision will be influenced at the point of sale. The holiday decision is not a spontaneous decision, but a joint decision between families and friends. In other words, the consumer's decision is not made in isolation. It is not surprising that our attitudes to products or activities are influenced by those we live and work with, and by the society and culture in which we live.

Generally, the decision can be influenced by family, social, cultural and personal factors.

Family Influences

For a large percentage of time, family holiday serves to strengthen family bonds. In the common situation where both partners are working full-time, the holiday represents a time when both can renew their relationship. More happily, holidays can provide a time when fathers can spend time with their young children, and so strengthen paternal bonding.

The marketer needs to understand the dynamics of the decision-making unit in order to sell to the family market(註11). For many important leisure purchases, the family acts as a single decision-making unit, because a family holiday has to provide something for every member of the household and all members of the family are users of the product.

Social Influences

A person may have different roles and status in each group and present a different aspect of his personality. He will want his appearance, his behavior and possessions to be acceptable and impressive to the others in these groups. He may also model his behavior on a group to which he would like to belong, and this could be his superiors at work or a higher social set in his neighborhood.

The holiday represents an important social forum for individuals where the normal conventions can be disregarded(註12). For a fortnight a group meets with a common experience, and without past knowledge of each other's backgrounds. The dynamics of such groups can be powerful determinants of the success or failure of the holiday. Holiday companies which specialize in holidays based on a hobby or leisure interests such as painting or sailing, or outdoor activity centers, recognize that one of the major determinants of the success of their holidays is that it creates a group of like-minded people with a common interest all sharing an experience. Other holidays are actually being designed for single people so that they can become part of a group and not feel isolated amongst the traditional family-orientated package holiday.

Role Models (Opinion Formers)

In each product area there are certain people willing to be innovators, to be eager to try out new experiences. They are opinion leaders who adopt new products or fashion first and influence the others to follow.

Status and social enhancement amongst one's peers can be temporarily gained on the basis of the destination chosen for the holiday. Certain destinations are fashionable, while others are not. The selection of a fashionable, or unusual and hence seen as exotic, destination will serve to confirm an impression about the holidaymaker. Holiday destination choice becomes a statement about life style. It is also not simply a question about destination, but also about the form of accommodation and activity. The desire for status enhancement needs not necessarily be confined to one's peers back home(註13). It can also be met by the role within the group of holidaymakers, or by the group creating a group identity whereby they perceive themselves as being superior to other groups of tourists, or the members of the host society(註14).

Culture Background

The sum of the shared attitudes, values and behaviors of the group is known as its culture. Culture is what the group has in common and which divides or distinguishes them from other groups. The effects on consumer behavior of cultural differences between nationalities are a major concern of international marketing. But within the same country or city, there are significant cultural differences, between ethnic minorities, between social classes, and even between age groups.

Personality

The personality is the expression of enduring inner psychological characteristics which govern how a particular individual responds to their own inner needs and to the influence of others(註15). The speed with which an individual within a group adopts an innovation will depend on their personalities.

Vocabulary 內文詞彙

explore	考察，研究
cater to	迎合（胃口／需要）
whereby	藉以，由此
self-identity	（自我）同一性，個性
highlight	強調，使突出
initiate	開始，著手實施，創始
priority	優先，重點，首位
distort	曲解，歪曲
preconception	先入之見
predictable	可預見的，可預言的
attribute	性質／屬性，人或地位之象徵
spontaneous	自發的，自然的
forum	講壇，論壇
dynamics	動態，運動與變化
innovation	改革，革新
exotic	外來的，奇異的
accommodations	方便設施，膳宿

Notes to the Text 內文註釋

1.Understanding how and why your customers make their choice of leisure services or products, or being clearly aware of each stage of marketing strategy in relation to the consumer decision in the consumer decision-making process is central to effective marketing.

有效市場營銷的關鍵在於瞭解顧客如何以及為什麼選擇休閒服務或產品，或者要清楚地瞭解針對顧客決策購買過程所採取的營銷策略的實施情況。

2.Marketing can persuade consumers to try some new way of meeting their needs, but it can not essentially create the needs. Therefore, understanding the needs of consumers is fundamentally crucial to successful marketing.

市場營銷雖然能夠引導消費者嘗試一些新辦法來滿足自己的需求，但是卻不能製造消費需求。所以，若想保證市場營銷成功進行，關鍵在於瞭解消費者的需求。

3.People's needs for leisure change with age and their stage in the family life cycle. At different ages, people have different preoccupations which manifest themselves in interests which are channeled into various leisure activities.

人們對休閒度假的需求隨著年齡和家庭生活的階段不同而有所改變。每個年齡階段都有令旅遊者專注的事情，這些事情表現為他們的興趣，並促使他們參與不同的休閒活動。

4.It is the result of a very subjective processing of the information to which the consumer has been exposed.

這就是消費者對所接受的資訊進行非常主觀處理的結果。

5.There is a believing that the mind is always trying to make new images and information fit into what it knows already, which helps to explain why people are selective in their attention, why advertising meanings can be distorted to fit their preconceptions, and why they remember some messages better than others.

有一種觀點認為大腦總是試圖將新鮮的形象和資訊同已知的形象和資訊相匹配，這種現象解釋了為什麼消費者的注意力有選擇性，為什麼消費者會曲解廣告含義來適應其原有的成見，還解釋了為什麼有些資訊容易被牢記，而另一些則很快就會被遺忘。

6.This element of surprise means that it is more likely to be ignored than something either completely unfamiliar or completely predictable.

能給人留下深刻印象的廣告通常以一種熟悉的情境或話語開始，中間稍做改動。但這種出人意料的元素與那些完全陌生的或完全在意料之中的情況相比，往往更容易被人忽略。

7.Then, the customer evaluates the alternatives and makes a choice by checking the features of the holiday against a mental list of attributes, his choice will depend on the relative value of each attribute to him, and how well they provide the key attributes.

之後，顧客對備選產品進行比較，將度假產品的各種特色和其心中的各種期待加以對照，並做出選擇。最後的選擇取決於各種心理期待對他的重要性，以及產品滿足其關鍵期望的程度。

8.to rank in importance the attributes they expect from a holiday：把他們對度假產品的各種期待按重要性排序。

9.The company then has the choice of changing the attributes of the brand or of trying to change consumer perceptions and attributes.

公司還可以改變品牌的特徵，或改變消費者的觀點和期望。

10.It is by no means certain that he will come out with the holiday he intends to book.

根本無法確定消費者一定會購買他打算預訂的度假產品。

11.The marketer needs to understand the dynamics of the decision-making unit in order to sell to the family market.

為了向家庭市場推銷產品，營銷人員需要對做出購買決定的團體的各個動態因素瞭如指掌。

12.The holiday represents an important social forum for individuals where the normal conventions can be disregarded.

度假旅遊為人們提供了一個可以將傳統生活規範通通拋在腦後的、意義重大的社會氛圍。

13.The desire for status enhancement needs not necessarily be confined to one's peers back home.

一個人希望提升身分檔次的願望並非一定要在其日常交往的人群中才能實現。

14.It can also be met by the role within the group of holidaymakers, or by the group creating a group identity whereby they perceive themselves as being superior to other groups of tourists, or the members of the host society.

這個願望也可以透過他在旅遊團內所扮演的角色來實現，或者透過旅遊團產生一種團隊共性，透過這種共性使他們認定自己優越於其他旅遊團，或者優越於當地社會的其他成員。

15.The personality is the expression of enduring inner psychological characteristics which govern how a particular individual responds to their own inner needs and to the influence of others.

個性是長期心理特徵的外在表現形式，它決定一個人如何應對其內心需求，如何應對其他人對自己的影響。

Useful Words and Expressions 實用詞彙和表達方式

購後體驗	post-purchase experience
複雜購買行為	complex buying behavior
減少分歧購買行為	dissonance-reducing buyer behavior
習慣性購買行為	habitual buying behavior
求異購買行為	variety-seeking behavior
商業資源	commercial resources
公共資源	public resources
品牌忠誠度	brand loyalty
品牌價值	brand value
品牌延伸	brand extension
附加服務	added services

強力推銷	aggressive selling
核心利益	core benefit
終端消費者	end-consumer
情感價值	emotional value
首次購買顧客	first-time customer
重複購買顧客	repeat customer
響應營銷	responsive marketing
預知營銷	anticipative marketing
創造營銷	creative marketing

Exercises 練習題

Discussion Questions 思考題

1.What is the first step to understand decision-making process?

2.How does human brain process advertising information exposed to them?

3.Can you add some other hidden psychological motivation in addition to the ones in this passage?

4.How can family affect decision-making by tourists?

5.How can role model influence the decision-making by tourists?

Sentence Translation 單句翻譯練習

1.市場就是消費者,而這些消費者,不論是個人也好,企業也好,當然都具有自主的意願,並根據這些自主的意願表達自己的意思,或者做出購買的判斷和決定。

2.從表面看,消費者的購買行為好像沒有什麼規律可循,購買商品或勞務有極為不相同的行為。即使對同一產品也各有所好,取捨不同。但事實上,這些千差萬別的購買行為是有一定規律的。

3.消費者的購買許多表現為即興購買(impulsive buying)。許多消費者原來並不打算購買某一商品,但當他在市場上受到某些營銷力量刺激後或受到相關群體影響時就會決定購買。

4.典型的購買過程由下列步驟組成:問題認識,資訊收集,可供選擇的方案評價,購買決策和購後行為(post-purchasing activity)。

5.旅遊經營商通常是以市場為導向而非產品為導向的,這主要是因為他們大多都不擁有屬於自己的產品或產品要素。

6.旅遊市場營銷的主體很廣,包括所有旅遊企業及宏觀管理的旅遊局。市場營銷是個人和群體透過創造並同他人交換產品和價值以滿足需求和慾望的一種社會和管理過程。

Passage Translation 段落翻譯練習

People have certain physiological needs, which are essential for their survival; they need to eat, to drink, to sleep, to keep warm and to reproduce, all needs which are essential to the survival of the human race. Beyond these needs, we also have psychological needs which are important for our well-being, such as the need to love and be loved, the need for friendship, the need to value ourselves as human beings and to have others value and respect us. Many people believe we also have inherently within us the need to master our environment, and to understand the nature of the society in which we live. Abraham Maslow (亞伯拉罕‧馬士洛，美國著名心理學家) conveniently grouped these needs into a hierarchy, suggesting that the more fundamental needs have to be satisfied before we seek to satisfy the higher-level needs.

Lesson 10 Ways of Segmenting the Market 如何細分市場

導讀：

根據消費者的年齡、職業、文化背景等諸多因素，可以將旅遊市場細分。其目的在於認清不同的消費人群，並針對不同的消費人群制定和實施相應的營銷辦法。本篇文章簡要地介紹了市場細分所遵循的原則，同時提醒旅行社經營中應該如何針對這些標準進行市場細分。

In very few cases are the products of one organization attractive to all consumers in the marketplace. It therefore makes good sense to target the products to specific types of consumers for which the product offers specific benefits, thereby making it more distinctive from its competitors(註1). This approach is known as market segmentation, the basis of which is that the company first determines the market or markets it will serve, and then develops its products to serve the needs of those markets(註2). A market segment can be defined as "a subgroup" of the total consumer market whose members share common characteristics relevant to the purchase of a product.

Generally speaking, the tourism product can be either product or market oriented. Product-oriented tourism emphasizes on the products and services of tourism supply, based on physical, cultural, historic, or folkloric attributes or a combination of several of them. This approach to tourism marketing does not take into account the desires of the potential tourists, particularly if the market is totally product oriented.

Theoretically, this marketing approach can be successful if demand exceeds supply, but competition among tourism sellers normally does not allow this. Market-oriented approach emphasizes on the needs and wants of potential tourists. It asks what will satisfy those needs and wants and when those needs and wants will occur and then tries to fulfill them. This marketing approach runs the risk of ignoring such things as local natural resources and culture and, for that reason, may alienate the local population(註3).

Market segmentation in tourism is a generally accepted approach to analyzing tourism demand. It is based on four assumptions:

◆ First, it assumes that tourists can be grouped into different market segments;

◆ Second, it assumes that people have different vacation/travel needs and preferences depending on their particular market segments;

◆ Third, it assumes that a specific destination or tourist experience will appeal to some segments of the market more than others;

◆Fourth, it assumes that tourism suppliers can improve their marketing efforts by developing products and services that appeal to specific market segments.

The process of dividing markets by their variables is known as market segmentation, and as few companies produce products which are in equal demand among all segments of population, similarly very few marketers will fail to break down the demand for their products by identifying those segments which purchase(註4). The market segmentation process begins by identifying the various segments by any one of the following methods or a combination of those methods.

◆ The first method or the most commonly used method is to identify a segment according to socioeconomic factors, such as age, education, and income factors;

◆ The second method is to segment people by geography, for example, climates, cultures, and scenery that can attract different kinds of tourist;

◆ The third method is to segment the market by psychographic factors, which focus on present and future buying behavior, physical needs, life-styles, and values, that is how purchasers behave. This method is often used to supplement the socioeconomic or geographic method.

Specifically, this process of market segmentation can be undertaken in four ways, by geographic variables, by demographic variables, by psychographic variables and by behavioral variables. We will examine each of these categories in turn.

Geographic Variables

The simplest way of dividing up our consumers is according to where they live. This can mean focusing marketing efforts on global areas, or on smaller elements of a country such as its regions, districts or towns. While there are cultural commonalities within a country, marketers need to be sensitive to the fact that cultural and other distinctions also exist both between contiguous countries and within countries(註5). Climate for example, can affect demand for products and services, as will be readily apparent in looking at the vast differences in climate between the northernmost and southernmost states in the USA, which are by no means restricted to the influence of climate alone. Even countries we might assume to share similar consumer traits, such as Denmark and Sweden, or Canada and the USA, demonstrate radically different patterns of consumer behavior.

Demographic Variables

In segmenting by demographic variable, marketers divide the population according to such characteristics as age, gender, family composition and size, life cyclec income, occupation, education or ethnic background. Marketers will be interested to know not only the present statistics of the population, but also any changing trends taking place in the population.

For example, if the number of young people in a country, found to be stabilizing or declining, while the number of those of retirement age is increasing, this will have important implications both for tour operators specializing in holidays for the elderly and for the young adult market. If we know something about the disposable income of these segments this will further aid our marketing strategy(註6). It is also a characteristic of the developed world's changing patterns of population that with lower birth rates the number of young people will continue to decline, while the number of those in later middle age will increase. We are likely to see much more attention focus on marketing new goods and services to the different segments in the future. The fact that some companies, for example, focus on the provision of youth holidays and others specialize in holidays for the over-50s reflects that concentrated marketing strategies lead to success.

If the tour operators have specialized in handling groups of tourists from specific countries, such as Japan or Israel, they would make it their business to employ nationals of their customer's countries to greet and deal with their clients, in order to ease communication and put their clients at ease.

As subcultures, ethnic groups, with their differing racial or religious characteristic, are among the most prominent in splintering the marketers' convenient behavioral models for a given national or regional market.

A popular means of exploiting marketing opportunities to differing segments of the demographic population has been the development of pinpoint geodemographic marketing(註7). Through analysis of census data and postal code areas it is possible to segment markets according to their geodemographic characteristics.

Aided by computer mapping, marketers can develop database selecting those elements of the population most likely to favor the company's products, and to target these by direct mail or other marketing activity. Travel agents can identify the residents within their branch catchments areas and target them through direct mail with appropriate message(註8).

Psychographic Variables

Just as with demographic segmentation, so can we segment by psychographic variables. We need to know much more about the cultural climate of a country and the psychological needs of its population.

Tourists can be categorized broadly as either psychocentrics or allocentrics. The former are self-inhibited, nervous and lack the desire for adventure, preferring well-packaged routine holidays in popular tourist destination, mainly of the "sun, sand, sea" variety, while the latter are more outgoing, have varied interests and are keen to explore new places and find new things to do(註9). Such tourists are more likely to travel independently. This model in itself is no doubt too simplistic. Most of us have some mix of these characteristics, and it is a noticeable fact that many mass tourists to popular destinations, who would fall into the psychocentric category, gain confidence after a number of trips abroad, and become more adventurous. Nevertheless, the model is helpful in thinking about the facilities we should provide to meet these differing needs.

Countries and regions develop their own unique cultures and values, which are learned rather than instinctive. Thus the British tend to seek a greater measure of privacy in their lives than do Americans, leading to a greater demand for products such as garden fencing. Life would be relatively simple if we could so conveniently classify people according to their nationality and national cultures. Unfortunately, regional differences within countries are also often pronounced, leading to different patterns of behavior, and of course the additional complexity of sub-cultural behavioral differences.

Within cultures, social class attempts to stratify societies according to criteria mainly based on the occupation of the head of household, now usually defined as the major income earner in the family(註10). Occupation is usually defined as a demographic variable, while class is generally seen as a psychographic variable, even though closely linked to occupation.

Of equal importance for those providing leisure services are the relative amounts of leisure time available for short breaks or holidays(註11). Many managers and professionals are obliged to take work home and give less time to relaxation than can the nine-to-five manual worker, who today will enjoy as many as four to five weeks holiday each year, and may take two or more foreign holidays.

Behavioral Variables

For a thorough understanding of consumers, we must also know how they act and react as individuals. Various models have been suggested by researchers of human behavior, who are in general agreement that the number of, and interrelationship between, variables affecting product choice is extremely complex(註12). The following is an analysis of consumer choice and a study of some of the factors which help understand marketing's function in aiding product choice.

Many models have been developed to show how consumers react to stimuli. Some experts have argued that consumers can be classified as being in one of three stages of behavior: an initial extensive problem-solving stage, where they have little knowledge about products or brands, and are seeking information from a wide range of sources; a stage of more limited problem-solving, where decisions have narrowed and information seeking has become more directed; and routinized behavior, where buying has based largely on habit and previous satisfaction with the product(註13).

Buyers choose products which they perceive as having the best potential to satisfy their needs; they will therefore be buying the benefits offered by the product. Buyers learn about such products partly through experience with the same or similar products in the past, and partly by seeking information. Information is sometimes sought actively, as when the buyer has an immediate need, or passively, where the buyer may be responsive to information and stores it away for future use. Sources of information may be the commercial world, or the buyer's social environment. The commercial world produces messages about products which act as stimuli, for example, advertisements which describe a product's quality, price, availability, service, and its distinctive qualities against its competitors. Social sources of information include word of mouth recommendation from friends or family, or articles about the product in newspapers, periodicals or other media. Our social class, personality, culture and group influences, as well as economic influences such as our financial means, pressure of time and the importance of the purchase, all interact with our internal state of mind to affect our decision-making. Internally, individual decisions are based on the way we perceive and learn about new products. Research has shown that our perception of products is highly selective. We tend to screen out information which is too familiar, or too complex to take in, while we are more receptive to information to which we are predisposed. If for example, we are thinking about a holiday, we become more aware of holiday advertisements. However, our perception of information is also biased: we tend to distort information to suit our own frame of reference(註14). For example, many people who have never visited Britain quite genuinely believe that the country is veiled in permanent rain and fog. Such preconceptions form a formidable problem to some travel agents when holding overseas marketing campaigns, but they can be modified by strong stimuli, such as the personal experience and recommendation of a member of the family or a friend(註15).

Vocabulary 內文詞彙

folkloric	民間傳說的，民俗的
exceed	（在數量和品質等方面）勝過，超過
alienate	疏遠，離間／使（感情）變淡漠，轉移（感情）
societal	社會的
assumption	認為當然的事情，假定，設想，臆斷
preference	偏愛物（人），嗜好物（人）
variable	可變物，易變的事物
socioeconomic	社會經濟（學）的，有關社會和經濟的
criterion（複數形式criteria）	（批評、判斷的）標準，準則，尺度
category	種類，類別
commonality	共性，共同特徵
contiguous	相接的，臨近的，毗鄰的，附近的
radically	極端地，徹底地
demographic	人口的，人口統計的
disposable	可自由支配的，可供自由使用的，可任意取用的

decline	（在品格、價值上）降低，降落，減退，走下坡路
geodemographic	地緣人口統計的，地緣人文的
psychocentric	自我中心的（人）
allocentric	異我中心的（人）
subculture	亞文化群（落）
prominent	突出的，顯著的，傑出的
splinter	使分裂成小類別
instinctive	本能的，直覺的，天性的
stimulus（複數形式stimuli）	刺激物，激勵物，促進因素
routinize	使成常規，使習慣於常規
recommendation	推薦，介紹，值得推薦的人或物
selective	選擇的，挑選的，選擇性的
predispose	預先處理，使傾向於，使易接受
stratify	分層

Notes to the Text 內文註釋

1.It therefore makes good sense to target the products to specific types of consumers for which the product offers specific benefits, thereby making it more distinctive from its competitors.

因此，使產品針對於特定的消費者類型、為他們提供特別收益的做法十分可取，這樣就使產品從眾多競爭產品中脫穎而出。

2.This approach is known as market segmentation, the basis of which is that the company first determines the market or markets it will serve, and then develops its products to serve the needs of those markets.

這種方法被稱為市場細分，它建立的基礎是公司首先要決定一個或多個目標市場，然後開發產品以滿足這些市場的需求。

3.It asks what will satisfy those needs and wants and when those needs and wants will occur and then tries to fulfill them. This marketing approach runs the risk of ignoring such things as local natural resources and culture and, for that reason, may alienate the local population.

這個方法首先要確定什麼東西以及何時滿足遊客的需要和要求。實施這種營銷方法存在的一個風險就是忽略了當地自然資源和文化等因素，並因此可能招致當地居民的反感。

4.The process of dividing markets by their variables is known as market segmentation, and as few companies produce products which are in equal demand among all segments of population, similarly very few marketers will fail to break down the demand for their products by identifying those segments which purchase.

根據市場變量對市場進行區分的過程被稱做市場細分。世界上沒有哪家公司生產的產品可以同時滿足各種細分人群的需求；同樣，也沒有哪個營銷者不透過劃分購買產品人群的類別來區分對產品的需求。

5.While there are cultural commonalities within a country such as its regions,

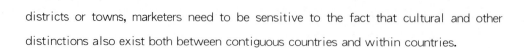

districts or towns, marketers need to be sensitive to the fact that cultural and other distinctions also exist both between contiguous countries and within countries.

雖然在同一個國家存在文化共性，如各地區、區劃或城鎮之間都有共性，但是市場營銷人員需要清醒地認識到相鄰的國家之間或在一個國家內部都還存在著文化的或其他方面的差異。

6.If we know something about the disposable income of these segments this will further aid our marketing strategy.

如果我們瞭解這些細分人群的稅後收入，那麼將會進一步幫助我們制定營銷策略。

7.A popular means of exploiting marketing opportunities to differing segments of the demographic population has been the development of pinpoint geodemographic marketing.

利用營銷機會來劃分人文細分市場的一種常用的方法就是開發精確的地緣人文營銷。

8.Travel agents can identify the residents within their branch catchments areas and target them through direct mail with appropriate message.

旅遊代理商可以先確定自己劃分地區內部的住戶，再透過直接郵寄的方式將合適的資訊傳遞給他們。

9.The former are self-inhibited, nervous and lack the desire for adventure, preferring well-packaged routine holidays in popular tourist destination, mainly of the "sun, sand, sea" variety, while the latter are more outgoing, have varied interests and are keen to explore new places and find new things to do.

前者內向拘謹，對冒險沒有興趣，傾向於全包常規旅遊，選擇多為「陽光—沙灘—海洋」這樣的大眾旅遊目的地；而後者較為外向，興趣廣泛，熱衷於嘗試新地點、新事物。

10.Within cultures, social class attempts to stratify societies according to criteria mainly based on the occupation of the head of household, now usually defined as the major income earner in the family.

在同一個文化社區內，劃分社會階層時主要的參考指標是一家之主的職業，目前通常定義為家庭主要經濟來源的提供者的職業。

11.Of equal importance for those providing leisure services are the relative amounts of leisure time available for short breaks or holidays.

短期休息或度假的時間長短對於提供休閒服務的公司同樣非常重要。

12.Various models have been suggested by researchers of human behavior, who are in general agreement that the number of, and interrelationship between, variables affecting product choice is extremely complex.

人類行為模式研究者提出了各種不同的行為類型，他們普遍認為對產品選擇產生影響的變量的數量及其內在關係都十分複雜。

13.Some experts have argued that consumers can be classified as being in one of three stages of behavior: an initial extensive problem-solving stage, where they have little knowledge about products or brands, and are seeking information from a wide range of sources; a stage of more limited problem-solving, where decisions have narrowed and information seeking has become more directed; and routinized behavior, where buying has become based largely on habit and previous satisfaction with the product.

有些專家認為可以把消費者行為劃分為三個階段：首先是泛泛的問題解決階段，此時，他們對產品或品牌幾乎一無所知，渴望透過各種廣泛的管道獲得資訊；其次是更加具體的問題解決階段，他們縮小決定涉及的範圍，對資訊的搜索也更加有針對性；最後是習慣性行為階段，購買行為主要建立在購買習慣和之前對某種商品的滿意度基礎上。

14.However, our perception of information is also biased: we tend to distort information to suit our own frame of reference.

然而，我們對資訊的接受同樣存在偏見：我們往往會歪曲不合乎我們原有觀點的資訊。

15.Such preconceptions form a formidable problem to some travel agents when holding overseas marketing campaigns, but they can be modified by strong stimuli, such as the personal experience and recommendation of a member of the family or a friend.

這些先入為主的想法會在旅遊代理商向海外市場推廣產品時形成嚴重的障礙，但是這些想法可以被強有力的外來刺激因素改變，這些因素包括個人經歷、家庭成員或親朋好友的推薦等。

★ ★ ★ ★

Useful Words and Expressions 實用詞彙和表達方式

代銷	sales on a commission basis
獨家經銷	contract for sales
自銷	sales through one's channel
試銷	test marketing

內銷	sell on domestic market
外銷	foreign export
搭銷	tied sale
傾銷	dumping sales
大眾化營銷	mass marketing
產品多樣化營銷	product-variety marketing
目標營銷	target marketing
無差異性營銷	undifferentiated marketing
差異性營銷	differentiated marketing
集中性營銷	concentrated marketing
市場定位	market positioning
競爭性定位	competitive positioning
地區分布	regional distribution
購買行為	buying behavior
核心產品	core product
輔助產品	augmented product

Exercises 練習題

Discussion Questions 思考題

1.Why is it necessary to divide the market into different segments?

2.Can you find some examples to explain the risk of market-oriented product?

3.Is there any difference between geographic and geodemographic variables in segmenting market? What is it?

4.What factors should be taken into consideration when segmenting market in terms of psychological variables?

5.What is behavioral variable and how does it affect market segmentation?

Sentence Translation 單句翻譯練習

1.在對市場需求進行調查和預測的基礎上實行市場細分化、目標化和定位是企業營銷戰略的核心，是決定營銷戰略成敗的關鍵。

2.市場細分還有利於企業掌握市場變化動態以及時調整市場營銷策略。

3.旅遊公司的市場營銷部門主要負責的工作是確定和策劃度假產品，來滿足潛在顧客的需求，並確保旅遊公司在適當的時間以適當的價格向適當的顧客推出適當的產品。

4.景區經營以遊客為中心，對遊客的調研自然是關鍵。

5.旅遊資源和旅遊環境品質是旅遊業賴以存在和發展的基礎，旅遊對環境尤其是自然環境造成的嚴重破壞不僅會阻礙旅遊業本身的持續發展，而且也會帶來相關的負效益。

Passage Translation 段落翻譯練習

The demand for business travel is quite different from that for leisure travel, since it is by nature less discretionary, that is, less a matter of personal choice. In considering the travel needs of the businessperson, the critical distinctions are, firstly, that such travel tends to be less price sensitive, since the company rather than the individual will be footing the bills. Additionally, businesspeople tend to make frequent short-duration trips, which are generally taken midweek rather than at weekends, and travel is not subject to seasonal fluctuations. Travel decisions often have to be taken at short notice, necessitating the availability of regular scheduled flights and a fast and convenient reservations service.

Lesson 11 Distribution—Getting Your Product to the Market 如何進行分銷

導讀：

要高效率、低費用地將旅遊產品投向市場，旅遊企業就必須為產品選擇合適的分銷管道。在選擇合適的分銷管道之前，必須要做好一系列的調研，比如目標市場的情況、旅遊中間商的情況以及如何降低銷售費用和提高銷售管道效率等。本篇文章系統地闡述了管道的選擇以及分銷當中的新趨勢等問題。

Some industries can use cars, trucks, ships or airplanes to transport manufactured goods to warehouses and retailers, and directly to customers. But there is no physical distribution system in tourism and hospitality, because services are intangible. So what is the best way to deliver hospitality and travel service to customers? Distribution system in this industry is both unique and complex. In order to get a better understanding of the system, we should clarify the concept of distribution channel and then correctly choose the channel.

Definition of Distribution Channel

A distribution channel is any organized and serviced system, paid for out of marketing budgets and created or utilized to provide convenient points of sale and/or access to consumers, away from the location of production and consumption.

The essence of this deliberately broad definition(註1) is that channels are carefully planned by marketing managers and serviced regularly through a combination of online access, call centers, sales visits, sales literature, multimedia options and in other ways. Each channel, once established, organized and serviced at a cost to be paid for out of marketing budgets, becomes in effect a pipeline. Through each pipeline flows a targeted volume of sales and revenue over a marketing campaign period.(註2)

The definition excludes the activities of sales representatives employed to negotiate individual contracts with corporate clients to deliver a specified number of products, over a specified period of time, at a specified price. The essence of any pipeline is that it is a non-personal system, set up in advance to facilitate targeted sales volume but the actual flow of sales achieved over the period of a campaign cannot be known in advance.(註3) The rate of flow may be strongly influenced, however, by marketing activities in the pipeline such as sales promotions and price reductions, or external to it, such as advertising.

Choosing the Channel

The Target Market

The choice of distribution channel depends on the target markets the organization wishes to reach. The questions the organization needs to ask are:

Where do customers normally look for information on this type of product?

Do they visit the travel agent or the tourist information center, or look at the holiday pages of the Sunday papers, the leaflets in the hotel lobby? Wherever they look, that is where the publicity material needs to be.

When and where do customers make the decision? Is there a conscious search, an extended problem-solving process, or is the decision taken on impulse(註4)? In the latter case, well-placed publicity and an attractive, well-signed exterior will be important.(註5)

Who influences the decision? Do customers come into the travel agency already knowing what they want to buy or do they take the advice of the agent? Once on holiday do they decide individually what to do each day, or do they take excursions pre-arranged by the tour company? Is the excursion decided in advance by the tour company or is it left to the coach driver to take passengers to the attractions which give him the best commission?

The Comparative Costs of Using the Channels

The use of intermediaries or agents has clear benefits for the producer, but it also creates additional costs, which must be paid for out of the sales revenue from the customers. The costs involved in both options need to be compared before the decision is made(註6). The following table shows a comparison of direct selling and using agents (assuming both methods need a computer reservation system and reservation staff).

Additional costs of direct selling	Additional costs of using agents
Consumer advertising	Trade advertising
Consumer promotions	Trade promotions
Staff to respond to customer enquiries and requests	Sales representatives to visit agencies
	Computer links to central reservation systems
Postage to customers	Bulk supplies of brochures
Wastage of brochures in direct mailing	Wastage of brochures not racked
	Educational and incentive trips[7]
	Commission

The Value Added by the Channel Members

The extra costs must therefore be justified either in terms of the additional business the organization will gain or the additional value the customers will gain(註8). To the producer, in this case the tour operator, the use of an intermediary such as travel agent offers:

Wider coverage: brochures displayed in many street shops.

Local selling: the travel agent talks to the customer face to face and can choose the best product, and the most effective sales message, for each individual.

Advance purchase: if the customer books in advance through an agent, the operator gets the money earlier and can earn interest on it.

Lower administrative costs: the travel agent deals with questions and problems that would otherwise involve the operator in additional work. Direct selling operators employ enquiry staff specifically to provide after-sales reassurance.

To the final customer, using a travel agent or local retailer has the following advantages:

Local purchase: it is more convenient to book the holiday during a regular shopping trip, and all the elements of the holiday (insurance, passports, currency, and the journey to the airport) can be bought at the same time — an example of what is known as "one-stop-shopping".

Local reputation: it is reassuring to know that if anything went wrong, there would be someone responsible with a local reputation to maintain who would therefore have an interest in settling the claim amicably. The brand of the retailer may be better known than that of the producer.

Comparison: customers can collect several brochures at one visit and choose the one that best suits their needs.

Demonstration: in a sports shop, the customer can try out the equipment. A travel agent will be able to give expert advice, look up information on the resort, or show a video.

New Trend in Distribution

The Internet emerged as a viable distribution channel during the 1990s and along with sophisticated on-line database programs, caused a trend that some call disintermediation (the decreasing importance of traditional travel trade intermediaries, especially travel agents). Emerging online technologies can effectively facilitate information flows and transactions, and improve efficiencies within the tourism distribution chain. Consumer travel decision-making processes are contracting, resulting in quicker decisions and shorter lead times prior to trips(註9). There is a greater need to strategically place information early in the consumer inquiry and decision-making cycle to meet these needs(註10).

So on-line travel services represent a brand new distribution channel for the hospitality and travel industry. There are now so many of these services, it is hard to

keep track of them(註11). The following table provides a partial list and identifies the major on-line travel services.

ON-LINE TRAVEL SERVICES	WEB ADDRESSES
Major On-Line Travel Services	
AOL Travel Channel (AOL)	◆ http://aolsvc.travel.aol.com/
Expedia (Microsoft)	◆ http://www.expedia.com/

(Continued)

Internet Travel Network (American Express)	◆ http://www.itn.com/
Travelocity (Sabre)	◆ http://www.travelocity.com/
Yahoo! Travel	◆ http://travel.yahoo.com/
Priceline	◆ http://www.priceline.com/
Specialized On-Line Travel Services	
Biz Travel	◆ http://www.biztravel.com/
Cheap Travel	◆ http://www.cheaptravel.com/
Last Minute Travel	◆ http://www.lastminutetravel.com/
Lowest Fare	◆ http://www.lowestfare.com/
Web Flyer	◆ http://www.webflyer.com/
Other On-Line Travel Services	
Bye Bye Now	◆ http://www.byebyenow.com/
Online Vacation Mall	◆ http://www.onlinevacationmall.com/
Travelscape	◆ http://www.travelscape.com/
Travel Now	◆ http://www.travelnow.com/
Travel Web	◆ http://www.travelweb.com/
Travel Zoo	◆ http://www.travelzoo.com/

The major world airlines are also combining to develop worldwide computer reservations systems (CRS) or global distribution systems (GDS). These offer the travel agent access not only to the CRS of the airlines themselves, but also to international hotel chains and car hire companies(註12). Major cruise lines and tour operators have also linked with the GDS, making them as important in leisure as in business tourism. The travel agency's terminal is a full personal computer (PC) which can also be used for office management purposes.

The on-line travel services provide several benefits for customers, the major of which are as follows:

Ability to self-book travel on-line;

Assistance in planning travel trips;

Availability of on-line pricing comparisons for hospitality and travel services(註13);

Convenience of accessing travel information at home or work;

Immediate confirmation of travel bookings;

Instant access to travel information;

Potential of securing lower prices on hospitality and travel services.

Hospitality and travel marketers are already quite involved in working with this new distribution channel(註14). In addition to having their own Web-based on-line booking systems, several organizations are buying banner advertising or offering special sales promotions on the on-line travel sites.

Vocabulary 內文詞彙

intangible   無形的

clarify   澄清，闡明

utilize	利用
deliberately	故意地
revenue	收入
essence	基本，本質
facilitate	推動，促進
excursion	遠足，遊覽
intermediary	中間者，中間商
bulk	大批，大量
rack	放在架子上
amicably	友善地
sophisticated	老於世故的；精細複雜的
exterior	外表，外觀
retailer	零售商
reassuring	讓人放心的，可靠的
contracting	收縮的
confirmation	確認，證實

Notes to the Text 內文註釋

1.The essence of this deliberately broad definition：這條特定意義廣泛的定義的實質是。

2.Through each pipeline flows a targeted volume of sales and revenue over a marketing campaign period.

經由每一條管道都流通著一定的預定銷售額和收入。

3.set up in advance to facilitate targeted sales volume but the actual flow of sales achieved over the period of a campaign cannot be known in advance：（分銷）系統會提前設立，以便更容易早日達到銷售額的預定目標，但是在這段時間裡實際所獲得的銷售量卻無法提前知曉。

4.Is there a conscious search, an extended problem-solving process, or is the decision taken on impulse?

是否刻意地搜尋過？是否經過了長時間的斟酌？抑或是一時衝動就定下來了？

5.well-placed publicity and an attractive, well-signed exterior will be important：（如果調研後發現，顧客容易憑一時衝動做決定的話）布置巧妙的宣傳廣告、標誌明確且頗具吸引力的外觀是十分重要的。

6.The costs involved in both options need to be compared before the decision is made.

在做決定之前，應該對兩種選擇所涉及的費用做比較。

7.Educational and incentive trips：教育或獎勵性旅遊。

8.The extra costs must therefore be justified either in terms of the additional business the organization will gain or the additional value the customers will gain.

額外費用必須有合理的理由，要麼是公司會得到附加的業務或者客戶會得到額外的價值。

9.Consumer travel decision-making processes are contracting, resulting in quicker decisions and shorter lead times prior to trips.

顧客對於是否出遊的考慮過程正逐漸縮短，於是顧客做決定的速度更快了，旅行前的準備時間也更短了。

10.There is a greater need to strategically place information early in the consumer inquiry and decision making cycle to meet these needs.

現在比過去更需要運用策略，及早地在消費者進行諮詢和做決定的過程中提供資訊，以滿足消費者的這些需求。

11.There are now so many of these services，it is hard to keep track of them.

現在這類的服務多得不勝枚舉。keep track of：——追蹤記錄下來。

12.These offer the travel agent access not only to the CRS of the airlines themselves，but also to international hotel chains and car hire companies.

這一切使旅行社不僅可以使用航空公司的全球電子預訂系統，而且還可以使旅行社方便地聯繫世界各地的連鎖飯店和汽車租賃公司。

13.Availability of on-line pricing comparisons for hospitality and travel services.

（消費者）可以在網上對飯店及旅行社的價格進行比較。

14.Hospitality and travel marketers are already quite involved in working with this new distribution channel.

很多飯店和旅遊公司都非常積極地使用這種新的分銷管道。

Useful Words and Expressions 實用詞彙和表達方式

（中國）一類社	China's category A travel agency
（中國）二類社	China's category B travel agency
（中國）三類社	China's category C travel agency
旅行計劃，行程表	itinerary
地陪，地方導遊	local guide
淡季	low season, off-peak season
最低旅遊價格	minimum tour price
會多種語言的導遊	multilingual guide
全陪，全程導遊	national guide
全國旅遊組織	national tourist organization
旺季	peak season
旅遊接待國	receiving country
旅遊安排	tour arrangement

旅遊小冊子	tour brochure
旅遊團目錄	tour catalog
旅遊代號編碼	tour code number
旅遊團陪同	tour escort/conductor/director
領隊，團長	tour leader

Exercises 練習題

Discussion Questions 思考題

1.What is the meaning of distribution channel?

2.Explain why the distribution systems in the hospitality and travel industry are different from those in other industries.

3.Why is each distribution channel referred to as "pipeline"?

4.What factors should be taken into consideration in choosing distribution channel?

5.Identify the major on-line travel services and the customer benefits in using them.

Sentence Translation 單句翻譯練習

1.旅遊產品的綜合性表現為它是由多種多樣的旅遊對象資源與旅遊設施和多種多樣的旅遊服務構成的。

2.旅遊產品資訊傳播速度快、效率高，對消費者的旅遊需求刺激影響大，其價值就易於實現。

3.旅遊活動的特點決定了企業的旅遊市場營銷必須在經過選擇的目標市場（target market）中，與現實的或潛在的旅遊者建立聯繫，瞭解旅遊者的願望和需要。

4.營銷觀念的形成是以賣方市場轉向買方市場為背景的，在當今國際和國內旅遊業競爭日趨激烈的大環境下，以顧客為中心的（customer-oriented）營銷意識衝擊著現代旅遊業的經營者。

5.旅遊服務是一種過程、一種行為，而不是一種有形的（tangible）實物，因此旅遊服務很難做到標準化，產品品質也難以控制。

6.旅遊的營銷管理不能只是以市場需求為最佳導向，在社會發展上也要以有利於社會發展為導向，旅遊企業才能長期存在。

7.旅遊產品不僅需要給予旅遊者生理上、物質上的滿足，還要給予他們心理上、精神上的滿足，所以旅遊產品的售後服務（after-sale service）是非常重要的。

8.旅遊者購買旅遊產品是為了得到它所提供的「觀賞和享用」實際利益，滿足自己「旅遊感受」和「旅遊經歷」的需要——這正是旅遊產品的促銷重點。

Passage Translation 段落翻譯練習

In business travel finding the right product to suit the business person's schedule has always required a high information content because of the individual nature of the trip. The plethora of options in terms of air schedules, types of ticket, class, hotels, etc. have to be sifted through to ensure that the most appropriate ones are chosen. Within leisure the emergence of a "new" tourism based on flexibility, variety and individualism has been well charted.

Lesson 12 Employees—the People Element in Service Delivery 僱員：服務業的人員要素

導讀：

旅遊行業是與人打交道的行業。作為旅遊企業與旅遊消費者之間的橋梁和紐帶，旅遊從業人員在企業市場營銷活動中發揮著重要的作用。本篇文章圍繞服務行業中一線人員所扮演的角色、服務客戶過程中所需要的一般性技巧以及銷售旅遊產品時應當運用的溝通手段進行了討論。

An often-heard quote about service organizations goes like this: "In a service organization, if you're not serving the customer, you'd better be serving someone who is." Front-line employees and those supporting them from behind the scenes are critical to the success of any service organization. Their performance can have a crucial impact on the way customers perceive your brand. These vital employees can build lifelong relationships with customers by delivering the right kind of experience through sales, service and delivery. Whether the front-line staff face the customer or not, the same principles apply; a well-organized front line is a decisive factor in any company's success.

The Roles Assumed by Service Employees

It is evident that all of the personnel participating in the delivery of a service provide cues to the customer regarding the nature of the service itself(註1). How these people are addressed, their personal appearance, their attitudes and behaviors all influence the customer's perceptions of the service.

The service provider or contact person can be so important that they are, in many cases, the service — there is nothing else. For example, in most personal services such as counseling, limousine services, and cleaning/maintenance, the contact employee provides the entire service singlehandedly. The offering is the employee. Even if the contact employee doesn't perform the service entirely or perhaps plays what appears to be a relatively small part in service delivery, he or she may still personify the firm in the customer's eyes(註2). Research suggests that even the provider like an airline baggage handler or an equipment delivery dispatcher can be the focal point of service encounters that can prove critical for the organization(註3). In a way, the contact employees are the organization in the customer's eyes.

What's more, because contact employees represent the organization and can directly influence customer satisfaction, they perform the role of marketers. They physically embody the product and are walking billboards from a promotional standpoint. Some may also perform more traditional selling roles.

Whether acknowledged or not, actively selling or not, service employees perform marketing functions. They can perform these functions well, to the organization's advantage, or poorly, to the organization's detriment.

The Use of Social and Personal Skills

In order to be competent for the roles of a service employee discussed above, he or she must grasp certain skills concerning the delivery of superior service in the first place. Two types of skills have to be employed when dealing with clients (and with other colleagues): personal skills and interpersonal, or social, skills, both of which involve verbal and non-verbal communication. Here we shall deal with some more important forms of communication between service employees and their clients.

Social Skills

In service delivery, employees must approach customers in a friendly and confident manner. This means a welcoming smile, eye contact, attentiveness and a willingness to listen. When shaking hands, a firm handshake will convey a sense of confidence and responsibility vital for the client seeking reassurance or help, or opening negotiations to buy a product(註4). The use of the client's name enhances the image of interest and attention (hotel porters are trained to read the labels of incoming guests' baggage, so they can use the client's name as early as possible in the host-guest relationship). The tone of voice is also important; voices should be well modulated and soothing, especially when dealing with an irate customer.

When handling complaints, the voice should convey concern. Many clients look for a sounding board to work off their anger when they have a legitimate complaint, and agreement rather than argument will help to modify their anger(註5). A wronged customer is seeking two things: an apology and a reassurance that action will be taken to investigate the complaint. It costs a company nothing to deliver both. Attentiveness to the client's needs can be demonstrated by volunteering an interest in the client(註6). A resort representative, for instance, can enquire in passing whether clients are enjoying themselves, or a counter clerk can ask a customer browsing through the brochures, "Is there any particular kind of holiday you have in mind?" to generate a sales sequence.

Personal Skills

In the initial encounter with clients, first impressions are crucial. The way travel agents, hotel receptionists or resort representatives appear and present themselves will set the scene for a successful company-client relationship. For this reason many companies impose strict rules on matters of appearance and grooming. Airlines, for example, will insist that cabin staff adopt a conservative and manageable hairstyle. Women who have formerly felt that the "natural" look suits them will be told to use make-up.

Needless to say, travel staff coming into close contact with customers must be fastidious about personal hygiene. Regular washing and bathing are essential, together with oral and dental care, and avoidance of food which may offend clients such as garlic or onions. The use of anti-perspirants are strongly recommended.

Deportment is important, too. We communicate non-verbally as well as verbally, and the way we walk, sit or stand reflects an attitude of mind towards the job. Staff will be expected to look alert and interested in their clients, to avoid slouching when they walk, to sit upright rather than slumped in a chair. The objective of most companies is to present a "uniform" appearance, to convey a corporate image of the company, and increasingly this means actually wearing a uniform.

Communication Skills in the Sales Sequence

In the travel and tourism industry, the front-line salespersons, retail counter staff, resort representatives and sales representatives continue to play a crucial role in the relationship between the company and its clients. They're generally the main point of contact between the two. These front-line employees undertake two tasks in their service delivery: to sell the company's products, and to match these products to client needs so as to ensure that the client receives satisfaction. To fulfill their roles effectively, salespersons will have to familiarize themselves with certain principles of communication skills particularly applicable in selling situations where client and sales staff come face to face(註7).

The principles are to be exemplified in the following five steps of a sales sequence a salesperson is required to follow.

Establishing Rapport

Given that the product sold can meet client needs so as to ensure satisfaction(註 8), the initial task for any salesperson is to engage the client in conversation, to gain the client's trust and learn about the client's needs. This process, known as establishing rapport, will reveal how open the client is to ideas, and how willing to be sold.

In order to strike up a conversation with a client, one must avoid the phrase "Can I help you?", common as it is(註9). The phrase simply invites the reply, "Thank you. No. I'm just looking." A more useful opening to generate discussion would be, "Do you have a particular kind of holiday in mind?", or to a customer who has just picked up a brochure, "That company has a particularly good choice of holidays this year. Were you thinking of a particular destination?"

The good salesperson must be something of a psychologist, judging from clients' facial expressions their frame of mind and their reactions to questioning. Above all, the salesperson should act as naturally as possible. Being yourself will best reassure clients that you are genuine in your desire to help and advice.

Investigating Needs

Having gained the client's trust, the next step is to investigate their needs. Once again it is necessary to ask open questions which elicit full answers, rather than closed questions which call for yes/no replies. The questions include who is traveling, when and how they wish to travel, how much they expect to pay, and etc.

Clients will not necessarily know the answers to all these questions themselves, so the salesperson needs to start out asking those that they can reply to easily, and gradually draw out their answers to questions they may not have thought about yet.

Needs must never be assumed.In any case, at each stage of the investigation, it is as well to make sure that the needs identified are agreed between the client and the salesperson(註10).

Presenting the Product

Once satisfied with enough information about the client's needs, the salesperson will then present the right product to meet the needs, in a way which will convince the client that it is the right product.

Here, the key to success is to mention not only the features of the holiday or product being sold, but also the benefits to the client. Obviously, product knowledge is crucial to the success of this stage, but personal experience of the resort itself is not always necessary; sound knowledge of the brochure material will generally suffice.

Even if the product you are offering is exactly what the client requires, it is always as well to offer one or two alternatives. Clients like to feel they are being offered a choice.

Handling Objections

One important aspect of the sales sequence which generally arises here is the need to handle objections from the client. If the product is more expensive than was originally envisaged, the client will need reassurance of the extra benefits included and that the product is offering real value for money(註11). This is best achieved by showing clients a product at the price they were willing to pay, and comparing the two, pointing out the additional benefits of paying a little more.

Whatever the reason for the objections, it must be identified and countered by matching all the client's needs to a product as closely as is possible to achieve(註12).

Closing the Sale

This stage means getting clients to take action and commit themselves. Although ideally the aim of all sales conversations is to close with a sale(註13), this is clearly not possible, and the important thing from the salesperson's point of view is to ensure that the best possible outcome is obtained. Clients may want to go home to talk over the product with their partner, but if they leave satisfied that they have received good service, there is a high likelihood that they will return to make the booking.

A good salesperson is continually looking for the buying signals emitted by clients: statements such as "Yes. That sounds good" clearly indicate a desire to buy. Where the signals are not clear, a comment from the salesperson such as "Would you like me to try and book that for you?" may prompt the client into action. However, clients should never be pushed into a decision; not only will they not buy, but also they may determine never to return again.

Vocabulary 內文詞彙

perceive	理解，領悟
cue	暗示，指示
perception	理解力，洞察力
limousine	豪華轎車
dispatcher	調度員
focal	焦點的
embody	體現，使具體化
detriment	損害，損害物
modulate	調解，調整
soothe	安慰，使平靜
irate	生氣的，發怒的

legitimate	合法的，合理的
modify	（尤指程度不大的）修改，更改
groom	修飾
fastidious	挑剔的，苛求的
hygiene	衛生
anti-perspirant	止汗露，止汗劑
deportment	風度，舉止
slouch	懶散，無精打采地坐、站、走
slump	懶散地坐著或站著
rapport	和諧，親善
exemplify	舉例說明
elicit	引出，得出
suffice	足夠
envisage	設想，預見
counter	對抗，反擊
emit	發出

Notes to the Text 內文註釋

1.It is evident that all of the personnel participating in the delivery of a service provide cues to the customer regarding the nature of the service itself.

顯然，顧客能夠從參與服務提供過程的所有工作人員的身上瞭解到服務本身的情況。

2.Even if the contact employee doesn't perform the service entirely or perhaps plays what appears to be a relatively small part in service delivery, he or she may still personify the firm in the customer's eyes.

即使與顧客打交道的某個員工並不提供全部的服務，或者也許只是扮演了服務提供過程中看似相對不起眼的角色，但可能在顧客看來他或她依然是公司的化身。

3.Research suggests that even the provider like an airline baggage handler or an equipment delivery dispatcher can be the focal point of service encounters that can prove critical for the organization.

研究表明，即便是像航空公司的行李裝卸員或負責設備遞送的調度員這樣的服務提供者，都可能成為對企業至關重要的為顧客服務的關鍵環節。

4.When shaking hands, a firm handshake will convey a sense of confidence and responsibility vital for the client seeking reassurance or help, or opening negotiations to buy a product.

握手時，有力度的握手會傳達一種自信，一種責任感；這種感覺在客戶尋求保證或幫助的時候，或是在客戶開始洽談購買產品的時候，都起著至關重要的作用。

5.Many clients look for a sounding board to work off their anger when they have a legitimate complaint, and agreement rather than argument will help to modify their anger.

許多客戶在有正當的投訴理由時，會尋求一個能使其淋漓盡致表達憤怒情緒的媒介。因此，認同的態度比爭論能更好地平息客戶的憤怒情緒。a sounding board本意為「（設在講臺、樂隊上方或背後以增強音響效果的）傳聲結構板」，此處是比喻用法，意為「能夠使其淋漓盡致表達憤怒情緒的媒介」。work off的意思是「發洩，排除」。

6.Attentiveness to the client's needs can be demonstrated by volunteering an interest in the client.

對客戶需求的關注可以透過主動對客戶表現出很在意而展示出來。

7.particularly applicable in selling situations where client and sales staff come face to face：尤其適用於銷售人員與顧客面對面進行銷售這種情況。

8.Given that the product sold can meet client needs so as to ensure satisfaction：倘若要使售出的產品滿足客戶的需求從而確保其滿意的話。given that是「如果考慮到，倘若」之意，它引導條件句。

9.In order to strike up a conversation with a client, one must avoid the phrase "Can I help you?", common as it is.

為了和一個顧客開始交談，應避免使用「我能幫忙嗎？」這句話，雖然通常人們都這麼說。strike up a conversation with sb.意為「開始與某人交談」。common as it is是將common提前的倒裝結構，正常語序是as it is common。

10.In any case, at each stage of the investigation, it is as well to make sure that the needs identified are agreed between the client and the salesperson.

不管處於哪種情況，在調查客戶需求過程的所有階段，最好還是要保證確定下來的需求是客戶和銷售人員雙方都認同的。

11.If the product is more expensive than was originally envisaged, the client will need reassurance of the extra benefits included and that the product is offering real value for money.

主句中need的賓語reassurance有兩個限定語：一個是of the extra benefits included這一短語，另一個是that引導的同位語從句。該句話的意思是「如果產品價格比客戶原來預見的要高，那麼需要讓顧客知道產品包含了額外的利益，是物有所值的，好讓他放心」。

12.Whatever the reason for the objections, it must be identified and countered by matching all the client's needs to a product as closely as is possible to achieve.

無論反對的理由是什麼，都必須把它明確下來，並透過提供儘可能完全準確滿足客戶所有需求的產品來扭轉局面。

13.Although ideally the aim of all sales conversations is to close with a sale：所有談話最理想的目標是成交。to close with a sale意為「談話以完成一樁銷售而結束」。

Useful Words and Expressions 實用詞彙和表達方式

勞動力的流動性	fluidity of labor
一線經理	first-line management
傭金	commission
漲價	escalation of prices; markup

交叉銷售	cross selling
贈券行銷法	couponing
買一送一，優惠	multi-pack offer
可信性	credibility
壟斷	monopoly
常客	regular customers
休閒市場	leisure market
市場領先者戰略	market leader strategy
市場挑戰者戰略	market challenger strategy
市場跟隨者戰略	market follower strategy
縱向一體化	vertical integration
橫向一體化	horizontal integration
水平一體化	lateral integration
市場涵蓋面	market coverage
高檔品市場	up market
低檔品市場	down market
入戶銷售	in-home selling

（廣告對顧客的）效果等級　　　hierarchy of effects

即興購買　　　　　　　　　　impulse buying

獎勵營銷　　　　　　　　　　incentive marketing

賺取現金的貨品　　　　　　　cash items

無特色產品　　　　　　　　　undifferentiated product

特約經銷點　　　　　　　　　tied shop

Exercises 練習題

Discussion Questions 思考題

1.How do you understand the two roles service employees play at work?

2.What skills should front-line employees learn to improve their clients'first impressions of them?

3.Explain the five steps salespersons in the travel and tourism industry generally follow in order to achieve successful selling.

4.Do you agree that "The salesperson must be something of a psychologist", and why?

5.When establishing rapport and closing the sale, what must salespersons take notice of in terms of effective communication?

Sentence Translation 單句翻譯練習

1.一個合格的銷售員（qualified salesperson）具備的一個最基本的能力就是懂得怎樣讓客戶敞開心扉（get things off one's chest），否則銷售根本就無法開始。

2.有研究表明，三分之一的顧客抱怨和不滿與顧客本身有關。服務中的一些錯誤或問題，即便是由顧客造成的，仍舊會導致（result in / bring on）顧客感覺不滿意。

3.銷售人員經常銷售服務，尤其是在他們實際提供服務之前；他們會宣傳新服務，但沒有確切的資訊表明何時新服務可以上市（go on the market）。

4.作為一個服務人員，內部的（internal）有效溝通（effective communication）也很重要。建立內部的良好溝通將有助於我們技術水平和解決問題能力的提高。

5.當客人向你走過來時，無論你在幹什麼，都應暫時停下來，主動和客人打招呼。

6.顧客的社交體驗（social experience）將會影響到顧客的滿意度和消費行為（consumer behavior）。一個帶給顧客美好社交體驗的餐館，能增加顧客重新惠顧（patronize）的意願。

7.隨著現代化資訊技術的不斷更新（update），顧客獲得資訊的途徑越來越多，也日益便捷（convenient）。

8.隨著中國大眾旅遊活動（mass tourism activities）和消費經驗的增加，越來越多的消費者依靠其經驗和愛好來購物，聽從導遊意見的人只占很少比例（proportion）。

Passage Translation 段落翻譯練習

The hallmark of a high-performance front line is the ability of staff to make good decisions and then execute them quickly and effectively. Front-line staff make critical decisions every day: "Should I accept that return?" or "How can we get this shipment out on time?" They play a vital role in determining the success or failure of strategies devised in the boardroom.

Organisations that excel at front-line execution know how to motivate employees, even in positions that involve seemingly uninspiring tasks. They manage to foster a connection between the front-line employee and his or her job. It could be that the employee belongs to the company's target market segment and thus understands the kind of extra help that will benefit the customer. The result is a virtuous circle. Organisations benefit from the energy unleashed by this connection, while employees feel more motivated and fulfilled.

Lesson 13 Public Relations for Tourism Industry旅遊公共關係

導讀：

　　一個公司不僅要提供品質上乘的產品和服務，還必須建立良好的公共關係，才能立足於這個高度競爭的經濟環境，並且長期立於不敗之地。本篇文章介紹了公共關係的含義、特點和意義所在，同時介紹了旅遊企業的公共關係部門在樹立公司形象、推廣公司產品上的作用和具體操作辦法。

Public relations (PR) includes all the activities designed to establish and maintain mutual understanding between an organization and the public, and it is not an optional part of the marketer's armory. All organizations have public relations, even if they do not consciously engage in PR activities.

The Characteristics of Public Relations (PR)

PR is best defined as a set of communications techniques which are designed to create and maintain favorable relations between an organization and its publics(註1).

The organization is seen by a number of different publics who may have an influence on its fortunes. The organization's actions and communications are unconsciously judged by everyone with whom it comes into contact, whether as direct customers or casual passers-by who notice the logo on the premises or vehicles. PR is concerned with controlling the impression thus created, to ensure that the image of the company is positive rather than negative. Companies will want to build good relations with their shareholders, suppliers, distribution channels, and where pertinent with trade unions. External bodies such as trade and professional associations and local chambers of commerce are other organizations that a company might wish to influence, while opinion leaders such as members of parliament — travel writers, hotel and restaurant guide publishers are yet more groups with which the organization must maintain good relations(註2). Finally, companies will wish to be on good terms with their neighbors, and will want to be seen as part of the local community and to support local activities.

As with other communications techniques, public relations plays a part in informing and reminding customers about the company and its products in order to generate an attitude towards the company favoring the purchase of its products(註3). In generating information, however, the PR message has to be seen as accurate and unbiased, while still reflecting the needs and interests of the company. This objectivity is essential if PR is to do its job effectively. However, it is the media that will determine what appears before the public. Since the aim is to ensure credibility, PR messages, with their perceived objectivity, are more convincing than advertising and in the long run are likely to have a greater impact on sales, if a far more subtle one(註4). This underlines the fact that public relations are essentially a weapon for long-term, rather than immediate, impact on a company's markets.

Because of the importance of travel and tourism as a service industry, the reputation of a travel company's products hinges on the quality of its staff, and the attitude of that staff to the company's customers(註5). When a company is carrying in excess of a million passengers abroad each year, it has to make greater and greater efforts to retain a friendly and personal image. PR can play a role in supporting and publicizing that image, although its creation must still lie with other marketing staff, whose role is to train and maintain quality control(註6).

In addition to creating favorable publicity for the company, PR is helpful in diminishing the impact of unfavorable publicity. The travel industry has more than its fair share of this, and there are some in the industry who feel that the media are concerned only to report the negative events, focusing on disasters such as overbooking, air traffic controllers' strikes, aircraft near-misses, ferry disasters(註7). However, it is a misconception that PR's role is to paper over the cracks which result from poor management or product faults. No amount of publicity will help a company which does not seek to correct underlying problems. PR must be used as an adjunct to good marketing practice, not as a substitute for it.

The Functions of PR Department

In some large companies PR activities may be carried out in the marketing department, while others are conducted quite separately. They are regarded as separate from the marketing function, located under such headings as corporate affairs. In any case, the PR department plays a role in maintaining the credibility of the company in the eyes of the public. As we all know that the credibility of the source of the message has an important influence on whether the message is accepted, and PR in its widest sense lays the foundations on which other forms of marketing communication build.

The work of the PR department can include:

Corporate Identity

The PR department is usually involved in the introduction or modification of the company's corporate livery(註8). The objectives of establishing a corporate identity are similar to those of branding: to create an image of consistency, reliability and professionalism, which is recognized by the public. Everything that the company owns or produces has to project the same image. The central symbol of the image is the logotype, or logo which should appear on all the publicity, correspondence, buildings, vehicles, uniforms, and merchandise, etc., and the design of which can instantly communicate the company and its image to the public(註9). The corporate image which should be instantly recognizable can be reinforced by advertising, by obtaining favorable news coverage and analysis in the media, and by sponsorship of charity and community ventures. Once adopted, the logo should be standardized and appear identically on every form of communication used by the company.

Lobbying

The organization's business may be affected by changes in the law or in government policy. It needs to make sure that the politicians are aware of the impact their decisions will have. Lobbying can be done by individual companies, professional bodies or by specially formed groups. Since lobbying is generally concerned with governmental or local authority issues, local organizations need to build good relations with their local councils, particularly in relation to planning decisions(註10).

Crisis Management

Crisis may arise any time and anywhere, and may at different levels. At a macro level, the impact of strikes or "go slows" by air traffic controllers or customs officers can create enormous disruptions to travelers(註11); at a micro level, the company can be affected by such diverse problems as fires in hotel lifts, and faulty gas heaters causing asphyxiation in self-catering facilities, to say nothing of major disasters such as aircraft crashes. Quite apart from disasters of this magnitude, many minor problems arise with which PR department must deal. Rumors of redundancy or takeovers can affect staff morale, resulting in the loss of key members of the company through resignation at a crucial time, and may sow seeds of doubt in the minds of the traveling public or within the trade, which can undermine the company's reputation and lead to its collapse(註12).

When a serious incident occurs, it is the job of the PR department to take the pressure off operational managers by handling media enquiries and ensuring that the organization's version of events is presented(註13). This will be easier to do if the PR staff has good relations with the local and trade press. The organization needs to be seen as acting swiftly, efficiently and responsibly to deal with the problem.

Internal Communications

Since the staff play an important role in creating the image of the company and the quality of the customers' experience, it is important that they are kept fully informed and made to feel part of the team. The PR function often includes improving staff morale, or staff management relations. In a large company, this will mean establishing a campaign just as is done with external publics. A common means of communication in the large travel firm is the house journal, an internal magazine of news and views about the company and its staff.

Customer Relations

Answering customer complaints and claims promptly and fairly can limit the bad word-of-mouth publicity dissatisfied customers can cause. This may be the responsibility of operation managers, a separate customer relations department, or the PR department.

Marketing Publicity

Marketing PR is part of the wider remit of the PR function and is part of the promotional mix. Its objective is to secure editorial space to achieve marketing goals. Editorial space in a newspaper, or indeed in a TV broadcast, is written or presented by a journalist as news or a feature story. As such, the story is likely to be perceived as unbiased, factual and more credible than an advertisement.

Means of Obtaining Publicity

To obtaining effective publicity, the PR department should carry out the following tasks: mounting a PR campaign, gaining publicity and building good press relations.

Mounting a PR Campaign

Favorable publicity for a company does not just happen, it has to be planned and programmed. Those responsible for PR must create news, as well as exploiting opportunities that arise to make news. As a starting-point to the campaign, the PR staff must know who the organization's publics are, and what their present attitudes towards the organization and its products are, so that there is knowledge of what needs to be done. While market research should already have a picture of the firm's consumers or potential consumers, additional research will probably be needed to establish the attitudes of other publics, such as staff and shareholder. This will provide an overall picture of the strengths and weaknesses of the company in its public affairs, which will allow a set of objectives to be drawn up for the PR campaign(註14).

The next step is to determine the strategies and tactics which are best suited to achieve these aims, and to decide what budget will be required to undertake the campaign.

Finally, the success or otherwise of the campaign must be monitored.

Gaining Publicity

If the objective is to generate publicity to develop a favorable attitude towards a local travel agency, then the first task is to ensure that the local catchment area is aware of the agency's existence, and of the products it provides. PR can support the advertising and sales promotion activities of the company by, for example, publicizing the opening of the offices. New shops and offices open all the time, so this is hardly newsworthy for the local press. It is the task of the PR to make it newsworthy, in order to attract visitors and gain media coverage. The important thing about the publicity is that it feeds on new ideas all the time, and the agent must continually be thinking up new gimmicks to gain attention(註15).

The second task comes after the opening; the PR must find ways of keeping the name in front of the public. Participation at local fairs, providing raffle prizes at fund-raising events or charities and other means all offer chances for building community links and generating local goodwill.

Sponsorship is a further means of achieving publicity for the name of a company. An organization might sponsor the publication of a book or film about the history of the company or the industry, which could not be a commercial success without subsidy. Other forms of sponsorship include financial support for the arts, theatre, fine art, concerts, festivals and sporting events. The attraction of this form of publicity is that it generates good will, while costs can be set against taxes.

Press Relations

Developing and maintaining links with the press and other media is a critical task of the PR department. If the organization plans to announce some prominent event, this may be sufficiently newsworthy to merit calling a press conference. This will entails invitations to travel journalists and other representatives from the trade, national and local media to attend a meeting at which senior executives will announce details of the new plan. The conference itself is usually presaged with a press release, or news release, which is thought newsworthy. Since the press release is the company's main form of communication with the media, it is important that it exemplifies the quality and efficiency of the organization. Once a press release has been issued, the company must be geared up to respond very quickly and efficiently to any press enquiries.

To build a long-term press relations needs press facility visits, which falls within the domain of the public relations department(註16). It aims to invite the media representatives — travel writers, journalists or correspondents from television and radio — to visit a particular attraction or destination, or to use the services of a particular travel company, in the hope that the trip will receive a favorable commentary in the media. This strategy is widely used by national or regional tourist offices, air and sea carriers, and tour operators, since a favorable press will have a huge impact on bookings.

Vocabulary 內文詞彙

armory	兵器庫，軍火庫
optional	可自由選擇的
unbiased	不存偏見的
pertinent	恰當的，適當的，貼切的
premises	房屋（及其周圍土地）
hinge on	取決於，關鍵在於
retain	保留，保持

diminish	縮小，減小，弄小
near-miss	幾乎成功之事，未完全成功之事
ferry	渡船
consistency	一貫，前後一致
logotype	（路標／廣告等用的）標誌，商標
venture	冒險，投機，嘗試
lobby	遊說
self-catering facilities	供房客自己做飯的廚房設施
redundancy	人浮於事，過剩
undermine	破壞，損壞
staff morale	員工士氣
remit	移交，提交
mount	發動，準備並實施
catchment area	服務範圍，接受服務的地區
adjunct	附屬物，伴隨物
prominent	傑出的，重要的
presage	預示

Notes to the Text 內文註釋

1.PR is best defined as a set of communications techniques which are designed to create and maintain favorable relations between an organization and its publics.

公共關係就是一套溝通技巧，它的作用在於營造並維繫一個公司同與其有關各方的積極的合作關係。publics在此之所以用複數形式在於公共關係的複雜性。

2.External bodies such as trade and professional associations and local chambers of commerce are other organizations that a company might wish to influence, while opinion leaders such as members of parliament, travel writers, hotel and restaurant guide publishers are yet more groups with which the organization must maintain good relations.

對於外部組織，如貿易和專業行業聯合會以及當地商會等組織，公司希望能夠對它們產生影響，同時，公司還必須與輿論領袖，如議員、旅遊記者、飯店餐館指南出版商保持良好關係。

3.As with other communications techniques, public relations play a part in informing and reminding customers about the company and its products in order to generate an attitude towards the company favoring the purchase of its products.

由於透過利用多種多樣的溝通技巧，公共關係部門可以幫助顧客瞭解本公司及產品，並不斷採取措施讓顧客牢記本公司，這一切都是為了讓顧客對公司產生良好印象並且樂於購買本公司的產品。

4.Since the aim is to ensure credibility, PR messages, with their perceived objectivity, are more convincing than advertising and in the long run are likely to have a greater impact on sales, if a far more subtle one.

因為公關的目標是確立可信度，所以公共關係部門傳遞出的資訊帶有明顯的客觀性，因而遠比廣告更有説服力，而且從長遠角度上看，這種資訊可能對銷售的影響更深遠，但也更微妙。

5.Because of the importance of travel and tourism as a service industry, the reputation of a travel company's products hinges on the quality of its staff, and the attitude of that staff to the company's customers.

由於旅遊和旅遊業作為服務行業具有重要性，一家旅遊公司所推出的產品聲譽如何不僅取決於公司員工的素質，也取決於員工對本公司顧客的態度。

6.PR can play a role in supporting and publicizing that image, although its creation must still lie with other marketing staff, whose role is to train and to maintain quality control.

公共關係在支持和宣傳公司形象方面承擔一定的作用，但是形象的創立還必須依靠其他負責培訓和負責維持品質控制的營銷員工。

7.The travel industry has more than its fair share of this, and there are some in the industry who feel that the media are concerned only to report the negative events, focusing on disasters such as overbooking, air traffic controllers' strikes, aircraft near-misses, ferry disasters.

旅遊行業受到的不利宣傳超過了其實際應受的數量，因此本行業中有些人覺得媒體只報導負面事件，只關注於超額預訂、航空罷工、誤機和渡船事故等這些災難性的事件。

8.The PR department is usually involved in the introduction or modification of the company's corporate livery.

公共關係部門通常參與公司企業形象的推廣或改變。

9.The central symbol of the image is the logotype, or logo which should appear on all the publicity, correspondence, buildings, vehicles, uniforms, and merchandise, etc., and the design of which can instantly communicate the company and its image to the public.

公司形象的主要象徵就是公司的商標或標識,該標誌應該出現在所有的宣傳、書信往來、建築物、交通工具、制服和產品上,而且其設計能夠不斷地將公司及其形象傳達給公眾。

10.Since lobbying is generally concerned with governmental or local authority issues, local organizations need to build good relations with their local councils, particularly in relation to planning decisions.

因為遊說一般是與政府或當地行政事務有關,所以地方公司必須與當地市政委員會建立良好的關係,尤其涉及規劃決策的問題時,更應如此。

11.At a macro level, the impact of strikes or "go slows" by air traffic controllers or customs officers can create enormous disruptions to travelers.

從宏觀角度而言,來自機場或海關方面的罷工或怠工可能對旅遊者造成重大的干擾。

12.Rumors of redundancy or takeovers can affect staff morale, resulting in the loss of key members of the company through resignation at a crucial time, may sow seeds of doubt in the minds of the traveling public or within the trade, which can undermine the company's reputation and lead to its collapse.

有關裁員或被兼併的傳言能夠影響員工的士氣,導致一些重要員工在關鍵時期辭職。這種傳言還可能在公眾中或業界播撒下疑慮的種子,從而影響公司聲譽並最終導致經營失敗。

13.When a serious incident occurs, it is the job of the PR department to take the pressure off operational managers by handling media enquiries and ensuring that the organization's version of events is presented.

一旦有嚴重事故發生，公共關係部門的作用是透過處理媒體詢問並確保公司針對該事故的相應解釋，以緩解各個執行經理的壓力。

14.This will provide an overall picture of the strengths and weaknesses of the company in its public affairs, which will allow a set of objectives to be drawn up for the PR campaign.

這將把公司在公眾關係方面的強項和弱點全面展示出來，為採取公共關係行動提供一系列工作目標。

15.The important thing about the publicity is that it feeds on new ideas all the time, and the agent must continually be thinking up new gimmicks to gain attention.

宣傳的重中之重是它永遠以新想法為源泉，因此公關代理人必須不斷花樣翻新以獲得公眾對公司的關注。

16.To build a long-term press relations needs press facility visits, which falls within the domain of the public relations department.

為了與新聞界建立長期的關係，需要為新聞界提供實地考察旅行，這也是公共關係部門的任務之一。

Useful Words and Expressions 實用詞彙和表達方式

口碑傳播	word-of-mouth

贊助活動	sponsorship activity
個人推銷	personal selling
自有品牌	own-label brand
直接再購買	straight rebuy
營銷網	marketing network
傳播管道	communication channels
供應鏈	supply chain
任務環境	task environment
外部營銷	external marketing
內部營銷	internal marketing
客戶數據庫	customer database
大數據營銷	database marketing
公司文化	corporate culture
客戶關係管理	customer relationship management
顧客平等權益	customer equity

Exercises 練習題

Discussion Questions 思考題

1.What is public relations and why is it so necessary in marketing?

2.What is the importance of public relations in tourism industry?

3.What is included in the domain of public relations department?

4.How are gaining publicity and recognition dependant of public relations department?

5.What is the difference between making advertisement and press releases?

Sentence Translation 單句翻譯練習

1.旅遊經營商在確定公司名稱時，可以選擇較為普通但是含義深刻的名稱，也可以選擇容易使人聯想到產品的名稱。

2.旅遊經營商除了使用標誌之外，還可以選擇與其產品有密切關聯的特殊形象，以使消費者迅速辨認出這些商品。

3.企業以消費者為中心展開的市場營銷活動，需要在企業與社會公眾互相瞭解和協調的行動中有效貫徹。

4.品牌權益（brand equity）是顧客對品牌的主觀上的無形評價和超出客觀上人們所理解的價值。

5.無論旅遊經營商在廣告宣傳及迎合新聞界方面的支出多少，最好的宣傳形式還是客人們良好的口碑。畢竟人們更容易相信親朋好友的話，而不是報紙的報導。

Passage Translation 段落翻譯練習

A travel agent who personally knows a destination is more likely to sell it with enthusiasm. There is no stronger force in a selling conversation with a customer than personal experience. Although agents cannot hope to have knowledge of every area of the world, most can reasonably be expected to have personal knowledge of the nearer and more frequently demanded destination. The accumulation of such knowledge is aided by the familiarization visits arranged by national tourist offices for travel personnel.

Lesson 14 Relationship Marketing關係營銷

導讀：

從1990年代至今，關係營銷受到了越來越多的關注。在飯店業和旅遊業，管理者們也將其作為提高常客的忠誠度、鞏固市場份額的一種有效的營銷手段。飯店業和旅遊業的關係營銷涉及企業如何維持和強化與顧客、供應商、分銷商、零售商、金融機構、內部市場及政府機構等多方面的現有關係，並如何擴大關係範圍。本篇文章著重介紹旅遊和飯店業如何保持和擴大與顧客的關係，從而鞏固其忠誠度。

Definition of Relationship Marketing

There has been a shift from transactions to a relationship focus in marketing(註1). Relationship marketing is a philosophy of doing business, a strategic orientation(註2), which focuses on keeping and improving current customers, rather than on acquiring new customers. This philosophy assumes that consumers prefer to have an ongoing relationship with one organization than to switch continually among providers in their search for value(註3). Building on this assumption and the fact that it is usually much cheaper to keep a current customer than to attract a new one, successful marketers are working on effective strategies for retaining customers.

Accounts of the value of long-term customer relationships have become common in the marketing and travel and tourism literature. One key construct within relationship marketing is customer loyalty: a customer's consistent and devoted relationship with a

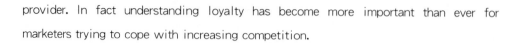
provider. In fact understanding loyalty has become more important than ever for marketers trying to cope with increasing competition.

Theoretical Background

In an interview, James L.Schorr, then executive vice president of marketing at Holiday Inns, illustrated the idea of relationship marketing in a very vivid way.In the interview he stated that he was famous at Holiday Inns for what's called the "bucket theory of marketing". By this he meant that marketing can be thought of as a big bucket: it's what the sales, advertising, and promotion programs do that pours business in to the top of the bucket. As long as these programs are effective, the bucket stays full. However, "There's only one problem," he said, "there's a hole in the bucket." When the business is running well and the hotel is delivering on its promises, the hole is small and few customers are leaving. When the operation is weak and customers are not satisfied with what they get, however, people start falling out of the bucket through the holes faster than they can be poured in through the top.

The bucket theory illustrates why a relationship strategy that focuses on plugging the holes in the bucket makes so much sense(註4). Historically, marketers have been more concerned with acquisition of customers, so a shift to a relationship strategy often represents changes in mind set, organizational culture, and employee reward systems. For example, the sales incentive systems in many organizations are set up to reward bringing in new customers. There are fewer (or no) rewards for retaining current accounts. Thus, even when people see the logic of customer retention, the existing organizational systems may not support its implementation(註5).

Goals of Relationship Marketing

◆ Building and maintaining a base of committed customers who are profitable for the organization is the major goal of tourist companies. In order to achieve this goal, a company has to understand the best target markets for building lasting customer relationships.

◆ Customer enhancement is another goal of tourist companies. Loyal customers not only provide a solid base for the organization, they may represent growth potential. In recent years, in fact, many companies have aspired to be the "exclusive supplier" of a particular product or service for their customers(註6). Over time these enhanced relationships can increase market share and profits for the organization.

Relationship Marketing in Tourism and Hospitality

With its long history of relational exchange, tourism has witnessed the introduction of many relationship marketing practices(註7). Airline frequent flyer programs, hotel frequent guest programs, and car-rental company customer preference schemes have all contributed to tourism being at the forefront of industries adopting relationship marketing.

Relationship Marketing in Airlines

The introduction of frequent flyer programs by airlines is one of their most dynamic marketing actions(註8). It allows them to understand their clientele better and target more precisely the message they want to convey to each client. Loyalty programs, known as Frequent Flyer Programs' (FFPs), were first launched by American Airlines. Today, most airlines offer a loyalty programs and the world-wide membership to these programs keeps growing. In mid-2000, for example, the Danish airline Maersk Air were using the Internet to develop their customer database with an appeal to existing customers to log on to their Web site and create your own personal profile and win two return tickets. "All profiles will be entered automatically into our competition held every month until the end of 2000."

The importance of FFPs in airline marketing strategies is increasing. In the UK,

FFPs are now linked to loyalty programs operated in other sectors. For instance British Airways' FFP is connected to the Air Miles Awards programs. Other participating partners come from a variety of sectors such as:

◆ The retail sector — Sainsbury's Homebase;

◆ Utilities — Scottish Hydro-Electric, Amerada gas;

◆ The telecommunication sector — British Telecom, Vodaphone;

◆ The financial sector — Diners' Club card, NatWest credit card;

◆ Selected restaurants.

Therefore, FFPs have become inter-sectoral(註9).

Relationship Marketing in Cruise Companies

Cunard, in common with many cruise companies, maintains contacts with former passengers through automatic membership of the Cunard World Club and regular distribution of a newsletter, the Cunarder.All members are notified of special offers, including heavy discounts on selected sailings, a Club Desk hotline, World Club representatives on board, and a members-only page on the Cunard website. A single voyage gives passengers Silver Cunarder membership of the Club, with additional benefits accruing to Gold and Platinum Cunarders, based on the number or lengths of voyages undertaken. These include the award of a Cunard pin, on-board World Club parties and, for the highest level of membership, priority check-in and embarkation at selected ports(註10) plus an invitation to the senior officers' party on board.

Relationship Marketing in Hotel Management

Most hotel groups also developed their membership clubs and other frequent user schemes during the 1990s, often supplying privileged user cards designed around the interests of their regular customers. The process is greatly facilitated by the sophistication of customer databases and techniques for data-mining, as well as the ability to use Web sites to identify customers' profiles. Some of these schemes offered credit facilities in addition to the normal range of benefits, such as rapid check-in and check-out, and upgrades of rooms if availability allows(註11). Some also offered awards through which frequent travelers could earn points for each stay, leading to attractive benefits according to the number of points collected over a given period.

Take the Ritz-Carlton Hotels for example. The chain maintains a computerized guest history profile of thousands of individual repeat guests(註12). This database notes, among other things, each guest's preferences and likes and dislikes. Ritz-Carlton employees are trained to keep track of this information for each hotel guest so that it can be recorded and used to provide more personalized service. Each hotel has at least one guest-recognition coordinator whose job is to identify repeat guests and to record new information on each guest within 24 hours of his or her departure. Once entered, this information is distributed system-wide to all other Ritz-Carlton Hotels. When guests visit another Ritz-Carlton, members of the staff already know about their likes and dislikes.

Tips for Retaining Customers' Loyalty

The ultimate goal of relationship marketing is to make the individual guest loyal to the organization. Retaining loyal, repeat customers is crucial because it is easy for people to switch between carriers, suppliers, and travel trade intermediaries. The key outcome of all relationship marketing efforts is to make individual customers feel special and to make them believe that the organization has singled them out for extraordinary attention(註13).

This individualization or customization can be achieved through the following procedures:

Managing service encounters: Training hospitality and travel organization staff members to treat customers as individuals, e.g., by using their names, knowing their preferences and interests, etc.

Providing customer incentives: Giving customers incentives or inducements to make repeat uses of the business, e.g., frequent-flyer and frequent-guest programs, preferred supplier arrangements, etc.

Providing special service options: Giving special extras to repeat or club customers, including, for example, upgrades to executive or concierge floors in hotels, airline club lounge memberships, and personalized baggage tags.

Developing pricing strategies to encourage long-term use: Offering repeat customers special prices or rates, e.g., annual memberships to theme parks, museums, zoos, and other gated attractions.

Maintaining a customer database: Keeping an up-to-date database on individual customers, including purchase history, preferences, likes and dislikes, demographics, etc.

Communicating with customers through direct or specialized media: Using non-mass media approaches to communicate directly with individual customers, e.g., direct mail, club newsletters, etc.

Knowing that repeat customers are important is hardly a new marketing insight(註14). It has been understood for centuries. What is new is the ability to recognize repeat buyers instantly and address them individually by name when organizations are dealing with tens of thousands or millions of customers a year. This ability provides the drive behind relationship marketing. Apart from the ability to target individuals, databases have a powerful market research value in generating detailed knowledge of repeat buyers and cutting out the cost of undertaking traditional usage and attitude studies among buyers.

Vocabulary 內文詞彙

orientation   方向，定位

illustrate   舉例說明，闡述

incentive   激勵的

retention   保持

dynamic   有活力的，強有力的

clientele   客戶

notify   通報

priority   優先權

embarkation   上船，登機

privileged   有特權的

sophistication   世故，複雜

accrue   自然增加，產生

database	數據庫
executive/concierge floor	（飯店的）行政樓層

Notes to the Text 內文註釋

1.There has been a shift from transactions to a relationship focus in marketing.

在市場營銷領域，人們關注的重點已經從交易營銷轉向了關係營銷。

2.a strategic orientation：一種策略性的定位。

3.This philosophy assumes that consumers prefer to have an ongoing relationship with one organization than to switch continually among providers in their search for value.

這種觀點認為，顧客寧願選擇與一家公司保持合作關係，而不願經常改變供應商。

4.The bucket theory illustrates why a relationship strategy that focuses on plugging the holes in the bucket makes so much sense.

這種「水桶理論」闡述了為什麼以堵漏洞為要務的關係營銷策略是很有道理的。

5.Thus, even when people see the logic of customer retention, the existing organizational systems may not support its implementation.

因此，就算是人們認識到了保住客戶的道理，現有的公司機制也可能會妨礙該理論的實施。

6.many companies have aspired to be the "exclusive supplier" of a particular product or service for their customers：許多公司渴望成為他們消費者所需的某種產品或服務的「獨家供應商」。

7.With its long history of relational exchange, tourism has witnessed the introduction of many relationship marketing practices.

由於旅遊業長期致力於發展關係交流，所以該行業在關係營銷方面有過不少的實踐。

8.The introduction of frequent flyer programs by airlines is one of their most dynamic marketing actions.

航空公司的「常客獎勵活動」是它們最有活力的營銷手段之一。

9.Therefore, FFPs have become inter-sectoral.

所以，「常客獎勵活動」已經成為跨行業的合作行為。

10.priority check-in and embarkation at selected ports：在指定口岸優先登記及上船的特權。

11.Some of these schemes offered credit facilities in addition to the normal range of benefits, such as rapid check-in and check-out, and upgrades of rooms if availability allows.

根據有的方案，顧客不僅可以享受到常規服務，而且還可以享受一些帶有獎勵性質的特殊服務，比如在飯店前台快速登記、結帳，如果條件允許的話，還可以更換更高級的客房。

12.The chain maintains a computerized guest history profile of thousands of individual repeat guests.

這家連鎖飯店將數以千計的老顧客的資料保留在電腦裡。

13.to make them believe that the organization has singled them out for extraordinary attention：使他們相信，企業對他們特意區別對待，以示尊敬。

14.Knowing that repeat customers are important is hardly a new marketing insight.

老顧客的重要性並不是什麼新的營銷概念。

Useful Words and Expressions 實用詞彙和表達方式

以市場為導向的	market oriented
市場定位分析	market positioning analysis
市場研究	market research
目標市場選擇	market targeting
市場開拓可能性	marketability
進入市場戰略	market-entry strategies
營銷策略	marketing policy
營銷研究	marketing research
營銷戰略	marketing strategy
商業批發商	merchant wholesalers

Exercises 練習題

Discussion Questions 思考題

1.What is relationship marketing?

2.What is "bucket theory marketing" according to James L.Schorr?

3.What is FFP? What is the benefit brought about by FFP?

4.How does the Ritz-Carlton Hotels obtain its regular customers' profiles and how does it apply the information to guest service?

5.In general, what steps should a hospitality and travel organization take to build long-term relationships with individual customers?

Sentence Translation 單句翻譯練習

1.在過去,之所以存在「消極的顧客」與「積極的廠商」,根本原因在於雙方溝通不方便,而不是顧客缺乏主動溝通的意願。

2.在交易營銷中,產品的多樣性滿足顧客特定需求,需求滿足導致顧客滿意,顧客滿意又引致重複購買,重複購買意味著雙方有可能建立長期關係。

3.對於飯店和旅行社來說,如果對飯店和旅行社的產品和服務感到滿意,顧客也會將他們的消費感受透過口碑(word-of-mouth)傳播給其他的顧客。

4.顧客滿意是指他們對某項產品和服務滿意,而顧客信任是顧客對該品牌產品以及擁有該品牌企業的信任感,他們可以理性地面對品牌企業的成功與不利。

5.老顧客是企業最寶貴的財富,一個老顧客的價值是巨大的。

6.在旅遊市場上，爭取一位新顧客的成本約比維持一位老顧客的成本多數倍，而且在成熟的、競爭性強的市場中，旅遊企業爭取到新客戶的困難非常大。

7.「一諾千金」（keeping　promise）對於企業來說是責任，對於顧客來說是價值。多次「一諾千金」有助於形成顧客信任，一次失約會導致顧客的背離。

8.服務品質是服務系統的核心和基礎，高品質的服務可以提高企業的可信度，增強顧客對服務價值的滿意感，產生有利的口碑宣傳效應。

Passage Translation 段落翻譯練習

Assuming they have a choice, customers will remain loyal to a firm when they receive greater value relative to what they expect from competing firms. Remember that perceived value is the consumer's overall assessment of the utility of a product based on perceptions of what is received and what is given. Value represents a trade-off for the consumer between the "give" and the "get" components. Consumers are more likely to stay in a relationship when the gets "quality, satisfaction, specific benefits) exceed the gives (monetary and non-monetary costs). When firms can consistently deliver value from the customer's point of view, clearly the customer benefits and has an incentive to stay in the relationship.

Lesson 15 Sales Promotion in Tourism 旅遊促銷

導讀：

促銷是企業運用短期誘因，鼓勵購買或銷售產品或服務的活動。它是企業或組織促銷組合策略當中舉足輕重的一項內容。本篇文章圍繞促銷的含義、功效以及企業採取促銷活動的原因進行了説明，並針對旅遊企業所採取的促銷技巧做了重點介紹。

What Is Sales Promotion

Sales promotion is a term which confusingly can have several meanings. However, its most common usage is to refer to promotional activities intended to induce buyers to purchase, or try, a product, or to stimulate the effectiveness of channel members. Sales promotions can add value to the product offering or create an incentive for certain behavior.

Sales promotion is a very effective promotional tool that has grown enormously in its usage since the 1980s. More money is spent on sales promotion than on advertising. The Institute of Sales Promotion (ISP)(註1), the body that represents all the major sales promotion practitioners in the UK, defines it as "a range of tactical marketing techniques designed within a strategic marketing framework(註2) to add value to a product or service in order to achieve specific sales or marketing objectives".

Added Value

Sales promotion comes after the product features have been designed, the unique selling points identified and the brand image established by an advertising campaign(註3). It is the additional incentive or discount offered to persuade the customer to buy now, from this company, rather than later, from someone else. In terms of AIDA(註4) and other hierarchical models, sales promotion is often designed to turn desire into action, although, as we shall see, it can play a role at any stage of the communication process.

Limited Tactical Objectives

Sales promotion works because it offers the customer a bargain and creates a sense of urgency. The offer only stands for a limited period and the customer therefore has to act quickly to take advantage of it. If the promotion were not limited it would become part of the normal product/price offer. It would lose its urgency and would simply add to the cost or reduce the price without stimulating sales. Sales promotions therefore have to be used sparingly; otherwise, consumers will come to expect discounts and will not buy at the full price. This has happened with the late-sale bargains(註5) offered by tour operators.

Another risk with promotions is that they will simply give added value, or reduced prices, to those who were going to buy anyway. To prevent this, they are often limited in validity as well as duration(註6).

Why Is Sales Promotion So Appealing

It's been acknowledged that there are at lease six main reasons why sales promotion appeals to the organization and the customer.

1.They work. Companies use sales promotions to the extent that they work because they have daily proof of their effectiveness.

2.Their effectiveness is easily measurable. A sales promotion is normally available for a specified period, and it is easy to measure its sales volume and profit consequences. For example, money-off coupons have to be handed in so they can be counted.

3.They can be closely targeted(註7). Thanks for computer databases, a special offer can be directed at specific groups of people within particular market segments. For example, online retailers might send out incentives to people who have registered but never bought.

4.They fit with niche marketing(註8). Niche markets often do not justify the level of spending needed for successful advertising(註9). Sales promotion is usually cheaper.

5.They are quick acting. The fortunes of brands and companies are increasingly volatile. Sales promotions can be devised and implemented, and take effect far more quickly than other forms of promotion.

6.They create interest. Sales promotion brings in an element of novelty, excitement and humour, which customers enjoy, and more importantly, respond to.

The Functions of Sales Promotion

It will be apparent from many examples that sales promotion can be used to achieve a number of different marketing functions, as well as that of creating an immediate purchase.

To create awareness and promote trial of a new product: Just as consumer goods manufacturers use free samples and coupons, leisure attractions can use free or discounted tickets to get people to try a new product.

To differentiate the product from competitors' offerings: Where the products are all similar, as with beach holiday packages, the free gift or discount can be the deciding factor.

To retain and reward regular customers: A club may include art incentive offer with its subscription renewal notices to persuade waverers to remain members; a promotion that requires a number of visits to obtain will encourage more frequent use and discourage brand switching(註10). Schemes such as Air Miles that involve collecting stamps or coupons towards an expensive item are examples of loyalty-building programmes(註11).

To change or reinforce the brand image: Mateus Ros (註12) achieved great success as "a wine for those who don't know much about wine" in the UK in the 1960s. Eventually, as wine drinking became more widespread, people were expected to know about wines, and drinking Mateus Ros became a joke. To change its image, Mateus ran competitions to win gourmet holidays in Portugal, positioning the wine as a distinctive part of Portuguese gastronomy(註13).

To sell excess capacity or channel demand to less popular periods.

To generate publicity and goodwill: The British Airways "Go for it, America!" campaign is a good example of this. Promotions linked to a charity are also likely to gain favourable press coverage and enhance the image of the company.

The Techniques of Sales Promotion

Before looking at the various techniques available, it will be helpful to identify all the tools in the sales promotion "armoury". These can be categorized as techniques aimed at those directed at consumers, those directed at intermediaries such as travel agents, and an organisation's own staff, such as sales representatives or counter sales staff.

Promotions Directed at Consumers (Either Through Retailers or Direct)

◆ Point of sale (POS) materia(註14) (window display, wall display, posters, counter cards, special brochure racks, etc.):

Sales literature and print;

Direct mail;

Free samples;

Discounted travel;

Money-off vouchers;

"Giveaways" (e.g. flight bags) and "self-liquidating offers" (products promoting the company's name, and sold at cost price by the company);

Joint promotions with non-travel companies (e.g. cheap weekends in a major city through the collection of washing powder vouchers);

Purchase privilege plans (e.g. "twofers" whereby two are charged the price of one for entrance):

Loyalty bonuses (e.g. airline frequent flyer programmes, or accumulating "honoured guest" points for frequent hotel stays).

Promotions Directed at Dealers or Retailers

"Giveaways" (pens, ashtrays, calendars, diaries, etc., usually bearing the principal's name);

Contests;

Trade shows;

Product/brochure launches (presentations, buffets, etc.);

◆ Direct mail (letters, circulars, etc.);

◆ Joint promotion schemes (financial, organizational help);

◆ Familiarization trips.

Promotions Directed at a Company's Staff

◆ Incentives (financial, travel, etc.) including exotic conference locations;

◆ Bonuses for targets achieved or other performance;

◆ Contests and competitions;

◆ Familiarization trips;

◆ Free gifts.

The list above is not intended to be exhaustive. Actually, the scope for new ideas in sales promotion is almost unlimited. Travel companies offer a huge range of giveaways to their clients, including flight bags, carrier bags, wallets for tickets and passport covers. Hotels offer a steadily increasing range of useful facilities to their guests, including shoeshine cloths, "first aid" sewing kits, shower caps and shampoo. Additionally, important clients might receive fruit, wine, flowers and/or chocolates in their room.

While many of these promotional tools are designed to do no more than create goodwill among clients and provide a sense of added value to the product, they will often also have an underlying purpose: that of ensuring the company or its products are remembered(註15). Therefore, the more exposure received by the item, the greater the impact. Ashtrays, paperweights and calendars, for instance, can all serve this purpose very well. Lists of useful telephone numbers which agents might want to keep in sight next to their desks will ensure that the principal's name is kept prominently displayed throughout the year, and aid recall. Such sales promotion aids serve similar purposes to advertising: they can be used to remind, to inform and to persuade customers to buy and retailers to sell.

Where the product is sold through retailers, the marketing manager can adopt one of two courses of action. One method is to aim the promotion at the consumer directly, in order to build brand awareness and create a demand that will pull people into the shops to buy the product. This technique is known as pull strategy, with the customer pulled into the shop by the effects of the promotion. In effect, to a considerable extent the client is pre-sold. Retailers will be persuaded to stock or sell the product simply by reason of demand. In the second method, sales promotion is geared to merchandising activities, which are designed to encourage retailers to stock the product and help them to sell it. This is termed push strategy, with promotion aimed to attract customer sales at the point of sale.

Cooperative promotions with non-travel companies are also proving a popular way of reaching the travelling public. Travel can be offered as an incentive to purchase other goods or services, or consumer durables can be offered to those booking holidays. Railway companies frequently team up with retailers or manufacturers of household goods to provide free rail travel against in-store purchases. Hoteliers have promoted short-break holidays in this way, too, while other examples of successful joint promotions include cross-channel ferry companies liaising with manufacturers of alcoholic drinks. Vouchers, redeemable for travel arrangements, have been successfully used as staff incentives in many large companies, particularly as rewards for the achievement of sales targets. Travel has been found to be a greater incentive than straight financial compensation in motivating staff.

Vocabulary 內文詞彙

induce	勸誘，促使，導致
stimulate	刺激，鼓勵
incentive	誘因，動機，獎勵
hierarchical	分等級的
practitioner	從業者，開業者
sparingly	節儉地
acknowledge	認識到，承認
consequence	結果，後果
justify	證明……是正當的
fortunes	時運，運氣
volatile	易變的，反覆無常的
novelty	新穎，新奇，新鮮
waverer	搖擺不定的人
scheme	計劃，方案
reinforce	加強，加固

gourmet	美食家，講究飲食的人
distinctive	與眾不同的，有特色的
gastronomy	烹飪法，美食法
generate	產生，發生
armory	軍械庫，武器廠
literature	印刷物，宣傳品
voucher	優惠購貨券；憑單，憑證
self-liquidating offer	自償贈品，自償廉售
circular	函件
exhaustive	詳盡的，無遺漏的
exposure	顯露；陳列，展出
paperweight	鎮紙，書鎮
prominently	顯著地
pull strategy	拉式策略
gear	使適應，使適合
merchandise	推銷（貨物或服務）
push strategy	推式策略

| liaise | 保持聯絡 |
| redeemable | 可贖回的，可彌補的 |

Notes to the Text 內文註釋

1.The Institute of Sales Promotion (ISP)：銷售促進協會。最初成立於1933年，它是一個代表所有涉及以促銷形式開展市場營銷活動的組織的行業協會，同時也是一個為個體從業者提供相關促銷知識和幫助的專業機構。

2.a range of tactical marketing techniques designed within a strategic marketing framework：在戰略性營銷框架內所制定出的一系列戰術性營銷技巧。

3.Sales promotion comes after the product features have been designed, the unique selling points identified and the brand image established by an advertising campaign.

銷售促進是在設計出了產品的特色、確定了產品的賣點和透過廣告大戰樹立了產品的品牌形象之後所要開展的活動。

4.AIDA：即顧客的認知（Awareness）、興趣（Interest）、決策（Decision）和行動（Action）模式。

5.the late-sale bargains：在旅遊產品（如某度假遊）的銷售期即將結束時被廉價出售的那部分產品。

6.To prevent this, they are often limited in validity as well as duration.

為防止出現這種情況，促銷活動往往會對其實行期限和有效性這兩方面作出限制。

7.They can be closely targeted.

促銷活動可以準確地針對目標顧客展開。

8.niche marketing：利基／補缺市場營銷，是指針對市場中通常為大企業所忽略的某些細分市場開展市場營銷活動。

9.Niche markets often do not justify the level of spending needed for successful advertising.

利基市場往往不能給企業提供充分理由讓它們把大筆資金花在廣告上。

10.A club may include art incentive offer with its subscription renewal notices to persuade waverers to remain members; a promotion that requires a number of visits to obtain will encourage more frequent use and discourage brand switching.

為了勸說猶豫不定的成員留下來，俱樂部可能會在其續訂通知中加入某種免費的藝術活動作為獎勵。那種要求多次參觀遊覽才可獲得的促銷獎勵將會鼓勵顧客頻繁使用該產品，並會防止品牌轉換現象的出現。

11.Schemes such as Air Miles that involve collecting stamps or coupons towards an expensive item are examples of loyalty-building programs.

諸如「航空里程」這種為了獲得某種昂貴產品而收集點數或優惠券的方案就是一種建立顧客支持度的計劃。

12.Mateus   Ros   ：產自葡萄牙的知名葡萄酒品牌，1970、80年代早期暢銷全球，目前已出口120多個國家。

13.To change its image, Mateus ran competitions to win gourmet holidays in Portugal, positioning the wine as a distinctive part of Portuguese gastronomy.

為改變這一形象，Mateus公司組織舉辦了一系列以前往葡萄牙享受美食度假為獎品的競賽，從而將該葡萄酒定位為葡萄牙美食烹飪中與眾不同的一部分。

14.point of sale (POS) material：在出售地用來為產品做廣告的資料，如海報。

15.While many of these promotional tools are designed to do no more than create goodwill among clients and provide a sense of added value to the product, they will often also have an underlying purpose: that of ensuring the company or its products are remembered.

儘管這其中很多促銷手段僅僅是為了在客戶中建立一種良好的印象，為了給產品提供一種有附加值的感覺，但它們往往還潛存著另一個目的，即保證該公司或其產品能被人們記住。

Useful Words and Expressions 實用詞彙和表達方式

（用以招攬客戶的）説明書，簡介	prospectus
折頁廣告	fold-out
外包裝廣告	on-pack promotion
促銷傳單	flier
信封廣告資料	envelope stuffer
教育性廣告（公益廣告）	educational advertising
強度滲透廣告戰役	saturation advertising
讀者廣告閱讀率	reading and noting rate

實地的，銷售現場的	in the field
實地調查，實地作業	field research
產品的撤除	product elimination
（產品）推陳出新	dynamic obsolescence
下降趨勢	downturn
差異營銷	divergent marketing
產品多樣化	product diversification
分銷成本	distribution cost
分銷統計	distribution census
虧本出售的商品	distress merchandise
特殊能力	distinctive competence
對大宗購買給予的折扣優惠	a discount on bulk purchases
現金折扣	cash discount
數量折扣	quantity discount
兌換贈品，享受折價	redeem
給回扣	rebate
新聞報導	press coverage

廉價櫃台   bargain counter

收費等級   scale of charges

Exercises 練習題

Discussion Questions 思考題

1.How do you understand the "limited tactical objectives" sales promotion can achieve?

2.Analyze the reasons why sales promotion appeals to organizations and customers alike.

3.Give examples to show that regular customers may be retained through sales promotion.

4.What techniques can be adopted when the promotions are directed at consumers?

5.What is meant by pull strategy and push strategy in sales promotion?

Sentence Translation 單句翻譯練習

1.如果促銷活動的時間（duration）太短，一些顧客可能無法重複購買，或由於太忙而無法利用促銷的好處。如果促銷時間太長，則消費者可能認為這是長期降價（price reduction），而使優待（favorable treatment）失去效力。

2.經營多品牌的店鋪應將其銷售促進預算（budget）在各品牌之間進行協調（coordinate），以取得儘可能大的收益。

3.銷售促進的對象主要是最終消費者（final consumers）。銷售促進對像是由產品的性質、營銷途徑、銷售促進的規模（scale）等多種因素所決定的。

4.近年來，由於商品產量和品牌數目大大增加，商品供過於求（supply exceeds demand），市場競爭激烈，人員促銷意識（sense）的增強等原因，都使得中國銷售促進的形式和手段日益繁多（vary）。

5.銷售促進最主要的作用是刺激需求（stimulate demand），增加銷售量。每次一種具體的銷售促進方式又有其不同的作用，主要是短期效果（short-term effect）。

6.值得注意的是（notably），有些產品在促銷期間銷量（sales volume）增加，促銷期後銷量就減少，出現了負效應（negative effect），這就說明企業採用的促銷方法不合適，沒有建立起品牌忠誠度（brand loyalty），需要改進。

7.作為一個銷售人員，在和客戶談話的過程中展現（exhibit）出自己的技術能力，不但可以提升（promote）本公司的形象還能使客戶更好地接受你。

8.僅僅以價格為基礎的銷售是最糟糕的一種銷售——它不能建立超越（beyond）價格的買賣雙方的關係。一旦有人開出更低的價格，顧客立刻就會離你而去。

Passage Translation 段落翻譯練習

Added-value packages, if used imaginatively, can help to attract attention to the product and reinforce the brand image. The difficulty is finding an additional incentive that is desirable enough to stimulate purchase in the way that cash saving does. The prize or gift has to be valuable enough to attract the customer, but the costs to the company must not outweigh the value of the extra business generated, as happened with the disastrous Hoover promotion offering free flights to the USA for any purchase worth over 200. This was such an attractive offer that it drew more people than Hoover could cope with administratively or financially. They attempted to control demand by introducing restrictions on the time and date of the flights, something that had not been mentioned in the offer. This made matters worse by attracting widespread media criticism and law suits.

There has to be a balance between making the gaining of the prize or gift too easy, so that it becomes uneconomic for the company, and making it too difficult, so that the customers do not think it worth trying for.

Lesson 16 Media Selection in Tourism Advertisement 旅遊廣告媒體的選擇

導讀：

旅遊產品的生產企業之間的競爭日趨激烈，旅遊產品的推廣，越來越多地藉助媒體廣告來擴大影響力，吸引客源。旅遊企業在發布旅遊廣告時，應結合旅遊推廣的目的和內容，充分考慮不同媒體在廣告宣傳上的優劣勢，正確選擇旅遊廣告媒體，才能達到預期的傳播效果。本篇文章介紹了媒體的分類、媒體選擇的策略，分析了選擇媒體廣告的時機以及對各類媒體的優劣進行系統的比較。

Media planning in tourism is very important. It is concerned with programming the ways in which advertisements will be seen and heard through media selection, scheduling and buying. The choice of media type is wide for travel and tourism. The range of media vehicles to carry the travel message is almost unlimited, and larger campaigns are best left in the hands of a professional media planner.

Categories of Media in Tourism Advertisement

There are two main categories of media — print and broadcast. The print media contains all advertisements that appear in print, including those in newspapers, magazines, direct mail, and outdoor advertising. Broadcast media are advertisements displayed by means of electronics; they encompass television (including cable), radio, videotape, and computer-generated graphic presentations.

Television (terrestrial and non-terrestrial) — including Teletext;

National press (daily and Sunday newspapers and magazine supplements);

Banners on Internet search engines and Web sites;

Regional and local press and free sheets (daily and weekly);

Consumer magazines and special interest magazines;

Business and professional magazines (e.g. travel trade press);

Directories and Yellow Pages;

Tourist board brochures, guides and directories;

In-house magazines (airline and hotel magazines selling space to other operators);

Radio (national and local stations);

Outdoor and transport poster sites;

Cinema;

Direct mail (using purchased address lists);

Miscellaneous space for sale or so-called ambient media (e.g. airport trolleys, towed aerial banners, balloon displays, bus tickets, petrol pumps, airline ticket wallets and visitor attraction tickets).

Considerations in Media Selection

Target markets and their reading, viewing, and listening habits.

Through marketing research, an organization should have established the media habits of chosen target markets. If potential customers live in defined metropolitan areas, then geographically specific media such as local newspapers, radio, television, direct mail, and outdoor advertising may be preferable(註1). On the other hand, specialized travel trade journals may be the optimum mode of communications if the targets are travel trade intermediaries (trade advertising). Customers with special interests, such as golf, tennis, or scuba diving, might be reached most effectively through special-interest magazines(註2).

Positioning approach, promotional goals, and advertising objectives.

The media, and media vehicles selected must support the image that the organization wants to convey, its promotional goals, and its advertising objectives. For example, if a company wants a luxury-oriented position, then upscale magazine advertising in publication such as Smithsonian may be the most appropriate(註3).

Media evaluation criteria.

· Costs. This represents the total campaign costs and the average cost per reader, viewer, or listener.

· Reach. The reach of a medium is the number of potential customers who are exposed to a given advertisement at least once(註4). The circulation of a newspaper or magazine is one measure of reach. Some of the print media have primary and secondary audiences. Most magazines, for example, are passed from the original subscriber or buyer to other persons, which results in additional reach.

· Frequency. Frequency refers to the average number of times that potential customers are exposed to a given advertisement or advertising campaign(註5).

· Waste. It represents the number of customers exposed to an advertisement who are not part of an organization's target markets. Newspapers, for example, are read by so many different types of people that significant waste circulation is often encountered.

· Lead time and flexibility. Lead time refers to the space of time between the design of an ad and its actual appearance in the selected medium(註6). The shorter the lead time, the greater the media's flexibility(註7).

· Clutter and dominance. Clutter represents the number of ads in one newspaper or magazine issue, or one radio or television program. Dominance means a sponsor's ability to dominate a particular medium at a specific time period.

· Message permanence. The permanence of a message refers to its life span and its potential for repeated exposures to the same customers(註8).

· Persuasive impact and mood. Some media and media vehicles have a greater persuasive impact than others. Mood is the added enhancement or feeling of excitement that a particular medium or vehicle gives to an ad.

Relative strengths and weaknesses of each media alternative.

For example, an ad placed in a special-interest magazine (e.g. Golf Digest) may have a smaller reach than if it appears in a major daily newspaper (e.g. the New York Times).

Creative requirements.

The creative format selected and the specific way it will be used also influence the choice of media and vehicles. For example, most travel destination ads require color and a visual presentation to have the greatest impact(註9). Magazines, television, and direct mail brochures work best, whereas radio and newspaper ads do not generate the same excitement or mood.

Competitive media placements.

Every organization must constantly keep one eye on its own marketing plan and the other on those of competitors(註10).

Approximate total advertising budget available.

Many small hospitality and travel businesses have limited budgets and must use the least expensive media and vehicles (e.g. newspapers and radio). Making the jump into television advertising is often one of the most difficult decisions for small-to medium-sized businesses(註11).

Timing of Advertisements

Another difficult decision must be made about when and how often to place the ads(註12). Different scheduling approaches are available, and the choice among them is based primarily on customers'decision processes and the sponsor's advertising objectives. Before looking at the alternative approaches, it is important to realize that there are really two decisions — macroscheduling and microscheduling. Macroscheduling means in which seasons or months to advertise, whereas microscheduling refers to specific times of the week and day. The three major scheduling approaches available are:

Intermittent.

Here ads are placed intermittently over a certain time period. The number of ads placed in each flight or wave may be level or uneven. Cruise lines might use this approach because they emphasize different cruising areas at certain times during the year (e.g., the Caribbean and Alaska).

Concentrated.

Using this approach, ads are concentrated in a specific part of the planning period and are not run at other times. Resorts open for only one season and downhill ski areas tend to use this approach by concentrating their ads in the months leading up to their peak operating periods(註13).

Continuous.

With the third scheduling methods, ads are spreading continuously throughout the planning period. Hospitality and travel businesses(註14) that need a steady, year-round and week-to-week flow of customers, including hotels and restaurants, tend to use this approach.

Benefits and Relative Merits of Different Advertising Media

Television.

· excels in reaching the mass consumer market;

· allows companies to keep product and brand presence in front of customers;

· influences the mass consumer market to convert long-term to a particular product;

· enables the promotion of corporate image nation-wide;

· is made more powerful by the combination of sound, color and movement.

Press.

· allows specific socio-economic groups to be reached;

- allows specific geographical regions to be reached;

- allows more complicated messages to be conveyed;

- is less expensive than television.

Radio.

- is good for geographical targeting;

- can reach identifiable market segments (youth, housewives);

- the costs of radio advertising are relatively low so repetition is easier.

Cinema.

- is good for reaching the youth market;

- is good for consumer-segment targeting;

- has good scope to use the impact of movement and sound;

- geographically separate markets can also be catered for.

Posters.

- are good for specific targets (shoppers etc);

- are low in cost.

National dailies.

- are expensive;

- are only suitable for large multiple chains with nation-wide customers.

Provincial dailies.

- are good for local markets;

- Evening locals;

- have high local coverage;

- have high readership.

Weekly locals.

- have high local coverage;

- have good readership over a period of seven days;

- are good for targeting housewives, senior citizens and long-term residents.

Trade magazines.

- are good for specific market segments.

Country magazines.

- are upmarket;

- are good for high socio-economic groups;

- have a high number of readers per copy (i.e. ones left in doctors' waiting rooms);

- are retained over a period of time.

Monthly/weekly magazines.

- are good for specific target segments;

- tend to be looked at more than once, by various members of a household.

As for the outdoor media, their merits are also obvious. For example, rail advertising offers an opportunity to reach a broad audience, from daily business commuters to leisure travelers; the underground is a compelling media proposition for advertisers wanting to reach young, affluent city dwellers, commuters and the millions of overseas visitors who flock to the city. With its permanently lit and highly visual environment, advertising on the underground weaves your product into the fabric of city life(註15). Bus advertising is certainly eye-catching and can take your message straight to the high street.

Vocabulary 內文詞彙

terrestrial	陸地上的，地球上的
miscellaneous	混雜的
ambient	周圍的
tow	牽引
preferable	更可取的
optimum	最適宜的

clutter	混亂
dominance	優勢，統治
enhancement	增進，增加
macroscheduling	宏觀安排
microscheduling	微觀安排
intermittent	間歇的
upmarket	高檔消費人群的
affluent	豐富的，富裕的

Notes to the Text 內文註釋

1.If potential customers live in defined metropolitan areas, then geographically specific media such as local newspapers, radio, television, direct mail, and outdoor advertising may be preferable.

如果潛在的客戶群生活在特定的大都市區域，那麼諸如當地報紙、廣播、電視、直接郵寄和戶外廣告等特定地理區域內的廣告媒體比較合適。

2.Customers with special interests, such as golf, tennis, or scuba diving, might be reached most effectively through special-interest magazine.

對那些對高爾夫、網球或自帶水下呼吸器潛水感興趣的客戶，透過特殊興趣雜誌來做廣告可能是最有效的方法。

3.For example, if a company wants a luxury-oriented position, then upscale

magazine advertising in publication such as Smithsonian may be the most appropriate.

比如，如果一家公司想將自己的產品定位在高端消費的檔次，那麼在諸如《史密森尼》等高檔雜誌上刊登廣告也許是最合適的。

4.The reach of a medium is the number of potential customers who are exposed to a given advertisement at least once.

媒體的影響範圍是指至少一次接觸某一廣告的潛在客戶的數量。

5.Frequency refers to the average number of times that potential customers are exposed to a given advertisement or advertising campaign.

頻率指潛在客戶接觸某一廣告或廣告活動的平均次數。

6.Lead time refers to the space of time between the design of an ad and its actual appearance in the selected medium.

前置時間指的是一條廣告從設計到真正出現在某一媒體上所需要的時間。

7.The shorter the lead time, the greater the media's flexibility.

前置時間越短，媒體的靈活度越大。

8.The permanence of a message refers to its life span and its potential for repeated exposures to the same customers.

廣告資訊的持久性指其存在的最長期限，以及該資訊重複影響同一組消費者的潛力。

9.For example, most travel destination ads require color and a visual presentation to have the greatest impact.

比如，許多旅遊目的地的廣告都需要有繽紛的色彩和鮮明的視覺感受，以此給消費者留下深刻的印象。

10.Every organization must constantly keep one eye on its own marketing plan and the other on those of competitors.

每個公司應該在關注自己的營銷計劃的同時，也留意競爭對手的計劃。

11.Making the jump into television advertising is often one of the most difficult decisions for small-to medium-sized businesses.

對那些中小型企業來説，決定花大量的資金在電視上做廣告不是一件容易的事。

12.place the ads：刊登廣告。

13.leading up to their peak operating periods：為他們的旅遊高峰季節做準備。

14.hospitality and travel businesses：飯店和旅遊公司。

15.With its permanently lit and highly visual environment, advertising on the underground weaves your product into the fabric of city life.

由於地鐵裡長期燈火通明，而且有著極佳的視覺效果，所以地鐵廣告將你的產品變為了都市生活不可或缺的一部分。

Useful Words and Expressions 實用詞彙和表達方式

姓名標籤   name tag

正常航班	regular flight
非正常航班	non-scheduled flight
國內航班	domestic flight
航空業務	airline operation
備用機場	alternate airfield
停機坪	landing field
國際航班候機樓	international terminal
控制台	control tower
旅客登機橋	air-bridge
迎送平台	visitors terrace
中央大廳	concourse
候機室至飛機的連接通路	loading bridge
機場內來往班車	shuttle bus

Exercises 練習題

Discussion Questions 思考題

1.What are the main categories of media in tourism marketing?

2.Which factors should be considered when selecting an advertising medium?

3.What are the advantages and disadvantages of the major advertising media alternatives?

4.What are the three major scheduling approaches in placing medium advertisement?

5.What are the major merits of outdoor media?

Sentence Translation 單句翻譯練習

1.酒店在節假日營銷中必須有針對性地選擇媒體，以求營銷效果最大化（maximize）。

2.在旅遊產品的推廣中，大眾媒體廣告效果十分明顯。

3.酒店應該根據營銷調查結果或者常識經驗（common sense）確定目標顧客經常接觸的媒體類別，這是酒店進行媒體類別選擇的基礎。

4.除了常規媒體外，還有許多非常規的媒體，比如飛機票、列車車廂隔間（train compartment）等，這些地方經過一定的處理均可成為營銷媒體。

5.由於網路營銷具有互動性（interaction），顧客可以遠在千里之外充分瞭解酒店的設施、服務、價位、節假日的營銷活動，酒店也可以充分瞭解顧客的特殊需求。

6.酒店要注意處理節假日的時間間隔（interval）問題。如12月和1月節假日較集中，為節省成本，酒店要有重點地選擇舉辦營銷活動的節假日，以免酒店裝飾的頻繁變換。

7.中小景區（scenic spot）的主要客源是在其景區附近的人群。因此，在廣告宣傳上，可選擇區域性的媒體。

8.國際廣告媒體的選擇和廣告資訊的設計也不是容易的事情，因為不同的文化有不同的媒體使用習慣，而且對資訊的理解方式也不同。

Passage Translation 段落翻譯練習

The decision on which particular medium to use for a campaign will be based on a number of criteria, of which financial constraint is only one. While only the largest travel companies can contemplate a national television campaign, there are still opportunities for spots on local television which are affordable by smaller organizations; for example, Bristol Zoo and other local attractions in the UK's West Country purchase spot advertisements on local television station HTV, and such advertisements reach not only local residents but visitors to the region staying in local accommodation.

Lesson 17 Direct Marketing 直接營銷

導讀：

隨著消費者的需求逐步多樣化及個性化，傳統的大眾營銷已不能滿足銷售者的需求。在這種情況下，20世紀初漸漸產生了一種新的營銷模式，被稱為直接營銷。直接營銷是一種相互作用的營銷系統，它利用一種或多種廣告媒體，在任何地方產生一種可衡量的反應或交易，如目錄郵購、面對面推銷、電話營銷、電視和其他媒體營銷和網上管道等。本篇文章介紹了直接營銷的概念，直接營銷的主要方式以及特點。

Direct marketing is one of the fastest growing areas of marketing and probably one of the least understood by outsiders(註1). It is often confused with direct mail, and is therefore dismissed as junk mail. After studying this unit, you may have a better understanding of direct marketing.

Definition of Direct Marketing

Direct marketing links producers with their customers in a two-way communication, using individually addressable media (such as mail, telephone and e-commerce). Interaction is organized through a database recording unique details of actual and prospective customers, including their geo-demographic profile, product purchasing behavior and their responses to different communications media.

The primary objective of direct marketing is to achieve more cost-effective use of marketing budgets based on a deep and evolving knowledge of customers and their behavior, and direct communication with them(註2). It is this objective which distinguishes direct marketing from traditional forms of direct selling.

Major Techniques in Direct Marketing

There are a series of directing techniques in use indicated below. However, these techniques are regarded as elements in the marketing campaign planning process, and any direct marketing campaign is likely to use a combination of these techniques rather than any individual one(註3).

Direct mail	➤ to previous customers
	➤ to purchased lists of targeted prospects
	➤ via lists owned by third parties
	➤ in response to enquiries/returned coupons from advertising
	➤ via joint mailing with relevant partners
	➤ to targeted households selected because they have characteristics matching those of known purchasers[4]
Telephone/telemarketing(via call centers)	➤ to targeted-customer lists
	➤ in response to enquiries
Door-to-door distribution	➤ to homes in targeted blocks of residential streets/roads
Travel related exhibitions	➤ to enquirers at stands, e. g. boat shows, travel exhibitions, and caravan and camping shows
Media advertising	➤ with coupons
	➤ with response telephone numbers, or 0800 lines
Websites and E-mail	➤ Internet access via PCs and interactive television in customers' homes and offices

Direct Mail

Direct mail is the technique whereby a company communicates directly with its potential customers through the post, in order to put across(註5) a sales message. The technique has the considerable advantage that letters can be personalized, and target markets can be clearly identified, so that customers should be expected to be reasonably interested in the product, providing the mailing list is sufficiently comprehensive(註6). Wastage is in this way minimized. The process has been greatly aided by the introduction of computer databases which can pinpoint specific target markets with far more comprehensive details of clients and their interest(註7). Lifestyle databases allow for(註8) very accurate selection of potential customers, based on information about age, income, type of occupation, hobbies, residential area including type of property occupied, and previous holidays.

Travel companies are increasingly aware that direct mail can play an important part in their own communications mix, and evidence suggests that travel-related mailings are far more successful than others. One piece of research revealed that over 90 percent of recipients of travel-related direct mail opened and read the material, with one third responding to it.

Direct mail can be used in:

◆ generating brochure requests for tour operators, especially where holidays are aimed at very well-defined groups(註9) (e.g. golfers), although bookings may still primarily be via the travel agent;

◆ generating late sales, especially when aimed at previous customers who booked late the previous year;

◆ channel support, whereby the travel company communicates sales benefits to the travel agent;

◆customer care, where the communication is to strengthen the brand image and customer loyalty(註10) for next season; for example a client returns from holiday to receive a personal letter from the principal of the travel agency where the holiday was booked.

Direct mail is now being supplemented by the use of direct fax, e-mail and voice mail. They can all prove useful tools, particularly at the speed with which information about products can be delivered. But there is real concern about the use of junk mail and spam. In addition, direct mail shots can take the form of a personal magazine, with accompanying letter. For a local travel agent, there is actually very limited opportunity to reach customers through local advertising, given that only about one-third of the homes in a given area regularly purchase a local paper(註11). An alternative is to create one's own medium for reaching the customer. Saga, the older people's specialist operator, has its own highly regarded (subscription) magazine(註12) dealing with matters that are of interest to that age group. This also acts as a regular sales brochure for the company, and separate travel brochures are also sent in regular mail shots to subscribers.

Telephone Marketing

Telephone marketing or telemarketing has developed massively in the 1990s through a combination of technology-led development of consumer databases, telephone communications and the creation of call centers. Many specific products, especially in financial services and insurance, have been developed for the purpose of dealing with customers on a direct-contact-only basis. Call centers may be reactive to enquiries and proactive to target customers(註13). In the last years of the twentieth century call centers have linked with Web sites and e-commerce as a highly cost-effective combined response mechanism for dealing with direct bookings from the public and these forms of communication are certain to play a larger part in overall travel distribution in the future.

There are constant refinements to telemarketing. One is the increasing emphasis on personal service, for which the telephone offers considerable scope. Training given to call center staff has moved away from insistence on the use of somewhat mechanistic stock phrases with which to reply to enquiries, towards encouraging a more personal and individual style of conversation to develop. While the original emphasis had been to minimize time spent on each call, the new customer-friendly approach takes better into account good customer relations management practice, and is designed to enhance the relationship between the organization's sales personnel and their customers, thus raising overall levels of customer satisfaction. Future developments encompassing computer integrated telephoning will further refine telemarketing. Calling line identification, for instance, allows the recipient of a call to identify who is on the line before answering, giving scope for redirecting the selection of replies, although this has not yet been approved for business practice.

Other Techniques

Door-to-door distribution costs of printed materials can be much cheaper per household than postal costs, and the ability to utilize this method more accurately using demographic targeting supported by database analysis has refined another of the important traditional direct marketing techniques. Interactive television for use by the general public in their own homes was developed in France using the Minitel system and in the UK using Teletext but, although the companies may survive in a different media, these are now yesterday's technology and latest estimates indicate that well over half of all homes in the main travel-generating countries will have direct access to the Internet via digital television within a decade(註14). At that point the Internet is expected to be the primary channel for direct marketing.

Impact of Direct Marketing

Precise targeting. The list selection can be very precise, reducing waste and allowing much focused copy and offers that reflect the prospect's likely requirements.

Personalized messages. The mailing can be personalized not only by name, but also by being accurately based on behavior and lifestyle of each individual customer. For example, as a valued customer who has booked with us three times before, we would like to extend you a special invitation. Messages that demonstrate knowledge of and feeling for the needs of the customer will inevitably be better received.

Response orientation. The medium generates high levels of response through coupons, reply cards and telephone. Internet and telephone communication encourages response through low price and instantaneous appeal. Direct marketing can be very sales orientated and directed.

Detail. Product descriptions, including complete information and terms and conditions of purchase, can be transmitted via print, while the Internet allows the added benefit of full color graphics to depict products — giving customers added confidence in buying.

Discreet. Television and press advertising will be immediately obvious to a company's competitors. With a little care, such as avoiding such obvious faux pas as including competitors on the mailing list, direct marketing campaigns will take longer to be noticed, and may even escape the competition's notice until well beyond their termination(註15).

Measurable. The medium generates response which can be tracked accurately, whether it is enquiries for more information or actual sales. Therefore the return on the costs of the promotion can be directly measured.

Vocabulary 內文詞彙

demographic	人口統計的
primary	主要的
distinguish	區分
previous	先前的
coupon	商家的優待券
caravan	房車
minimize	最小化
pinpoint	精確，查明

spam	兜售的資訊，非索要資訊
alternative	可供選擇的辦法
proactive	積極主動的
refinement	精緻，改進
encompass	環繞，包含
graphic	圖形的，用圖表示的，生動形象的
discreet	慎重的
faux pas	失言，失禮
prospective	預期的

Notes to the Text 內文註釋

1.Direct marketing is one of the fastest growing areas of marketing and probably one of the least understood by outsiders.

直接營銷是市場營銷領域發展最快的營銷方式，可能也是局外人最難以理解的方式。

2.The primary objective of direct marketing is to achieve more cost-effective use of marketing budgets based on a deep and evolving knowledge of customers and their behavior, and direct communication with them.

直接營銷的主要目的在於，透過對客戶及其行為不斷深入的瞭解以及透過直接與客戶交流，最終使用於營銷的預算更加具有成本效益。

3.and any direct marketing campaign is likely to use a combination of these techniques rather than any individual one：任何一種直接營銷活動都不會孤立地使用某一種方式，而是將多種方式結合起來。

4.to targeted households selected because they have characteristics matching those of known purchasers：寄給一些目標家庭，這些家庭的選定是根據他們與已知的消費者之間的相似性。

5.put across：使被理解，使被接受。

6.The technique has the considerable advantage that letters can be personalized, and target markets can be clearly identified, so that customers should be expected to be reasonably interested in the product, providing the mailing list is sufficiently comprehensive.

這種方法具有相當大的優勢，因為這種方法使信件更加人性化，還能使目標市場變得十分明確。因此假如郵件清單足夠全面的話，就有理由期待客戶對產品產生興趣。

7.The process has been greatly aided by the introduction of computer databases which can pinpoint specific target markets with far more comprehensive details of clients and their interest.

電腦數據庫的應用極大地推動了這一過程的發展，因為該數據庫能準確定位目標市場，並能查明客戶的全面資訊及他們的興趣。

8.allow for：考慮到，估計到。

9.well-defined groups：類型明確的客戶。

10.to strengthen the brand image and customer loyalty：鞏固品牌形象，加強客戶

忠誠度。

11.For a local travel agent, there is actually very limited opportunity to reach customers through local advertising, given that only about one-third of the homes in a given area regularly purchase a local paper.

倘若在一個特定的地區只有約三分之一的家庭定期購買當地的報紙,那麼對於一家地方旅行社來說,透過在當地做廣告的方式來吸引顧客,其收效微乎其微。

12.has its own highly regarded (subscription) magazine:擁有自己的著名刊物。

13.may be reactive to enquiries and proactive to target customers:既可以答覆各種諮詢,也可以主動地聯繫目標客戶。

14.these are now yesterday's technology and latest estimates indicate that well over half of all homes in the main travel-generating countries will have direct access to the Internet via digital television within a decade:這些技術在現在看來已經成為了歷史,而最新的評估表明,在旅遊業興旺的國家,半數以上的家庭可以在十年之內以數位電視的方式直接接觸到網際網路。

15.direct marketing campaigns will take longer to be noticed, and may even escape the competition's notice until well beyond their termination:直接營銷就不太會招惹對手的注意,直到你遠遠超過他們。

Useful Words and Expressions 實用詞彙和表達方式

房價	room rate
標準價	standard rate

套房	suite
家庭套房	family suite
訂金	advance deposit
登記	registration
房價表	rate sheets
價目表	tariff
取消預訂	cancellation
總統套房	presidential suite
高級套房	suite deluxe
簡單套房	junior suite
小型套房	mini suite
蜜月套房	honeymoon suite
樓頂套房	penthouse suite
未清掃房	unmade room
貴重物品	valuables
託運行李	registered/checked luggage
手推車	trolley

行李間　　　　　　　　　　　　　storage room

Exercises 練習題

Discussion Questions 思考題

1.What is direct marketing?

2.What is the primary object of direct marketing?

3.What problems may be brought about by direct mail?

4.What is the new trend in telephone marketing?

5.Summarize the impact of direct marketing.

Sentence Translation 單句翻譯練習

1.旅遊電子商務（e-commerce for tourism）是指透過現代網路資訊技術手段實現旅遊商務活動各環節的電子化，包括透過網路發布、交流旅遊基本資訊和旅遊商務資訊，進行旅遊宣傳促銷、開展旅遊售後服務。

2.互聯網路是一種功能強大的營銷工具，它同時兼具管道、促銷、電子交易以及市場資訊分析的多種功能。

3.過去，由於直接營銷人備有客戶的姓名和地址等詳細資料，他們在生意上會比其他企業營銷人員略勝一籌（to gain an advantage over）。

4.旅遊和飯店業的直接營銷人員應該首先記住客戶是如何向你講述他們的喜好的，然後結合他們的喜好來設計產品、服務和交流方式，這樣就可以更好地預測並滿足他們的需求。

5.企業和消費者的互動性增強,這使得直接營銷企業能更多地瞭解其客戶,但帶來了很多數據管理(data management)的麻煩。

6.網路世界的欺詐行為會嚴重影響飯店的品牌和信譽,所以飯店直接營銷人員必須採取必要的行動,以培養、尊重和保護他們的客戶。

7.根據美國的相關法律,直接營銷企業必須公開他們獲取顧客資料的方法,當顧客需要時,他們必須說出他們是如何獲得或共享這些個人資訊的細節。

8.現在,直接營銷更傾向於與顧客建立長期的關係(long-tern relationship)。如航空公司及飯店集團透過「親和卡」計劃(Affinity Credit Card Program)以建立強有力的顧客關係。

Passage Translation 段落翻譯練習

The ultimate purpose of marketing, advertising and sales initiatives is to get the potential customer to do something. In most cases, this means moving that customer from the education and consideration stage to the purchase stage. Direct response advertising and marketing is one of the more immediate tools in the marketers' arsenal to move potential customers into action. At its core, direct response advertising is a marketing message that incorporates a "call to action." While usually thought of in terms of television advertising, direct response advertising can actually be a part of just about any marketing media from direct mail to billboards, print advertisements and online ads. The distinguishing characteristic, of course, is the call to action. The idea is to broadcast a marketing message and encourage potential customers to act on that message while it is still fresh. The hook for the call to action can include special promotions such as a 10 discount on long distance "if you call now," solicitations to purchase products or services, or a packet of information.

Lesson 18 Differentiated Marketing and Niche Marketing

差異性營銷和補缺性營銷

導讀：

企業在進入市場時，有多種營銷策略可以選擇：無差異性營銷、差異性營銷和補缺營銷。現代旅遊企業一般都會選擇差異性營銷和補缺營銷，因為這兩者更有助於識別旅遊市場機會，能夠更好地滿足遊客的需求，也因此能獲得更多的收益。本篇文章主要討論差異性營銷和補缺性營銷，重點介紹兩種營銷的概念和優缺點，以及在選擇這兩種營銷策略時應注意的問題。

Once a firm has segmented its market, it will then usually proceed to decide which or how many segments it can serve effectively and profitably. The outcome is often that the firm decides to pursue one of the following three marketing strategies:

◆ Undifferentiated marketing;

◆ Differentiated marketing;

◆ Niche marketing.

An undifferentiated marketing strategy is one that overlooks segment differences, and uses the same marketing mix for all market segments(註1). The firms using undifferentiated marketing believe that there is little basis for segmenting a market and develop a destination or tourism offering which it considers suitable for the entire market. This is sensible in some situations, such as the marketing of capital cities where the appeal is very broad(註2). But, generally, they start out trying to be all things to all tourists and end up meaning nothing to anyone. As a result, most of the tourism marketers have greater interests in differentiated marketing and niche marketing.

Differentiated Marketing

In differentiated marketing, the firm operates in several market segments and design different marketing programs for each segment(註3). Most tourism businesses have adopted a differentiated marketing strategy.

Tourism supplier can segment itself to try to reach more than one segment. For example, some hotel chains have two or more distinct classes or types of hotels, with each class appealing to a different market segment(註4). Some airlines also do this on the same plane by offering first-class, business class, and coach or economy-class seats, often at vastly different prices.

However, some tourism suppliers will provide services for almost every market segment and use a unique marketing mix to promote to each market separately(註5). Ramada Franchises Enterprises(註6) offers lodgings for a variety of guests: Ramada Limited for economy travelers; Ramada Inn for those seeking a mid-priced full-service hotel; Ramada Plaza, a new offering in the upper-mid-priced service; Ramada Hotels offering three-star service; and Ramada Renaissance hotels, offering four-star service. Here Ramada attempts to serve all customers with all the products that they might need. This approach, which is known as full market coverage strategy, is the most expensive marketing strategy and only very large firms can undertake it.

Tourism suppliers can also offer a single product that serves the needs of several market segments. Some hotels segment themselves within a single property and have guest rooms that offer more or fewer features for different customers(註7). Most independent hotels and resorts usually use this approach. Faced with direct competition from national chains, they provide uniquely designed properties, added services, or personal touches to attract business and pleasure travelers(註8).

The Advantages of Differentiated Marketing

Differentiated marketing can create a more fine-tuned product offer and price it appropriately for the target customers, thus increasing the total sales(註9).

Tourists are not identical. Some tourists will want additional features and benefits not included in the offer, while others would gladly give up something that they don't want very much. For example, affluent guests in hotels may want more amenities, and some guests may want to find more items in their room, such as a fax machine, while others may prefer fewer amenities and a lower price. In this sense, differentiated marketing can better meet the needs of different market segments than undifferentiated marketing and attract more customers.

Moreover, the hotels or the airlines that use differentiated marketing will price their different products at vastly different levels. As a result, differentiated marketing can increase the total sales for the firms.

Differentiated marketing can help overcome the problem of peaks and troughs in demand.

For leisure centers, bowling, skating and similar activities, the peaks and troughs are daily. To overcome this they can target young professional for early morning exercise before work; housewives, mothers and toddlers, or senior citizens during the day; school children in the late afternoon/early evening; and working couples or teenagers in the evenings. Also, the hotels market for business people in the week and leisure travelers at weekends.

This also occurs at many destinations where different features or sectors of a resort are targeted to different segments. For example, Alpine ski resorts repackage themselves as "lake and mountains" destinations in the summer(註10), targeting walkers and those looking for relaxation and scenery.

Differentiated marketing can spread the risks by catering for more than one market segment.

This strategy has the advantage of diversifying the firms' risks. A particular market segment may turn sour, or a competitor may invade the segment. But with differentiated marketing, the firms can spread the risks and continue to earn money in other segments.

The Disadvantages of Differentiated Marketing

Although differentiated marketing typically creates more total sales and spreads risks, it has some disadvantages:

◆ Because each segment has different needs and different price sensitivities, much more efforts will be needed in marketing planning.

◆ It may require additional promotion costs because different promotional approaches will probably have to be used with each different segment.

◆There may be higher administrative costs because a separate marketing plan is sometimes needed for each different segment.

◆ There may be additional research and forecasting cost.

◆ The product may have to be modified, or in some cases completely redesigned, to match the needs of a particular market.

Since differentiated marketing leads to both higher sales and higher costs, nothing general can be said regarding this strategy's profitability(註11). And tourism marketers should be cautious about oversegmenting their market.

Niche Marketing

A niche is a more narrowly defined group, typically a small market whose needs are not being well served(註12). Niche marketing strategy is one that identifies a niche from several market segments or subsegments, and market exclusively to it. An advertising agency executive wrote, "There will be no market for products that everybody likes a little, only for products that somebody likes a lot." In many markets today, niches are the norm.

Identifying the Niche

Marketers usually identify niches by dividing a segment into subsegments. Business travel can be broken down into subsegments such as personal, regular business, meetings and conventions, and incentive travel(註13). The niche of incentive travel is so large that the number of companies specializing in incentive travel arrangements has grown from a handful to several hundreds.

Pleasure travel can be subsegmented into individual travel and organized group travel. Individual travel is done by individuals, couples, families, groups of friends, and so on. Group travel is typified by a group with a common interest that has had its entire trip organized by a third party such as a tour wholesaler(註14). Pleasure travel can also be subsegmented according to the attractions and products offered at the destination. For example, a resort area with a choice of several golf courses would appeal to the golfing segment of the pleasure travel market.

An attractive niche is characterized as follows:

◆ The customers in the niche have a distinct and complete set of needs;

◆ The customers will pay a premium to the firm best satisfying their needs;

◆ The nicher gains certain economies through specialization(註15);

◆ The nicher has the required skills to serve the niche in a superior fashion;

◆ The niche is not likely to attract other competitors or the nicher can depend on itself;

◆ The niche has sufficient size, profit, and growth potential.

The Advantages of Niche Marketing

Niche marketing can help smaller firms avoid competing with larger firms

by targeting small markets of little or no interest to the larger firms.

The essence of niche marketing is to avoid head-to-head competition with industry leaders. Therefore, it is very popular with smaller and low-market-share organizations. In the long term, it is hoped that a strong association with the target market, as well as a reputation of excellent service to that market, will be developed(註16).

A good example in the hospitality and travel industry is "conference-center" resorts. The developers of these properties spotted the need for specialized resorts exclusively serving smaller corporate and association meetings and conferences. The real strength of their approach is specialization and close attention to the needs of a specific target market. Most other hotels and resorts accommodate convention/meeting groups of all sizes, in addition to other business and pleasure travelers. Unlike most major hotel chains and convention/visitor bureaus, conference resorts do not pursue the major association conventions. Instead, they rely on sophisticated audiovisual equipment, purpose-built meeting facilities, and high level of personal service in arranging and coordinating their customers' meetings(註17). They provide the added touches and services that many larger hotels and resorts overlook or cannot justify.

There are many other examples of market specialization in tourism industry. Most small, independent restaurants specialize by only serving a well-defined local market. A growing number of travel agencies concentrate exclusively on corporate accounts. Now, even large tourism businesses are increasingly setting up their units to serve niches.

In some cases, niche marketers meet their niches'needs so well that their customers willingly pay a price premium.

Linblad Travel gets a high price on offering exclusive, luxury tour packages, often to unusual places. Small, regional airlines serve specific geographic areas with routes and schedules that major airlines find uneconomical(註18). As a result, the nicher can charge a substantial markup over costs because of the perceived added value. The nicher achieves high margin, while the mass marketer achieves high volume(註19). The firms with low shares of the total market can also be highly profitable through smart niche marketing.

The Major Risk of Niche Marketing

However, niche marketing carries a major risk in that the market niche might dry up or being attacked. For example, small independent operators first developed tours to Turkey. But within a few years, the specialist operators began tours to Turkey, major companies like Intasun started to include the destination. The resulting rush to develop new hotels threatened to ruin the appeal of the resorts for the smaller companies' clients(註20). The main problem with niches is that they only exist if the demand is large enough to sustain a small business venture, but not large enough to interest the major companies.

Vocabulary 內文詞彙

undifferentiated marketing   無差異性營銷

differentiated marketing   差異性營銷

niche marketing   補缺營銷

tourism offering   旅遊產品

appeal   吸引力

tourism supplier   旅遊供應商

upper-mid-priced   中高檔價位的

property   指飯店、汽車旅館或其他住宿設施

touch   特色，點綴

fine-tuned   經過精心調整的

amenity   娛樂、消遣設施

peak   高峰

trough   低谷

repackage   重新包裝

diversify   分散

over-segment   過度細分

niche   （指縮小經營範圍，集中目標於某一個特定市場上）補缺，補缺市場

sub-segment   子細分市場

norm	標準，規範
incentive travel	獎勵旅行
golf courses	高爾夫球場
premium	因稀有而超過一般價值的價格
economy	節約，經濟
conference-center resorts	會議中心度假地
spot	找出，識別出
sophisticated	高級的
substantial	實質性的，巨大的
markup	加價，提價
dry up	枯竭
margin	贏利，利潤
independent operator	獨立的經營商
specialist operator	專營某種旅遊項目的經營商

Notes to the Text 內文註釋

1.An undifferentiated marketing strategy is one that overlooks segment differences, and uses the same marketing mix for all market segments.

無差異性營銷策略忽略市場的差異，把同樣的營銷組合運用於所有的細分市場中。

2.This is sensible in some situations, such as the marketing of capital cities where the appeal is very broad.

在某些情況下運用無差異性營銷是明智的，比如，因為首都的吸引力非常大，所以可以對首都城市採用無差異性營銷。

3.In differentiated marketing, the firm operates in several market segments and design different marketing programs for each segment.

差異性營銷指企業在多個細分市場上經營，並為每個細分市場設計不同的營銷方案。

4.For example, some hotel chains have two or more distinct classes or types of hotels, with each class appealing to a different market segment.

比如，有些連鎖旅店擁有兩個或兩個以上不同級別或類型的酒店，每一種酒店所吸引的細分市場都不相同。

5.However, some tourism suppliers will provide services for almost every market segment and use a unique marketing mix to promote to each market separately.

但是，有些旅遊供應商為幾乎所有的市場都提供服務，並分別用不同的營銷組合來推廣每一個市場。

6.Ramada Franchises Enterprises：華美達國際酒店集團是國際最著名的十大酒店名牌之一，在包括美國在內的全球134 個國家中開設有1000 多家連鎖酒店。1997年與全球著名酒店集團——萬豪（Marriott）國際集團合併。

7.Some hotels segment themselves within a single property and have guest rooms that offer more or fewer features for different customers.

有些酒店在其內部進行細分，它們所提供的客房可以根據顧客的不同增減特色。

8.Faced with direct competition from national chains, they provide uniquely designed properties, added services, or personal touches to attract business and pleasure travelers.

面對來自於遍布全國的連鎖酒店的競爭，它們提供設計獨特的酒店建築、額外的服務或人性化服務來吸引商務旅行者和觀光遊客。

9.Differentiated marketing can create a more fine-tuned product offer and price it appropriately for the target customers, thus increasing the total sales.

差異化營銷可以創造經過精心設計的產品，並根據目標顧客設定合適的價格，因此可以增加總銷售額。

10.Alpine ski resorts repackage themselves as "lake and mountains" destinations in the summer：在夏季重新包裝阿爾卑斯山滑雪勝地，使其成為「湖光山色型」目的地。

11.Since differentiated marketing leads to both higher sales and higher costs, othing general can be said regarding this strategy's profitability.

因為差異性營銷既能產生高銷售額，也會產生高額成本，因此很難估計該策略的贏利情況。

12.A niche is a more narrowly defined group, typically a small market whose needs are not being well served.

補缺市場可解釋為比較狹窄的群體，是一個典型的需求還未得到充分滿足的小市場。

13.Business travel can be broken down into subsegments such as personal, regular business, meetings and conventions, and incentive travel.

商務旅行可以細分為一些子細分市場，比如個人商務旅行、常規商務旅行、會議和獎勵旅行等子細分市場。break down into：把……分類，分解為。

14.Group travel is typified by a group with a common interest that has had its entire trip organized by a third party such as a tour wholesaler.

典型的團體旅行指一組有共同興趣的群體將其整個旅程交給第三方來組織，比如交給組團旅行社組織。be typified by：以某一形象或典型來代表。

15.The nicher gains certain economies through specialization：補缺者透過專業化而獲得了一定規模的經濟利益。

16.In the long term, it is hoped that a strong association with the target market, as well as a reputation of excellent service to that market, will be developed.

從長期看，希望能與目標市場建立緊密的聯繫，同時也會在該市場樹立起服務優良的聲譽。

17.Instead, they rely on sophisticated audiovisual equipment, purpose-built meeting facilities, and high level of personal service in arranging and coordinating their customers' meetings.

相反，它們依靠先進的視聽設備、特別設計的會議設施以及高水平的個性化服務來安排和協調其顧客的會議。purpose-built：特別設計的。

18.Small, regional airlines serve specific geographic areas with routes and schedules that major airlines find uneconomical.

區域性的小型航空公司為特殊地理區域提供那些大公司認為不經濟的航線和航班。

19.The nicher achieves high margin, while the mass marketer achieves high volume.

補缺者能夠獲得高額利潤，而大眾化營銷者則獲得高銷售額。

20.The resulting rush to develop new hotels threatened to ruin the appeal of the resorts for the smaller companies' clients.

所導致的興建新旅店的「熱潮」對小公司造成了極大的威脅，很有可能會毀掉這些旅遊勝地對小公司客戶的吸引力。

Useful Words and Expressions 實用詞彙和表達方式

地理細分	geographic segmentation
人口細分	demographic segmentation
消費心態細分	phychographic segmentation
行為細分	behavioral segmentation
產品專業化	product specialization
市場專業化	market specialization

產品差異化	product differentiation
服務差異化	service differentiation
管道差異化	channel differentiation
形象差異化	image differentiation
按要求提供的服務項目	customized services
特別服務項目	tailor-made services
團體旅行	group tour
團體包價旅行	group inclusive tour
友好旅行團	friendship group
駕駛員導遊（既當導遊又當駕駛員）	driver-guide
地方導遊，地陪	local guide
翻譯導遊	interpreter-escort
旅行團領隊	tour conductor
旅遊宣傳冊	tour brochure
冬季旅遊日程	winter itinerary
敲竹槓的旅館、餐館或商店	tourist trap

Exercises 練習題

Discussion Questions 思考題

1.What is undifferentiated marketing?

2.What are the advantages of differentiated marketing?

3.Why nothing general can be said about the profitability of differentiated marketing?

4.What is niche marketing？ And why is it popular with smaller firms?

5.What is the major risk of niche marketing?

Sentence Translation 單句翻譯練習

1.大型會議團體（convention group）因為其規模很大可以迫使各酒店相互競爭以降低房費，並因此減少會議代表的住宿成本。

2.如果選擇高收入的精英群體（elite group）為目標市場，那麼就要開發能夠吸引他們的產品，這種產品的價格相應也會很高。

3.旅遊企業可以透過增加新的服務，提高服務品質，增加在營銷上的支出以及收購（acquire）與其競爭的企業來擴大市場份額。

4.透過使用產品差異化策略，旅行社能夠實現更多的銷售量，並樹立穩固的市場地位。

5.差異性營銷的優點在於能夠分散（diversify）企業經營的風險，但是正因為如此，差異性營銷的成本遠遠高於無差異性營銷。

6.另一種常用的細分市場的方法是地理細分，旅遊供應商運用這種方法主要是因為很容易根據消費者或潛在消費者所在的地理區域劃分（categorize）消費者類型。

7.面對成熟市場，酒店或航空公司應該把重點放在尋找新的分銷管道（distribution channel）上，比如尋找新的旅行社、組團旅行社（tour wholesaler）或專門策劃獎勵旅行（incentive travel）的機構。

8.市場補缺者通常都是小型企業，它們不會和大型企業直接競爭，也不會緊緊追隨大型企業，相反，它們努力尋找自己的補缺市場。

Passage Translation 段落翻譯練習

Once the segments have been classified, the marketing manager must identify the ones that he or she will use to attract potential tourists. The ones selected are commonly referred to as the target market. Target marketing requires analyzing the sales potential of each segment or segments. This analysis includes assessing the number of both current and potential new tourists as well as their likely per person per diem spending. Selection of target markets makes it easier to determine appropriate promotion media for reaching them. For example, suppose that a target market has been determined that comprised young singles with interest in outdoor daytime recreational activities along with nightlife. Without segmentation of that market, any advertising done might otherwise have been placed in media that would not specifically reach that audience. Target marketing should also consider the competition for that segment, the cost of developing a product for the target market, and the financial and managerial capability of the supplier to handle or server that target market. The final decision concerning target markets can be made only after considering which segments will be most beneficial.

Lesson 19 Internet Marketing 網路營銷

導讀：

網路營銷是企業整體營銷戰略的一個組成部分，是為實現企業總體經營目標所進行的、以互聯網為基本手段營造網上經營環境的各種活動。本篇文章重點介紹了網路營銷的幾個要素，包括品牌建設、直銷、線上銷售、客戶支持、市場研究、產品（服務）拓展與檢驗等，同時指出了網路營銷目前所面臨的問題、挑戰與機遇。

Tourism Marketing Today

The global economy has evolved from one of excess demand to one of excess supply(註1). A growing number of marketers are thus attempting to expand existing markets or develop new markets, and multinational competition has increased dramatically in recent years. Organizations operating in major industrial economies must treat the world as a source of supply and demand. A one-world market exists for products ranging from cars to computers(註2). There is no question that the development of the Internet has become the most important communication and marketing media breakthrough since the printing progress in the mid-fifteenth century. It has fundamentally reshaped understanding of sales and marketing.

On-line marketers are fast pushing the boundaries of(註3) the field through a combination of creative content, the use of in-depth market knowledge, and the deployment of interactive and analytical technological tools. Targeted on-line marketing has emerged as a viable form of reaching customers on the Internet. In addition to providing a cheap and effective way of reaching qualified and interested end customers, it offers several other advantages in the way marketers can establish long-term customer relationships, leading ultimately to retention and loyalty.

Internet Marketing Concepts

The Internet can be a highly efficient tool in overall event management organizations' marketing program. At the same time, it can be a major financial burden if an event management organization does not formulate specific goals for its Internet marketing policy. The objectives for each event management organization may vary depending on organization size, dynamics of operations, financial and staff resources, location, overall development strategy, and client base. The website for a small event management startup will differ from that of a large multinational event management conglomerate. Major marketing concepts enhanced by online tools include brand building, direct research, and product or service development and testing.

Brand Building

Online marketing combined with television, media, and a print is a major brand-building tool. The biggest advantage the Internet has over television and old-fashioned media is the favorable cost/benefit ratio(註4). Event management organizations can achieve a much higher return on their marketing investments in Internet promotions than in a traditional campaign. The research conducted by Millward Brown Interactive, a 20-year-old international advertising research group, found that an organization could achieve significant progress in brand recognition simply by placing its logo on banners of search engines or online database(註5).

Direct Marketing

Online marketing radically changes the way in which information about customers is collected, analyzed and put to use(註6). The competitive dynamics of the direct marketing industry are changing fast with the advent of the Internet. Households are online. It comes as no surprise that online advertising has emerged as one of the hottest growth areas for direct marketers. Direct marketers are flocking to the Internet, drawn by the promise of(註7) cheaper marketing, deeper customer relationships, and access to a worldwide audience. With the ability to connect instantly to the customer, the Internet promises to become the ultimate one-to-one marketing vehicle.

According to the research, more than 80 percent of personal computer owners have at least one college degree. Their average household income is about 50000 per year, well above the 35000 US household average. Customers with household income of less than 40000 per year often cannot afford to contact a professional event manager. By placing well-designed information and ads about your event management services on the Internet, you gain immediate direct contact with your target market group(註8). In addition, larger competitors have no significant advantage over small organizations on the Internet.

On-line Sale

An on-line sale is more applicable to organizations that sell consumer goods, not services(註9). However, event management organizations can still benefit greatly from electronic commerce features. Event management organizations conduct registration, ticket sales, and distribution of materials over the Internet. All of these are segments of event sales. By putting them online, management organizations achieve savings and preserve resources that can now be reallocated.

Among the most important problems of online commerce is a problem of security. If an event management organization conducts financial transactions over the Internet, security of clients' personal financial information is the top priority(註10). Data that contain such information as credit card and social security numbers are very sensitive. It is important to ensure that these data be protected. Since this is a crucial point, it is highly recommended that you involve security professionals in this aspect of your website development(註11).

Customer Support

Incentive-based marketing, a major customer support method, is a technique where the consumer is rewarded or compensated for completed purchase transactions. Similar to the concept of "rebates" in the physical marketplace, online marketing "incentives" are

driving the explosive growth in advertising and marketing revenues.

One of the key objectives of online marketers is to increase their look-to-buy ratio(註12). In addition, they want to build relationships with customers so that they return and be retained for repeat purchases. In addition to a major new marketing channel, the online world offers a cheap and cost-effective way of reaching a large number of qualified customers. The online channel is particularly attractive because advertisers can use tools that are not available in traditional media, such as measurement of "click-through" rates and one-click response to e-mail offers. Further, online sites can record and track user behavior, and these data can be used in conjunction with responses to online advertising messages. These tools give advertisers rapid feedback on their marketing campaigns. This feedback can be used to tailor new messages and targeted offers, when integrated with existing data about customers, and purchase and post-purchase behavior.

Market Research

Increasingly, event management organizations are recognizing the Internet potential for market research. Using the Internet technology, the organization was able to bring together participants from different parts of the world for small, real-time chat sessions. Clients can observe these chat sessions from anywhere in the world. Web sites can be used to conduct market research by surveying visitors. This information can be effective if the process is well planned. Unfortunately, many websites require users to complete online registration forms without providing incentives. As a result, users often submit incorrect information or simply ignore the forms. This behavior can be explained by the desire of users to guard their privacy online. The best way to overcome this constraint is to build a sense of trust between organization and clients or to compensate users for submitting their data.

Products or Service Development and Testing

The Internet is an ideal place for event organizations to test new products/services before they are launched. An event organization can post information about a conference that it is planning to organize online and monitor the interest that users express(註13) toward the conference before they invest large amounts in actual planning. This refers to the first stage of successful event management research. One of the biggest advantages that Internet has over other marketing tools is real-time contact. Marketing professionals use a number of special technical features to leverage this point. Chat rooms, live broadcasting, and time-sensitive promotions are only a small part. The Internet allows marketing professionals to change and update content in almost no time, hence to ensure that customers have the most recent information(註14).

Challenges and Future Directions

There are increasing demands by customer advocacy groups to protect online privacy. Some of these demands are justified, as eager marketers have jumped on the online bandwagon without heed for the fundamental ethic of protecting consumer interest(註15). Growth in credit-card fraud and junk mail solicitations is a direct result of such exuberance. Over time, marketers will have to strike a balance between(註16) online privacy and the ability to provide more targeted campaigns and one-to-one marketing efforts.

Further, it should be realized that the Internet fundamentally alters traditional marketing models. First, the networked model of competition dramatically increases the speed of change in every part and function of the organization, be it in building and delivering a marketing campaign or altering product or service characteristics based on feedback(註17). By its very nature, it leads to discontinuous innovation that can supersede existing modes or channels of doing business. Second, the Internet gives small marketing outfits the ability to extend market reach and impact using technological excellence and know-how, and an aggressive partnering strategy. Thus, a successful business model can be scaled dramatically, and threaten existing players.

Finally, the rate of innovation diffusion through the online medium is faster than through conventional channels, and thus requires organizations to be acutely aware of their "time to market", and the "time to market response". In addition, many Web-based organizations have discovered that wired customers make their views and opinions known, and are extremely involved with their consumption experience. The feedback loop between buyers and sellers is shrinking fast(註18).

Organizations who seek to compete in this domain need to understand the dynamics of viral digital marketing(註19), and the formation of extremely loyal customer communities. By constantly listening to what customers have to say, observing their purchase and consumption behavior, and interacting with them in a dynamic environment, marketers will be able to fine-tune the products or services offered(註20). Customers are demanding convenience, participation, and anticipation — the organizations that deliver these effectively will be tomorrow's winners.

Vocabulary 內文詞彙

multinational	多國的，跨國公司的
dramatically	戲劇性的，引人注目的
breakthrough	突破
retention	保持
formulate	明確表達，闡述
dynamic	運動、行為方式
startup	小企業

conglomerate	聯合企業
advent	來臨
flock	聚集，蜂擁
reallocate	再分配
real-time	即時的，實時的
leverage	槓桿作用
advocacy	擁護，主張
bandwagon	花車，潮流
heed	留心，注意
fraud	欺詐
solicitation	誘惑，懇求
exuberance	茂盛
supersede	代替
outfit	機構，配備

Notes to the Text 內文註釋

1. The global economy has evolved from one of excess demand to one of excess supply.

全球經濟已經從需求過剩演化為供給過剩。

2.products ranging from cars to computers：從汽車到電腦的各種產品。

3.fast push the boundary of：快速地拓寬領域、快速地發展。

4.The biggest advantage the Internet has over television and old-fashioned media is the favorable cost/benefit ratio.

同電視和其他老式的媒體相比，網路最大的優勢是有利的成本利潤比。

5.could achieve significant progress in brand recognition simply by placing its logo on banners of search engines or online database：能夠在品牌認知上取得顯著的進步，而其方式僅僅是把其企業徽標放在了搜尋引擎或網路資料庫的網幅圖像廣告上。

6.Online marketing radically changes the way in which information about customers is collected, analyzed and put to use.

網路營銷極大地改變了蒐集、分析和使用有關顧客資訊的方式。

7.Direct marketers are flocking to the Internet, drawn by the promise of：受……承諾的吸引，大批直銷商湧入網路市場。flock to：成群地聚集、湧向。

8.By placing well-designed information and ads about your event management services on the Internet, you gain immediate direct contact with your target market group.

透過把精心設計的關於你專案管理服務的資訊和廣告發布到網上，你能夠迅速地和你的目標群體取得直接聯繫。

9.An on-line sale is more applicable to organizations that sell consumer goods, not services.

　　網路營銷更適合於出售產品而不是服務的公司。

　　10.If an event management organization conducts financial transactions over the Internet, security of clients' personal financial information is the top priority.

　　如果專案管理公司透過網路進行資金交易，那麼客戶的個人經濟資訊將成為首要考慮的問題。top priority：優先權、首要地位。

　　11.it is highly recommended that you involve security professionals in this aspect of your website development：強烈建議你在網路發展方面使用網路安全專業人士。

　　12.increase their look-to-buy ratio：提高他們的觀望／購買比率。

　　13.can post information about a conference that it is planning to organize online and monitor the interest that users express：可以發布有關它計劃在網上組織的會議資訊，監控用戶所表達的興趣。

　　14.hence to ensure that customers have the most recent information：因此可以確保消費者獲得最新的資訊。hence：副詞，意思是「因此」，相當於therefore。

　　15.as eager marketers have jumped on the online bandwagon without heed for the fundamental ethic of protecting consumer interest：因為許多銷售商迫不及待地搭上網路這股潮流，但他們沒有考慮保護消費者利益這個重要的道德規範。

　　16.strike a balance between：取得平衡。

　　17.be it in building and delivering a marketing campaign or altering product or service characteristics based on feedback：其中的「be it...or」...在這裡是虛擬語氣，意思是「無論……還是……」。

18.The feedback loop between buyers and sellers is shrinking fast.

買方與賣方之間的回饋週期極大地縮短了。

19.Organizations who seek to compete in this domain need to understand the dynamics of digital marketing：想在這個領域競爭的公司需要瞭解數碼營銷的運作方式。

20.to fine-tune the products or services offered：對提供的產品或服務做出精細的調整。

★ ★ ★ ★

Useful Words and Expressions 實用詞彙和表達方式

橫幅廣告	banner
收視次數	impressions
廣告瀏覽量	ad view
點擊次數	clicks
點擊率	click rate
千人成本	cost per thousand impressions（CPM）
點擊	click
訪客流量統計文件	log file
心理篩選	psychological screens

參照人群	reference groups
經銷商市場	reseller markets
選擇性感知	selective perception
單獨用戶	unique users
訪客量	user sessions
品牌興趣	brand interest
影響中心	centers of influence

Exercises 練習題

Discussion Questions 思考題

1.What is the main difference between Internet marketing and traditional marketing?

2.What is the trend for tourism marketing today?

3.What is incentive-based marketing?

4.What are the challenges and main problems of Internet marketing?

5.What do you anticipate the future of Internet marketing?

Sentence Translation 單句翻譯練習

1.隨著資訊社會（information society）的到來，營銷環境（marketing

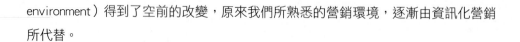
environment）得到了空前的改變，原來我們所熟悉的營銷環境，逐漸由資訊化營銷所代替。

2.網上銷售是企業現有營銷體系的有利補充（complement）。

3.網路營銷的外部環境為開展營銷活動提供了潛在用戶（potential client），而且還向用戶傳遞營銷資訊的各種手段（means）和管道。

4.我公司一直從事網路營銷的研究，我們根據您的特定用戶群的需要幫您制定貼心的網路營銷計劃。

5.對那些想在傳統營銷領域取得突破（breakthrough）的公司來説，網路無疑提供了一個新的傳播載體。

6.中國家電行業互聯網應用已達到較高水平，這不僅體現在網站數字比例（proportion）上，而且也體現在網路意識和重視（awareness）程度上。

7.調查顯示，81.5%的企業認為選擇CN域名是國內企業的明智做法。

8.對於中國企業的網上推廣（promotion）活動，完全中文化的通用網址也同樣受到企業的認同和讚揚。

Passage Translation 段落翻譯練習

Since the process of changing the marketing variable and collecting the responses cannot interfere with the normal operation of the site, we first describe the site and highlight how the change in the marketing variable is achieved. We assume that there is a Web site whose pages comprise content typical of online sites. In particular, there are some navigation controls, there is some space for horizontal and/or vertical banner advertisements, and there is space for the main content of the page. Hyperlinks or "hot spots" embedded within the main content or navigation controls allow a visitor to navigate the site and engage in transactions offered by the site. The content of the banner advertisements is chosen by logic embodied in the recommender subsystem of the commerce server on which the online site is developed. Certain activities (for example, a purchase) require the individual to log in, while other activities do not require identification to the system. For the latter, the individual can browse the site as an anonymous user.

Lesson 20 Travel Brochures 旅遊宣傳冊

導讀：

旅遊宣傳冊不僅是遊客瞭解旅遊產品資訊的主要來源，同時也是旅遊經營機構宣傳和推銷產品的重要營銷工具，它是影響顧客決策的重要因素。本篇文章不僅介紹了傳統宣傳冊的作用、樣式、布局、封面、設計、選紙和分銷管道，而且對目前頗為流行的各種電子宣傳冊也進行了詳細的闡述。

The travel brochure is a vital marketing tool. Much of the information it contains is designed to answer the questions which consumers may generally want to ask. It informs consumers about the product and attracts bookings. On the other hand, many brochures also have a symbolic role. It can act as a substitute for a product which cannot be physically seen or inspected prior to purchase. With brochure at hand, consumers can see the descriptions of the product in advance, to refer to the material during the trip and to look it over at a later date when recalling the trip.

For these reasons, very large sum are invested in the brochure itself, and in advertising to persuade the customers to enter the travel agent and pick the brochure up.

Style and Format

Travel brochure must be distinctive and attractive. In it, the organization must communicate its brand image, determine its product positioning and convey enough information to reassure the consumer of the organization's strength and reliability(註1). Usually, consumers weigh up a number of factors to gauge a "good" brochure(註2), including:

◆ The appeal of the front cover;

◆ The paper quality and its "glossiness";

◆ The use of colors and their appeal;

◆ The number and quality of photographs and other illustrations;

◆ The thickness of brochures;

◆ The clarity of the text, and prices where appropriate;

◆ The relevance and appeal of the products on offer.

Most of the travel brochures follow a typical three-section pattern:

◆ A set of introductory pages;

◆ The contents pages, which in the case of large companies can run to 500 pages(註3);

◆"extra" or exit pages.

The introduction establishes the company's style, makes statements about policies and commercial practices, reassures the consumers of the company's stability, promotes its unique selling points and "bargain" offers(註4), and preferably (though not invariably) contains an index.

Contents pages tend to be arranged in sections defined by destination country(註5). Most companies lead with their strongest destination, but it is not unknown for the first to be a resort that they wish to emphasis for other reasons (such as when launching a new destination)(註6). Typically, most destination will include a simple map locating hotels, photographs of a hotel interiors and exteriors (almost inevitably with a swimming pool, descriptive text, and a price box with details of flights, departure points, durations and dates(註7), either on the same page or in the exit pages).

The final section of the brochure contains details of booking conditions, extraneous information, insurance schemes and all the other "small print" details required by law and regulatory bodies(註8). The booking forms is frequently to be found on the back cover or on one of the last pages in the brochure, but should not be printed on the back of any booking conditions, since such contractual information should be retained by the customer. The larger tour operators no longer carry booking forms in their brochures but instead provide retail agents with separate booking form pads.

Print material in other sectors is less constrained. Tour operating brochures are required to carry prices, and these are required to be clear and comprehensive, i.e. inclusive of tax or other levies. With the more fluid pricing policies among tour operators now, this can lead to the need to republish brochures at frequent intervals, adding to cost(註9). A hotel chain has greater freedom, and typically will publish its prices in the form of a loose-leaf insert(註10), which can be changed each year, or more frequently where necessary. Destination brochures seldom include any details of prices, although some will include accommodation guidelines for a commercial consideration, in which case they, too, will need regular updating, at least annually.

Cover

The design of the brochure cover is the key to persuading consumers to consider any product. Tour operators therefore put considerable effort into the design of the front cover. The choice of design is a difficult one, but typically the cover will feature:

◆ Spectacularly attractive photograph of one or more destinations;

◆ An attractive holiday situation, such as a family group enjoying themselves in the water;

◆ A pictorial amalgam of the contents;

◆ A statement of what is contained or of sales features.

Whatever design style is chosen it is wise to ensure that it is relevant to the contents, not merely attractive in itself(註11). Another aspect is that most brochures will be displayed in standard racks within travel agencies. This means that their design is to some extent predetermined — company names must appear along the top of the page so that if overlapped by lower racks the name will still appear prominently.

Design and Print

Designing a brochure goes beyond merely cobbling together graphics(註12) and copy; it incorporates artwork, the ability to recommend and use certain fonts and typefaces in the copy which reflects the company's image, and a flair for what will be both attractive and commercial to the reader.

The brochure can be printed in landscape format (in which the top and bottom sides of the page are longer) or portrait format (where the left and right sides of the rectangle are longer, i.e. upright). Because most brochures are designed to fit into standard racks, A4 sized portrait is now the common shape, but companies dealing direct with their customers can choose to be a little different and produce a landscape design.

If there are many pages the company will wish to reduce the weight by using thinner paper. This may need to be compensated for by using a heavier paper for the cover to prevent floppiness(註13). If the brochure contains few pages, then extra weight may be less important and the "feel" can be improved by using heavier than average paper(註14).

When it comes to pictures, the base rule is — good quality, to professional standards. Photographs should be high in contrast. Almost without exception, brochures today will incorporate color, which greatly heightens the appeal of beach scenes, landscapes and action shots.

Distributing the Brochure

Customers seeking information on travel and tourism have a variety of ways in which to obtain their brochures. Holiday brochures are still largely collected from travel agencies while destination brochures are frequently sent through the mail to customers responding to advertising. All of the following are typical methods of distribution used by the trade to get brochures into the hands of their customers. These methods may be used either to initiate an enquiry for a brochure, or in some cases to distribute the brochure itself:

Method of Distribution:	Appropriate For:
Travel agencies	Tour operators, cruise and ferry companies
Door-to-door circulars, newsletters	Travel agents, local airport, coaches
Tourist information centers	Tourist attractions, destinations, hotels
Hotels	Tourist attractions, destinations
Websites	All travel principals
Magazine inserts, press supplements	All travel principals, especially destinations and tourist attractions
Coupons in magazines and newspapers	All travel principals
Direct mail	Travel agents and principals
Exhibitions, trade fairs	Destinations, attractions, operators and transport principals
Airports	Airlines, hotels, attractions
Travel agents' presentation events	Tour operators and other principals
National or local television/radio	National destinations, large operators, travel agency, chains, popular attractions

The E-brochure

The development of modern technology is opening up new ways of presenting travel products to the public, and the ability to display moving and still pictures alongside text(註15) on a website is beginning to change the long-standing reliance on hard print(註16), in a way that could scarcely be imagined a decade ago. This ability had developed in following stages since the 1990s.

Stage1. In this stage, the video cassette made it possible for travel companies to commission a variety of video programs that offered in-depth information about particular holiday areas and types of holiday, with accompanying pictures of hotel interiors and exteriors. This gave consumers a far better impression of a resort and its facilities, and proved a valuable supplement to the brochure.

Stage2. This stage offered far more versatility. The development of the CD-ROM, which can hold photographic images of every hotel for the complete season, resulted in a very powerful promotional tool which could be produced at modest cost(註17). The difficulties inherent in videotape are overcome in using a CD-ROM, which can be viewed by anyone with access to(註18) a modern personal computer.

Stage3. This stage was reached when website providers, prompted by the greatly increased capacity of personal computers, began to add still and moving pictures of their facilities to the sites. This is currently in the process of rapid expansion(註19), and more and more data will become available as the power of PCs expands exponentially. In 2003, Kuoni launched a full-color e-brochure on its website which allowed agents to download information and pictures of hotels and destinations in which their clients were interested, thus building a personalized brochure. This company is one of several now placing their brochures online, reducing costs and storage for both agents and operators and providing immediate delivery of information to agents and their clients.

Finally, Thomas Cook has experimented with Check-T cards, a system in which clients search for a holiday of their choice on a series of cards generated by computer. Those selected can then be scanned by a bar code reader(註20), and details of the holidays appear on the agent's screen. This also reduces cost and wastage for the agent, who can provide hard copies of the screen data for their customer. This is not only cuts the costs of brochure production and wastage, but also opens up the prospect for the sale of holidays and travel through other retail outlets.

Vocabulary 內文詞彙

travel brochure   旅遊宣傳冊

symbolic   象徵的

description	描寫，描述，介紹
distinctive	與眾不同的，有特色的
brand image	品牌形象
gauge	衡量，評判
glossy	平滑的，有光澤的
extra	額外的
selling point	賣點
extraneous	無關係的，外來的
contractual	契約的，合約的
constrained	被約束的，強迫的
levy	徵稅
fluid	不固定的，靈活的
update	更新
pictorial	用圖說明的，有插圖的
amalgam	混合體
prominently	顯著地
cobble	把……草率地（匆忙地）拼湊在一起

incorporate	合併，包含
font	字體
typeface	字體，字樣
flair	鑑別力，眼光
rectangle	長方形
floppy	鬆鬆垮垮的，鬆垂的
shot	快照，拍攝
circular	傳單，廣告，函件
newsletter	時事通訊，簡訊
insert	夾在報刊中的散頁廣告
supplement	增刊，附錄
coupon	優惠券
presentation event	展示活動
versatility	多用途，多功能
inherent	固有的，內在的
website provider	網站服務商
exponentially	以乘方的速度（增大），迅速地

Notes to the Text 內文註釋

1.the organization must communicate its brand image, determine its product positioning and convey enough information to reassure the consumer of the organization's strength and reliability：企業必須宣傳自己的品牌形象、確立產品定位、傳播足夠的資訊，以便讓顧客瞭解企業的優勢，相信企業是可靠的。

2.consumers weigh up a number of factors to gauge a "good" brochure：顧客從很多方面來判斷一個宣傳冊的好壞。weigh up：估量，掂量。

3.The contents pages, which in the case of large companies can run to 500 pages：主要內容部分，對有些大公司來說，可能會達到500頁之多。

4.promotes its unique selling points and "bargain" offers：宣傳其獨特的賣點和「物超所值」的項目。

5.Contents pages tend to be arranged in sections defined by destination country.

主要內容部分一般按目的地細分為幾個部分。

6.Most companies lead with their strongest destination, but it is not unknown for the first to be a resort that they wish to emphasize for other reasons (such as when launching a new destination).

大部分企業首先列出自己最好的目的地，不過，我們也經常見到，出於某些原因，企業會把自己想重點突出的某個度假地放在第一個（例如要推出一個新的旅遊目的地）。

7.almost inevitably with a swimming pool, descriptive text, and a price box with details of flights, departure points, durations and dates：幾乎都包括游泳池、描述性文字以及具體航班資訊、出發地點、逗留時間和日期等詳細資訊的價格表。

8.all the other "small print" details required by law and regulatory bodies：以及法律和有關管理部門規定必須含有的其他資訊，這部分通常用「小號字體」印刷。

9.this can lead to the need to republish brochures at frequent intervals, adding to cost：這將需要經常重新印製宣傳冊，也增加了成本。

10.loose-leaf insert：活頁的價格表。

11.Whatever design style is chosen it is wise to ensure that it is relevant to the contents, not merely attractive in itself.

無論挑選什麼樣的設計，都應確保它與內容相關，而不僅僅只是設計本身具有吸引力。

12.Designing a brochure goes beyond merely cobbling together graphics：宣傳冊的設計不僅僅是把圖片和文字拼湊在一起。

13.This may need to be compensated for by using a heavier paper for the cover to prevent floppiness.

為了彌補這一點，可以選用厚實一些的紙張作為封面來避免給人鬆散、不整齊的感覺。

14.If the brochure contains few pages, then extra weight may be less important and the "feel" can be improved by using heavier than average paper.

如果宣傳冊只有幾頁，那麼重量就不太重要，這時就可以選用比普通紙厚實一些的紙張來增加它的質感。

15.to display moving and still pictures alongside text：在展示文本文件的同時可以展示動態和靜態的圖片。

16.change the long-standing reliance on hard print：改變了長期以來對印刷文字的依賴。

17.resulted in a very powerful promotional tool which could be produced at modest cost：成為一個製作成本適中的強有力的營銷工具。

18.with access to：有能力使用，有權力使用。

19.This is currently in the process of rapid expansion：目前正處於快速發展時期。

20.Those selected can then be scanned by a bar code reader：那些被選中的就可以透過條碼讀取器掃描了。

Useful Words and Expressions 實用詞彙和表達方式

營業時間	Business Hours
失物招領處	Lost and Found
禁止吸煙	No Smoking
請勿拍照	No Photos
遊人止步	No Visitors
禁止入內	No Entry
閒人免進	No Admittance

禁止鳴喇叭	No Honking
免費通行	Toll Free
（郵政）特快專遞	EMS
車輛修理	Mechanical Help
此處插入	Insert Here
此處開啟	Open Here
此處撕開	Split Here
禁止掉頭	No U Turn
本處職工專用	Staff Only
勿亂扔雜物	No Littering
請勿觸摸	Hands Off
酒店	Pub
咖啡館、小餐館	Cafe
酒吧	Bar
洗衣店	Laundry
置於陰涼處	In Shade
謹防扒手	Beware of Pickpockets

意見箱	Complaint Box
滅火專用	For Use Only in Case of Fire
麵包店	Bakery
問訊處	Information
禁止通行	No Passing
對號入座	Seat by Number
愛護公共財物	Protect Public Property
售票處	Ticket Office (or: Booking Office)
免費入場	Admission Free
自行車存車處	Bike Park (ing)
婦女、兒童優先	Children and Women First
小心輕放	Handle with Care
禁止攜犬入內	Dogs Not Allowed
切勿近火	Keep Away From Fire
減速行駛	Reduced Speed Now
馬路施工，請繞行	Roadwork Ahead
請勿倒立	Keep Top Side Up

當心不要丟失東西	Take Care Not to Leave Things Behind
用畢放回架上	Please Return It Back After Use
行李存放處	Luggage Depository

Exercises 練習題

Discussion Questions 思考題

1.Why is a travel brochure regarded as a marketing tool?

2.How do customers usually judge a "good" brochure?

3.What is called landscape format in the printing of brochure?

4.How do we choose paper for brochures?

5.What do you know about e-brochures?

Sentence Translation 單句翻譯練習

1.越來越多的機構使用網站來促銷會展活動（convention and exhibition），每當需要更新（update）日程、酒店和交通等資訊時，只需把資訊放進網站（website），然後給所有與會者發送一封電子郵件（E-mail）通知更新即可。

2.外觀漂亮誘人的（eye-catching）宣傳冊較之外觀平淡普通的（plain）宣傳冊自然具有優勢（have advantages over）。

3.制定營銷計劃（marketing plan）前要對目標人群（target customer）的需求、期望等進行深入（in-depth）的調查和瞭解。

4.20多年前，大多數來自香港、臺灣及其他地方的美國華人（Chinese American），從唐人街（Chinatown）搬出來後，在這裡建起了新的居住中心（residential center）和商業中心（business center）。

5.這裡超級市場（super market）和購物中心（shopping mall）林立，真是一個週末遊玩、參觀和購物的理想地方。

6.我們有健身娛樂中心（fitness center），有設施完善的健身房（bodybuilding gym），裡面有最新的運動器械（apparatus），如拉力器械（pull weights）和自行車機等。

7.中國菜分成八大菜系（eight big cuisine），或者說是八大風味（style），如粵菜（Cantonese food）、京菜和川菜等。

8.中醫的治療方法以中草藥為主（center on Chinese herbal medicine），以針灸、推拿（medical massage）和氣功（Qigong）為輔（to be supplemented by）。

Passage Translation 段落翻譯練習

The sum of the shared attitudes, values and behavior of the group is known as its culture. Culture is what the group has in common and which divides or distinguishes them from other groups. Historically, each nation developed its own distinctive culture protected from outside influences by geographical, language and religious barriers. Today, on the surface these barriers are being broken down by the ease of travel and communication across frontiers. We all live in what McLuhan called the Global Village, watching the same news and programs on our televisions. Nevertheless ethnic strife and civil wars currently raging throughout the world should warn us that despite, or even because of, this global culture, the need to identify with one's own small group and to defend its culture against others is still very powerful.

The effects on consumer behavior of cultural differences between nationalities are a major concern of international marketing. But even within the same country or city, there are significant cultural differences, between ethnic minorities, between social classes, and even between age groups. These are likely to be seen in attitudes to the family, to work, to the role of women and to the way relationships are conducted in business and society.

Lesson 21 Experiential Marketing 體驗式營銷

導讀：

　　隨著體驗經濟的到來，人們越來越認識到體驗式營銷的重要性。傳統的營銷方式注重產品的利益和特色，而體驗式營銷則注重消費者的感受，透過為消費者創造一種難以忘懷的體驗經歷來吸引消費者。本篇文章重點介紹了體驗的定義、體驗與傳統產品和服務的區別、體驗式營銷與傳統營銷的區別，以及體驗式營銷在旅遊業中的應用。

Experiential Marketing is an important trend upon entering the new age of experience economy. Experiential marketing focuses on the customer experience by providing them information on the actual consumer experience or interactions with products for the purpose of driving the sale of the product(註1). It's about creating the "ah ha" with the consumer and when applied correctly, will lead to greater impact for the consumer, increased effectiveness for the marketers, and even cost savings relative to traditional advertising or marketing techniques(註2).

What Is Experience

To understand experiential marketing, it is important to comprehend what is meant by the term experience and its difference from goods and services.

Experiences are a fourth economic offer, one that is distinctly different from the traditional commodities, goods and services. Using a theatrical analogy, some experts describe "services" as the stage used to create experiences and "goods" as the props that are used in planning and sequencing series of memorable events(註3).

For example, the primary goods a hotel offers is a temporary bed. People are buying a place to sleep. Hotels adjust their market position, audience and price point of their goods by the quality of the rooms, amenities available, and services offered. Service offers may include a concierge, rolling the sheets back in the evening, room service, fax delivery to the room, or an on-site or on-call doctor or exercise advisor. These are traditional goods and services.

Hotels that want to build visitor experiences for their markets needs to examine their attributes differently. For example, a 2-night weekend package at an historic hotel or castle could include a heritage tour of the building by a staff member or a reputable, experienced local interpreter. An opportunity to tour the grounds with the head gardener or to go behind-the-scenes and discover how the chef at a five-star hotel spends his day could be added to the package and used to attract different markets. Either of these two packaged weekends would provide a very different visitor experience than that received by the person who merely reserves a room.

There are five experiential realms, each of which offers a type of value to the travel consumers:

Entertaining experiences are primarily passive yet can be highly absorbing such as watching how the chef chops up vegetables, cracks eggs, flips dough in the air, then giving it a try;

Educational experiences are informative, increase knowledge, skill, and engage the minds. They can be passive, such as reading, interpretive panels at an historic site, or involve active participation such as cooking with a chef, or becoming an archaeologist for a day;

Aesthetic experiences are passive but have the ability to totally immerse people in an experience(註4). For example, walking the grounds of a castle resort, smelling the fresh flowers, listening to a waterfall, and feeling the breeze;

Escape experiences involve active participation and immerse people in an activity such as a spa weekend or visiting a variety of homes on a private garden tour and meeting the owners;

Social experiences involve finding ways to make people feel "welcome" and create opportunities for them to socialize and even develop new social bonds(註5), whether they are traveling in a group, with families and friends, or alone.

The five experiential realms are the key elements for tourism marketers to successfully creating memorable travel experiences.

Why Experiential Marketing

Experiential Marketing and Traditional Marketing

Traditional marketing is based on a features-and-benefits approach(註6). It presents a rational, analytical view of customers, products and competition. In traditional marketing, consumers are thought to go through a considered decision-making process, where each of the features or characteristics of a particular product or service are seen to convey certain benefits, and these are all assessed by the potential consumers(註7). However, this is far too limited a way of viewing the purchase decision, with excessive emphasis on the rational and logical elements of the decision, and not enough on the emotional and irrational aspects involved in the purchase(註8). Unfortunately, traditional marketing and business concepts offer hardly any guidance to capitalize on the emerging experience economy.

Whereas, experiential marketing focuses on consumer experience, including sense, feel, think, act, and relate(註9). These are the factors greatly influencing traveler's choices and travelers are willing to pay a premium for them. Companies that can successfully create memorable traveler experiences will get much more profits than companies using traditional marketing tools.

The Need for Experiential Marketing

Tourism, by its very nature, is an experiential business. Visiting a destination for the first time is an experience, attending a special cultural event is an experience, and struggling to order food in a foreign language while leafing through a dictionary is an experience. But in today's environment of ever more sophisticated consumers, those who deliver outstanding and memorable experiences consistently create superior value and competitive advantage(註10).

Travel consumers want to be "emotionally" moved, educated, challenged, involved, entertained, and even surprised. They are selecting travel destinations based on the delivery of "experiences" rather than the physical attributes of a resort, a city, a province, or a country. Customers don't remember the event; they remember the experience. It is not the place they just visited, but how they feel after they visited it. It's all about experience. At the heart of this demand are people who are willing to pay more to participate in travel that offers something different, engaging experiences that go beyond traditional goods and services.

Responding to this demand are travel suppliers, tour operators and travel marketers. These companies are developing new, and refreshing existing products in ways that are designed to create long lasting memories with their niche or mainstream travelers. Experiential marketing offers these companies an excellent framework for involving the travel consumers in a series of memorable activities that are inherently personal, engage the senses, and make connections on an emotional, physical, spiritual or intellectual level.

For example, the high-end travel experience Swimming with Sharks at Orlando's Sea World. Participants learn facts about sharks, visit the food preparation room, touch a shark and dive, in a steel cage with Plexiglas window, into a shark encounter pool(註11). And cruise ships are expanding the travelers' on-board learning activities. The travelers have fun and learn at the same time and choose to take advantage of the many classes, workshops, and programs that are available onboard daily.

Some Cases of Experiential Marketing

Like all big "new" ideas, the idea of experiential marketing is not new. The origin of experiential marketing can be dated back to Walt Disney and the creation of Disneyland in 1955. The way Disneyland welcome guests, engage visitors, and provide an endless array of interactive experiences is the first example of experiential marketing(註12).

Case One: JetBlue Airways(註13)

Airlines also have struggled with its application for years.Just think of JetBlue Airways. JetBlue does the little things right to provide a consistent experience. They do not nickel-and-dime the consumer; headsets and snacks are free. Flight attendants are renown for their friendliness and helpfulness. When the weather slows down or cancels a flight, customers get a flight credit right away, often without even asking for it. At JFK Airport, for instance, JetBlue operates two "caf s" where delayed passengers can relax and get free refreshments, and harried parents can watch their kids play in JetBlue play areas.In smaller airports, JetBlue requires its managers to be proactive in servicing customers, going so far as to order pizzas from a local restaurant to serve to hungry passengers. It's no wonder that JetBlue is ranked at the top for best service in the airline industry.

Case Two: IKEA(註14) Hotels

Given the lack of differentiation of many hotel chains like Hampton Inn, Fairfield Inn, Red Roof Inn, etc., imagine if a particular chain partnered with IKEA to decorate their rooms with simple, clean and comfortable bedroom furniture(註15). This fact alone would give that hotel chain a significant point of selling. The hotel chain also gets the economic benefit of furniture at prices that are even better than wholesale prices on generic furniture(註16). Visitors who go to the hotel will undoubtedly get enough first-hand experiential information of the hotel and of the IKEA furniture. Finally, some creative "consumer insights research" opportunities can even be built in(註17), such as allowing visitors to select from among differently decorated IKEA hotel rooms and tracking such decisions to gather which items are most popular or even how to make IKEA's in-store bedroom sets more appealing. In summary, both the hotel and IKEA achieve "experiential marketing" which drives greater marketing effectiveness (i.e. hotel chain differentiates themselves from others; IKEA lets customers actually experience their products prior to going to a store), delivers a more impressive experience to customers, and even reduces costs for both parties.

The business successes achieved by focusing on customer experience is exactly why experiential marketing is becoming increasingly important to any company's marketing mix. It may be a modest percentage now, but it will inexorably grow(註18). Companies will soon be forced by the consumer to adopt experiential marketing tactics and strategies in order to reach them.

Some Guidelines for Devising an Experiential Marketing Strategy

Determine what types of experiences you want to market for travelers.

Are there any opportunities to build contact with local people, through engaging your travelers in the local community? Is there a special behind-the-scenes activity or access to a special unforgettable place that would create wonderful memories for your travelers? Do you want your travelers to learn or discover something new?

Select a consistent theme that will guide and harmonize the types of activities that will be included in the tour and review the sequencing of experiences and activities.

For example, in Hong Kong there is a themed program called the "Cultural Kaleidoscope". The primary objective of this program is to meet people, spend time with artisans that can teach the art of making tea, tai chi, learning how to distinguish jade, etc. This could be offered as a stand-alone program, or packaged as an introduction to a country/community and followed by visits to attractions and places associated with the people the traveler has met(註19).

Offer memorabilia and cue that create and sustain the memories.

The use of memorabilia and cues in recording and sustaining visitors, memories was a good technique to build customer loyalty and foster word of mouth promotion(註20). The range of cues and memorabilia used by different organizations included: pre-trip items for travelers, photo logs, travel journals, visitor profiles, personal letters, post-trip videos and certificates of recognition(註21).

Deliver a premium travel experience that engages all the senses and provides value for money.

Vocabulary 內文詞彙

experiential marketing   體驗式營銷

drive	驅動，推動
economic offer	經濟產品
analogy	比擬，類比
audience	受眾
concierge	公寓管理員
on-call	隨叫隨到的
exercise advisor	健身教練，健身顧問
interpreter	解說員
experiential realm	體驗領域
entertaining experience	娛樂體驗
aesthetic experience	審美體驗
immerse	使沉浸於，使專心於
escape experience	散心體驗
leaf through	匆匆翻閱
refreshing	使人振作的，令人耳目一新的，提神的
high-end	高端的
plexiglas	有機玻璃

nickel-and-dime	對……很吝嗇
flight credit	飛行里程積分卡
harry	使苦惱，不斷煩擾
proactive	主動採取行動的，積極主動的
Cultural Kaleidoscope	文化萬花筒
stand-alone	獨立的
memorabilia	與名人或重大事件有關的紀念物
cue	提示物
certificates of recognition	認證書

Notes to the Text 內文註釋

1.Experiential marketing focuses on the customer experience by providing them information on the actual consumer experience or interactions with products for the purpose of driving the sale of the product.

體驗式營銷注重顧客的體驗，透過為顧客提供有關真實體驗的資訊或顧客與產品的互動來達到推動產品銷售的目的。for the purpose of：以……為目的。

2.It's about creating the "ah ha" with the consumer and when applied correctly, will lead to greater impact for the consumer, increased effectiveness for the marketers, and even cost savings relative to traditional advertising or marketing techniques.

體驗式營銷能使消費者發出驚嘆，感到滿意，如果運用恰當，它還會對消費者

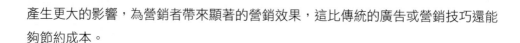

產生更大的影響，為營銷者帶來顯著的營銷效果，這比傳統的廣告或營銷技巧還能夠節約成本。

3.Using a theatrical analogy, some experts describe "services" as the stage used to create experiences and "goods" as the props that are used in planning and sequencing series of memorable events.

一些專家用戲劇來類比說明體驗、產品和服務的關係，認為「服務」是用來創造體驗的舞臺，「產品」則是用來計劃和安排一系列值得回憶的事件的道具。

4.Aesthetic experiences are passive but have the ability to totally immerse people in an experience.

審美體驗是被動的，但是它能夠使人們完全沉浸於體驗之中。

5.Social experiences involve finding ways to make people feel "welcome" and create opportunities for them to socialize and even develop new social bonds：社交體驗包括找到一些方法使人們感到「受歡迎」，為他們創造一些機會進行聯誼，甚至建立起新的社會關係。

6.Traditional marketing is based on a features-and-benefits approach.

傳統營銷是以特色和利益為基礎的營銷。

7.In traditional marketing, consumers are thought to go through a considered decision-making process, where each of the features or characteristics of a particular product or service are seen to convey certain benefits, and these are all assessed by the potential consumers.

傳統營銷認為，消費者會經歷一個深思熟慮的決策過程，在這個過程中，某個產品或服務的特色或特點都代表一定的利益，潛在的消費者會對這些特色和利益進行比較。

8.with excessive emphasis on the rational and logical elements of the decision, and not enough on the emotional and irrational aspects involved in the purchase：過分重視決策中的理性和邏輯因素，而忽視了購買中的情感因素和非理性因素。

9.Whereas, experiential marketing focuses on consumer experience, including sense, feel, think, act, and relate.

但是，體驗式營銷注重消費者的體驗，包括感官、情感、思考、行動、關聯五個方面。

10.But in today's environment of ever more sophisticated consumers, those who deliver outstanding and memorable experiences consistently create superior value and competitive advantage.

但是在現在的環境下，消費者越來越有經驗，只有那些一直能夠提供非比尋常的、值得回憶的體驗的企業才能創造出更高的價值，才能獲得競爭優勢。

11.Participants learn facts about sharks, visit the food preparation room, touch a shark and dive, in a steel cage with Plexiglas window, into a shark encounter pool.

參與者獲得有關鯊魚的知識，參觀為鯊魚準備食物的地方，觸摸鯊魚，並且乘坐一個裝有有機玻璃窗戶的籠子潛入鯊魚池中。

12.The way Disneylands welcome guests, engage visitors, and provide an endless array of interactive experiences is the first example of experiential marketing.

迪士尼樂園歡迎遊客，吸引遊客並且為遊客提供大量互動式體驗的方式，可以說是體驗式營銷的首例。an array of：一長列，一系列。

13.JetBlue Airways：美國捷藍航空公司。1998年成立，公司總部設在紐約甘迺迪國際機場。這家航空公司是一家小型特色低成本航空公司。「捷藍的旅行體驗」包括捷藍航空的新飛機、真皮坐椅、24個頻道機載衛星電視服務。還包括無正餐供應，只提供飲料和零食；顧客自己指定座位；不使用紙製機票；無超售航班；無頭等艙；無週六晚上停留限制；駕駛員座艙防彈門；機上瑜伽；等等。

14.IKEA：瑞典宜家（IKEA）是全球最大的家居用品零售商，1943年初創。

15.imagine if a particular chain partnered with IKEA to decorate their rooms with simple, clean and comfortable bedroom furniture：想像一下，如果某個連鎖酒店與宜家進行合作，用宜家簡潔舒適的臥室家具來裝飾客房。partner with：與某人合作、合夥。

16.The hotel chain also gets the economic benefit of furniture at prices that are even better than wholesale prices on generic furniture.

該連鎖酒店也能夠獲得經濟利益，因為它購買家具的價格甚至低於購買大批家具時的批發價。

17.some creative "consumer insights research" opportunities can even be built in：甚至還會出現一些創造性的「消費者評價調查」的機會。

18.It may be a modest percentage now, but it will inexorably grow.

現在體驗式營銷所占的比例並不顯著，但是它將來肯定會增長的。

19.This could be offered as a stand-alone program, or packaged as an introduction to a country/community and followed by visits to attractions and places associated with the people the traveler has met.

可以把這作為一個獨立的旅遊項目，也可以作為套裝行程的一部分，把它當做是對國家、社會的介紹，之後再參觀與旅遊者所遇到的人相關的旅遊勝地和地點。

20.The use of memorabilia and cues in recording and sustaining visitors memories was a good technique to build customer loyalty and foster word of mouth promotion.

運用紀念物和提示物來記錄旅行過程並保持遊客對旅行的回憶是一種非常好的方法，它能夠提高遊客的信任度，形成良好的口碑。

21.The range of cues and memorabilia used by different organizations included: pre-trip items for travelers, photo logs, travel journals, visitor profiles, personal letters, post-trip videos and certificates of recognition.

各種機構所使用的提示物和紀念物包括：旅行前發給遊客的一些小東西、照片日誌、遊記、遊客特寫、信件、旅行後的錄影帶和認證書。

* * * *

Useful Words and Expressions 實用詞彙和表達方式

品牌忠誠度	brand loyalty
（航空）包價旅遊票價	tour-basing fares
包機航班	charter flight
機上雜誌	in-flight magazine
承載能力	carrying capacity
預付款遊覽機票	advance purchase excursion tickets
候補票價（起飛前的剩餘票價）	stand-by fares

「飛機常客獎勵」計劃	"frequent flyers" program
訂了座位而未到的人	no-shows
幹線航空公司	trunk route airlines
地方短距離航空公司	"commuter" airlines
支線	feeder/local line
旺季價	high season fare
高端產品	high-end product

Exercises 練習題

Discussion Questions 思考題

1.What is experiential marketing?

2.What is experience? What is the difference between experience and goods and service?

3.What are the differences between experiential marketing and traditional marketing?

4.Why experiential marketing is becoming popular now?

5.When devising an experiential marketing strategy, what should we pay more attention to?

Sentence Translation 單句翻譯練習

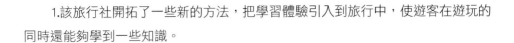

1.該旅行社開拓了一些新的方法，把學習體驗引入到旅行中，使遊客在遊玩的同時還能夠學到一些知識。

2.把意想不到的或潛在的負面事件（negative events）轉化為正面回憶（positive memories）的關鍵在於導遊，訓練有素的（well-trained）導遊能夠利用所有的機會，確保遊客整個旅行愉快。

3.體驗營銷的目標就是增強顧客的信任度，建立情感紐帶（emotional bond），使他們成為回頭客。

4.隨著越來越多的旅遊企業開始掌握體驗產品的特點，知道如何開發、營銷和提供體驗，消費者對體驗產品的需求會逐漸上升。

5.為了保證遊客的體驗能夠從旅行之前開始，並且持續到旅行結束後的很長一段時期，旅遊營銷者就用紀念物（memorabilia）來吸引遊客，保持和遊客的聯繫。

6.體驗產品的提供需要把自己的企業想像成一個劇院，把環境當做舞臺，把產品、建築物、交通、遊覽區當成道具，把員工當成演員，他們的主要任務是吸引遊客。

7.為了能夠從體驗經濟中策略地獲利，旅遊企業必須瞭解體驗與傳統的產品和服務的區別，而且要能夠給顧客提供一系列不同的選擇。

8.到當地人家中參觀（home visits）能夠使遊客和當地人進行近距離接觸，使他們對當地人的生活和生活方式有比較深入的瞭解，這是一種親身體驗目的地的方式。

Passage Translation 段落翻譯練習

The importance of the tour director and tour guides cannot be overstated. These people are a critical element of any tour. Their knowledge, skill, and ability to balance group situations along with individual needs is essential to group travel. Tour directors and guides are credited with creating terrific visitor experiences and positive memories by their ability to manage spontaneity, find opportunities, take care of problems, ensure a good time for all, make travelers feel welcome and part of the group and create a dynamic that leads to friendship between strangers and connect travelers to the communities they visit.

The element of surprise was consistently mentioned in discussing how to create memorable experiences. Surprises can be pre-planned or opportunistic, for despite all the planning in the world, something is bound to go wrong. The beauty of surprise situations is that they create unique opportunities for human interaction, generate a special connection with the place, and build a common bond between travelers. They also can be the foundation of some of the best stories people tell when they return home.

Part III

Lesson 22 Marketing for Theme Parks 主題公園營銷

導讀：

迪士尼在美國和其他地區的成功在世界各地掀起了主題公園熱。由於主題公園蘊藏的巨大的經濟潛力，許多投資者和開發商紛紛把目光投向主題公園的建設，但這並不意味著所有主題公園都會成功。財務管理、設計、接待能力上的問題、缺乏有效的管理等因素都可能導致開發的失敗。本篇文章將介紹主題公園開發中要注意的一些基本知識。

Economics and Finance

Theme park development projects typically consist of: "hard" costs applied toward construction of facilities, fabrication and installation of rides and shows(註1); and "soft" costs for financing, design, legal and other fees, pre-opening expenses, and other miscellaneous costs(註2). In the U.S. theme park industry, "hard" costs usually represent about 70 percent of the total project development cost and "soft" costs about 30 percent. This ratio helps ensure that at a given budget level the theme park product being built will have the entertainment and market impact necessary to meet attendance projections(註3). At some of the new attractions, "soft" costs have escalated to a disproportionately large amount of total investment(註4). Since the visitor does not benefit directly from these "soft" costs, these parks did not have the market impact they should have had.

The "hard" costs of developing a theme park can be conveniently categorized into four areas which are developed sequentially:

◆ land and infrastructure;

◆ structures;

◆ rides and shows;

◆ theming including landscaping, facades, streetscaping, and furniture, fixtures, and equipment (FF & E)(註5).

The components which have the highest visitor impact and provide the attraction with its critical ambience — rides, shows, and theming — occur at the latter end of the development and budgetary time line. At the later stages of a project, which is overrunning its budget, these components are the only things left to cut.If these critical elements are subjected to schedule crunches and budget cuts(註6), and do not survive at the level necessary to present the public with a complete product, an insufficiency in themed landscaping can be noted in the newly developed parks, which will be opened with just the "bare bones"(註7) — very little theming, landscaping or other soft features. These "finishing" touches of an attraction are very important to solidify its entertainment value(註8). The development process of a theme park requires careful management to ensure that sufficient budget is available at the end of the process to provide for those key elements.

To develop the necessary information to answer the questions as to how the project will operate economically, a series of tasks will need to be performed:

◆ Prepare projections of potential income to the project on the basis of analysis of market characteristics, spending behavior, visitation potential, anticipated guest composition, facility sizing, attraction content and pricing policies(註9). These projections are made for a 10-year period, to reflect growth of visitation and visitor spending.

◆ Project the cost of operations including labor and materials. Investigate the implications of local labor laws and employment conditions to accurately reflect labor costs.

◆ Prepare a 10-year cash flow projection, taking into account expected revenues and expenses, development costs, financing, tax treatment and other factors as a basis for estimating project value as well as rates of return for investors.

The key to understanding these requirements and meeting them is having a realistic financial plan, including a cash flow projection, which will support the technical work and avoid unproductive "trial and error" spurts of effort which, inevitably, can only add cost to the project(註10). Even for smaller projects, the risks of embarking on a well-intentioned project without a sound business plan are significant(註11).

Design

Planning a theme park requires special skills in terms of combining creative and commercial ability. Theme park design is crucial in determining the success of a park.

Theme parks represent a highly specialized type of land use and tourism planning. The circulation, entertainment and the feeding of great numbers of people demand highly skilled technicians and creative designers working together. To optimize the delivery of the theme park product to the consumer and prevent or at least minimize the problems that might be generated, theme parks must be planned in a controlled, integrated and sustainable manner, responsive to market demands(註12).

In terms of theme park design, several different levels can be distinguished. First, rides, activities and exhibits have to be designed attractively and effectively both in terms of initial appeal and usage. Second, landscaping and urban design are required to integrate the different single facilities into a whole based on the selected theme for the park(註13). Finally, activities and services need to be arranged that can support and increase consumer experiences of the physical elements in the park.

The design of the park needs to facilitate tourism consumption but also needs to support organizational objectives of the theme park manager (e.g. in areas such as logistics). When demand for rides, activities and facilities fluctuates during the day this can cause problems for the park, such as congestion and time specific peaks at the rides, activities and facilities. For theme park managers, capacity planning and routing(註14) is therefore an important task to deal with these problems.

Although design flaws may not be the primary reasons for the underperformance of some new parks, there are some design lessons to be learned. A lack of understanding of market distinctions might contribute to certain problems. Probably the most notable lesson to be learned is the need to understand culture and habits particular to the market. For example, in France such habits include such factors as eating at certain times, and a strong preference for attending attractions on Sunday. In Universal Studios(註15), Osaka(註16), Japan, such concerns also carry over into the menus at the park's 20 restaurants. While the food is predominantly American, much of it has Japanese touches in some ways(註17). The company tested 4000 different menu items over three years to get the right combinations.

Several serious design flaws include a limited number of attractions spread too thinly over the site, limited or ineffective theming, and poor landscaping.There has also been a tendency in certain attractions towards themes which are too lofty for the lay person(註18). Highly intellectual, scientific, cultural, or overly educational themes may lead to mixed reception from the public; be difficult to support with marketing; and have limited repeat visitation potential. For example, the underlying principal of a theme park product is that it provides a day of fun for the family. Deep or intellectual themes have difficulty producing the emotional experience necessary to attract this family market.

Visitor Use Planning

Planning effective visitor use of the park and avoiding serious environmental or social problems are very important.Congestion and over-usage of specific attractions are difficult to avoid and may cause severe problems for a theme park. Therefore, control of visitor use and flows is a basic consideration in theme park planning. It is imperative to establish carrying capacities of attractions and apply techniques to organize visitor flows and to control over-usage.

The main objectives in visitor use planning are as follows:

◆ To allow visitors ample opportunity to enjoy, appreciate, and understand the attraction features;

To make sure visitor use does not reach a level that results in excessive congestion that depreciates visitor enjoyment of the park, and leads to irritation of the visitors;

To restrict visitor use so that it does not result in environmental degradation of the future;

To allow residents in the area to visit and enjoy their own attractions.

In the theme park context, handling large number of visitors at major rides and exhibits often implies visitor queuing, visitors waiting in line to get entrance to the facilities. These queues of visitors waiting for rides, facilities and exhibits may engender a loss of personal control and overestimation of time spent in waiting along with boredom, irritation and discomfort for many visitors(註19). There are techniques that can be applied to make queues more acceptable to tourists. Some suggestions include:

Providing live entertainment to amuse visitors waiting in a queue;

Using interesting and surprising queue shapes and forms;

Incorporating queues physically in the exhibit space;

Giving greater attention to physical comfort and service facilities for visitors waiting in queues.

Also, capacity planning and routing may be used to optimize visitor distribution over the park and therefore to reduce visitor queuing. Signs and information boards as well as leaflets may be used to guide visitors through the park and to provide them with information to help them decide how to best spend their time on site. Differential pricing for specific parts of the day is another technique that may shift some demand from peak hours to off-peak periods. Also, extra services can be offered during peak times to reduce overuse of other facilities.

It is common for theme parks to experience demand fluctuations caused by seasonality effects. This leads to underusage of the facilities in the park during certain periods of the year, and often to excessive demand at other times. Various techniques can be applied to reduce seasonality and more evenly distribute tourist use throughout the year. Specific low season activities can be developed to make it more attractive to visitors to travel to the park in the low season. This can be seen in parks like Euro Disney offering special holiday shows and themes in the winter periods with special highlights around Christmas and New Year.

Management

Experienced management is the engine of the theme park industry. Particularly in the areas where mature and competitive markets have squeezed profit margins, strong management is essential.

There are at least three important factors, called performance measures, which park management attempts to control. The first performance measure, in-park revenue, refers to the income derived from the in-park purchase of goods and services by park customers. Management attempts to maximize in-park revenue. The second performance measure, called operating costs, refers to the costs associated with operating the park. These costs consist of two components: facility operating costs and labor costs. The facility operating costs are usually fixed at or near some average value which is predicted based upon historical records. The labor costs are heavily dominated by the wages paid to the seasonal operating staff, many of whom are part-time employees. This labor cost represents the single largest controllable operating expense. The day to day staffing levels can be adjusted with very short lead times through careful management of work schedules and by holding a portion of the workforce in an on-call status(註20). Clearly it is important for management to keep labor costs as small as possible. Third performance measure, called customer wait-time, is a measure of the perceived service experienced by customers. Since theme parks depend heavily on word-of-mouth advertising and repeat customer business, it is essential for management to keep the customer wait-time as small as possible. This performance measure is usually monitored as the percentage of the total in-park time spent waiting for access to attractions and services(註21).

One of the main control variables exercised by management is staff level control. As mentioned previously, the staff level can be adjusted very rapidly, often within one-third day intervals. Additional staff control is available by changing staff assignments. Each staff member is cross-trained to perform several different services or support functions so that a staff member can be shifted from one task to another within a few minutes. Other important control variables are the operating schedule and throughput time of attractions. Attraction operating schedule control refers to the closing of certain attractions during periods of very low demand. For example, an attraction for toddlers may be heavily subscribed(註22) during the afternoon hours, but have no demand during the evening hours. Closing this attraction during the evening hours decreases the staff requirement without affecting the perceived customer quality of experience. For many attractions, it also is possible to control the attraction throughput time. This is accomplished by adjusting the attraction cycle time; that is, the time required to service one set of customers. Similar control is possible with service facilities such as dining facilities, concession areas, and ticket gates. These facilities usually have a number of service lines, and the number of service lines open at any given time is easily adjusted according to the anticipated customer demand.

It is clear that management cannot optimize all performance measures. At some point, reducing labor costs will begin to impact negatively on customer wait-time and on in-park revenue. The very best that management can do is to achieve some reasonable compromise among the conflicting performance measures.

Vocabulary 內文詞彙

fabrication	構造
miscellaneous	各種各樣的
escalate	逐步增長或發展
sequentially	按順序地
ambience	環境，氣氛
budgetary time line	預算時間表
projection	估計，估測
spurt	迸發
logistics	物流
fluctuate	波動
congestion	擁擠
carrying capacity	接待能力
depreciate	降低價值，貶值
degradation	下降，退化
differential pricing	差別定價

profit margin   利潤率，利潤空間

cross-train   對……進行多種職業培訓，對……作交叉訓練

throughput time   開放時間

concession area   租地營業商區

Notes to the Text 內文註釋

1.rides and shows：娛樂設施和表演項目。

2.and "soft" costs for financing, design, legal and other fees, pre-opening expenses, and other miscellaneous costs：間接成本，包括融資、設計、法律等方面的相關費用，還包括營業前支出和其他一些雜費。

3.This ratio helps ensure that at a given budget level the theme park product being built will have the entertainment and market impact necessary to meet attendance projections.

這個比率有助於確保在建主題公園產品能夠在既定預算範圍內具有達到預計遊客量所必需的娛樂和市場影響力。

4.At some of the new attractions, "soft" costs have escalated to a disproportionately large amount of total investment.

在一些新景點的建設中，間接成本在總投資中所占的比例太大。

5.theming including landscaping, facades, streetscaping, and furniture, fixtures, and equipment (FF&E)：園林設計、門面、街景、擺設、內部裝置以及設備的主題化。

6.If these critical elements are subjected to schedule crunches and budget cuts：如

果這些關鍵因素受到預計時間不足以及預算削減的影響。

7.bare bones：基本框架。

8.These "finishing" touches of an attraction are very important to solidify its entertainment value.

對景點所做的這些最後的潤色對鞏固景點的娛樂價值非常重要。

9.Prepare projections of potential income to the project on the basis of analysis of market characteristics, spending behavior, visitation potential, anticipated guest composition, facility sizing, attraction content and pricing policies.

在分析市場特點、消費行為、訪問潛力、預計遊客構成、設施規模、景點內容以及定價政策基礎上對項目的潛在收入進行預估。

10.which will support the technical work and avoid unproductive "trial and error" spurts of effort which, inevitably, can only add cost to the project：這將會支持技術工作並且能避免那些徒勞的反覆嘗試努力，這些努力只會不可避免地增加項目成本。

11.Even for smaller projects, the risks of embarking on a well-intentioned project without a sound business plan are significant.

即使對較小的項目來說，沒有一個穩妥的經營計劃而著手一項用意良好的項目所要承擔的風險也是很大的。

12.theme parks must be planned in a controlled, integrated and sustainable manner, responsive to market demands：主題公園規劃必須是有控制的、協調的、可持續發展的，並且能夠考慮市場需求。

13.landscaping and urban design are required to integrate the different single facilities into a whole based on the selected theme for the park.

園林和城市設計要根據公園所選主題將不同個體設施融為一體。

14.capacity planning and routing：接待能力計劃和行程安排。

15.Universal Studios：環球影城

16.Osaka：大阪（日本本州島西南部港市）。

17.While the food is predominantly American, much of it has Japanese touches in some ways.

儘管食物主要是美國出產的，但是其中的某些方面帶有日本風格。

18.There has also been a tendency in certain attractions towards themes which are too lofty for the lay person.

在一些景點還有一種趨勢，那就是公園主題太深奧，以至於外行人難以理解。

19.These queues of visitors waiting for rides, facilities and exhibits may engender a loss of personal control and overestimation of time spent in waiting along with boredom, irritation and discomfort for many visitors.

排隊等候使用遊樂設備、公共設施以及等待參觀展覽的遊客過多，可能會導致人員失控，很多遊客會因感覺等候時間過長而感到無聊、煩躁和不安。

20.The day to day staffing levels can be adjusted with very short lead times through careful management of work schedules and by holding a portion of the workforce in an on-call status.

每日的員工人數可以透過對工作時間的精心安排、透過掌握一部分隨時候召員工在很短的時間內進行調整。

21.This performance measure is usually monitored as the percentage of the total in-park time spent waiting for access to attractions and services.

這種業績測度通常是由等待進入娛樂設施和獲得服務所花時間占在園內總時間的百分比來監控的。

22.an attraction for toddlers may be heavily subscribed：針對學步兒童的景點可能會爆滿。

Useful Words and Expressions 實用詞彙和表達方式

世界旅遊日	World Tourism Day
世界旅遊組織	World Tourism Organization (WTO)
太平洋亞洲旅遊協會	Pacific Asia Travel Association (PATA)
中國國家旅遊局	China National Tourism Administration (CNTA)
省／市旅遊局	provincial/municipal tourism administration
世界旅遊業職業道德規範	the Global Code of Ethics For Tourism
國家級歷史文化名城	state-list famous historical and cultural cities
自然景觀	natural attraction
避暑勝地	summer resort

世界文化遺產　　　　　　world cultural heritage

國家公園　　　　　　　　national park

Exercises 練習題

Discussion Questions 思考題

1.Describe the major factors that must be taken into account when a firm assesses its financial plan for developing a theme park.

2."Planning a theme park requires special skills in terms of combining creative and commercial ability." How do you interpret this statement?

3.What measures would you take to alleviate the problem of over-crowding in a theme park?

4.In order to alleviate the financial pressure of operating a theme park, what would a manager usually do? Why?

5.Choose some well-known theme parks and analyze why they are well received.

Sentence Translation 單句翻譯練習

1.為了從旅遊活動中獲得更多的收入，主題公園開始朝度假（resort）目的地方向發展，增添住宿設施、高爾夫球場（golf courses）和其他活動以使遊客逗留更長的時間。

2.隨著人們越來越關注動物保護，這意味著到動物園、馬戲團（circus）、鬥牛場（bullfights）這樣的傳統動物景點的遊客人數會下降。

3.由於越來越多的人希望在一日遊（day trips）和度假時透過主動參與學習新知

識，許多景點透過工藝品製作演示（craft demonstrations）或體驗型科學展覽（hands-on science exhibitions）等特別活動為遊客提供學習機會。

4.景點規劃和設計人員透過虛擬現實技術（Virtual Reality）創造出所開發景點的真實3D畫面（realistic three-dimensional pictures），以便從遊客的角度審視未來的景點。

5.隨著旅遊景點的規模不斷擴大和重要性日益得到承認，教育和培訓領域開設旨在提高景點管理人員和員工素質的課程，包括研究生、本科生、國家高等技術學校學歷生（at postgraduate，undergraduate and HND level）的正規課程，以及在職培訓課程（in-service training courses）。

6.景點是整個旅遊業的核心（core），是吸引人們出遊的重要因素。不管是遊覽金字塔、欣賞埃及文化遺產的兩週假日遊，還是到離家幾英里遠的主題公園的一日遊，都是這樣。

7.溫泉城（spa towns）也是一種景點，目前溫泉城不但為病殘客人（invalid guests）提供醫療服務，還滿足了休閒遊客（relaxing tourists）的需要。

8.對導遊員進行註冊（register）、培訓以確保導遊的接待品質（the quality of hosting）和他們提供的歷史等資訊的準確性是非常重要的。

Passage Translation 段落翻譯練習

The theme park business is extremely marketing sensitive. A visit to a theme park is a temporal product which requires intensive marketing to successfully compete among the many other forms of leisure and entertainment. In new markets, heavy marketing is required to establish identity and to build awareness of the product.

Allocating a significant portion of operating expenses towards marketing has been the practice of U.S. theme parks for years. Typically, major U.S. parks spend from 10 to

15 percent of total operating expenses on marketing. Directed and focused advertising, promotions, special events, and group sales programs are key elements of theme park marketing success.

Group sales account for a large share of theme park attendance in the U.S. Effective use of this marketing approach is usually critical to an attraction's success. U.S. parks and established European parks typically receive from 35 to 50 percent of their annual attendance in the form of groups. Asterix, the highest attendance park of the new French attractions, did a very strong group business, and succeeded in attracting about 50 percent of its annual attendance from groups.

Lesson 23 Hotel Marketing 飯店營銷

導讀：

隨著飯店產品和服務的日新月異，飯店的營銷手段也在不斷改進。當今的飯店必須把傳統的廣告、公關、促銷等營銷方法與新的營銷手段結合起來，才能在日益激烈的競爭中保持優勢。本篇文章將介紹飯店營銷的一些新概念、新方法：內部營銷、透過品質建立顧客滿意度、針對重點顧客市場、綠色營銷。

Internal Marketing

When it comes to marketing, people usually think of efforts directed externally toward the marketplace(註1), but a hotel's first marketing efforts should be directed internally to employees, since in the hotel industry employees are part of the product. Marketing in the hospitality industry must be embraced by all employees; it cannot be left up to the marketing or sales department(註2). Marketing should be part of the philosophy of the organization, and the marketing function should be carried out by all line employees. The hotel's external marketing brings guests to the hotel but does little good if the employees do not perform to the guest's expectations.

Marketers must develop techniques and procedures to ensure that employees are able and willing to deliver quality service. Internal marketing ensures that employees at all levels of the organization experience the business and understand its various activities and campaigns in an environment that supports customer consciousness. The objective of internal marketing is to enable employees to deliver satisfying products to the guest.

Internal marketing can include the following factors:

◆ Establishment of a service culture;

◆ Development of a marketing approach to human resource management;

◆ Dissemination of marketing information to employees;

◆ Implementation of a reward and recognition system.

A service culture is an organizational culture that supports customer service through policies, procedures, reward systems and actions(註3). An organizational culture is a pattern of shared values and beliefs that gives members of an organization meaning, providing them with the rules for behavior in the organization.

Development of a marketing approach to human resource management involves the creating of positions that attract good employees, a hiring process that identifies and results in hiring service-oriented employees, initial employee training designed to share the company's vision with the employee and supply the employee with product knowledge(註4), and finally continuous employee training programs.

Often the most effective way of communicating with customers is through customer-contact employees. Employees should receive information on promotions, marketing campaigns, new products and product changes from management, not from advertisements meant for external customers(註5). Hospitality organizations should use printed publications as part of their internal communication. They can also use technology and training to provide employees with product knowledge. Moreover, the actions of management are one way an organization communicates with its employees. Management at all levels must understand that employees are watching them for cues about expected behavior(註6).

Employees must know how they are doing to perform effectively. Communication must be designed to give them feedback on their performance. An internal marketing program includes service standards and methods of measuring how well the organization is meeting these standards.

If a hotel wants customer-oriented employees, it must seek out ways to catch them serving the customer(註7), and reward and recognize them for making the efforts.

Building Customer Satisfaction through Quality

Today's hotels face their toughest competition in decades, and things will only get worse in years to come. The answer to the question how hotels can go about winning customers and outperforming competitors lies in the marketing concept(註8) — in doing a better job of meeting and satisfying customer needs. To succeed, companies must be customer centered; they must deliver superior value to their target customers, which is achieved through a service quality program.

A service quality program involves a cooperative effort between marketing and operations. To develop quality service, a firm must follow certain principles. The following principles of quality service offer a framework for a quality service program:

Leadership. The CEO of the organization must have a clear vision for the company, and communicate that vision and convince employees to believe in and follow it. Good leaders communicate their dedication to service quality through actions to both employees and customers(註9).

Integrate marketing throughout the organization. Marketing functions in a hospitality organization are the responsibility of people throughout the organization.

Understand the customer. Companies with quality products know what the market wants. The product must be designed for and aimed at a target market.

Understand the business. Delivering quality service takes teamwork(註10). Employees must realize how their job affects the rest of the team. Many firms that deliver quality service use cross-training, which exposes employees to different perspectives and encourages them to view the operation from other perspectives(註11).

Leverage the freedom factor(註12). Employees must have the freedom to shape the delivery of the service to fit the needs of their guests. They shouldn't be bound to strict procedures and inflexible rules(註13). Mangers should support and guide the staff, rather than provide barriers with rules and regulations that prevent the employees from serving the customer.

Use appropriate technology. Technology should be used to monitor the environment, help operational systems, develop customer database, and provide methods for communication with customers.

Good human resource management. A firm needs to hire the right people. Employees must be capable of delivering the services promised to the customer.

Set standards, measure performance, and establish incentives. The most important way to improve service quality is to set service standards and goals and then teach them to employees and management. Employees who deliver good service should be rewarded.

Targeting Profitable Consumer Segments

Planning resources for the marketing effort begins with identifying specific company needs and targeting consumer segments that can most profitably meet those company needs.

Segment profitability is determined by analyzing the revenue and profit generated through the sale of products and services to a particular type of consumer or market segment. As in all businesses, some customers are more profitable to serve than others. A hotel can determine the profitability of market segments by reviewing purchasing patterns of past customers. Historical information from guest folios shows the number and types of purchases made by customers grouped into the market segments under analysis. Although the profitability of market segments varies from property to property, the segment profitability ranking that follows could apply to many hotels(註14):

◆ International executives on unrestricted expense accounts with multiple night stays(註15);

◆ Executives on relatively unrestricted expense accounts;

◆ Individuals attending a corporate group meeting, conference, or convention;

◆ Individuals attending an association group meeting, conference, or convention;

· Second honeymooners;

· Regional sports clubs and teams;

· Families with children;

◆ Individuals on restricted expense accounts.

Let's assume that the analysis of a 1000-room hotel's current pattern of business shows that, on average, only 330 rooms are sold on Friday nights and only 250 rooms are sold on Saturday nights. With 33 percent and 25 percent occupancy rates respectively, Friday and Saturday are clearly areas of company need for building more business. Marketing's task is to target specific consumer segments that could provide the most profitable business for the hotel on these nights.

Based on the results of internal and external analysis, targeted pleasure market segments can be ranked in order of potential business volume(註16). For example, a partial listing might include:

◆ Second honeymooners;

◆ Families escaping for the weekend;

◆ Regional sports teams.

Given the need of the hotel in our example to build weekend business, the first reaction might be to focus resources on attracting business from second honeymooners. However, before spending precious marketing dollars, it's important to examine if it's possible to get a multiple sale for the same cost involved in securing a single sale(註17). That is, can the marketing efforts attract a group, such as family reunions, that will fill many rooms instead of filling rooms one at a time with marketing activities directed at individual second honeymooners? Failing this, perhaps booking weekend business from sports clubs and teams would prove more profitable in terms of the return on investment of marketing dollars(註18) than promoting weekend stays to individual second honeymooners.

Going Green

Guests are now starting to pay attention to how businesses treat the environment, and are trying to seek out those who are greener. Green marketing is becoming an effective and powerful marketing tool to attract loyal guests in the hotel industry. With easy-to-implement green actions, a hotel can save significant money and enhance its public perception — leaving guests and employees alike with a good feeling about themselves. It's indeed a rare win-win-win(註19).

Many hotels have asked their guests to participate in a water-conservation program, giving them the option of having towers and sheets cleaned when requested or daily(註20). This practice has not only shown the environmental consciousness of the hotels but, because of reduced energy and water consumption, has also saved them huge sums of money. Traditionally hotels preferred to keep behind-the-scenes operations quiet. But after they found out that guests liked what they were doing, and encouraged them to do more, they began to integrate green actions into marketing plan.

Just as guests view a hotel's water-and energy-conservation measures as positive and a sign of corporate responsibility, they will appreciate the other environmentally friendly programs as well. "Free" green steps a hotel can take include fixing leaks — air and water; turning lights off in rooms when guests are out of the hotel; using recycled paper; changing the thermostat one degree, and offering non-smoking guestrooms. Green steps you can take that may have a slight initial investment, but will have immediate and long-term paybacks, include educating your staff and guests about your commitment to the environment and your green action plan; installing low-flow shower heads and low-flush toilets; providing recycling bins in guestrooms and throughout the hotel property; converting your garden to a xeric garden-using native plants that don't require much additional water; serving organic and locally grown food; and buying compact fluorescent light (CFL) bulbs.

The lodging industry is by nature a wasteful industry. You can make a difference with each green action you adopt and implement. Spreading the word is part of that action, so be sure to clearly state what green actions you are taking and why it benefits the earth and your guests. Your green actions will lead to green deposits — in your bank account.

Vocabulary 內文詞彙

consciousness	意識，覺悟
dissemination	散布，傳播
publication	出版物，刊物
dedication	貢獻，奉獻
integrate	整合，（使）一體化
database	數據庫
segment profitability	細分市場贏利能力
folio	對摺紙
occupancy rate	客房出租率
thermostat	溫度自動調節器，恆溫器
low-flow shower head	節水淋浴噴頭
low-flush toilet	節水馬桶
recycling bin	可回收物垃圾桶

xeric garden	旱生植物園
CFL bulb	節能燈泡
lodging industry	住宿業

Notes to the Text 內文註釋

1.When it comes to marketing, people usually think of efforts directed externally toward the marketplace：當提到營銷時，人們常常認為這是針對外部市場所做的工作。

2.Marketing in the hospitality industry must be embraced by all employees; it cannot be left up to the marketing or sale department.

飯店業的營銷工作必須被所有員工所理解和接受，不能僅僅由營銷或銷售部門來做。

3.A service culture is an organizational culture that supports customer service through policies, procedures, reward systems and actions.

服務文化是透過政策、程序、獎勵制度和行動支持消費者服務的組織文化。

4.initial employee training designed to share the company's vision with the employee and supply the employee with product knowledge：旨在使員工瞭解公司目標和產品知識的初級員工培訓。

5.not from advertisements meant for external customers：而不是來自針對外部顧客的廣告。

6.Management at all levels must understand that employees are watching them for cues about expected behavior.

各個階層的管理人員必須明白員工們都在看著他們，以他們的行為為榜樣。

7.If a hotel wants customer-oriented employees, it must seek out ways to catch them serving the customer：如果飯店需要以顧客為中心的員工，就必須找到在員工為顧客服務時監督他們的方法。

8.the answer to the question how hotels can go about winning customers and outperforming competitors lie in the marketing concept：酒店如何贏得顧客並戰勝競爭者取決於營銷理念。

9.Good leaders communicate their dedication to service quality through actions to both employees and customers.

優秀的領導者把他們對服務品質的推崇透過行動傳達給員工和顧客。

10.Delivering quality service takes teamwork.

提供優質服務需要團隊合作。

11.Many firms that deliver quality service use cross-training, which exposes employees to different perspectives and encourages them to view the operation from other perspectives.

許多提供優質服務的企業運用交叉培訓，讓員工瞭解不同的觀點並鼓勵他們從不同的視角看企業。

12.Leverage the freedom factor.

藉助於自由因素。

13.They shouldn't be bound to strict procedures and inflexible rules.

他們不應該受嚴格程序和僵化規則的束縛。

14.Although the profitability of market segments varies from property to property, the segment profitability ranking that follows could apply to many hotels.

儘管每個飯店細分市場的贏利能力不同，下面細分市場贏利能力的排行榜適用於許多飯店。

15.International executives on unrestricted expense accounts with multiple night stays：逗留數日、開銷無限制的國外經理。

16.Based on the results of internal and external analysis, targeted pleasure market segments can be ranked in order of potential business volume.

根據內部和外部分析結果，娛樂細分目標市場可按潛在業務量排列。

17.if it's possible to get a multiple sale for the same cost involved in securing a single sale：是否可能用獲得一次銷售的同樣花費來贏得多次銷售。

18.in terms of the return on investment of marketing dollar：就營銷支出的投資回報而言。

19.It's indeed a rare win-win-win.

這實際上是一種三贏策略。

20.giving them the option of having towers and sheets cleaned when requested or daily：是要求換洗毛巾和床單的服務還是每天都換洗的服務由他們選擇。

Useful Words and Expressions 實用詞彙和表達方

式

星級飯店	star-rated hotel
涉外旅遊飯店	hotels catering to overseas tourists
廉價旅館	budget hotel
青年旅館	youth hostel
辦理登記手續	to go through the registration procedure
旅館登記表	hotel registration form
定金	advance deposit
贈送／免費飲料	complimentary drinks
客房出租率	room occupancy rate
健身房	fitness room
三溫暖按摩中心	sauna and massage center
保齡球室	bowling room
閉路電視	in-house movie
電子門鎖系統	electronic key card system

Exercises 練習題

Discuss Questions 思考題

1.What is the significance of internal marketing?

2.Why is it important to explain advertising campaigns to employees before they appear in the media?

3.Choose a quality hotel product you are familiar with and explain how its quality service is achieved.

4.What marketing efforts can you make during the peak season to maximize your profit?

5.If you were the marketing manager of an environmentally friendly hotel, how would you communicate your commitment to your customers?

Sentence Translation 單句翻譯練習

1.越來越多的商務旅行者重視品牌而不是星級水準（star ratings），大多數商務旅行者認為飯店的品牌對他們決定住哪家飯店有很大或相當大的影響。

2.電信業的發展使得越來越多的個人透過他們自己的通訊設備（有線電視、傳真機、私人電話、網際網路、私人電腦）直接與飯店的預訂中心（reservation center）接洽。

3.獨立的飯店已經形成營銷聯盟（marketing consortia），以抵禦著名飯店集團的競爭。加入獨立飯店聯盟使飯店能從聯合營銷（joint marketing）中獲益，也能利用通常只有大飯店集團公司才有的國際預訂系統（international reservation systems）。

4.近年來大學和教育機構（educational establishments）進入了市場，在假期中把學生宿舍改成舉辦會議和培訓班（conference and course markets）的住所，利用校內娛樂設施（built-in recreation facilities）推出體育假期和其他特別興趣產品

（special-interest products）。

5.飯店可以在房屋造型、室內裝修（interior decoration）、服務人員服飾、服務形式、飲食文化、背景音樂、娛樂活動等方面突出表現（highlight）本地方特點，以吸引顧客。

6.飯店內部營銷（internal marketing）不需要有廣告、公關（public relation）等專門的經費投入，是節約營銷成本的最好策略。

7.顧客經常惠顧飯店是要得到回報的，獎勵常客（frequent guest）是回報的一種形式。目前，中國不少飯店推出了「常客獎勵計劃」（Frequent Guest Program），以免費住宿（complimentary room）、價格優惠（favorable price）等形式獎勵常客，以培養對本飯店忠誠的顧客（loyal customer）。

8.品牌是飯店重要的無形資產（intangible asset），它具有極大的經濟價值。利用品牌進行營銷是一種非常有效的市場方法。

Passage Translation 段落翻譯練習

The empowerment of service employees is considered to be one of the best options available to hospitality and tourism managers when dealing with the problems of customer complaints and operational bottlenecks. Employees who perceive that they have the right and the responsibility to solve problems themselves are more effective in handling all manner of day-to-day service difficulties. Many leading service organizations utilize this philosophy successfully — seeking ways to encourage and reward their employees for exercising initiative in their day-to-day work.

Superior service does not result from employees undertaking systemized tasks according to set procedures with management adopting a training role. Rather, excellence in service comes from employees showing initiative in a trusting work environment in which management assumes a supporting role. Management must therefore ensure that it establishes appropriate strategies and systems whereby employees will be able to exercise trust.

Lesson 24 Database Marketing in Travel Industry 旅遊業中的大數據營銷

導讀：

技術和通訊的飛速發展大大改善了旅遊產品和服務，同時也提高了消費者的期望。21世紀的市場是個性化的市場。為了適應新的形勢和變化，一種新的營銷方式——大數據營銷悄然而生。本篇文章介紹大數據營銷的好處以及在旅遊業中的應用。

Why Database Marketing

The conventional ways of looking at consumer behavior — especially in tourism and leisure — are becoming outdated. No longer are the purchasing habits of the leisure customer predictable by labeling a group as a segment of the market and describing it with average characteristics(註1). More and more, marketers are turning to tailored and targeted marketing to individuals. This is now possible through new technology with sophisticated database management systems and immense amounts of historical and purchased information on individual preferences and purchase behavior. This trend is particularly appropriate for tourism marketing since there is a world of paradoxes in leisure behavior. The multi-profile leisure customer is difficult to motivate by traditional institutional means. A market of individuals, individually addressable and open to interactive communication, threatens the very existence of established marketing techniques and trade relationships(註2).

Database marketing is the technique of gathering all the information available about your customer into a central database and using that information to drive all your marketing efforts. The information is stored in a marketing database and can be used at both the strategic and tactical levels to drive targeted marketing efforts(註3). A company that utilizes database marketing continually gathers, refines, and analyzes data about their customers, their buying history, prospects, past marketing efforts, demographics, and so forth. They analyze the data to turn it into information that supports all their marketing and sales programs. More enlightened marketing companies also use customer and prospect interests and preferences, generally gathered on their web sites, to tailor marketing efforts right down to the individual level.

The single most important benefit of database marketing is the ability to target your marketing efforts, which means specific groups in your marketing database get specific messages that are important to them. You will focus your marketing dollars on customers that are most likely to buy and spend less on customers that are less likely to buy. Database marketing lets you work more intelligently by making marketing decisions based on facts gleaned from your marketing database. The result is enhanced sales with limited marketing expenses — and better return on your marketing investment.

Applications of Database Marketing in Transportation

One of the pioneers in identifying and contacting individual customers was American Airlines. Back in the 70's, airlines began to realize that 80% of their business came from 20% of their customers, the frequent-flying business traveler. But the airlines did not know who these people were and what to do about it. They had a name on an airline ticket but no address. They kept no permanent record of the customer's destination or how frequently he or she traveled. Furthermore, government regulations forbade giving away to passengers anything of value which would upset the mandated standard pricing(註4). But as airline deregulation approached, American Airlines realized the opportunity they had to identify their best customers and cultivate them with special rewards. The airline began in secret to plan the Advantage Program, the first frequent-flyer plan with bonuses recorded and administered by means of a membership database. Introduced in 1981, it was an instant success, and it took most other airlines years to catch up. American Airlines management has repeatedly described their Frequent Flyer program as the single greatest marketing achievement of the 80's.

In the 70's, the airline advertising budgets were devoted almost entirely to image-making in television, magazine, and newspaper advertising. Now the ability of each airline to talk directly to their best customers has resulted in a complete turnaround in marketing thinking. The image advertising remains, but a significant amount of each year's budget has been shifted to communicating directly with and cultivating their best customers. Of course, no marketing advantage lasts forever. Soon all the airlines with frequent-flyer programs were embroiled in a free mileage and price-cutting war(註5), with each airline offering more free bonus miles than the next. Even with these costs, however, frequent-flyer programs reinforce an extremely sound business philosophy: inducing frequent or repeat customers to maintain a long-term relationship with a carrier is a lot more profitable and less expensive than trying to build traffic and profits by selling airline seats one ticket at a time to new customers. A frequent-flyer program addresses an airline's need to build long-term relationships by offering a combination of special services, benefits, and customer recognition.

Amtrak(註6) has built a multi-million name database over the past four years through its own reservations and toll-free information systems. The data is being used to deliver specific travel opportunities to Amtrak's most potentially lucrative niche markets. In fact, direct mail now accounts for approximately 15% of Amtrak's total annual marketing budget of 45 million. The database is managed by Boston-based Epsilon (subsidiary of American Express)(註7), which captures names and addresses from incoming callers to the Amtrak toll-free information number and from customers who buy tickets from the Amtrak reservations system. According to Epsilon, demographic overlays are used extensively to segment the database into target markets(註8). Amtrak then targets specific travel products to each of these defined markets using direct mail. For example, the Autotrain, running from Virginia to Florida, transports passengers with their cars. Amtrak is targeting this service to "snowbirds" — those senior citizens who head south in the winter. Epsilon has on file both the summer and winter addresses for these retirees who receive targeted promotional material about one month prior to when they normally migrate(註9). The Autotrain direct marketing effort to the snowbird market has paid off in a 5-to-1 return on investment.

Applications of Database Marketing in Accommodations

Hotel organizations around the world have started to utilize various applications of database marketing. Database marketing affords hotels an excellent opportunity to learn more about their regular customers, and can be used to build customer loyalty very effectively. Indeed, database marketing can provide a hotel with the critical edge in customer service. Customer records can be sorted and enhanced to produce useful information on target markets. Innovative applications have produced profitable new marketing programs for many hotels.

Database marketing creates new customer profiles and/or adds to existing customer profiles. Each customer has his or her own demographics and spending patterns. The objective of database marketing is to identify demographic patterns among hotel's best customers, the aim being to build customer loyalty and to reduce the cost of marketing by increasing its precision. The database provides marketers with an understanding of the complex expectations and attitudes of customer. Hotels are therefore able to preplan services, even before the customers arrive, with a view to(註10) exceeding the expectations of the customer.

In some chain hotels, the customer database is used to ensure that preferred products and services are supplied at each and every hotel in the chain. With regard to the choice of newspaper, modern technology can mean that if a guest stays at the San Diego Marriott and requests a copy of the London Times, the Miami Marriott should also have a copy of the Times available if the same guest later checks in there!(註11)

While most programs are similar in principle, they vary in design according to the marketing objectives and market position of the particular properties. When Sheraton(註12) finds that their guests are primarily interested in additional hotel service features during their stay rather than price factors, their program tends toward room upgrades and benefits such as late check-outs. Westin's(註13) program follows much the same theory. Their documentation states "guests are interested in immediate tangible benefits during their hotel stays." On the other hand, Ramada(註14) has identified that its guests primarily check into Ramada properties for price reasons. Consequently, the rewards of the program revolve around escalating discounts.

With frequent guest program databases running into the millions, hotels are able to run numerous different offers, or send out whatever specialized messages they choose. Days Inns(註15), for example, recently mailed out an offer to 400000 September Days club members. This drew a response rate of around 4 percent — far higher than general mailing could expect.

Applications of Database Marketing in Attractions

One of the most surprising yet logical places for sophisticated database marketing to niche markets is in the casino industry. Faced with fierce competition in a crowded industry, the smartest casinos have been leaders in building a database and using it for direct marketing. Harrah's(註16) core marketing strategy is to foster and then cater to a relatively small group of dedicated gamblers by building brand loyalty. The company uses various strategies including a proprietary database marketing system and casino hosts whose sole responsibility is to develop relationships with regular gamblers. The key to building a database is Harrah's Gold Card. When presented at a gaming table or inserted into gambling machines, the Gold Card records how much an individual spends in the casino. To encourage use of the card, gamblers earn bonus points toward non-gambling amenities and find it easier to cash checks in the casino. Harrah's uses Gold Card information to develop customer profiles for marketing pitches and complementary services. Each card holder's gaming patterns are statistically analyzed to determine the expected house win from each customer. The customer is then "graded" as to the type and value of complementaries he is offered(註17).

Casinos want to know everything — your age, birth date, and anniversary, how often you come to gamble, what you play, where you like to stay, how you travel to the casino, what your budget is. They even want to know about your cars, pets, and favorite sports. With this information, the casino can devise specific promotions for different customer segments and individual customers within the database. For example, if you are a slot-machine or blackjack player(註18), you will receive an invitation to a slot or blackjack tournament. If you are a fan of boxing, you will be notified when there is going to be an event that you will love. If you are a big spender, you may receive a birthday card and your favorite chocolates (just so you will know they really care).

The databases also tell the casinos where their customers come from and how they travel. By analyzing which zip zones have the most customers, the casino can get a better fix on where advertising should be concentrated and where charter bus service can be most productive(註19). Now casinos are working on using their databases to reach beyond the 10% of their customers who are the high rollers and to identify, cultivate, and build casino-specific loyalty in a much larger market niche, the middle-market recreational gambler(註20).

One of the most remarkable third-party database marketing programs in the U.S. is Walt Disney's Magic Kingdom Club. It was originated in 1959, two years after the original Disneyland had opened in California. Walt Disney came up with the idea of going to nearby companies and offering to enroll their employees in Walt Disney's Magic Kingdom Club. Members could obtain ticket books at a single price which presented a substantial discount off buying the tickets separately.

In 1971, Walt Disney World opened in Orlando, Florida, and the program went nationwide with dramatically increased benefits, including group travel packages, discounts on car rentals, special hotel rates, a newsletter, and much more.

Today club membership is free, and the Club has enrolled as members some six million employees of 30000 companies. Disney's communication is primarily with the companies and only secondarily with the members themselves. A very sophisticated computer program permits them to select and track the most promising companies for each park location. Disney provides each company with a variety of collateral materials — newsletters, membership guides, brochures, posters, etc.

Other parts of the Disney empire are involved through giving Club members in the database the Disney mail-order catalog, a 10% discount at Disney stores, special offers on Disney videos, and so on. It is a prime example of synergistic interaction among many different divisions of the same enterprise(註21). Every Disney division is directed by corporate headquarters to work in concert with(註22) all the others to maximize the benefits of dealing directly with identified individual customers.

Vocabulary 內文詞彙

database marketing	大數據營銷
paradox	矛盾，悖論
demographics	人口統計數據
glean	蒐集（消息、情報等）
mandated	依法的，法定的
deregulation	撤銷管制

turnaround	徹底的改變
embroil	捲入，糾纏
carrier	航空公司
toll-free	免費的
lucrative niche markets	有利可圖的補缺市場
snowbird	冬季到南方過冬的旅遊者（尤指退休人員）
casino industry	賭博業
bonus points	紅利點數
amenities	便利設施
marketing pitches	市場營銷廣告
complementary services	附加服務
house win	莊家贏
collateral materials	附屬材料
synergistic	協同作用的

Notes to the Text 內文註釋

1.No longer are the purchasing habits of the leisure customer predictable by labeling a group as a segment of the market and describing it with average characteristics.

休閒消費者的購買習慣再也不能透過僅僅把一個群體歸為某個細分市場、描述其普遍特徵來預測了。

2.A market of individuals, individually addressable and open to interactive communication, threatens the very existence of established marketing techniques and trade relationships.

個人市場是一個可以直接向個人發送訊息,並可以進行雙向交流的市場,這種市場威脅到了現有市場方式和交易關係的生存。

3.The information is stored in a marketing database and can be used at both the strategic and tactical levels to drive targeted marketing efforts.

資訊儲存在營銷數據庫中,可以在戰略和戰術的層面上使用,以推動有針對性的營銷活動。

4.Furthermore, government regulations forbade giving away to passengers anything of value which would upset the mandated standard pricing.

而且,政府條例也不允許把可能會影響法定標準價格的任何有價值的東西贈與旅客。

5.Soon all the airlines with frequent-flyer programs were embroiled in a free mileage and price-cutting war.

很快所有採用常客計劃的航空公司都捲入到了免費乘機里程和機票降價大戰之中。

6.Amtrak:美鐵,(美國)全國鐵路客運公司,成立於1971年。

7.The database is managed by Boston-based Epsilon (subsidiary of American Express).

這個數據庫是由波士頓的愛普西龍公司（美國運通公司的子公司）管理的。

8.According to Epsilon, demographic overlays are used extensively to segment the database into target markets.

據愛普西龍公司說，人口統計重疊數據被廣泛用於將數據庫劃分為不同的目標市場。

9.Epsilon has on file both the summer and winter addresses for these retirees who receive targeted promotional material about one month prior to when they normally migrate.

愛普西龍公司將這些退休人員的夏季和冬季住址存檔，在正常遷移前一個月，這些退休人員可以收到相關的促銷材料。

10.with a view to：目的在於。

11.With regard to the choice of newspaper, modern technology can mean that if a guest stays at the San Diego Marriott and requests a copy of the London Times, the Miami Marriott should also have a copy of the Times available if the same guest later checks in there.

關於報紙的選擇，現代科技意味著如果一位客人住在聖地亞哥萬豪酒店時要了一份倫敦《泰晤士報》，那麼如果同一位客人後來入住邁阿密萬豪酒店，那裡也應該為他準備好一份《泰晤士報》。

12.Sheraton：喜來登飯店集團。

13.Westin：即Westin Hotels & Resorts，威斯汀飯店集團，是北美地區歷史最悠久的飯店經營管理公司。

14.Ramada：華美達酒店集團。

15.Days Inns：戴斯酒店集團。

16.Harrah：即Harrah's Entertainment，（美國）哈拉斯娛樂公司，是全球的博彩業巨頭。

17.The customer is then "graded" as to the type and value of complementaries he is offered.

然後根據顧客所得到的附加服務的類型和價值來給他「定等級」。

18.slot-machine or blackjack player：吃角子老虎機或二十一點玩家。

19.By analyzing which zip zones have the most customers, the casino can get a better fix on where advertising should be concentrated and where charter bus service can be most productive.

透過分析哪些郵政區域擁有最多的消費者，賭場可以更好地確定廣告應集中在哪裡，在哪裡提供包租大轎車服務最得益。

20.Now casinos are working on using their databases to reach beyond the 10% of their customers who are the high rollers and to identify, cultivate, and build casino-specific loyalty in a much larger market niche, the middle-market recreational gambler.

現在賭場正致力於利用自己的數據庫來爭取占賭場10%的大客戶以外的顧客，在一個更大的市場，即在中產市場中的娛樂性賭博者中，確認、培養和建立他們對自己賭場的特有忠誠度。

21.It is a prime example of synergistic interaction among many different divisions of the same enterprise.

這是同一個企業不同部門之間協同互動的典型例子。

22.in concert with：與……一致。

Useful Words and Expressions 實用詞彙和表達方式

旅遊旺季	tourist peak season
旅遊淡季	tourist off-peak season
經濟遊	economy tour
豪華遊	luxurious tour
環球旅行	round-the-world tour
觀光旅行	sightseeing tour
蜜月旅行	honeymoon tour
背包徒步旅行	backpack tour
公費旅遊	travel at public expense
地陪	local guide
全陪	national guide

領隊	tour leader
海外領隊	overseas escort
會多種語言的導遊	multilingual guide
註冊／持證導遊	registered/licensed guide
索取傭金	to demand commissions
投訴	lodge claims
退款政策	refund policy
旅遊出版物	travel publication

Exercises 練習題

Discuss Questions 思考題

1.Describe the concept of database marketing.What is the role of technology in database marketing?

2.In what field was the database initially made use of? Why? What is the significance of Frequent Flyer Program?

3.Use examples to illustrate how database can be utilized to improve the service quality of a hotel.

4.Explain how casinos have tried to develop the relationships with their regular gamblers.

5.Summarize the benefits of database marketing.Is there any disadvantage involved in database marketing?

Sentence Translation 單句翻譯練習

1.獎勵旅遊（incentive travel）被認為是商務旅行市場（business travel market）中發展最快的細分市場。這個市場的消費幾乎是最高的，因為獎勵旅遊的目的是為了用獨特的度假形式獎勵銷售人員。

2.匯率（currency exchange rates）對國際旅遊者的流向（flows）起決定作用。比如，如果美元堅挺（strong），就有很多美國人到歐洲去，如果英鎊比美元強勢，就有更多的英國人去遊歷美國。

3.大多數發達國家的老年人口比例都在不斷上升。對許多老年人來說，個人養老金方案（private pension schemes）的完善和醫療保健（health services）的改善意味著他們有足夠的錢和健康的身體成為旅遊市場的積極參與者。

4.英國一些大的旅遊經營商（major tourist operators）採取了縱向聯合策略（a strategy of vertical integration）以控制包價旅遊市場（package holidays）並從中獲利。

5.旅遊外匯收入（foreign exchange earnings from tourism）是指透過向外國旅遊者出售商品和服務賺取的非本國貨幣收入。外匯可分為兩種：強勢貨幣（可兌換貨幣）（hard/convertible currencies）和弱勢貨幣（不可兌換貨幣）（soft/non-convertible currencies）。

6.政府從旅遊業獲得的稅收（contributions）有直接的，也有間接的。直接稅收來自於所得稅（income tax），比如旅遊從業人員個人所得稅和旅遊企業的所得稅。間接稅收主要來源於各種旅遊商品稅和旅遊服務稅。

7.旅遊業可長期保護有美學和文化價值（aesthetic and cultural value）的自然風

景，保護祖先的遺產和文化環境，並且促進地方工藝品（local arts and crafts）和傳統文化活動的復興。

8.旅遊對社會文化的影響是覺察不到的（imperceptible），是慢慢累積起來的（cumulative），需要很長時間才顯現出來。

Passage Translation 段落翻譯練習

In order to start the process of direct mail, either through a newsletter or promotional pieces, a travel agency must build a database, which can be done through developing a questionnaire for current and new customers that can be filled out quickly and that includes an offer that will spur a response. A wealth of information about clients can be stored, including detailed information on when and where clients like to travel, their favorite activities and their budgetary preferences. Then when a tour company announces a biking tour of Beijing or an Italian art tour, you can quickly call up names for a selective mailing. In addition, the database can separate out corporate and individual clients and break them down further by frequent flyer or other club memberships. Then when you know when vendors are offering discounts and specials, you can let them know by means of direct mail. Direct mail always include a letter that personalizes the promotion. Feature a reply device and capture information on customer lifestyles, noting such things as marriage, birth of children, retirement and other changes. From this information, the agency can develop targeted offers, such as retirement trips or anniversary vacations, among others.

Lesson 25 Destination Marketing Strategy：Image-making
目的地營銷策略：形象塑造

導讀：

與世界其他著名旅遊勝地相比，香港、佛羅里達、拉斯維加斯等旅遊目的地的旅遊資源相對貧乏，但它們卻打造了現代旅遊業的神話。究其原因，旅遊目的地營銷策略的成功實施是促進其旅遊業在短時期內迅速騰飛的重要因素之一。本篇文章將闡述旅遊目的地營銷的一個重要戰略：形象塑造。

Creating and Projecting a Public Image

Of all the destination marketing tasks, one of the most important is to develop or maintain the destination image in line with the visitor groups being targeted. Image is therefore considered integral to the destination and is a well-researched area in tourism.

The success of a destination, to a great extent, is reliant on its image. The image is the cluster of all perceptions the customers hold for that destination. It is the aggregate of all the ideas, impressions and beliefs derived from direct experience and/or indirect information sources. Image is not static and homogeneous. It evolves and changes due to the internal and external factors.

Place image is heavily influenced by pictorial creation of the destination in movies or television, by music, and in some cases by popular entertainers and celebrities. Irelands exploits the John Wayne-Maureen O'Hara Quiet Man film(註1) as a successful image of the Irish, while Austria still relies on The Sound of Music image of its country's beauty and people. Television also affects destination attractiveness. The pub site for the television hit "Cheers" became an overnight tourist bonanza in Boston, while the Public Broadcasting System serialization of English dramas opened Britain to American audiences.

As major events are regarded as tourist attractions, they have become an integral part of tourism destination marketing strategies. Nations and cities take advantage of events to reinforce their favorable image in the international tourism marketplace. Such an image allows countries or cities to foster tourism promotion and foreign investment.

Major sporting events such as the Olympics or the FIFA World Cup serve a super-magnetic role in attracting international tourists to the venues and beyond. A host city receives considerable television coverage during the sporting events. It is estimated that more than six billion people from more than 190 countries watched the, 2002 Korea/Japan World Cup. The primary functions of mega sporting events for a city/region are to present itself as an attractive vacation destination and to improve its image as a tourism destination. For instance, as a result of hosting the Centennial Olympic Games in 1996, Atlanta, Georgia emerged as a world-class destination.

A destination's image can be ruined by violence, political instability, natural catastrophe, adverse environment factors and overcrowding. Once the image of a destination is in some ways damaged, quick and effective measures must be taken to rebuild its image. After the outbreak of SARS, the Hong Kong Government, the Hong Kong Tourism Board and the private sector launched unprecedented joint efforts to promote tourism and local spending(註2). As early as 1 May 2003, the "We Love Hong Kong" Campaign was launched as a self-help movement for Hong Kong businesses to encourage the Hong Kong public to go out and spend. The event greatly improved the image of Hong Kong as a popular tourist destination. Moreover, attention to and emphasis on cleanliness and hygiene have increased considerably in order to prevent a similar incident from occurring(註3), resulting in an improvement in the environment in Hong Kong, thereby increasing the region's attractiveness to inbound tourists.

Effective destination imaging requires a congruence between advertising and the place. Glossy photographs of sunsets, beaches, buildings, and events need to have some relationship to what tourists actually experience; otherwise destinations run the risk of losing tourist goodwill and generating bad word of mouth(註4).

Branding as a Technique to Communicate an Image

Brands are a fundamental part of commercial activity. Destinations need brands as well, because, destinations, like companies, must communicate to a broad market of consumers what they are, why they offer what they do, and the consistency and quality of their offerings. This is accomplished by the brand.

Branding is defined as the use of a combination of name, logo and design standards which make up a core identity for a product or service which differentiates it from competitor offerings(註5). The brand is the abstract of the destination's identity, the way the destination wants to project itself in the market and be recognized. Brand is a promise, an anticipation and an expectation.

Successful destinations all have branded the value proposition in a communications program that is substantial and consistent(註6). Orlando is the far-and-away leader in creating share of mind as well as share of heart throughout the entire world. It has cultivated a powerful brand essence: "The World's Favorite Place for Family Fun". Chicago's marketing theme — "Chicago's Got It" — featured pictures of its famous architecture, lakefront, symphony, world's tallest building, financial exchanges, and Wrugley Field (home of the Chicago Clubs) to suggest that the city had everything: business, culture, entertainment, recreation, and sports. In contrast, San Francisco played off its well-developed image as seductive and mysterious(註7): a photo of a foggy, softly lit Golden Gate Bridge(註8) with the copy, "In the Beginning, God Created Heaven and Earth. San Francisco Took a Little Longer."

Changing an image is more difficult. Las Vegas, for example, was once seen as a vice capital known for sex and gambling. In 1998, Las Vegas Convention and Visitors Authority (LVCVA)(註9) launched a five-year ad campaign, which included ads promoting Las Vegas as a family vacation destination. The 27 million campaign was considered a significant departure from traditional advertising of gambling and show girls in "Sin City," as Las Vegas was commonly called. In January 2003, the LVCVA launched a 58 million ad campaign called Vegas Stories and featured the tag line(註10), "What happens here, stays here." The campaign was based on consumer research. Extensive brand planning has revealed that the attitude most likely to encourage visitation to Las Vegas is an assumption about the level and kind of indulgence and liberation Las Vegas is believed to offer, which cannot be found in any other destination. This is Las Vegas' brand essence; it is the emotional connection to the destination that underlies millions of peoples' thoughts about Las Vegas(註11). The major thrust of this marketing program, then, is to brand Las Vegas as a place to escape, let loose, indulge, and do things you couldn't or wouldn't do anywhere else. It's about embracing the true sense of adult freedom that moves Las Vegas into a category of one(註12).

Having an effective brand essence does not require that the destination must be one-dimensional in its appeal(註13). In successful destinations, beneath the brand essence are a family of diverse offerings, each of which has a brand of its own. This form of marketing is called multi-branding. It is motivated by the findings of the market research that most visitors are seeking a varied experience that includes several distinctive attractions. In most cases, a premier attraction functions as a hook to bring in tourists, who will ultimately spend money on many other items. Visitors to these destinations will inevitably experience far more than the hook attraction. Multiple values are each branded and communicated to the potential customer as a total diverse experience.

Marketing the Image

Before marketing the image, tourism boards of destinations must address three important questions concerning the marketing of their sites to the public:

◆ Are the true values and significance of the site being projected in the current Master Plan and in previous marketing efforts?

◆ Is there a legitimate need for any further, large-scale, commercial marketing of the site?

◆ If the site needs to be marketed, what is the controlling image to project to the public?

Armed with a clear vision, they will develop overall marketing concepts; craft a dignified and popular logo; place stories or information in magazines, newspapers, specialized newsletters and travel guides; prepare press kits for researchers and writers.

Here are some of the marketing tools you can develop to sell the image of the place.

Press Relations and the Press Kit

Travel magazines, travel sections of major newspapers and tourism industry newsletters are among the most widely read and important print media in which to market a destination. Publishers, editors, reporters and writers should all be especially welcomed at the site and provided with an effective and informative press kit. The written and published products of such visits have the potential to reach millions of people in a worldwide audience. Ideally a press kit should include: a destination brochure; a one-or-two page fact sheet about the history and international significance of the destination; the destination's priority conservation issues; a map showing the location of the destination in relation to the surrounding area; one or two high-quality black and white photographs; a list of upcoming public events; and a sheet with complete names, addresses and telephone numbers for those seeking further information. The contents of these press kits should be updated at least once a year. Many writers will visit the destination as part of "familiarization tours" organized by national tourism offices, airlines, tour companies, etc.

Feature Books, Movies and Videos

The image and popularity of a destination can be enhanced by making available to visitors the books, movies and videotapes that feature it. If famous authors have used the place in travel books or in fiction, these books should be stocked, which will project a fine image. If current or earlier movies have included scenes at destinations and, if available on cassettes, they should be stocked for sale to visitors. Videos about the site have become almost a basic requirement for any visitor attraction. These are commercially produced, and bids should be submitted(註14) to be sure the best product is produced. Cassettes of television documentaries are now available and can also be stocked if they are relevant. There are different electronic formats for these cassettes, and care should be taken to order what customers want and can use in their equipment when they return home.

International Museum Exhibits

The opportunity to participate in international museum exhibitions can be fruitful. Increasingly, large exhibitions of works of art are being organized for international tours. Such exhibitions are prestigious, serious and scholarly efforts undertaken at great expense(註15). Moving art pieces always involves a risk, but these relics can be superb ambassadors to increase international exposure for your place. The licensing of the rights for reproductions of items included in such exhibitions — jewelry, small sculptures, images, etc. — can also be an important source of income.

Postcards and Posters

Postcards and posters are splendid, profitable and reliable marketing tools if they are well produced. It is not necessary to have a whole rack of choices(註16). A few good ones will suffice. But it is necessary to get experienced and qualified firms to submit bids on postcards and posters and have professionals help select the pieces that best present the image that you want to project.

Travel and Trade Exhibitions

Major international travel-trade shows are held annually at regional, national or state levels. These are trade shows where the national tourist office (NTO) presents the travel products of the country to international tour organizers. These are important visitor-generating events and expensive to attend. Hence it is vital that the destination's marketing image is represented properly in the show by their respective NTOs.

Commercial and Corporate Alliances

In some situations it is possible to appropriately and advantageously fit a site to the commercial marketing interests of corporate officials(註17). They should be asked to make substantial financial donation, or provision of needed equipment or supplies, in exchange for photographing their product on site, making a television commercial or filming a movie. Again, it is important to have expert help to negotiate the best possible contract.

Special Events

Destinations may be expected to host a variety of special events. Planned and conducted in a professional and sensitive manner, such special events can be significant marketing opportunities. They have the potential of introducing the destination to important and influential people — political, diplomatic, corporate and private.

 Vocabulary 內文詞彙

integral   構成整體所必需的

cluster	一簇，一群
aggregate	總計，合計，總量
homogeneous	同類的，同性質的
bonanza	財源，好運
serialization	連載，連播
super-magnetic	非常有吸引力的
venue	（事件的）發生地點
catastrophe	大災難
adverse	負面的，不利的
congruence	適合，一致
glossy	有光澤的，光亮的
value proposition	價值主張
Orlando	奧蘭多（美國佛羅里達州中部城市，是世界上著名的旅遊勝地之一）
lakefront	湖邊
Wrigley Field	瑞格利球場（美國職業棒球聯盟芝加哥總部）
multi-branding	多品牌策略

hook attraction	吸引遊客的主要景點
master plan	總體設計，總體規劃，藍圖
newsletter	時事通訊，業務通訊
press kit	（提高知名度用的）新聞發布資料
feature book	專題書
suffice	足夠，滿足要求

Notes to the Text 內文註釋

1.John Wayne-Maureen O'Hara Quiet Man film：由約翰‧韋恩和瑪琳‧奧哈拉主演的電影《蓬門今始為君開》。

2.the Hong Kong Government, the Hong Kong Tourism Board and the private sector launched unprecedented joint efforts to promote tourism and local spending：香港政府、香港旅遊發展局和私營部門開展了前所未有的聯合行動來促進旅遊業的發展，增加本地居民的消費。

3.attention to and emphasis on cleanliness and hygiene have increased considerably in order to prevent a similar incident from occurring：為了防止類似事件的發生，對清潔與衛生的關注和重視程度已經有了很大的提高。

4.otherwise destinations run the risk of losing tourist goodwill and generating bad word of mouth：否則目的地就會有失去遊客的好感、產生較差口碑宣傳的風險。

5.a core identity for a product or service which differentiates it from competitor offerings：區別於競爭對手所提供的產品或服務的核心特徵。

6.Successful destinations all have branded the value proposition in a communications program that is substantial and consistent.

成功的旅遊目的地都透過大量的、一貫的宣傳活動標明他們的價值觀念。

7.San Francisco played off its well-developed image as seductive and mysterious：舊金山推出了它精心設計的形象，即一個有魅力的、神秘的城市。

8.Golden Gate Bridge：金門大橋。

9.Las Vegas Convention and Visitors Authority：（美國）拉斯維加斯會議和旅遊局。

10.the LVCVA launched a 58 million ad campaign called Vegas Stories and featured the tag line：美國拉斯維加斯會議和旅遊局投入了5800萬美元發起了一場名為賭城故事的廣告活動，突出宣傳其廣告語。

11.it is the emotional connection to the destination that underlies millions of peoples' thoughts about Las Vegas：數百萬人對拉斯維加斯的看法都是基於這種情感紐帶。

12.It's about embracing the true sense of adult freedom that moves Las Vegas into a category of one.

正是由於推崇成人自由的真正意義使得拉斯維加斯成為一個獨樹一幟的目的地。

13.Having an effective brand essence does not require that the destination must be one-dimensional in its appeal.

擁有一個有效的品牌要素並不意味著目的地只有單一的一種吸引力。

14.bids should be submitted：應該進行競標。

15.Such exhibitions are prestigious, serious and scholarly efforts undertaken at great expense.

這些展覽聲譽很高，很嚴肅，具有學術價值，而且舉辦時都不惜重金。

16.It is not necessary to have a whole rack of choices.

沒有必要做大批的可供選擇的明信片和海報。

17.In some situations it is possible to appropriately and advantageously fit a site to the commercial marketing interests of corporate officials.

在某些情況下，適當地使目的地的形象符合公司經理們的商業營銷利益是可能的，這樣做對目的地也是有益的。

Useful Words and Expressions 實用詞彙和表達方式

客源輸出國	tourist-generating country
開發旅遊資源	to tap tourist resources
配套設施建設	the construction of supporting facilities
出入境口岸	entry and exit point
入境手續	entry formality
外幣兌換商店	currency exchange shop

兌換率	exchange rate
旅行支票	traveler's check
免稅商店	duty-free shop
行李領取處	luggage claim
出租車乘車點	taxi pick-up point
候機室	departure lounge
登機牌	boarding pass
報關物品	goods to declare

Exercises 練習題

Discussion Questions 思考題

1.What are the factors which help to create the image of a destination?

2.Have you ever known a case in which the image of a destination is badly affected because of natural disaster, violence, terrorism, political instability, etc? How did it try to rebuild its image?

3.When marketing an image, what tools are commonly used? Why?

4.Using examples to illustrate how successful destinations have branded its value and built up its solid image.

5.Choose what you believe to be a good tourism promotion for a city, a region, or a country and tell why you think it is effective.

Sentence Translation 單句翻譯練習

1.旅遊對目的地的經濟影響主要包括：賺取外匯、增加政府財政收入（government revenues）、創造就業機會、刺激地區經濟的發展（regional development）。

2.當旅遊者來到目的地國時，他們不僅僅帶動了消費和基礎設施（infrastructure）的建設，更重要的是，他們的行為可能會徹底改變當地的社會習慣。

3.旅遊目的地營銷的目的是提高這些地方的價值和形象，以促使潛在旅遊者充分認識到該地區與眾不同的優勢（distinctive superiority），宣傳和促銷整個地區的產品和服務，使遊客把這些地區當做理想的旅遊度假地。

4.香港針對不同的目標市場（target markets）制定了相應的市場營銷戰略，例如對亞洲遊客突出宣傳香港是「購物天堂」，而對歐美遊客則重點宣傳香港的傳統東方色彩。

5.旅遊產業各部門（the trade contributors to the tourism industry）可按其直接的相互依賴關係（direct interdependence）和從旅遊業獲得的直接收入水平（the level of direct earnings）來劃分。

6.一類旅遊行業指交通、旅行社、住宿餐飲（accommodation and catering）和旅遊景點（tourist attractions）。這其中包括旅行方式、支持系統（support system）和旅行動機。

7.二類旅遊行業指直接從旅遊消費（the tourist spend）中獲益的行業，主要有商店，還有娛樂休閒活動（entertainment and leisure activities）和個人服務業、理髮業（hairdressing）、洗衣業、保險業和銀行等。

8.三類旅遊行業是指間接從旅遊消費中獲益的行業，如信用卡公司、出版和印刷業（publishing and printing）、提供旅遊產品的批發商和製造商（wholesalers and manufacturers）以及其他許多支持旅遊基礎設施的行業。

Passage Translation 段落翻譯練習

It is quite conceivable to regard tourism as a kind of theatrical performance that is played out on a stage called "Destination", but in a relationship between host and visitor that pays regard to human dignity and the cultural identity of the hosts. Nevertheless, the question must be asked: is there sufficient recognition of the fact by both the industry and the public sector that they are condemned to partnership? With regard to sustainability, will they have the courage to move on from lip-service declarations to confront the moment of truth for tourism? If we wish to achieve the strategic goals of sustainability, we must first define the role of the relevant indicators that must be found at the economic, social and environmental levels. As time passes, the careful and wise use of the natural environment is becoming the key factor for the attractiveness of tourism destinations of all sorts. In the 21st century, we who work in tourism must find a clearly defined policy of "qualitative growth". This means that we must again recognize that the capital assets of tourism consist of elements that are easily destroyed, namely our human capital, our culture, nature and the environment. We must learn to use these assets — but not to use them up! Tourism can only generate stable employment if the environment is tolerable for the local inhabitant and the visitor alike. We should welcome the warnings that sustainability is a long-term concept which creates added value by the law of the optimization and not the maximization of income.

Lesson 26 Marketing and De-marketing for Eco-tourism 生態旅遊營銷和反營銷

導讀：

生態旅遊作為日漸興起的一種旅遊形態，其目的在於保存和維護當地現有的旅遊資源，這同對生態旅遊所進行的市場營銷自相矛盾。本篇文章介紹了生態旅遊和持續性旅遊與替代旅遊兩個概念之間的關係，同時解釋了對生態旅遊的市場營銷和反市場營銷兩個概念並介紹了生態旅遊中的反銷售技巧。

Sustainable tourism, Alternative Tourism and Ecotourism

Ecotourism, a new concept in tourism field, is the object of intense scrutiny, debate and controversy. Whenever ecotourism is concerned, sustainable tourism and alternative tourism, which are two ecotourism affiliates, can not be ignored.

Sustainable Tourism

The concept of sustainable tourism is inextricably linked to the ethic of sustainable development, which in theory advocates that people strive to meet their present needs without compromising the ability of future generations to meet their own needs, presumably measured against the standard of living currently enjoyed(註1). Sustainable development is essentially a trade-off between the needs and aspirations of the present and those of the future.

Some researchers equate sustainable tourism with alternative tourism, although it seems clear that most, if not all, modes of tourism can be potentially sustainable in the sustainable development sense, if managed in a appropriate way within suitable settings.

Alternative Tourism

The term of alternative tourism has been used in a number of distinct ways, with the common characteristic of representing an alternative to mass or large-scale tourism(註2). The characteristics of alternative tourism present polar opposites to those ascribed to mass tourism, where mass tourism is large-scale, alternative is small-scale; where mass tourism leads to the homogenization of the tourism product, alternative tourism promotes desirable differences between destinations; where mass tourism is high-impact, alternative tourism is low-impact, etc. Usually included under the alternative tourism rubric are such interrelated activities as ecotourism, home stays, vacation farms, and other specialist accommodation such as guest-houses, nature retreats, cottages, bed and breakfast, hunting lodges and health farms(註3).

Ecotourism

Ecotourism is widely perceived as a subset of alternative tourism which places primary emphasis on the natural environment as the main motivation for travel.

Ecotourism is tourism that consists in traveling to relatively undisturbed or uncontaminated natural areas with the specific objective of studying, admiring, and enjoying the scenery and its wild plants and animals, as well as any existing cultural manifestations (both past and present) found in these areas. In these terms, nature-oriented tourism implies a scientific, aesthetic or philosophical approach to travel, although the ecological tourist need not be a professional scientist, artist, or philosopher(註4). The main point is that the person who practices ecotourism has the opportunity of immersing himself/herself in nature in a manner generally not available in the urban environment(註5).

Ecotourism can be segmented into active and passive ones. The active ecotourism tend to emphasize that ecotourism entails a behavioral/lifestyle change in the participant, and that must involve actions that contribute to the well-being of the environment. The passive ecotourism does not ascribe such a transformational character to ecotourism and require only that the activity does not result in negative impacts on the physical environment.

Marketing in Ecotourism

The classic marketing techniques could be utilized to help achieve more sustainable forms of ecotourism. Firstly, this means seeking to understand our customers in terms of their motivations and determinants, reflecting the consumer-led concept of modern marketing(註6). You cannot influence a tourist's behavior unless you understand how they think, what they are looking for and the factors which influence their purchase decisions.

Then the organization, be it a destination marketing agency or a tour operator or a hotel, needs to scan its business environment for relevant data that might determine the stance it takes towards ecotourism(註7). This scanning could involve considering:

◆ Government legislation on environmental issues,

◆ The economic climate,

◆ The level of public concern over the social and environmental impacts of tourism(註8),

◆ The potential influence of technological innovations such as virtual reality(註9). The organization or destination would then look at itself and its current marketing situation through a SWOT analysis. This should give it a realistic view of both its current situation in relation to sustainable tourism and future opportunities and threat(註10). It would then be in a position to devise its strategy.

Once the strategy is agreed, then the next challenge is to implement it through the manipulation of the four Ps and the marketing mix, namely, product, price, place and the promotion.

Product: The product dimension of achieving ecotourism involves: developing products which are more environmentally-friendly in nature and moving away from offering products which are not natural.

Price: Traditionally the main emphasis in pricing in tourism has been on low prices to encourage high volume to provide adequate profit levels for enterprises. However, if we are to develop more sustainable ecotourism, we must recognize the price paid by the tourist has to cover the full cost of their holiday.

Place: The issue of place, or rather distribution, has two main implications in relation to ecotourism. First, the trend towards direct selling should be encouraged to leave out the marketing intermediaries so as to result in a better price for the consumer. Second, when an agent is used, action should be taken to ensure that the way they sell a product is ethical and does not raise unrealistic expectations in the minds of the tourists(註11).

Promotion: Promotion is a vital element in creating more ecological forms of tourism. Tourism organizations and destinations can use literature and advertisements to raise tourist awareness of key issues relating to ecology and nature.

De-marketing in Ecotourism

To keep ecotourism a sustainable industry, some researchers begin to suggest that organizations may explore some techniques to divert, change or even deny consumer demand by de-marketing. De-marketing is a relatively recent phenomenon, which involves manipulating the marketing mix to discourage rather than encourage potential tourists to visit particular destinations(註12). De-marketing concerns with the following three aspects in terms of eco-tourism: de-marketing places, peak period and people.

De-marketing Places

It is generally believed that some destinations are over-crowded with tourists. Let's look at how the four Ps might be manipulated to achieve the aim of de-marketing those destinations.

Product-related: In the most radical solution access to the product could be restricted(註13). Take Venice for example, it might operate a ticket-only system, allowing access to the city to only a certain number of people each day.

Price-related: Economists would argue that the most effective way of reducing overall demand for famous destinations would be to raise prices.

Place-related: The distribution of the product could be constrained by restricting the sale of package holidays to the destination, particularly at peak periods.

Promotion-related: We could reduce the amount of literature and advertising that is designed to attract tourists to the famous destinations.

These four types of strategy can be seen as negative in nature. Perhaps a more positive way to de-market world-renowned destinations would be to promote alternative destinations of the same sorts. Another positive move could be to try to encourage people to stay in the destination overnight rather than just visiting for the day, so that at least they spend more money in the city. However, the latter approach, while helping maximize the benefits of tourism for the host community, would do little to reduce the overcrowding problem.

De-marketing Peak Periods

To some tourist attractions the main problem is not the overall volume of visitors, but rather their concentration on particular days of the year. De-marketing of the peak periods might involve the following actions:

Product-related: The worst aspect of the peak period in the tourist attractions is traffic congestion as most of the visitors arrive by private car. Therefore one approach would be to regulate the use of cars on peak days and insist that visitors use more environmentally friendly rail or bus services or cycle transport.

Price-related: De-marketing the peak periods could mean either increasing the fees for tickets and parking or introducing an entrance charge to the attraction on peak days.

Promotion-related: Initiatives could involve actively producing brochures or placing advertisements that might publicize the problems of congestion that visitors will face if they visit at peak times.

De-marketing People

Young, badly behaved, heavy-drinking, so-called "lager louts" have become an unwanted phenomenon in many resorts. While they spend a lot of money in bars, their presence in a resort can blight its image and discourage other market segments from visiting the resorts. De-marketing this particular segment would involve the following approaches:

Product-related: Action could involve trying to re-position the resort to make it less attractive to "lager louts". Clubs and bars could be closed and accommodation establishments could introduce rules banning single sex groups of young people.

Price-related: Most "lager louts" appear to look for cheap, basic accommodation so they can spend as much as possible on drinking and partying. Therefore, they could be de-marketed by raising accommodation prices to the point at which they do not leave the tourist enough money to have a "good time" in the resort.

Place-related: Certain tour operators which specialize in "hedonistic" holidays for young people could be discouraged or even prevented from organizing holidays to the destination.

Promotion-related: Promotional activities could be geared to selling messages about the resort that will appeal to other groups and put off the "lager louts"(註14). This may involve emphasizing cultural attractions rather than night-life and stressing the fact that for most of the year the resort is quiet. The campaign could also stress the resort's desire to be seen as up-market and selective. Brochures and advertisements could feature illustrations of older visitors and families.

Vocabulary 內文詞彙

scrutiny	細心的觀察，詳細的檢查
controversy	爭辯，辯論
ascribe to	將……歸因於
homogenization	均勻化，同質化
nature retreats	自然修養所
perceive	察覺，發覺
stance	想法，立場，態度
divert	使轉向，改換用途
sustainable	能保持的，能維持的，能持續的
aesthetic	（有關）美學原理的，美學的；審美的

premium	（為推銷商品等的）優惠，贈品
immerse	使專心於，使浸沒於
de-marketing	（透過廣告宣布）壓縮對熱門商品的需求，（用廣告）減少（對熱門商品的）市場需求，反銷售
manipulation	熟練地使用、操作、處理，操縱、控制
access to	接觸（使用或進入的）機會或途徑
initiative	主動的行動、倡議
lager louts	（Br.E）酒後鬧事的年輕人
hedonistic	享樂主義者

Notes to the Text 內文註釋

1.The concept of sustainable tourism is inextricably linked to the ethic of sustainable development, which in theory advocates that people strive to meet their present needs without compromising the ability of future generations to meet their own needs, presumably measured against the standard of living currently enjoyed.

可持續性旅遊與可持續性發展的原則密切相關。因為在理論上，後者提倡人類在盡力滿足眼前需求不能犧牲後代滿足其自身需求的能力，所謂後代的需求是以目前的生活水準為衡量依據的。

2.The term of alternative tourism has been used in a number of distinct ways, with the common characteristic of representing an alternative to mass or large-scale tourism.

替代旅遊一詞雖然被應用於各種不同的場合，但卻具有同一種特徵，即它是大

眾旅遊,也稱大規模旅遊的替代品。

3.Usually included under the alternative tourism rubric are such interrelated activities as ecotourism, home stays, vacation farms, and other the specialist accommodation such as guest-houses, nature retreats, cottages, bed and breakfast, hunting lodges and health farms.

在替代旅遊的類目之下通常包括如下相關活動,如生態旅遊、民宿、度假農場和其他專業膳宿服務,旅遊設施包括招待所、自然休養所、農舍、早餐民宿、狩獵農舍和健身農場。

4.In these terms, nature-oriented tourism implies a scientific, aesthetic or philosophical approach to travel, although the ecological tourist need not be a professional scientistartist, or philosopher.

這樣看來,以自然為導向的旅遊意味著科學性、美學性或哲學性的旅遊,雖然這種生態旅遊者並不一定真的是科學家、藝術家或哲學家。

5.The main point is that the person who practices ecotourism has the opportunity of immersing himself/herself in nature in a manner generally not available in the urban environment.

重要的是進行生態旅遊的人有機會沉浸於自然,這在都市環境中一般是無法做到的。

6.The classic marketing techniques could be utilized to help achieve more sustainable forms of ecotourism. Firstly, this means seeking to understand our customers in terms of their motivations and determinants, reflecting the consumer-led concept of modern marketing.

傳統營銷技巧可用來幫助獲得更具持續性的生態旅遊。首先,這意味著努力去理解我們顧客的購買動機和決定購買的因素，思考以顧客為導向的現代營銷理念。

7.Then the organization, be it a destination marketing agency or a tour operator or a hotel, needs to scan its business environment for relevant data that might determine the stance it takes towards ecotourism.

其次，不論是目的地銷售代理商還是旅行社或是飯店，該企業需要快速審視其業務環境，以便找出那些可能決定其對生態旅遊所持態度的資料。

8.The level of public concern over the social and environmental impacts of tourism：公眾對於旅遊給社會與環境所帶來的影響的關注程度。

9.The potential influence of technological innovations such as virtual reality：諸如虛擬現實一類的科技創新所具有的潛在影響。

10.The organization or destination would then look at itself and its current marketing situation through a SWOT analysis for example. This should give it a realistic view of both its current situation in relation to sustainable tourism and future opportunities and threat.

然後，旅遊公司或目的地可以透過SWOT分析來審視自己及現有的營銷情況。這樣就應該可以真實客觀地瞭解在可持續旅遊方面企業的現狀和未來的機遇與風險。

11.The issue of place, or rather distribution, has two main implications in relation to ecotourism. First, the trend towards direct selling should be encouraged to leave out the marketing intermediaries so as to result in a better price for the consumer. Second, when an agent is used, action should be taken to insure that the way they sell a product is ethical and does not raise unrealistic expectations in the minds of the tourists.

銷售或者說分銷對於生態旅遊而言有兩種含義。首先，應該鼓勵直接銷售來避免中間商環節，這樣就可以讓消費者獲得更加優惠的價格。其次，在使用代理商的情況下，應該採取措施確保他們銷售產品的方式合乎道德規範，不會讓遊客產生不切實際的期望。

12.De-marketing is a relatively recent phenomenon, which involves manipulation the marketing mix to discourage rather than encourage potential tourists to visit particular destinations.

反銷售是一個比較新鮮的現象，它涉及運用營銷組合來阻止而非鼓勵潛在遊客去某個目的地旅遊。

13.In the most radical solution access to the product could be restricted.

在最極端的情況下，可以限制獲得產品的途徑。

14.Promotional activities could be geared to selling messages about the resort that will appeal to other groups and put off the "lager louts".

進行促銷行動時修改度假勝地的訊息，使之對其他消費群體更具吸引力，又讓這些「年輕的鬧事者」失去興趣。

Useful Words and Expressions 實用詞彙和表達方式

促銷活動	promotional campaigns
峰值週期，高峰時期	peak periods
替代旅遊	alternative tourism

東道國經濟	host economy
當地自然環境	host natural environment
到自然景區旅遊	nature-oriented tourism
旅遊容量	tourism carrying capacity

Exercises 練習題

Discussion Questions 思考題

1.Comment briefly on the functions of marketing and de-marketing in ecotourism.

2.What are sustainable tourism, alternative tourism and ecotourism?

3.How can the classic marketing techniques help achieve more sustainable forms of ecotourism?

4.What are de-marketing people,peak period and places?

5.Will de-marketing affect the development of some resorts negatively?

Sentence Translation 單句翻譯練習

1.真正的生態旅遊是一種學習自然、保護自然的高層次的旅遊活動和教育活動，而單純的贏利活動是與生態旅遊背道而馳的。

2.生態旅遊是一項科技含量很高的環保產業，需要認真研究生態環境和旅遊資源的承受能力。

3.生態旅遊學是研究生態旅遊活動規律與生態環境倫理的一門學科，是介於生態學和旅遊學之間的一門交叉性學科。

4.生態旅遊是為體驗、瞭解、認識、欣賞、研究自然和文化而開展的一種對環境負有真正保護責任的旅遊活動，它是旅遊的一種特殊形式。

5.旅遊美學（tourism aesthetics）指導人們透過觀賞來進一步瞭解一個國家和地區的自然風光、文化藝術和民情風俗，加深對人類文明的瞭解，並得到更深的美感享受和審美教育。

6.生態旅遊應倡導愛護環境，或者提供相應的設施及環境教育，以便旅遊者在不損害生態系統或地域文化的情況下訪問、瞭解、鑑賞、感受當地的自然及文化。

Passage Translation 段落翻譯練習

It is ironic, but perhaps not unreasonable, to postulate that the high profile of ecotourism is directly dependent upon the existence of well-developed mass-tourism sectors, (which account for most of the participants. Furthermore, the characteristics of much of the PCPD (popular, casual, passive, diversionary) ecotourism market, such as organized group travel, mid-centric profile and the actual volume of visitation, suggest that a rethinking of ecotourism as an alternative tourism-only type of activity is merited; it may even be necessary to use terms such as mass ecotourism, normally an oxymoron, to describe the increasingly common intersection of sustainable mass-tourism and non-consumptive nature-viewing.

Lesson 27 Marketing to Luxury Travelers 豪華旅遊市場營銷

導讀：

　　在大多數消費群體之外還存在著這樣一種消費人群，他們由於職業需要、生活方式或私生活等諸多原因而選擇的旅遊產品價格昂貴，品味很高。這就是所謂的高端旅遊市場。旅行社對此需要有充分的認識才能做出恰當反應。本篇文章介紹了高端旅遊者的年齡分布、職業分布、旅遊動機、旅遊期望及消費習慣。

　　While the luxury market was previously dominated by purchasing expensive brand goods, there has been a shift away from that trend. Real affluence today is often measured not by what you own, but by what you do and where you go. Many of today's affluent consumers, who grew up in middle-class families, use the money they earn to realize their dreams; there are also consumers who think it is important to experience places and adventures first, before others. Travel, especially the luxury travel, is seen by many as the number one non-material way to express success.

Analysis of Luxury Travelers

　　Who buys the luxury and tailor-made holidays and what distinguishes them from others going on holiday? While there are other groups that enjoy luxury holidays, surveys have shown that there is a high correlation between being affluent and buying luxury or tailor-made holidays(註1).

Age

　　Typically the affluent are middle-aged. They are business people or professionals and the majority of the clients are in the 30-40 age group. Most of them have families.

When they travel they need huge accommodations; they need four or five bedrooms, because they bring their children, extended family and even nannies. The 55-60 age bracket shows a similar disproportionate representation of affluent households(註2). Many of these people are empty nesters, feel comfortable enough in their career to take a holiday and have often inherited money. This group now has a unique combination of available time, money and good health. Besides these baby boomers there are also the affluent that do not fit this age description. There are the young affluent; people who have high-paying jobs or other means of income that give them the resources to spend on luxury holidays. This last group, often called the emerging rich, has become an important segment within the luxury travel market.

Profession

More than 60% of all affluent travelers are either professionals or work in a management position. Another group that is well represented as luxury travelers are retirees.

Motivation

Why are people taking luxury or tailor-made holidays? While the wealthy seem to be the natural market for luxury and upscale holidays since they have the money to spend, there are also other groups of people motivated and able for luxury travel. This can be used as a guide for segmenting the market as follows:

◆ Traditional high-end travelers for whom luxury travel is the standard: these are typically older and wealthier people who are often loyal to individual properties or traditional luxury brands.

◆ Corporate travelers whose expenses are paid for by the company: most high-ranking executives expect to fly at least business class and stay at luxury hotels. Companies do this not only to satisfy their employees, but also to keep up a certain image with the outside world. Conference attendees are also part of this market. In order to attract high-ranking executives to a conference or seminar, meeting planners are well aware of the fact that they have to offer luxurious accommodation.

◆Lifestyle travelers who are able to pay for the best and who look for features such as exclusivity and individuality: this group is different from the first group as the traditional high-end traveler is looking for a guaranteed standard of luxury in accommodation and comfort while the lifestyle traveler is looking for something unique(註3). The lifestyle traveler is looking to enrich his or her life while traveling and is willing to pay for something exclusive. Lifestyle travelers also like to stay in trendy, upscale hotels.

◆ Once-in-a-lifetime luxury travelers who cannot afford luxury travel with the same frequency as other groups: this group is willing to save and sacrifice other things in life in order to enjoy a unique and expensive holiday. An example of this group is the honeymooner. Especially in the US, newly married couples are known to spend much more on their honeymoon than they would spend on average for any other travel experience. Another group, often older people, is consumers who are wiling to save up for a trip they have looked forward to all their life. People who have a clearly defined special interest, such as bird-watching, are often also willing to pay a premium they would not pay for their typical holidays.

For the luxury market, the overall motivation to spend more than average on a holiday is to receive satisfaction, exclusivity and high-quality, and outstanding customer service(註4). With an increase in the number of affluent people, it has become harder for the super affluent to differentiate them from others. Now that more and more people are able to afford luxury travel, the very wealthy are looking for experiences that are inaccessible for others or in other words, those travel experiences that are extraordinarily expensive. This upward shift in demand for exceptional and exceptionally expensive products suggests opportunities for super-luxury in people(註5).

Frequency and Travel Companions

People who take luxury holidays go on more than one trip per year. Two thirds of the respondents of a 2004 American Express survey amongst affluent Americans mentioned that they take an average of six personal trips per year. This is not only due to the overall trend to take more but shorter holidays, but also because most affluent travelers have a higher-than-average annual number of holidays. They also spend more on each trip than the average traveler.

Most luxury and tailor-made holidays are taken by couples. However, the market for luxury holidays catering to families has experienced an interesting growth over the last few years. Parents and grandparents are increasingly interested in bringing children and grandchildren on luxury trips, often these are tailor-made trips.

Marketing in Luxury Travel

A new trend that has been seen in the US, Europe and Japan is that of trading up. People are sometimes prepared to pay significantly more for luxury products and services than for regular products. They have to compensate this trading up with trading down for products they consider less important(註6). For example, consumers are willing to shop year-round for groceries in discount warehouse stores in order to splash out on a luxury holiday. Luxury has become more about the ability to realize a passion, not just about expensive and trendy brand names(註7).

Though many affluent households have a high disposable income, they are still very careful with what they spend their money on. Most of the affluent are cautious, risk-averse and protective of their financial resources(註8). They are willing to pay full price on luxuries they desire, but often still seek out bargains for other products and services they need. The affluent consumers today see themselves as independent thinking, savvy, careful consumers who will not pay for hollow prestige, but will always be ready to pay for real quality(註9). They like to find a bargain and enjoy free extras(註10). A survey showed that 65% of the people always or often fly coach class, which is an interesting fact, especially as 64% of this same group always or often stay in luxury hotels. It can be concluded that many affluent do not mind flying coach class, but are willing to pay extra to stay in luxury accommodation.

Evoking a Sense of Luxury

Selling holidays to the luxury travelers is to find out what travel product is catering to and can really satisfy the luxury travelers. Product to evoke a sense of luxury in travelers is an answer(註11).

Luxury and luxury travel can have different meanings for different people. The following four factors can evoke a sense of luxury in people:

Cost.

Often an item or experience is considered luxury because it is expensive, especially when the product does not have a tangible quality that increases with the price(註12).

Time.

Luxury is often not just perceived as pampering, but as convenient and hassle-free travel. With time being one of the most precious resources in many people's lives, giving travelers back time can be perceived as luxury(註13). Examples of this kind can be breakfast served in bed or a helicopter service from the airport to the resort.

Prestige/social status.

This is created by the belief that other people perceive a product or experience as a luxury, giving the buyer a certain prestige. For example, if a traveler tells an acquaintance about staying in a resort with private butler service, the listener is believed to think more highly of the teller.

Uniqueness.

A unique product or experience will be able to create a sense of luxury, as the traveler knows that the product is not in the reach of everybody. Having meals made of unique ingredients or enjoying a new type of spa experience can evoke a sense of luxury. The affluent are not buying luxury brands because of what the brand says about them; they are interested in the brand from a standpoint of quality(註14). They also want something special and authentic, not mainstream.

The Luxury Travel Product

The luxury market has become much more diverse over the years. Many affluent travelers have also become more concerned about privacy and are willing to pay for the privacy of villas with private pools and spas. Over the last years the luxury travel product has changed from the traditional luxury products such as standard old-world five-star resorts and hotels, to a wide variety of exclusive and unique experiences. What people like to do and what is offered appears to be limitless as offerings expand.

Luxury travelers are willingly to engage in a variety of leisure activities, such as luxury cruises, yacht rentals or vacation home rentals. Meanwhile, luxury travelers have extraordinarily unusual booking requests for their holidays, such as space training in Russia, a holiday using dog sleds as the mode of transportation and a suite at a hotel made of ice as the accommodation. Such luxury travel products are often being packaged by specialized tour operators and are being sold through travel agents. These products can be roughly divided into the following categories:

Luxury resorts/hotels;

Private villas;

Luxury cruises;

Private islands;

Yacht rentals (including crew);

Adventure travel;

Luxury special-interest travel;

Private jet holidays;

Tailor-made tours.

Tailor-made holidays can lead travelers to all parts of the world by offering trips to unique places that are less well known and off the beaten track. Although the accommodation might not always be five-star in standard during these tailor-made holidays, the personalization of the trip and the remoteness of the location can make it expensive, and thus it is viewed as a luxury trip(註15).

There is a tremendous growth in luxury travel market, which is never ending, so the tour operators and travel agencies have to be a step ahead, and have to look at the future. The most important thing of all is that the product has to be better than the next person.

Vocabulary 內文詞彙

extended family	幾代同堂的大家庭
age bracket	年齡段
correlation	關聯性，相關性
inherit	繼承（財產、頭銜等）
disproportionate	不相稱的，不均衡的，不成比例的，懸殊的
seminar	年會，研討會
cater to	迎合
trade up	購買更高價的物品
trade down	購進低價（或低檔）物品（或財產）
evoke	引起，喚起（記憶、情感）
prestige	聲望，顯赫
pamper	縱容，嬌養
diverse	不同的，多種的
off the beaten track	人跡罕至的
empty nesters	空巢家庭
high-end traveler	高端遊客
corporate traveler	團體遊客

hiking trip	遠足旅行
once-in-a-lifetime luxury traveler	一生僅此一次的高端遊客
luxury accommodation	豪華飯店
tangible quality	有形的品質
hassle-free travel	毫無麻煩的行程
butler service	管家式服務
leisure activity	休閒活動
specialized tour operator	特色旅行社
yacht rental	遊艇租賃服務
tailor-made tour	量身訂製的旅遊行程，訂製旅遊
luxury lodging property	豪華住宿

Notes to the Text 內文註釋

1.While there are other groups that enjoy luxury holidays, surveys have shown that there is a high correlation between being affluent and buying luxury or tailor-made holidays.

各種調查表明雖然高端旅遊也涉及一些其他的消費群體，但是高端旅遊或訂製旅遊與高收入之間的關係非常大。

2.The 55-60 age bracket shows a similar disproportionate representation of affluent households.

55到60歲年齡段的遊客中同樣有絕大部分都來自富裕家庭。

3.Lifestyle travelers who are able to pay for the best and who look for features such as exclusivity and individuality: this group is different from the first group as the traditional high-end traveler is looking for a guaranteed standard of luxury in accommodation and comfort while the lifestyle traveler is looking for something unique.

注重生活方式的旅遊者有能力購買最優質的產品和服務，同時也希望獲得具有獨享性與個性等特徵的商品。這一人群與第一類消費群體的區別在於，傳統高端遊客是在追求豪華住宿和豪華享受的品質保證，而講究生活方式的遊客是在追求與眾不同。

4.For the luxury market, the overall motivation to spend more than average on a holiday is to receive satisfaction, exclusivity and high-quality, outstanding customer service.

對於高端旅遊市場而言，花費高於普通旅遊支出的動機是要獲得滿足感、獨占權、高品質和非凡的售後服務。

5.This upward shift in demand for exceptional and exceptionally expensive products suggests opportunities for super-luxury in people.

對獨特產品以及天價產品的需求不斷增加，這是旅行社向消費者推銷超高端旅遊的機會。

6.They have to compensate this trading up with trading down for products they consider less important.

他們必須透過低價購買自認為不太重要的商品來補償這種高價消費。

7.Luxury has become more about the ability to realize a passion, not just about expensive and trendy brand names.

豪華消費越來越和實現夢想的能力相聯繫，而不僅僅是單純的高價位以及時尚品牌。

8.Most of the affluent are cautious, risk-averse and protective of their financial resources.

大多數家境富裕者非常謹慎、知道迴避風險，對自己的收入有保護意識。

9.The affluent consumers today see themselves as independent thinking, savvy, careful consumers who will not pay for hollow prestige, but will always be ready to pay for real quality.

今天經濟條件富裕的消費者大多是一些思想獨立、洞察力敏銳且謹慎理智的消費者，他們不會購買有名無實的產品，但對貨真價實的品質卻肯慷慨解囊。

10.They like to find a bargain and enjoy free extras.

他們希望獲得低價，並享受到免費的額外服務。

11.Selling holidays to the luxury travelers is to find out what travel product is catering to and can really satisfy the luxury travelers. Product to evoke a sense of luxury in travelers is an answer.

向高端遊客出售度假產品的關鍵在於發現何種旅遊產品可以取悅並能夠真正滿足高端遊客的需求。而這種產品恰恰就是能賦予遊客豪華感覺的產品。

12.Often an item or experience is considered luxury because it is expensive, especially when the product does not have a tangible quality that increases with the price.

某種產品或旅行是否高端往往取決於它的高昂價位，尤其是當這種產品還不具備可以隨價格增長而增加的有形品質的時候。

13.With time being one of the most precious resources in many people's lives, giving travelers back time can be perceived as luxury.

既然對於許多人的生活時間是最寶貴的資源之一，那麼為旅遊者節省時間的做法必定被視為一種豪華的享受。

14.The affluent are not buying luxury brands because of what the brand says about them; they are interested in the brand from a standpoint of quality.

富裕階層購買奢侈品牌並不是因為品牌自身的含義，而是對品牌所具有的品質感興趣。

15.Although the accommodation might not always be five-star in standard during these tailor-made holidays, the personalization of the trip and the remoteness of the location can make it expensive, and thus it is viewed as a luxury trip.

雖然訂製旅遊中的住宿條件不可能總是五星級標準，但是行程的個性化和偏遠的住宿都不可避免地提高了價格，該行程也因此被認為是豪華遊。

Useful Words and Expressions 實用詞彙和表達方式

市場走勢	market behavior

打入市場	find inroad into the market
銷貨回佣	sales rebate
銷貨毛利	gross margin on sales
淨利	net profit
銷售平淡	lackluster sales
訂貨不足	insufficient order
銷路好	in good demand
銷售刺激因素	sales stimulation factor
突擊銷售法	shotgun approach
厚利多銷	large profits and quick turnover
薄利多銷	small profits and quick turnover
硬性推銷	hard selling
淡季	period of slack sales
電子轉帳	electronic funds transfer
銷售發票	sales invoice
銷售合約	sales contract
總成交額	total contract value

| 銷售最大化 | sales maximization |
| 操縱市場 | manipulating the market |

Exercises 練習題

Discussion Questions 思考題

1.How many customer types are likely to take luxury travel according to the text? Are there other potential customers?

2.Can you give some examples to show how tour operators adopt different ways to sell their products to different luxury travelers?

3.What is the key consideration when tour operators are marketing luxury travels to consumers?

4.What leisure activities are most preferred by luxury travelers according to the text, and are there other activities you can suggest?

5.What motivates consumers to take luxury travel?

Sentence Translation 單句翻譯練習

1.營銷環境的多變性（variability）是由於其自身存在的狀況決定的。在一個致力於經濟快速發展的社會裡，每個環境因素都隨著社會經濟的發展而不斷變化，而這種變化在大多數情況下有時難以控制。

2.隨著旅遊者的經驗越來越豐富，旅遊經營商（tour operators）出售的包價旅遊產品的選擇餘地也越來越大，方式越來越靈活。有些旅遊經營商還可以根據客人的特殊需要量身訂製特別的包價旅遊。

3.遊輪旅遊（cruise tour）主要吸引的是年齡較大的遊客，他們當中許多人的年齡在55歲以上；然而，這又是一個以旅遊目的地為導向的市場，加勒比海地區（the Caribbean）被視為是稍微年輕一些的遊客的旅遊目的地。

4.野生動物觀賞遊（wildlife tour）是激動人心的行程，遊客們可以置身於非洲叢林、遠離城市喧囂，並可以近距離地欣賞各種野生動物在它們的棲息地悠然自得地生活的情形。

5.有些旅行社在推出適合年輕消費群體的不同尋常的探險旅遊（adventure travel）項目時規定了最高年齡和最低年齡的限制。由於時間較長，此類度假產品似乎較為昂貴，但是，以平均每週的費用來計算則絕對是物有所值。

Passage Translation 段落翻譯練習

Luxury travelers use a variety of resources for obtaining travel information. These resources are often used in a certain sequence. For example, a traveler could potentially hear form a friend about a certain destination or resort or read about it in a magazine. While friends and acquaintances are an important and very influential source of information for people who are looking for an exclusive or tailor-made experience, another important source is magazines. There are a variety of magazines catering to the upscale travel market. There are also a number of travel-related companies that publish and distribute their own magazine. Next, the traveler potentially tries to find additional information using the internet. There are also a large number of websites and newsletters catering to the upscale market. They then receive information from the travel agent, where he or she books the holiday.

Lesson 28 Heritage Tourism Marketing 文化遺產旅遊營銷

導讀：

以文物古蹟資源作為主要旅遊吸引物的文化遺產旅遊已成為20世紀以來推動世界旅遊業迅速發展的重要因素之一，而中國的文化遺產旅遊也隨著旅遊業的飛速發展而不斷繁榮。本篇文章對文化遺產旅遊涉及的相關問題及文化遺產旅遊者進行了概述，並圍繞其營銷活動中的營銷組合確定問題、目標市場營銷及影響方式選擇等方面作了討論。

About Heritage Tourism

The Concept of Heritage Tourism

Heritage tourism is a loose term that can be interpreted broadly or narrowly. For the purposes of this discussion it will be defined as tourism which is based on heritage where heritage is the core of the product that is offered and heritage is the main motivating factor for the consumer. It is based on the view that heritage is only heritage in tourism terms when it is of interest to, and accessible to, tourists(註1).

In this context heritage is taken to mean history, culture, and the land on which people live. It includes both tangible and intangible elements and therefore includes the following, for example:

◆ Historic buildings and monuments;

◆ The sites of important past events like battles;

◆ Traditional landscapes and indigenous wildlife;

◆ Language, literature, music and art;

◆ Traditional events and folklore practices;

◆ Traditional lifestyles including food and drink and sport.

It covers the aspects of heritage that are consciously owned and managed by the public, private, and voluntary sectors and those elements which are not owned by anyone(註2).

How old something has to be to be considered as heritage is an arguable point, but the period seems to be becoming shorter and shorter. There are museums now which have exhibits based on life in the 1960s and even later(註3).

Heritage tourism can take place at individual sites, as well as, increasingly, in "heritage areas" and along "heritage routes," "corridors" and "trails" (e.g., the Coal Mining Heritage Route in southern West Virginia, South Carolina National Heritage Corridor, and Maine Maritime Heritage Trail)(註4). In some cases, cities may promote themselves, or districts within them, as heritage destinations.

The Nature of the Heritage Tourism Products

The heritage tourism product is heterogeneous. Sometimes it is tangible and takes the form of buildings and monuments, while at other times it is intangible such as a folklore event or a particular language. The product can be natural or man-made and may be a single attraction, a destination area, or a whole country. Some heritage is consciously owned and managed so as to attract tourists while other heritage features are managed with the aim of reducing the problems caused by unwanted tourism(註5). The heritage product is controlled by different types of organizations with differing objectives. Private-sector-owned attractions are often driven by the profit motive, while those in the public sector tend to be managed with wider social objectives in mind, including education and providing leisure facilities for the community. Those in the stewardship of the voluntary sector are often only made available to tourists as a means to another end, for example, to generate revenue to fund conservation work(註6). Finally, some of the heritage products are totally authentic, while others are less than authentic.

Even if we focus just on single-site, individual, man-made heritage attractions rather than destinations, there is great diversity. Seventeen different types have ever been identified, ranging from nature trails to "historic" adventure theme parks, and from historic gardens to breweries. These attractions also vary in that some are themselves old while others are very recent developments. Some charge a market price while others make no charge.

One of the major ways in which the heritage product is almost infinitely varied is in terms of the benefits bestowed on users and those which users seek from it(註7). These tend to vary depending on the type of attraction but include the following: status, inexpensive family day out, an opportunity to learn something new, relaxation, healthy exercise, nostalgia, aesthetic pleasure, exhilaration and excitement, being awe-inspired, entertainment, participating in activities, and meeting like-minded people.

The Market for Heritage Tourism

The heritage tourism market is also heterogeneous and again varies depending on the type of heritage. Some of the ways in which the market is heterogeneous include the following:

Some tourists are almost obsessed by heritage, for others it is a minor interest, while for some people it holds no interest whatsoever;

The market for some heritage attractions and destinations means mainly a day-trip market, while the market for others is made up, almost exclusively, of people on holiday;

Heritage may appeal to an international or to a mainly national, or even just a local audience;

The market for different types of heritage can often be segmented on the basis of factors such as age, sex, class, and race;

Certain sorts of heritage appeal to mass markets while others have narrow, small niche markets;

Differences exist in people's ability and willingness to pay to enjoy heritage products.

About the Heritage Tourist

Throughout the world, the number of tourists seeking some kind of heritage experience during their vacation continues to increase.

According to numerous analyses, the typical heritage tourist is of middle age or older, and of above-average levels of education and income.

The heritage tourist tends to seek more in the type of experience and benefits expected than other types of tourists. Heritage tourists usually seek an informed visitor experience rather than merely gazing.

They also expect outcomes that include learning about their destination and gaining an insight into its past. While enjoyment is still crucial, the heritage tourist often expects a greater degree of involvement with, or immersion into, the site(s), with a heavy educational component. The heritage tourist may be described as a "thoughtful consumer," one who is of above-average cultural competence and wary of the "dumbing down" so prevalent in today's culture(註8).

Of special interest to tourism providers, the heritage tourist also typically stays longer in an area than the average tourist, as well as spends more money. A study conducted by the Travel Industry Association of the U.S. found that cultural/heritage tourists spent an average of 623 per trip, compared to the typical American tourist's expenditure of 457, and that a higher proportion were likely to spend in excess of 1000 (19 percent compared to 12 percent). While the typical tourist's trip lasted 3.4 nights, the cultural/heritage tourist spent an average of 5.2 nights at the destination.

Marketing Activities of Heritage Tourism

Determining the Marketing Mix

As part of marketing activities, managers must determine the most correct marketing mix for achieving their stated goals and objectives. The market mix, which is simply a set of variables that can be manipulated to achieve goals and objectives, is important in allowing the heritage attraction to compete for selected target markets. Traditionally, the marketing mix has consisted of various elements related to product, price, promotion and place (the four Ps). In heritage terms the product can be seen as the physical characteristics of the attraction, the historic relics, methods of interpretation, the staff, support services, image and branding. Price covers a range of issues like admissions, discounts, concessions, value, methods of payment, and cost of getting to the site. Promotion deals specifically with issues such as marketing endeavors, advertising, various promotional media and media design. Finally, place generally refers to the location of the experience and the distribution of the product.

Recent thinking has expanded the original 4 Ps to include elements such as people, programming and partnerships. Each of these has been examined in considerable detail, and a summary is provided below:

◆ People — from a marketing perspective, the focus is often on the product itself, with less attention to the experiences on offer. The heritage industry has emerged from how a region's past has been commodified and sold to the visitor, where emphasis has been on the tangible products of the industry. The "people" element suggests that equal attention be focused on the experiences behind the heritage settings themselves, and that while tourism is product driven, ultimately tourists are in search of the intangible within settings where focus is on the actual experiences they seek to take away from visits(註9). This experiential dimension to heritage is often tied to the learning aspect of heritage tourism.

◆ Programming focuses on how the products and experiences can be better packaged for the customer. In tourism this is often in the form of running special events, and in the case of heritage tourism much attention has focused on festivals and how they can be representative of places themselves. In addition, packaging can involve putting together a mix of product and experience by linking a number of attractions together. Recognized as cluster development, or attraction clusters, this type of programming is often only accomplished through the presence of partnerships between tour operators(註10).

◆ Partnership is linked to wider ideas of collaboration and network development. Defined as regular, cross-sectoral interactions between parties, based on at least some agreed rules or norms, intended to address a common issue or to achieve a specific policy goal or goals, partnership is emerging as almost standard practice within tourism management to involve some sort of partnership agreement, or dialogue between different parties(註11). It is not a new concept, but one that has been around for several decades particularly within management and corporate sectors. It is relatively new within tourism research circles, where the focus has been descriptive and centred around presenting case studies. There has emerged some work that has developed a conceptual dimension to this area of inquiry focusing on heritage tourism(註12). Two experts working in the context of World Heritage Sites ever stressed the importance of three key elements within any partnership: type (informal to formalized), the approach taken (grassroots to agency led) and the extent of co-operation between partners (full to limited).

Target Marketing

Another marketing activity used to achieve a site's objectives is target marketing, wherein heritage managers decide which specific groups of visitors they will focus on in their marketing efforts. The identification of target markets involves three stages. First, there must be a decision about how many market segments will be targeted. This will usually be based on its management objectives and the nature of the heritage resources. Second, managers must develop a clear market profile for each segment. Finally, a marketing strategy needs to be developed that is appropriate to the heritage site and the selected market segments.

Optional Ways of Marketing

Heritage managers can market in a number of different ways. One way is to offer the same marketing mix to all potential visitor groups. This approach, usually known as undifferentiated marketing, has the advantage of reaching a wide range of market segments and people who fall within more than one category(註13). It is a "one size fits all" approach and can involve some wasted financial resources on groups that might not be interested in visiting a particular type of heritage site(註14).

Single segmentation, or differentiated marketing, is where a specific target market is selected. This has the advantage of directing all resources to a single segment that managers know will have an interest in visiting. Instead of aiming for a small share of the larger market, an attraction can aim at getting a large share of the specific market that has been identified.

Another approach is selective segmenting, which lies somewhere between undifferentiated and single segmenting. Here, a few groups are chosen, which provides some of the advantages of single segmentation while eliminating some of the risks. Several approaches have been used in attraction marketing. A common one is to identify attraction clusters, and market around the mix of attractions making up individual clusters. One more approach that has been used in Canada is marketing through what are known as product clubs, which have a specific clientele.

Vocabulary 內文詞彙

millennia	千年（millennium的複數）
indigenous	土生土長的，本地的
heterogeneous	不同種類的，混雜的
stewardship	管理，經營
authentic	真實自然的
brewery	釀酒廠
bestow	給予，授予
nostalgia	懷舊之情，鄉愁
exhilaration	愉快，高興
awe-inspired	產生敬畏的
like-minded	具有相似意向或目的的
immersion	沉浸，浸沒，專心
wary	謹慎的，謹防的，小心翼翼的
the dumbing down	（為智力弱的人而做的）簡化

prevalent	普遍的，盛行的，流行的
in excess of	多出，超出
manipulate	（熟練地）操作，操控
historic relics	歷史遺蹟
methods of interpretation	表現手法
concession	讓步，妥協
endeavour	竭盡之舉，努力之舉
cluster development	集群開發
attraction clusters	旅遊吸引物的集群
grass roots	基層，基層民眾
a market profile	市場概況

Notes to the Text 內文註釋

1.It is based on the view that heritage is only heritage in tourism terms when it is of interest to, and accessible to, tourists.

文化遺產旅遊的概念是建立在這樣一種認識基礎之上的，即遺產僅僅是旅遊範疇內的遺產，是遊客感興趣並且可以接觸到的遺產。

2.It covers the aspects of heritage that are consciously owned and managed by the public, private, and voluntary sectors and those elements which are not owned by anyone.

它涵蓋了那些由公有、私營以及志願部門所擁有和管理的遺產，以及那些還未確定擁有者的遺產。

3.There are museums now which have exhibits based on life in the 1960s and even later.

如今有的博物館中的展品反映的是1960年代，甚至是更近年代的生活。

4.Heritage tourism can take place at individual sites, as well as, increasingly, in "heritage areas" and along "heritage routes," "corridors" and "trails (e.g., the Coal Mining Heritage Route in southern West Virginia, South Carolina National Heritage Corridor, and Maine Maritime Heritage Trail)".

文化遺產旅遊活動可以在獨立的遺址地進行，但也越來越多地出現在「遺址區」內和「遺址路線」、「廊道」及「小徑」等沿線上（例如，西弗吉尼亞南部的「煤礦開採遺產路線」，「南卡羅來納國家遺產廊道」和「緬因州沿海遺產小徑」）。

5.Some heritage is consciously owned and managed so as to attract tourists while other heritage features are managed with the aim of reducing the problems caused by unwanted tourism.

有的遺產是為了吸引遊客而有意識加以擁有和管理的，而另外一些遺產景觀的管理是為了減少由不希望發生的旅遊活動所引發的各種問題。

6.Those in the stewardship of the voluntary sector are often only made available to tourists as a means to another end, for example, to generate revenue to fund conservation work.

處於志願部門管轄範圍內的旅遊吸引物常常是為達到別的目的才向公眾開放的，比如為遺產的保護工作提供資金。

7.One of the major ways in which the heritage product is almost infinitely varied is in terms of the benefits bestowed on users and those which users seek from it.

文化遺產旅遊產品的變化幾乎是無窮盡的，變化的一種主要形式是就提供給使用者的利益以及使用者從產品中所尋求的利益而言的。

8.The heritage tourist may be described as a "thoughtful consumer," one who is of above-average cultural competence and wary of the "dumbing down" so prevalent in today's culture.

進行文化遺產旅遊的遊客可以被形容為「認真思考型的消費者」，他們的文化能力超出了一般水平，並且對當今文化中盛行的「簡化」現象有所警惕。

9.The "people" element suggests that equal attention be focused on the experiences behind the heritage settings themselves, and that while tourism is product driven, ultimately tourists are in search of the intangible within settings where focus is on the actual experiences they seek to take away from visits.

「人」的因素意味著遊客除了參觀遺產景觀本身之外，還要追求一種個人的體驗；儘管旅遊活動是以產品為核心驅動的，但最終而言，遊客是要透過旅遊在景點中找尋並能帶走一種無形但真切的精神感受。

10.Recognised as cluster development, or attraction clusters, this type of programming is often only accomplished through the presence of partnerships between tourist operators.

這種類型的規劃被視為集群開發或旅遊吸引物的集群化，它通常只能透過旅遊經營商之間的合作來實現。

11.Defined as regular, cross-sectoral interactions between parties, based on at least some agreed rules or norms, intended to address a common issue or to achieve a specific policy goal or goals, partnership is emerging as almost standard practice within tourism management to involve some sort of partnership agreement, or dialogue between different parties.

合作關係是指雙方面定期的、跨部門的相互協作，這種協作至少是基於某些約定的規則或準則，並且是為瞭解決一個共同問題或是為實現某一個或一些具體政策目標而開展的。合作關係在旅遊管理中正成為一種幾近標準的做法，它涉及某種合作協定或者各方之間的對話。

12.There has emerged some work that has developed a conceptual dimension to this area of inquiry focusing on heritage tourism.

對於這一探索領域，已經有人做了一些工作，建立起了文化遺產旅遊的概念範疇。

13.This approach, usually known as undifferentiated marketing, has the advantage of reaching a wide range of market segments and people who fall within more than one category.

這一方式通常被稱為無差異營銷，其優勢在於它所能影響的細分市場類型廣泛，並可以作用於同時屬於多種類型的人群。

14.It is a "one size fits all" approach and can involve some wasted financial resources on groups that might not be interested in visiting a particular type of heritage site.

這種「一碼通用」的辦法可能會導致把一些財源浪費在那些對參觀某一特定類型的遺產地點不感興趣的團體身上。

Useful Words and Expressions 實用詞彙和表達方式

原汁原味的文化	authentic culture
傳統的僵化	the freezing of traditions
少數民族村寨	ethnic minorities villages
少數民族文化生態遊	ethnic cultural eco-tourism
鄉村旅遊	rural tourism
農家樂旅遊	happy farm households tours
符號化旅遊	symbolized tourism
遺產廊道	heritage corridors
文化路線	cultural routes
風景小道	scenic byway
風景駕車道	scenic drive
自然風景路	nature beauty roads
工程路線	engineered routes
商旅管理	enterprise travel management

運營模式	operation mode
重訪率	repeat patronage rate
旅遊傾向	travel propensity
旅遊者偏好	tourist preference
旅遊者決策	tourist decision
知覺風險	perception risks
環境感知因素	factors of environmental perception
遊客利益細分	benefit segmentation of tourists
供求彈性	elasticity of supply and demand
市場失靈	market failure
地格	sense of place or locality
漏損	revenue leakage
剝離	divestment

Exercises 練習題

Discussion Questions 思考題

1.What is meant by heritage in the context of heritage tourism?

2.Why are both the product and the market of heritage tourism heterogeneous?

3.What differences are there when the heritage tourist is compared with other types of tourists?

4.Which three elements other than the traditional 4 Ps have to be taken into account when determining the market mix in heritage tourism?

5.How many ways can heritage managers market?

Sentence Translation 單句翻譯練習

1.當前旅遊業發展的一個特點（prominent feature）是旅遊文化性競爭日益激烈，利用文化來發展旅遊、繁榮經濟（promote economic prosperity），已成為世界旅遊發展的大趨勢和主潮流（major trend）。

2.伴隨著旅遊業的發展，散落（spot）在廣袤（vast）非洲大地上的非物質文化遺產（non-material cultural heritage）集中於各大旅遊景點（tourist attractions），這些遺產充實了旅遊市場，豐富了旅遊文化生活。

3.旅遊是一種文化，作為文化本身的旅遊業正發揮著繼承（inherit）文化、發展文化、保護文化遺產的功效。旅遊業的發展造成了保護非物質文化遺產的作用，可謂是意外（unexpected）收穫和特殊功勞（contribution）。

4.中國「遺產資源」非常豐富。旅遊經濟的興起（rise）和興旺（prosperity）也使中國成為全球最具潛力的旅遊目的地。

5.曾幾何時，旅遊被認為是保護遺產的一種手段，因為參觀與旅遊能帶來更多的收入。而現在人們越來越關心旅遊所帶來的威脅，特別是對無形遺產和其自然狀態（authenticity）的威脅。

6.任何一個旅行社的經濟資源（financial resources）都是有限（boundary）的。企業在此界限內為顧客提供旅遊產品，尚可保證（guarantee）產品品質超越了這個界限所生產的產品必然沒有品質保證。

7.特殊活動的類型複雜多樣（complicated and varied），在客源市場（source market）方面也有其特殊性。一些小型的、單調的傳統活動主要吸引但當地人觀看，而大型的國際活動，如奧林匹克運動會，吸引著世界各地的遊客。

8.主題產品（theme product）設計的關鍵是產品要與眾不同（differentiation），形成鮮明（distinct）、唯一的特性，以滿足遊客的不同需求，從而形成主題產品的核心競爭力（competitive edge）。

Passage Translation 段落翻譯練習

Heritage-based travel, like all segments of the tourism industry, offers the potential for numerous economic benefits in destination areas. The attraction of new visitors to a site or area increases spending and may lead to the creation of new jobs and businesses, thereby stimulating the local economy both directly and indirectly, through the multiplier or trickle-down effect. Taxes on spending can be used to benefit all members of a community, not just those directly involved in the tourism industry, through the improvement of physical infrastructure.

In addition to the economic benefits that the attraction of tourists to a heritage site or area can generate, the recognition of such locations may also bring with it a number of other advantages. Identification of a site or area as of historic, cultural or natural importance should promote greater awareness of, and appreciation for, its value, thereby increasing the chances of its preservation in the future. Realization of the existence and significance of its unique resources by local residents is likely to enhance community pride and help strengthen a sense of place and identity.

Lesson 29 Timeshare Marketing 分時度假營銷

導讀：

分時度假，作為國際上已經流行多年的旅遊度假方式，是一種將房地產、酒店住宿和休閒度假完美結合在一起的新型投資模式。本篇文章概述了分時度假的概念、起源及其發展，並就全球最大的分時度假交換公司——RCI在新世紀所具備的營銷優勢及其分銷問題進行了討論。

The Concept of Timeshare

The concept of timeshare, also known as vacation ownership or holiday ownership, offers purchasers the right to use a specified resort based apartment, villa, chalet or other accommodation facility for a specified number of days at the same time of year, every year. Buyers usually purchase their time slots in modules of a week and keep the right to use their days — or exchange the right for the use of accommodation in another resort — for a specified number of years or in perpetuity. Annual maintenance charges are payable and ownership rights can be sold and, in some circumstances may appreciate in value. Although resorts vary in size and sophistication, most modern timeshare accommodation is provided in secure enclosed resorts that contain a range of associated facilities that make them largely self-contained(註1). Resorts are located around the world in attractive environments with shops, restaurants, bars, clubs and a wide variety of health and sports and recreation facilities normally provided as important elements in the overall product offer. In other words, the purchase by individuals of an ownership right to use accommodation is the basis for developing sophisticated and highly efficient leisure, retailing and catering complexes at the leading edge of tourism accommodation development and marketing around the world(註2).

History and Development

History

If you play golf, you do not need to buy a golf course to indulge in the sport: you join a club and play when you want to. The principle of timeshare is very similar. The concept of holiday timeshare started in the late 1950s, with an idea conceived by a Swiss, and put into practice in a hotel which he ran. The idea evolved into Hapimag, a Swiss-based company, which offered its shares for sale. The ownership of shares conveyed the right to use the holiday properties on a regular basis(註3).

In 1967, an enterprising hotelier at Superdevoluy in the French Alps started what has become the more common form of timeshare — the sale of right-to-use "fixed" weeks in the hotel for holiday purposes — sold with the slogan "stop hiring a room, buy the hotel, it's cheaper!"

At that time, however, the concept of timeshare did not spread any further in Europe. It caught on rapidly when it was dramatically expanded in the early 1970s in the USA by the urgent need to find revenue streams for blocks of condominiums in California and Florida, which had been built but could not be sold as whole units in the immediate aftermath of the 1970s international oil crisis(註4). The combination of energy crisis and the associated global economic downturn hit the leisure/vacation property market badly and timeshare was an excellent short-term solution.

A particular problem which salesmen of condominiums soon came up against was: while the potential client liked the timeshare accommodation and the resort on offer, he did not like the prospect of having to return to the same place at the same time for his holiday year after year.

At the same time, in Indianapolis, Jori and Christel DeHaan had begun a private "swap" system with their friends, trading weeks in each others' holiday homes(註5). When this swap system was applied to the timeshare idea, the timeshare sales problem was solved. Thus, a company called RCI was founded in 1974 as a timeshare exchange organization to enable purchasers of timeshare to exchange the weeks they owned each year for weeks in different resorts. A second exchange organization, Interval International, came along two years later. Between them, these two companies acted as the catalyst which started a boom in timeshare sales in the USA during the following 10 years. The success in North America turned timeshare into the internationally successful phenomenon as it is today.

Development

Market growth around the world over the 1990s has been estimated at a remarkably high compound rate of approaching 15 per cent per annum-much faster than any vacation product of equivalent global size, with the possible exception of parts of the cruise market. Over a decade this translated into a 260 per cent increase in the number of owner families and a 230 per cent increase in timeshare sales while the number of resorts more than doubled.

At the turn of the millennium timeshare resorts were located in over eighty countries around the world with more than 4.0 million households in 175 countries owning timeshare units in some 5000 holiday resorts. Since a family typically averages around three persons, the timeshare market is now dealing with over 12 million customers with every prospect of further major growth because the economics are right for the developers, the resort operators and their marketing agencies(註6). In particular, the product is attractive to prospective customers, reflecting the continuing growth of independent rather than package tour holidays and the recent introduction of stronger consumer protection legislation, notably the implementation from 1997 of the European Timeshare Directive(註7).

RCI Europe: Marketing for a Timeshare Exchange Company

Introduction to the Company

Resort Condominiums International (RCI) is a leading global provider of innovative products and services to the global travel and leisure industry.

Founded in 1974 as an exchange service for condominium owners, RCI quickly became a driving force for growth within timeshare, and has been at the forefront of the vacation ownership industry ever since. It is consistently the global leader in membership, resort affiliations, and exchanges, confirming almost twice the number of vacations of its nearest competitor(註8).

RCI's core business is to organize, market and develop a membership organization or club dedicated to facilitating exchanges for its members and providing associated travel products(註9). Today, RCI provides its subscribing membership of more than three million timeshare owners worldwide with quality exchange vacation experiences at more than 3700 resorts in 101 countries through its week-for-week (RCI Weeks) and points-based (RCI Points) timeshare exchange networks(註10).

In addition to exchanges, the company offers seats (scheduled and charter), car hire travel insurance and other travel offers such as cruises, short breaks and packaged holidays. It has broadened its product range for members beyond timeshare by forging new relations with small specialist operators of products likely to be of interest to its membership(註11).

Marketing Advantages for the New Millennium

Compared with traditional tour operators dealing primarily via travel agents as their major source of distribution or traditional resort hotels competing within a destination to market their bedspaces, mostly to new customers every year timeshare exchange companies have powerful and vital marketing advantages for the next millennium(註12):

◆ Most resorts get as close to year-round occupancy over 90 per cent as is possible, partly because of their design and location but primarily because of the nature of the ownership structure and the exchange options.

◆RCI and its competitors can control quality by trading only with resorts that meet their criteria for affiliation. As the largest operator with the capacity to deliver business, almost like turning on or off a tap, RCI has obvious leverage to exercise over its affiliate resorts(註13). Dis-affiliation is an effective threat if resorts fall below customer satisfaction targets.

◆ Customer satisfaction is relatively easy to measure for every aspect of the business, bearing in mind that RCI is dealing with frequent, repeat users who are also club members in a clear relationship with the company(註14).

◆ The timeshare purchase process delivers a loyal client base for RCI, with a frequent repeat purchase and communication potential which most tour operators can only dream about(註15).

◆ Relationship marketing is highly efficient as the comprehensive details of members and enquirers are all on corporate databases. There is virtually total information on geodemographics, lifestyle, holiday purchase preferences and patterns, number of years of ownership, expenditure on site, time of year chosen, and type of resort preferred. Individual customer satisfaction ratings are also incorporated into the database.

◆The exchange company mines and analyses its customer database continuously and practices highly sophisticated segmentation of its membership base. There is obvious scope also to engage in cross-selling and for doing deals with third party companies which work to the same brand values as the timeshare company.

Distribution Issues

Direct Response Mechanisms: Call Centres.

Distribution decisions for RCI stem directly from the marketing process identified above. Within the travel and tourism industry, RCI is unusual in that it has very narrow distribution channels because it is a membership club. Members write or more usually telephone RCI directly and RCI products have not been available through retail travel agents. Accordingly, RCI operates primarily by telephone call centres which still handled over 99 per cent of its travel sales at the end of the 1990s.

Up to 1997 it is estimated that more than 95 percent of member contacts had been organized through call centres established in local markets wherever there was a viable membership base. In early 1998 there were fifteen call centres in operation throughout Europe serving between 10000 and 200000 members each. Across Europe RCI employed more than 1100 people, of which some 45 per cent were in the call centres with another 15 percent providing call centre support. Clearly, this represents the major distribution cost which has recently been under scrutiny.

A Consolidated Pan-European Call Centre Strategy for the Late 1990s.

As part of its globalization ambitions, the company decided in late 1997 that it would be more effective to shift the responsibility for call centres from its national centres into key locations only. It announced the consolidation of nine of the current call centres into a major international centre based in the Republic of Ireland with a 25 million investment that became fully operational by the end of 1999. Using the latest "intelligent" telecommunications technology and local call rates, the call centre delivers higher levels of efficiency and employs around 500 holiday and travel consultants speaking some seventeen different languages.

Use of the Internet.

RCI in North America started to encourage its members to undertake transactions via its Internet site in April 1997. By early 1998 the RCI site was receiving about

6000 hits a day from North American members who had been provided with an acceptably secure means to make their bookings on the system. A further 5000 hits a day was being received from members who were not able to make bookings on the system but could browse the Web pages for information. At that time the proportion of e-commerce bookings was tiny (probably less than 2 per cent), but the cost per enquiry and booking was much lower than for telephone servicing at call centres and the growth potential of the system was obvious.

RCI in Europe developed its first Internet strategy in 1997 and the first phase, with E-mail and telephone directions for specified customer actions, was running in 1998. Within five years RCI was projecting that up to 15 per cent of bookings could be Internet generated and was investing accordingly in its systems and links with the call centres. Full transactional capability (online e-commerce) was planned for introduction in 2000. As at least half of all timeshare owners either are or will be Internet users on PCs or interactive televisions at the turn of the millennium, an e-commerce strategy is logical, and its use will further reinforce the company's knowledge of consumers and enhance the efficiency of the timeshare exchange business model.

Vocabulary 內文詞彙

villa	別墅
chalet	（休假營地的）小屋
time slot	時間檔期
module	模數，模塊
in perpetuity	永遠，永存

appreciate	增值，漲價
convey	傳遞，蘊涵
catch on	流行，風行
condominium	由許多私人擁有的公寓住宅單位組成的公寓大樓
aftermath	結果，後果
swap	交換
annum	年，歲
translate	轉化，轉變為
affiliation	加盟，合作關係
forge	建立，鑄造
specialist operators	專業（旅遊）經營商
via	透過
geodemographics	地域人口統計
rating	等級級別
incorporate	合併，併入
mine	挖掘

scrutiny	詳細審查
consolidate	加強，鞏固
phase	階段
project	設計，計劃

Notes to the Text 內文註釋

1.Although resorts vary in size and sophistication, most modern timeshare accommodation is provided in secure enclosed resorts that contain a range of associated facilities that make them largely self-contained.

儘管度假區在規模和複雜程度上變化多樣，但大多數現代化的分時度假住宿處都設在安全的、封閉式的度假區內；這些度假區備有一系列的相關設施，使它們成為基本獨立的場所。

2.In other words, the purchase by individuals of an ownership right to use accommodation is the basis for developing sophisticated and highly efficient leisure, retailing and catering complexes at the leading edge of tourism accommodation development and marketing around the world.

換言之，個體對住宿使用所有權的購買是發展複雜的、高效率的休閒、零售和餐飲服務綜合體的基礎，並使其在全球旅遊住宿業的發展和營銷方面占領先地位。

3.The ownership of shares conveyed the right to use the holiday properties on a regular basis.

對時段的擁有就表示擁有定期使用度假房產的權利。

4.It caught on rapidly when it was dramatically expanded in the early 1970 s in the USA by the urgent need to find revenue streams for blocks of condominiums in California and Florida, which had been built but could not be sold as whole units in the immediate aftermath of the 1970 s international oil crisis.

美國1870年代早期，在加利福尼亞和佛羅里達州，由於迫切需要為一幢幢的公寓大樓尋找帶來收入的管道，分時度假有了出人意料的發展，從而迅速流行起來。這些已經建成的大樓受到1870年代全球石油危機的影響而無法整套銷售出去。

5.At the same time, in Indianapolis, Jori and Christel DeHaan had begun a private "swap" system with their friends, trading weeks in each others' holiday homes.

與此同時，在印第安納波利斯，喬里和克里斯特爾·德漢已經和朋友開始了一種私人的「交換」系統，他們拿各自的度假處以星期為單位相互交換使用權。

6.Since a family typically averages around three persons, the timeshare market is now dealing with over 12 million customers with every prospect of further major growth because the economics are right for the developers, the resort operators and their marketing agencies.

由於一般家庭平均人數在3 個左右，因此分時度假市場目前要接納的就是超過1200 萬的顧客。因為經濟情況適合於開發商、度假區經營商和其營銷代理社的發展，這一市場有進一步大規模增長的前景。

7.In particular, the product is attractive to prospective customers, reflecting the continuing growth of independent rather than package tour holidays and the recent introduction of stronger consumer protection legislation, notably the implementation from 1997 of the European Timeshare Directive.

尤其是，分時度假產品還吸引著未來的顧客群，這就說明散客度假旅遊而非團體度假旅遊的人數在持續增長，同時說明近期對消費者更大力度的保護立法在逐個推出，其中特別引起注意的是自1997年起實行的「歐洲分時度假指示」這一立法。

8.It is consistently the global leader in membership, resort affiliations, and exchanges, confirming almost twice the number of vacations of its nearest competitor.

它一貫保持著在會員制、度假區聯盟以及交換等方面的全球領先地位,確保其度假數量是緊隨其後的競爭對手的兩倍。

9.RCI's core business is to organize, market and develop a membership organization or club dedicated to facilitating exchanges for its members and providing associated travel products.

RCI的核心業務是對會員制企業或俱樂部進行組織、營銷和開發,這些企業或俱樂部致力於為其會員提供便捷的交換服務,並提供相關聯的旅遊產品。

10.Today, RCI provides its subscribing membership of more than three million timeshare owners worldwide with quality exchange vacation experiences at more than 3700 resorts in 101 countries through its week-for-week (RCI Weeks) and points-based (RCI Points?) timeshare exchange networks.

如今,RCI透過其周對周和以點數為基礎的這兩種分時交換網路,為全球超過三百萬分時度假會員在101個國家的3700多個度假村提供了高品質的交換度假體驗服務。

11.It has broadened its product range for members beyond timeshare by forging new relations with small specialist operators of products likely to be of interest to its membership.

透過與有可能有興趣成為其成員的小型專業化產品經營商建立新的關係,該公司擴大了產品的範圍,為其成員提供分時度假形式以外的服務。

12.Compared with traditional tour operators dealing primarily via travel agents as their major source of distribution or traditional resort hotels competing within a destination to market their bedspaces, mostly to new customers every year timeshare exchange companies have powerful and vital marketing advantages for the new millennium.

　　與利用旅遊代理商作為主要分銷管道進行運作的傳統旅遊經營商相比，或者與在旅遊目的地範圍內進行競爭以銷售其床位的傳統度假區飯店相比，分時度假交換公司在新千年中，尤其在爭奪每年出現的新顧客方面具有強大而重要的營銷優勢。

13.As the largest operator with the capacity to deliver business almost like turning on or off a tap, RCI has obvious leverage to exercise over its affiliate resorts.

　　RCI作為最大的經營商，具有幾乎可以説是收放自如地進行業務遞送的能力；它顯然能夠對其加盟的度假區施加影響。

14.Customer satisfaction is relatively easy to measure for every aspect of the business, bearing in mind that RCI is dealing with frequent, repeat users who are also club members in a clear relationship with the company.

　　對於開展的所有業務活動而言，顧客的滿意程度相對來説比較容易測量。要知道　RCI應對的是頻繁的重複使用者，而這些人同時也是與公司有著明確關係的俱樂部成員。

15.The timeshare purchase process delivers a loyal client base for RCI, with a frequent repeat purchase and communication potential which most tour operators can only dream about.

　　分時度假這一購買方法為RCI創造了一個常客基礎；顧客頻繁的重複購買，以及其間蘊涵的溝通潛力都是大多數旅遊經營商可望而不可及的。

Useful Words and Expressions 實用詞彙和表達方

式

飯店分等定級	hotel classification
飯店星級評定	the star rating system
超豪華級飯店	super deluxe hotel
高檔小飯店	boutique hotel
全套房飯店	all-suite hotel
連鎖飯店公司的下屬飯店	chain affiliate
溫泉旅館	thermal hotel
自有公寓旅館	resort condominium
夫妻旅店	mom-and-pop hotel
汽車露營地	auto-campsite
度假地	vacation spot
特大型度假地	mega-resort
陽光充足的海灘	sun-drenched beaches
特許經營	franchising
旗艦產品	flagship product
醒目裝，降價裝	flash pack

需求高峰期	time of peak demand
負需求	negative demand
賒帳支付	payment on account
交貨付款	payment on delivery
搶購	panic buying
缺貨，脫銷	out of stock
一站式購物，一站式服務	one-stop shopping

Exercises 練習題

Discussion Questions 思考題

1.What is timeshare?

2.What services or products does RCI offer to its customers?

3.Why do we say that RCI, as a timeshare exchange company, has powerful and vital advantages for the new millennium?

4.How important is the call center to RCI as a distribution channel?

5.Is it logical and beneficial for RCI to develop an e-commerce strategy?

Sentence Translation 單句翻譯練習

1.隨著越來越多的中國人旅遊消費方式（consumer mode）從「走馬觀花」

（merely touring around and gazing）步入「娛樂休閒」（recreation and leisure），中國巨大的「分時度假」消費市場潛力正日益突現（prominent）。

2.分時度假概念和其產品於90年代末由英美企業傳入（introduce）中國。2001年，RCI中國會員達到2500人，加盟RCI的酒店或度假村13個。

3.由於分時度假者與度假村之間建立了穩定的服務關係，度假村可以根據客人在度假、社交、商務接待等方面的要求提供個性化訂製（customized）服務。

4.顧客可以用自己購買的時段（time slots）去「交換」同屬於一個交換服務網路中的任何一家酒店或度假村的另一個時段，從而達到前往不同地方旅遊住宿的目的。

5.北京地區已經有專門經營分時度假產品銷售業務的公司成立，它不參與分時度假房產的開發（development），只負責銷售、推廣，經營的產品仍為傳統類型的分時度假產品。

6.分時度假是現今旅遊業中成長最快的一個行業，過去10年裡，分時度假計劃的銷售額每年增長16%，分時度假業在全球的營業額（turnover）達到67億美元。

7.中國人口基數龐大（enormous base），占全球人口的四分之一，分時度假市場前景廣闊（broad prospects），並且國內的休假制度（holiday system）已經開始實施。

8.越來越多的消費者對分時度假產品的靈活性提出了更高的要求。比如，有的消費者希望每年居住時間能少於一週，有的則希望能自由出租部分單元。

Passage Translation 段落翻譯練習

When a project is confined to a single site, the marketing of an urban timeshare development is a much more difficult problem. The key issue is balancing the need to generate leads and achieve a high conversion rate, whilst minimizing marketing costs. The Manhattan Club, for example, sends targeted mailings through credit card companies, and advertises in publications such as theatre brochures and broadsheets. The timeshare achieves a 20-25 percent conversion rate with 400-500 families visiting the site a week.

The Edinburgh Residence, on the other hand, uses a third-party company to do its marketing. Like The Manhattan Club, it relies on direct mail and displayed advertisements in the broadsheets. However, it also gains a substantial proportion of its customers through in-house affinity relationships in the form of promotional deals. Its total marketing costs amount to only 18 percent of the cost base, which is substantially lower than the industry as a whole. Conversion rates are approximately 30 percent, in contrast to the average market rate of approximately 15 percent.

Lesson 30 Cross-cultural Tourism Marketing 跨文化旅遊營銷

導讀：

　　全球化已經成為當今世界的一個重要趨勢。旅遊企業應當充分認識到文化多樣性給營銷活動帶來的影響，並制定具有針對性的營銷策略來應對全球市場。本篇文章主要介紹了文化多樣性在全球營銷中的重要地位，文化因素對消費行為等方面產生的影響，以及在跨文化背景下旅遊市場的營銷策略。

Cultural Influence on Tourism Marketing

Culture is the human-made part of human environment. It is the combination of knowledge, beliefs, art, morals, laws, customs, and habits acquired by humans as members of society.

Since culture deals with a group's design for living, it is necessary for the enterprises with the aim at international tourism market to study the cultural role in the foreign marketing. Since the aim of marketing is the satisfaction of consumer needs and wants at a profit(註1), the successful marketer is actually a good student of culture. What a marketer deals with is the culture of the people (the market). When designing a product, the style, uses, and other related marketing activities must be made culturally acceptable. In fact, culture is pervasive in all marketing activities — in pricing, promotion, channels of distribution, product, packaging, and styling. And the judgment of a marketer's success is made in a cultural context for acceptance, resistance, or rejection(註2).

Tourism, one of the largest businesses in the world, is even more influenced by cultural diversities than other industries. Tourism is not uniform across the globe(註3). While most tourists visit industrialized countries, they are increasingly visiting those developing countries. Therefore, frequent cross-cultural contacts of tourists in a foreign land are inevitable.

Elements of Culture

In his book Man and His Works, Melvin Herskovits classifies the elements of culture into five categories. They are:

◆ Material culture

· Technology

· Economics

◆ Social institutions

· Social organization

- Education

- Political structures

◆ Humans and the universe

- Belief system

◆ Aesthetics

- Graphic and plastic arts

- Folklore

- Music, drama, and dance

◆ Language

Material Culture

Material culture influences the level of demand, the quality and types of products demanded, and the means of production of these goods and their distribution. Particularly, economic characteristics and distribution of income may limit the desirability of products. Luxurious tourist products are acceptable in some high-income households, but in those low-income households, they might be unwanted because disposable income could be spent more meaningfully on clothing, food, shelter or transportation(註4). According to the report paper written by William J. Allett for Bureau of Transportation Statistics, U.S. Department of Transportation, when traveling long distance low-income adults under 65 more often travel intercity to visit friends and relatives and for personal business than other income groups. The paper also shows that low-income individuals travel shorter distances than people in higher income groups. Most of this is related to the fact that the low-income individuals travel much less often by air. Low-income individuals stay longer than other groups when they travel long distance, however. Low-income people averaged 5.2 nights per trip compared with 3.9 nights for high-income persons. Longer stays are associated to some extent with the fact that low-income individuals travel more often to visit friends and relatives. Trips tend to be longer in duration; business trips tend to be short.

Social Institution

Social organization, education, and political structures can influence the way in which people relate to one another, organize their activities to live in harmony with one another. The position of men and women in society, the family, social classes, group behavior, and age groups are interpreted differently within every culture. For example, travel advertising in culturally divided Canada pictures a wife alone for the English audience but a man and wife together for the French segments of the population because the French are traditionally more closely bound by family ties. Another interesting cross-cultural tourism example is that of promoting India to the U.S. tourist market. The cultural difference between India and the United States provides an explanation for the campaign conducted and the poor response received. India and the United States differ considerably in two dimensions: individualism and power. American individualism requires that all promotional appeals be directed toward an American traveler; the message must be addressed to and made relevant to the individual as well as reflect friendliness and informality(註5). The prospective American traveler needs to be assured of adequate free time to relax or explore, ample opportunities for shopping, and the flexibility to select activities that suit the individual(註6). The fun aspect of vacation travel should be emphasized. The original Indian approach that stressed typical Indian values failed; the revised approach that appealed to American values was considerably more successful.

Humans and the Universe

The influence of belief or religion cannot be overestimated(註7), because belief or religion influences people's outlook on life, choice of food and beverage, acceptance or rejection of promotional messages, etc. A marketer has to take religious factors into his consideration(註8) when he advertises tourist products in a certain nation, and never offend those religious customers. For example, McDonald's 100 percent pure vegetarian dishes served in India demonstrate its adaptation to Hindu requirement of forbidding the consumption of beef as well as to local consumers' taste.

Aesthetics

Aesthetics are of particular interest to the marketer. Insensitivity to aesthetic values can offend, create a negative impression, and, in general, render marketing efforts ineffective(註9). Strong symbolic meanings may be overlooked if one is not familiar with a culture's aesthetic values. The Chinese, for example, revere the dragon as being auspicious for it is said to be the governor of rainfalls in Chinese culture; in Western culture, however, dragon is portrayed as a mysterious animal. The Japanese adore the crane as being very lucky for it is said to live a thousand years; however, the number four should be completely avoided since the word for four, shi, is also the Japanese word for death.

Language

Good communication plays an important role in achieving effective marketing, and good command of a certain language is a key to the good communication(註10). A dictionary translation does not equal to idiomatic interpretation, and seldom will the dictionary translation suffice(註11). For example, one airline's advertising campaign designed to promote its plush leather seats urged customers to "fly on leather"; when translated for its Hispanic and Latin American tourists, it told passengers to "fly naked". Language is regarded as the most difficult cultural element to master, but it is the most important to study in an effort to acquire some degree of empathy. One authority

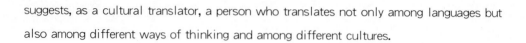

suggests, as a cultural translator, a person who translates not only among languages but also among different ways of thinking and among different cultures.

Cross-Cultural Marketing Mix

In cross-cultural marketing the marketing mix consists of a set of tools or strategies designed to meet customers' expected values in a manner that is in agreement with(註12) their culture. These strategies must match the customers' cultural preferences and expectations. In their paper Cross-Cultural Tourism Marketing, Po-Ju Chen and Abraham Pizam elaborate on several strategies, the most important of which are as follows.

Product and Service Strategy

There are three approaches used in the design of cross-cultural product/service strategies: global, national and combined. The global approach takes the stand that the world is a single market(註13) and, therefore, a standard products and marketing strategy on a global basis is more advantageous (e.g. Hilton International). The national approach focuses on designing products and the layout of marketing strategies according to specific nations (e.g. Sol Melia Hotels). The combined approach assumes that globalization is feasible for some of their products and other products are nation or culture-specific (e.g. McDonald's, Best Western International Hotels).

People's tastes worldwide on some products and service are on the converging path, but corporations must comply with certain national regulations and local cultural considerations. The use of native motifs is a good example for reinforcing the local flavor in global brand images. For example, Witkowski et al. (2003, p.77) report that a Starbuck's in Shanghai has a Ming Dynasty facade and the entrances of some Chinese KFC restaurants are guarded by full-size, fiberglass models of Colonel Sanders who, in his Asian reincarnation, looks a little portly like a Buddha.

Branding Strategy

Branding has an important role in service companies. Brand enables consumers to visualize and understand the intangible aspects of the service including the quality of the people who provide the service(註14). Hilton Hotels uses the service brand to guide their geographical and culturally different markets. For example, Hilton Hotel Corporation's service brand Equilibrium was aimed at catering to all types of customers. But its Japanese service brand Wa No Kutsurogi was tailored specifically for serving Japanese tourists and business travelers.

Pricing Strategy

There are several cross-cultural considerations when planning pricing strategies. Consumers' cultural norms and the host country political, social and legal environments (e.g. state-controlled prices and consumers'attitudes toward quality and price relationships) affect pricing strategy.

The propensity to haggle varies from culture to culture(註15). In many Latin America, for instance, cultural attitudes favor price haggling; while in Europe and the USA, haggling is not as common. In some developing countries, where imported products are scarce, a low-priced product such as a budget hotel could be viewed as low quality. Therefore, marketers have to take all these factors into their consideration when they conduct pricing strategy.

Promotion Strategy

This strategy consists of a number of promotion mix components that marketing professionals can choose from. First, in order to achieve smooth communication, a company must try to remove language barrier and avoid source effect by downplaying its country of origin in cross-cultural marketing. Secondly, advertising strategy should include the developing of a corporate platform with possibilities to incorporate meaningful host country extensions so that building a relationship and trust with consumers is possible. Thirdly, personal selling processes vary from culture to culture, so cultivating relationships and building trust are essential skills required for sales personnel to do personal selling in this type of cultural environment. Fourthly, to gain positive publicity, hospitality and travel companies may engage in activities such as press releases, event sponsorship, community involvement and good will activities. The involvement with the host country community and government, especially with countries that have significant controls over foreign investments, is essential for building long-term relationships and enhancing corporate images.

Distribution Strategy

Many companies such as hotels or airlines use their central reservation systems to facilitate sales directly to customers. Customers may use toll-free telephone numbers to make reservations or access the company's website through the Internet. Besides, many hospitality companies also provide localized websites with several languages.

Vocabulary 內文詞彙

pervasive	普遍深入的
inevitable	不可避免的
aesthetics	美學，審美學
punctuality	準時
dimension	維度
strategy	策略

reinforce	加強
visualize	想像
equilibrium	平衡，均衡
propensity	傾向
haggle	討價還價
motif	主題，主旨
segment	片段，組成部分
prospective	預期的
revere	尊敬，敬畏
auspicious	吉祥的，幸運的
idiomatic	符合語言習慣的
empathy	同感，共鳴
converging	趨同的
feasible	可行的
downplay	不予重視

Notes to the Text 內文註釋

1.Since the aim of marketing is the satisfaction of consumer needs and wants at a profit：既然市場營銷的目的是滿足消費者的需求同時使企業獲利。

2.And the judgment of a marketer's success is made in a cultural context for acceptance, resistance, or rejection.

對商家成敗的評判往往是看他在一定的文化背景下是否被接納、抵制或拒絕。

3.Tourism is not uniform across the glob.

全球的旅遊業並不是同一個模式的。

4.disposable income could be spent more meaningfully on clothing, food, shelter or transportation：可支配的收入如果花在衣食住行方面可能更有意義。

5.the message must be addressed to and made relevant to the individual as well as reflect friendliness and informality：這樣的訊息不僅要反映出友好和隨意，並且要針對個人，並與個人相關。

6.The prospective American traveler needs to be assured of adequate free time to relax or explore, ample opportunities for shopping, and the flexibility to select activities that suit the individual.

潛在的美國遊客需要有充分的自由時間進行休閒遊和探險，有大量購物的機會，同時還要保證他們可以靈活自由地選擇適合自己的活動方式。

7.The influence of belief or religion cannot be overestimated：絕不能低估了宗教或信仰的影響。

8.take religious factors into his consideration：將宗教因素考慮在內。

9.Insensitivity to aesthetic values can offend, create a negative impression, and, in general, render marketing efforts ineffective.

對審美觀的麻痺會冒犯他人、造成不良影響，並且會使所有的營銷努力化為泡影。

10.and good command of a certain language is a key to the good communication：熟練地掌握一門語言是成功交流的關鍵。

11.and seldom will the dictionary translation suffice：只憑詞典翻譯（對於成功的交流）是不夠的。

12.in agreement with：相符，一致。

13.The global approach takes the stand that the world is a single market.

全球營銷方式的基本觀點是，整個世界就是一個大市場。

14.Brand enables consumers to visualize and understand the intangible aspects of the service including the quality of the people who provide the service.

品牌使消費者能夠想像出並瞭解服務中無形的成分，如服務人員的素質等。

15.The propensity to haggle varies from culture to culture.

不同的文化對討價還價的認可程度各有不同。

★ ★ ★ ★

Useful Words and Expressions 實用詞彙和表達方式

全球精英消費品市場   global elite consumer segment

全球機會戰略   global niche strategy

全球標準化戰略　　　　　　global standardization strategy

全球青少年市場　　　　　　global teenage segment

全球化　　　　　　　　　　globalization

全球市場擴張　　　　　　　global-market expansion

競爭性平價定價法　　　　　going-rate/competitive parity pricing

政府管制　　　　　　　　　government regulation

產業動態　　　　　　　　　industry dynamics

產業評估　　　　　　　　　industry evaluation

產業演變　　　　　　　　　industry evolution

商業資訊廣告　　　　　　　infomercials

資訊時代　　　　　　　　　information age

資訊蒐集　　　　　　　　　information search

國際分銷管道　　　　　　　international channels

Exercises 練習題

Discussion Questions 思考題

1.Discuss "Culture is pervasive in all marketing activities."

2.Why should a successful marketer be a good student of culture?

3.Give examples to illustrate how social institutions influence tourism marketing in a variety of ways.

4.Visit various national and global brand websites and determine whether they have a domestic, global or multinational orientation. Take some of them for instance to examine how many countries they cater to.

5.Prepare a cultural analysis for a specific country and tourist product.

Sentence Translation 單句翻譯練習

1.開發宗教文化資源,對旅遊業的發展具有重要的意義;而旅遊業的發展,也有利於宗教文化的繼承、傳播、交流和研究。

2.目前,各種宗教信徒總數約占世界人口的60%以上,許多國家都非常重視宗教文化資源的開發,因為人們虔誠(pious)的宗教信仰和強烈的求知慾望都會轉化為旅遊動機。

3.如果具有某一宗教信仰的人占到相當大的比重,那麼投資的飯店必須有相適應的設施及膳食供應,絕對不能對客人的宗教信仰和風俗習慣有所違背和觸犯。

4.每一種促銷方法都有其適用性,而且各國對促銷方式的限制也有所不同。

5.由於歐洲的迪士尼最初拒絕採取適應歐洲顧客的飲食服務方式,其虧損額在1993年達到十億美元。為了改變現狀,歐洲的管理層對菜單進行了改革。

6.麥當勞是一家非常成功的跨國企業,因為企業管理人員認識到,在給顧客提供相同的飲食體驗的同時,也必須密切關注當地的飲食習慣。

7.歐洲的迪士尼從麥當勞的全球化成功中學到了兩點。第一,如何制定戰略並在本地化(localize)過程中採取適當的戰術。第二,如何處理歐洲和美國飲食文化的重大差異。

8.文化差異會帶來無形的（intangible）貿易障礙，所以精明的國際推銷商懂得如何兼顧全球和本地顧客；同時，那些不同的文化也創造了新的市場機會。

Passage Translation 段落翻譯練習

In conclusion, when marketing hospitality/tourism products cross-culturally it is necessary to adopt the "riffle approach" which matches each individual marketing strategy with the values and norms of the target market. However, this approach can be successful only if the specific target market's needs and wants can be clearly identified. The unique cultural profile of each target market plays an essential role in the identification of the target market's needs and wants.

Lesson 31 Marketing for Convention Tourism 會議旅遊營銷

導讀：

眾所周知，雖然自從有人類以來，人們就有了聚集、開會的歷史，但會議旅遊業的真正發展卻是從20世紀開始的。近年來，伴隨世界經濟和技術的發展，會議旅遊業在世界各國都呈現出興旺蓬勃之勢。本篇文章簡要介紹了會議旅遊市場的兩大支柱客戶，並詳細闡述了會議目的地的營銷組合。

Marketing convention tourism requires, first, an understanding of the customers of the meeting and conventions industry, and second, the principal elements of the convention destination marketing mix.

Two Main Customers in the Market

Corporations

The corporate market is the largest single market segment, accounting for over 65 percent of meetings (Lawson, 2000). Corporate meetings are essentially driven by the needs of individual businesses. They take a variety of forms, including board, management, and shareholder's meetings; training seminars; meetings with partners, suppliers and clients; sales conference; product launches; strategic planning retreat; and incentives.

The corporate market has a number of unique characteristics. Corporate meetings tend to be small with delegate numbers generally fewer than 100. Furthermore, they are mostly short in duration. Corporate meetings are also characterized by short lead times, typically much less than a year(註1). In the United States, the average length of time to plan corporate meetings was 6.7 months in 2000. In view of the relatively small size of corporate meetings, most are typically held in hotels, with the remainder taking place in dedicated conference centers, training centers, universities or the company's own facilities. Due to the inherent nature of incentive meetings, the venues for them are often rather unusual and of high standards.

Associations

The largest meetings and conventions held throughout the world each year are not conducted by individual corporations, but by the enormous number of associations that exist to present and promote the interests of their members. The association market incorporates professional and trade associations, voluntary associations and societies, charities, religious organizations, political parties and trade unions. Associations hold a variety of meetings, including training and development programs, networking functions and seminars. The most visible and desirable gatherings, from a destination point of view, however, are the annual conventions that can attract thousands of delegates.

Even though associations are typically of a nonprofit nature, annual conventions often have a profit objective. Apart from a professionally run convention, the selection of an appropriate convention destination that can boost attendance numbers is critical to achieve profit objectives. This is especially important because, in contrast to the corporate market, delegates at association conventions must cover the cost for attending themselves and may also decide to bring their families(註2). Attractive partner and social programs in addition to pre-and post-tour options are important in view of the influence family members can exert on the potential attendee's decision to participate in a convention.

Higher attendance numbers and longer duration for the association market are further distinguishing characteristics from the corporate sector. Conventions attracting several thousand delegates are common. In Las Vegas in 1999, sixty conventions attracted more than 7000 delegates each, the largest of which was attended by more than 100000 delegates. In view of the size of conventions, the diversity of member needs, associations' decision-making procedures and resulting complexity of association conventions, lead times can be substantial. According to a survey, in 1992, the average lead time in the United States was 3.9 years. Ten years or more is also not unusual for the largest conventions that are restricted to very few cities that can accommodate them(註3).

"7Ps" Mode in Convention Destination Marketing Mix

The convention destination marketing mix are represented by the "7Ps":

◆ Product,

◆ Place,

◆ Promotion,

◆ Price,

◆ People,

◆ Physical Evidence,

◆ Process.

Product

Convention tourism involves the buying and selling of convention destination services. Corporate or association customers seek meeting and related facilities provided by alternative destination suppliers to satisfy their need for holding gatherings of various kinds. The convention tourism product, therefore, is clearly a service. More specifically, the product is the total experience that the client and its employees or members receive when a convention is held at a particular destination. Although various meeting, accommodation and other facilities are central to this service, they are not the product per se; that is, the client does not purchase these facilities. Rather, these physical features of a convention destination provide the ability to deliver the convention tourism product (services), but they do not form part of the product itself. Hence, the convention tourism product is created from the combination of physical facilities, branding (destination image), service performance and quality, accessory services (e.g. audio-visual services), and packaging. Successful convention destination marketing recognizes the product as consisting of all influences affecting the convention experience of the client(註4).

Place

The place element of the marketing mix relates to all factors that are involved in connecting convention customers to convention products. The traditional marketing channel roles of wholesaling and retailing play no part in the meeting industry because there is little scope for the sorting, assembling and reselling of convention services. Most transactions are handled on a direct basis between the user of convention facilities and the provider, with assistance often provided by meeting planners, destination management companies, and convention and visitors bureaus(註5). These intermediaries, however, do play a critical role in the selling function and can significantly influence the convention site selection decision.In this context, the reputation of the convention destination and word of mouth are critical too. Transportation is also an important place element, but in this instance, it brings the customer to the product rather than distributing the product to the customer, as occurs in many other marketing situations(註6).

Promotion

Convention destinations engage in all forms of promotional activity(註7). Destinations often advertise their convention facilities in meeting-industry magazines. Sales promotions are also offered to attract conventions through price discounts, subsidies, and other inducements. Public relations and publicity assist in developing a strong, positive image of a successful convention destination. However, personal selling is probably the most important promotional method used in the meetings and conventions industry. Personal contact and interaction between sales representatives of a destination and meeting planners, association executives, and professional conference organizers are vital elements of the promotional effort. Indeed, for most conventions, a site visit, including the assessment of meeting, accommodation, and other facilities, is critical.

Price

The price of a destination as a convention site is a critical marketing variable. Major convention destinations such as New York, London, Hong Kong and Sydney are normally more expensive, as the higher cost of real estate and facilities drives up the price of meeting space, accommodations, and the cost of other services(註8). In recent years, so-called "second-tier" cities have become more price competitive while still offering good meeting facilities in less congested but attractive environments(註9). Second-tier cities are suburbs of major cities or smaller cities that differ from fist-tier cities in the hotel room inventory, the size of the convention center, and the citywide hotel rack rates.

Although clearly important, the prices of meeting and accommodation services are only one part of the total price of a destination. Marketers must also consider the accessibility and cost of transportation to the destination, local destination, food services etc. Although price cannot be set and controlled by a convention destination in quite the same way as occurs in other product contexts, it is nevertheless a significant marking variable.

People

The role of people is key in the successful marketing of services because the convention tourism product is, in essence, an experience(註10). The experience of an association or corporation holding a convention or meeting occurs in real time simultaneously with the delivery and performance of the service by the destination(註11). Therefore, the actions of service personnel and their interactions with customers are critical in governing overall service quality. Hence, service personnel perform a marking function, not just an operations function. The recruitment, training, and motivation of all service personnel affecting the convention experience are therefore vital. Service recognition and reward programs are often implemented by destinations to acknowledge the important role of people. Indeed, all human interaction, not just with employees, must be considered. For this reason the friendliness and hospitality of local residents are also important.

Physical Evidence

The convention service experience occurs in the context of an inanimate environment. The physical design and layout of the convention facilities is clearly of paramount importance, but the importance of decor, ambiance, lighting, signage, temperature control, aesthetics, equipment, employee dress, etc. should not be overlooked. Indeed, all physical evidence conveys important information about the type and level of service anticipated and perceived. This perspective can be extended beyond the meeting space itself. The whole feeling or ambiance of the city hosting the convention is also critical. The climate, perceptions of individual safety and general attractiveness of the city are significantly shaped by all elements of physical evidence that the delegate experiences.

Process

The final element of the extended marketing mix recognizes that the delivery and operation of the convention service experience occurs through a process. A convention product is produced in the presence of the convention customer. Consequently, the convention customer's experience is not just a function of some end result(註12). The whole flow and mix of activities from the beginning to the end of the process will govern the customer's overall experience and perception of the destination as a convention site(註13). Indeed, this process does not begin and end with the convention itself. The selling and planning stages leading up to the convention and the post convention activities, such as follow-up marketing research, satisfaction surveys, and resolution of any complaints, all shape the perceived quality of the experience.

Conclusion

Continued economic development, world trade and globalization will stimulate continued growth in convention tourism, spurring even greater competition among convention destinations. Cites now have to market themselves more aggressively than ever before to attract major convention and other events. In this environment, the practice of relationship marketing and an improved cross-cultural understanding will take on critical roles.

Destinations that are consistently able to meet or exceed the expectations of their convention customers enjoy a strong reputation and positive word of mouth, which leads to repeat business and new customers that can become an important source of referral business. Many associations rotate the location of conventions to provide a variety of meeting environments. Nevertheless, destinations that enjoy a strong relationship with association executives and meeting planners can expect continuity and stability in their convention customers. The costs of serving the needs of repeat customers are also lower, increasing the attractiveness of maintaining strong relationships. Of course, some meeting planners serve the needs of several associations; destinations that are able to develop strong relationship with these planners enjoy a competitive advantage.

The global competition among convention sites will require convention marketers to increase their sensitivity to cultural and social issues, particularly in the case of international conventions spanning diverse cultural, religious and social groups. Convention destinations must develop cross-cultural skills in their efforts to position themselves as a major host site for international conventions.

Vocabulary 內文詞彙

convention destination   會議舉行地

corporate market   公司市場

board   董事會

seminar	研討會
sales conference	銷售會議
product launches	產品發布會
retreat	靜休會
conference center	會議中心
association market	協會、社團市場
society	社團，協會
trade union	工會
networking	人際交流
annual convention	年會
exert	產生影響，施加壓力
diversity	差異，多樣性
decision-making procedure	決策過程，決策步驟
complexity	複雜性
lead time	籌備時間
per se	本質上，本身
accessory	輔助的

intermediary	中介，中間人
site selection	選址
inducement	優惠，誘惑
assessment	評估，估價
real estate	房地產，不動產
first-tier city	一類城市
second-tier city	二類城市
recruitment	招聘，補充員工
inanimate	單調的，無生氣的
paramount	極為重要的
lighting	照明，燈光效果
follow-up	後續的
continued growth	持續增長
spur	刺激
relationship marketing	關係營銷
cross-cultural	跨文化的
referral	舉薦的

rotate	輪換
repeat customer	回頭客

Notes to the Text 內文註釋

1.Corporate meetings are also characterized by short lead times, typically much less than a year.

公司會議的另一個特點是籌備時間比較短，通常少於一年。

2.delegates at association conventions must cover the cost for attending themselves and may also decide to bring their families：協會會議的與會者必須自己支付出席會議的費用，有時他們還會攜帶家庭成員同來。

3.Ten years or more is also not unusual for the largest conventions that are restricted to very few cities that can accommodate them.

對大型會議來說，籌備期長達10年或10年以上的並不少見，這些會議通常只侷限於那些具備舉辦能力的極少數城市。

4.Successful convention destination marketing recognizes the product as consisting of all influences affecting the convention experience of the client.

成功的會議地點旅遊營銷應該把產品看做是由所有影響與會者經歷的各種因素的總和。

5.Most transactions are handled on a direct basis between the user of convention facilities and the provider, with assistance often provided by meeting planners, destination management companies, and convention and visitors bureaus.

大部分的交易是在會議策劃者、目的地管理公司以及會議和遊客管理局的幫助下，在會議設施的使用者和提供者之間直接進行的。

6.it brings the customer to the product rather than distributing the product to the customer, as occurs in many other marketing situations：它把顧客帶到產品面前，而不是像其他營銷那樣把產品送交給顧客。

7.Convention destinations engage in all forms of promotional activity：會議目的地會從事所有形式的促銷活動。

8.as the higher cost of real estate and facilities drives up the price of meeting space, accommodations, and the cost of other services：因為土地、設施的較高成本促使會議地點、膳宿以及其他服務的價格都上漲。

9.In recent years, so-called "second-tier" cities have become more price competitive while still offering good meeting facilities in less congested but attractive environments.近年來，一些被認為是「二類」的城市越來越有價格上的競爭力，它們不太擁擠，環境優美，而且也能提供良好的會議設施。

10.The role of people is key in the successful marketing of services because the convention tourism product is, in essence, an experience.

人是服務營銷成功的關鍵因素，因為會議旅遊產品從實質上說是一種經歷。

11.occurs in real time simultaneously with：與……同時發生。

12.Consequently, the convention customer's experience is not just a function of some end result.

因此，會議顧客的經歷不僅只是一些最終產物所產生的影響。

13.The whole flow and mix of activities from the beginning to the end of the process will govern the customer's overall experience and perception of the destination as a convention site.從頭到尾整個會議過程中所舉辦的各種活動以及進展情況都將對顧客的總體經歷和對會議舉辦地的看法產生很大影響。

Useful Words and Expressions 實用詞彙和表達方式

會議，代表大會	conference
會議，年會，例會	convention
博覽會，展覽會	exposition
會議策劃人	meeting planner
行業展示會，展覽會	trade show
全體大會	general session
研討會	workshop
論壇	forum
座談會	symposium
研究會	seminar
座談小組	panel
辯論會	debate

學術討論會	colloquium
網路會議	Web casting
年會，年度大會	annual convention
全國性會議	national meeting
新產品發布會	new product introduction
管理層會議	management meeting
獎勵會議	incentive meeting
商務會議	business meeting
教育會議	educational meeting
宗教會議	religious meeting
董事會和委員會會議	board and committee meeting
開幕會	opening meeting
全會	plenary session
分會	session
歡迎招待會	welcome reception
會間休息	break
會議前期準備時間	lead time

會議入場方式	admission system
臺面型展覽	table top exhibit
分區型展覽	area exhibit
展位型展覽	booth exhibit
島形展位	island booth
半島形展位	peninsula booth
環形展位	perimeter wall booth
線形展位，排式展位	in-line booth/standard booth/linear booth

Exercises 練習題

Discussion Questions 思考題

1.What are the characteristics of corporate market?

2.What are the characteristics of association market?

3.Describe the differences between the corporate market and association market.

4.How do you understand the element of physical evidence in convention marketing mix?

5.What impact will the convention tourism bring on the local economy?

Sentence Translation 單句翻譯練習

1.近年來，在旅遊客源市場（tourist generating market）有兩個組成部分發展迅速，一是老齡（aging）旅遊者，二是有特殊興趣（special interest）的旅遊者。

2.旅遊業的顯著特徵之一是具有季節性，即淡、旺、平三季。

3.向顧客提供全方位服務的旅行社要代售機票、遊船票、火車票和長途汽車票，代租汽車（car rental）、代辦旅館食宿及包價旅遊，也要提供輔助性的服務，如旅遊保險、旅遊支票和外幣兌換（foreign currency exchange）等。

4.旅遊者的湧入，無論其數量大小，都會對接待地區造成一定的影響，其影響程度取決於旅遊者的數量以及這一地區所吸引的遊客類型。

5.中國目前的包價旅遊有全包價（full inclusive）和半包價（semi-inclusive）兩種。

6.導遊員一般有四種：全陪（national guide）、地陪（local guide）、領隊（tour leader）和講解員（lecturer）。

7.導遊員始終要以熱情好客的眼光關注旅遊者、預測旅遊者需求並及時提供服務，使旅遊者時刻感受到導遊員在關心自己。

8.景區可以是風景名勝區，如北京的八達嶺長城，也可以是城市，如義大利的羅馬、中國的西安這樣的著名風景和歷史文化名城。

Passage Translation 段落翻譯練習

The growth of the convention industry since the 1950s is due to a number of factors on both the supply and demand sides. Some of these factors are closely related to factors that supported the growth of tourism in general. For example, the increase in disposable income, the greater propensity to travel, increased leisure time, and improvements in transportation and technology have all facilitated the growth of the convention industry.

Resulting from the greater demand for conventions and meetings and in view of the industry's potential economic benefits, many destinations around the world invested heavily in infrastructure development. National and local convention bureaus actively promote destinations' facilities and other attributes that influence the site selection process. Furthermore, industry representation and coordination through international, national, and regional associations have also improved significantly.

Today, the convention industry is regarded as one of the most buoyant sectors of the tourism industry. It is least responsive to price changes and helps to reduce "peak-trough" seasonal patterns. The convention industry has the potential to attract high-spending visitors who often stay longer at and make repeat visits to a destination. Furthermore, it is seen as prestigious to host international conferences, with tourism authorities throughout the world being keen to attract convention visitors to their destinations. Yet it is also important to consider the effects of economic conditions on the growth of the industry to truly understand the development of the sector.

Lesson 32 Marketing Festival，Fairs and Special Events
節慶、展會和特別活動營銷

導讀：

節慶、展會和特別活動不是一般的旅遊產品。隨著會展業的發展，這一特殊旅遊產品在中國越來越受到重視。面對這一特殊產品，我們應該如何做好營銷工作呢？本篇文章為此詳細地闡述了七大注意事項。

Today's festivals, fairs and special events are more varied and sophisticated than ever before. Marketing these unique types of events requires unique and innovative tactics. In other words, the success of an event may not only depend on the type of event, the star attraction, or the cause of the event(註1), but also on how well a marketer takes advantage of certain factors of the event. These factors include:

Location,

Competition,

Weather,

Cost,

Entertainment,

Media,

Schedule.

Location

The selection and marketing of the location has a significant impact on attendance and the resulting success of an event. Is it centrally located or in a distant suburb? Is there easy road access from interstate highways or is there a subway stop within walking distance(註2)? Promoting easy access, a central location, or a new venue can contribute to great attendance at your event. In addition, marketing the convenience of the location can increase acceptance of the event, and combining the historic or resort attributes can excite the potential attendees.

Competition

Promoting your event as unique, different and better than the competitors' can be as important as the event itself. A marketer needs to advertise and promote the advantages of the event by showcasing the interesting and unique features. This requires a fully prepared marketing strategy. Sometimes using a marketing strategy in which you point out your differences can be effective, but there is also a risk in doing so(註3). To name the competition can only give these competitors credibility and recognition(註4). Unlike consumer products, which advertise the fact that it is of the same quality as other brand names but costs less, it is hard to use this as a marketing advantage in events.

When an event is successful, there can, and will be, imitators who market their events the same way, copying advertisement and themes as well as the look of the events. This can not only add to confusion for the public, but also hurt both the original event and the imitator in the end. Lollapalooza, a summer concert tour featuring a very diverse assortment of musical rock groups attracting fans in their teens and twenties(註5), became a surprise runaway success in the concert business, breaking attendance records across the United States(註6). After the second year of the tour, there were countless imitators marketing their tours in similar fashions, eventually giving music fans comparable choices(註7).

Weather

Unlike a consumer product that is marketed on its own virtue, the weather can be an advantage or disadvantage in selling a special event. Weather can set the mood for the participants or consumers of the events(註8). For example, consumer ski and travel shows typically take place in early November, a time that enables attendees to preview the latest ski equipment and ski resorts. Research has shown that, when the weather was cold, the show's attendance increased measurably. On the other hand, when the weather was unseasonably warm during the show(註9), attendance declined dramatically. In these cases, the weather had a significant effect on the outcome of the event.

Indoor shows or events can be adversely affected if the weather is ideal. However, when the weather turns undesirable, it can keep people from outdoor leisure activities and bring them indoors to special events. A sophisticated marketer will be ready in these situations with advertisements on standby. When rain is forecast, the marketer will run local radio or TV advertisements promoting the public to come indoors in the wet weather.

There are hundreds of arts-and-crafts shows that are held in outdoor locations with exhibitors under portable pop-up tents(註10). The success of these events depends on good weather, but everyone participates in these events with this understanding. One way marketers can ensure their success in promoting events that can be affected by the weather is to pre-sell as many tickets as possible, sometimes at a deep discount, to guarantee attendance at these events(註11). At the Vintage Virginia Wine Festival, tickets at a discount are sold in advance to guarantee substantial attendance. The success of marketing a golf tournament is better in May than in November.

Cost

The word "free" is used in fair, festival and other special event advertisements because it attracts attention. If the cost is set at an attractive level, it needs to be included in the advertising. Cost and price can also be determining factors in marketing events. When advertising a show, a marketer wants to be able to attract as wide an audience as possible to the event(註12). For this reason, some events and shows that sell front-row seats at a premium do not even list the price of these tickets in advertisements but instead say "special seating available"(註13).

Sometimes a strategy with a high price can be successful when the event is positioned as something special. At other times, a value price that a larger, broader market can afford would be more successful(註14).

The use of coupons can also make an event more attractive. When planning an event, the marketer generally tries to find a retail partner that can distribute discount coupons to attract a larger audience. Typically, retailers that feature these discount coupons are supermarket chains, drug stores, fast-food restaurants, and even pizza delivery chains. Another important source of discount coupons is in print advertising. By tagging a coupon in a print advertisement, there is the inclination for the public to tear out the advertisement, thus adding another reminder about the upcoming event(註15).

Entertainment

The success of an event is also dependent on the marketing of the entertainment. There are many types of entertainment that can be marketed in a variety of ways. For big-name stars, an interview on a radio station and a press release announcing tickets going on sale are effective for a quick sellout(註16). Different and new types of entertainment, on the other hand, may require larger marketing and public relations budgets.

When "Defending the Caveman", a one-man comedy show, started playing in Washington, DC, there was a need for numerous newspaper advertisements and a public relations campaign to promote this alternative to the typical comedy club show. At the onset of the show, there had never been a truly successful one-man comedy show outside of Broadway. After the show ran in five cities and began to receive strong public relations support and word of mouth(註17), it began selling out across the country, leading to Broadway's longest running comedy show. As the show moved from San Francisco to Dallas to Washington, the marketing was altered and became more sophisticated. What started with newspaper advertisements eventually moved to radio and direct mail.

Media

Certain types of media will help elevate the excitement of events. For visual events, the marketer looks to use television advertisement. When print advertisements are desired, the use of color can lead to extra attention. Radio advertisements can set a mood or a theme and attract attention.

Musical events, for example, are difficult to describe. However, by the use of radio advertisement, prospective spectators can gain a sense as sound is the key to these types of programs.

If you are marketing the annual home and garden show, do not randomly run advertisements in a local newspaper(註18). Instead, target media that have a connection to the event. In the newspaper, target the weekly home or garden section. On radio, promote the event on the Saturday morning garden shows. On television, target cable TV networks like the Home and Garden network. By spending advertising dollars on media that relate directly to the product, you are being efficient with your media dollars(註19). The marketer must look at the event and find the advertising opportunities that best fit the event.

Schedule

The promotion of festivals, fairs and special events requires a different schedule than other types of events. In promoting first-time events, one needs to educate the public to promote the new event. First-time events need to cut through the clutter. The consumer needs to be exposed to many different media, ranging from radio advertisements that heighten interest, to TV advertisements that visualize and excite, to print advertisements that give information, to Web sites that provide a comprehensive overview(註20). In contrast, having a big-name band or movie star at an event will certainly contribute to its success, but needs to be promoted in a different way. There is a seesaw effect in scheduling a proper marketing program for this type of event.

You may want to allow extra time to promote the event. If promotions start too far out, however, it will be difficult to get the market to focus on the event(註21). If promotions start too close to the event, there will not be enough time to educate the audience about your event.

Vocabulary 內文詞彙

innovative	創新的，革新的
tactic	戰術的
contribute to	引起，帶來
showcase	展示
credibility	可信性，信譽度
recognition	讚譽，認可
imitator	模仿者，效仿者
runaway	巨大的，遙遙領先的
consumer product	消費品
adversely	相反地，不利地
special event	特殊活動
standby	待命，備用的

arts-and-crafts show	工藝品展覽會
exhibitor	展商
Wine Festival	葡萄酒節
golf tournament	高爾夫錦標賽
premium	高價的，額外費用的
fast-food restaurant	快餐店
pizza delivery chain	披薩外賣連鎖店
press release	新聞稿
sellout	全部售出，脫銷，客滿
comedy show	喜劇演出
onset	開始
elevate	提升，促進
cable TV	有線電視
heighten	提高，升高
visualize	使形象化
big-name	知名的，著名的，眾所周知的
seesaw	一起一伏的交替過程，輪流

Notes to the Text 內文註釋

1.In other words, the success of an event may not only depend on the type of event, the star attraction, or the cause of the event：換句話說，一個活動的成功與否可能不僅取決於活動的類型、明星的效應或者舉辦活動的原因。

2.Is there easy road access from interstate highways or is there a subway stop within walking distance?

是否可以方便地通達州際高速公路，或附近是否有步行可以到達的地鐵站？

3.Sometimes using a marketing strategy in which you point out your differences can be effective, but there is also a risk in doing so.

有些時候，運用營銷策略突出自己與眾不同的特色可能很奏效，但這種方法也存在著一定的風險。

4.To name the competition can only give these competitors credibility and recognition.

指明競爭的存在只會增加競爭對手的信譽和知名度。

5.a summer concert tour featuring a very diverse assortment of musical rock groups attracting fans in their teens and twenties：一個由多個不同搖滾樂隊參與、對年齡在十幾到二十幾歲的音樂愛好者有很大吸引力的夏季巡迴演唱會。

6.breaking attendance records across the United States：在全美打破觀眾人數紀錄。

7.there were countless imitators marketing their tours in similar fashions，eventually giving music fans comparable choices：無數效仿者運用類似的手段來營銷

他們各自的演出活動，結果使音樂愛好者們有了品質相當的多種選擇。

8.Weather can set the mood for the participants or consumers of the events.

天氣會影響參與者或顧客的心情。

9.when the weather was unseasonably warm during the show：指在推展期間天氣異乎尋常地熱，與時令不合。

10.There are hundreds of arts-and-crafts shows that are held in outdoor locations with exhibitors under portable pop-up tents.

有成百上千的工藝品展會是在室外舉辦的，展商們的展品就放在方便搬運和搭建的活動帳篷裡。

11.sometimes at a deep discount, to guarantee attendance at these events：有時打的折扣非常大以便保證觀眾的數量。

12.a marketer wants to be able to attract as wide an audience as possible to the event：營銷人員想吸引儘可能多的觀眾來參加活動。

13.do not even list the price of these tickets in advertisements but instead say "special seating available"：他們在廣告中甚至都不列出票的價格，只是説「提供特殊座位」。

14.At other times, a value price that a larger, broader market can afford would be more successful.

另一些時候，能夠為較大市場接受的公平價格（策略）會更加成功。

15.By tagging a coupon in a print advertisement, there is the inclination for the public to tear out the advertisement, thus adding another reminder about the upcoming event.

在印刷品廣告中附上一個優惠券，讀者就有可能會撕下優惠券，這樣優惠券就成為另一個提醒讀者參加即將舉辦的活動的東西。

16.For big-name stars, an interview on a radio station and a press release announcing tickets going on sale are effective for a quick sellout.

對於那些有大牌兒明星參加的活動，可以透過做電台採訪或發布新聞稿的方式來告知市場票已開始發售，這些做法對提高售票數量非常有用。a quick sellout：很快銷售一空。

17.After the show ran in five cities and began to receive strong public relations support and word of mouth：在五個城市巡迴演出以後，演出開始贏得了公關方面的有力支持，並獲得了良好口碑。

18.If you are marketing the annual home and garden show, do not randomly run advertisements in a local newspaper.

如果你在為每年一度的家居和園藝展做營銷的話，那麼不要盲目地在當地報紙上做廣告。

19.you are being efficient with your media dollars：你就有效地利用了在廣告上的開支。

20.to Web sites that provide a comprehensive overview：到可以提供更周到全面資訊的網路。

21.If promotions start too far out, however, it will be difficult to get the market to focus on the event.

但是，如果營銷工作開始得太早，那麼就很難讓市場的注意力集中到所策劃的活動上去。

Useful Words and Expressions 實用詞彙和表達方式

信函	letter
傳單	flyer
單頁傳單	single sheet flyer
宣傳冊	brochure
郵遞插頁	mailing inserts
海報	poster
明信片	postcard
街頭演示	street demonstration
電子商務	e-commerce
收入增幅	income range
所在行業	trade or profession
地理位置	geographic location
婚姻狀況	marital status

家庭結構	family size
媒體提示	media alert
報導要求	request for coverage
新聞背景故事	background news story
文件夾	folder
特殊廣告物品	advertising specialty item
公共關係	public relations
交叉促銷	cross promotion
夥伴營銷	partnership marketing
街頭促銷	street promotion

Exercises 練習題

Discussion Questions 思考題

1.How does the selection of location influence the attendance of festival, fairs and special events?

2.What do you think can help cope with the competition in the special event market?

3.Why is the weather element so important in festival and fair events?

4.How to make use of the coupons?

5.When developing a marketing schedule for festivals and fairs, what would you pay attention to?

Sentence Translation 單句翻譯練習

1.傳統節日與一個民族的歷史發展、風俗習慣（custom and folkway）、宗教信仰（religious belief）和道德標準（moral principals of a nation）密切相關。

2.獎勵旅遊（incentive travel）是一些大公司、大企業為獎勵（reward）優秀員工（employee）或零售商（retailer）而組織的旅遊活動。

3.節日慶典活動、民族生活方式和傳統的民俗（folk-custom）活動往往對旅遊者有很大的吸引力。

4.獎勵旅行團一般在購物上的消費大大超過普通旅行團，所以不少獎勵旅行團實際上就是豪華旅遊團（deluxe）。

5.汽車旅行（car-driving travel）是現代很流行的一種旅行方式，這種方式使旅行變得更加隨意，旅遊者可以自由控制行車路線和途中停車地點。

6.活動的宣傳促銷技巧包括廣告、公共關係促銷、交互促銷（夥伴促銷）、街頭促銷、引人注目的活動（stunts）和公益節日的公共服務（public service for cause-related events）。

7.互聯網提供了一系列（a wide array of）為市場營銷節約成本（cost-saving）的方法，透過在網上將資訊傳達給更多的人（reach more people），廣告開支獲得了更大的收益。

8.不管是大型購物中心（a shopping mall）的隆重開張（grand opening），還是

舉辦汽車展覽（auto show）或者新代理商（dealer）的開業剪綵（cut a ribbon），內部和外部的溝通都非常重要。

Passage Translation 段落翻譯練習

In order to develop awareness and increase sales for events, we should keep in mind the three Es of event marketing: entertainment, excitement and enterprise.

Entertainment is available everywhere in our society. Years ago, people had to make a special effort to leave their homes to attend the theater or a sporting event to enjoy entertainment. They are now saturated with convenient home entertainment options on television, CDs and DVDs, computers, and videos. Key to your marketing success is the need to provide entertainment that will once again compel your audience to leave home to experience something they will not find there, because what you are offering is different, unique, and designed just for them.

Excitement may seem intangible, but it is real.It is key to making an event memorable. Excitement may be generated by entertainment that "blows the doors off the place": the great band, the dazzling magician, the fabulous party staged in the atrium lobby of a resort hotel. Entertainment may also be part of a tribute to an industry leader, a new corporate logo introduced at a sales conference, or a celebration of an association's anniversary. The point is that it should always be considered as part of an effective marketing plan.

Enterprise is a "readiness to take risks or try something untried; energy and initiative". It is the characteristic of the pioneers in event marketing. It is the willingness to drive marketing's original landscapers into the imagination and conscience of the publics.

Lesson 33 Marketing Sport Event Sponsorship 體育賽事贊

助營銷

導讀：

隨著社會的發展和進步，人們越來越重視體育活動，各種類型的賽事也層出不窮，體育活動的營銷和管理也隨之成為一個重要的領域。那麼，在體育活動的營銷工作中，如何拉取贊助以及向誰拉取贊助呢？本篇文章正是從以上兩個問題著手，詳細闡述了營銷贊助的對象以及如何有效地獲取贊助。

The sport event management and marketing field is big business and has grown enormously during the last few decades. From small participatory events to the mega hallmark events seen by millions, this industry has mirrored the explosive growth of media, entertainment and tourism.

In order to market sport sponsorship successfully, you should:

◆ Seek funding, create a business plan in which you meticulously list all of your procedures for capitalizing and producing the successful sport event in a profitable manner;

◆ Consider prosperous individuals, corporations, foundations, venture capitalists and public entities as potential sources of funding;

◆ Seek sponsorships early and prepare an attractive sponsorship proposal that lists various levels and categories of investment and describes in detail the benefits the sponsor will enjoy;

◆ Take advantage of the packaging technique.

Who Are Likely to be Sport Event Sponsors

Once you have prepared your plan, it is time to shop for prospects to invest in your sport event(註1). The sources of funding broadly fall into the following groups:

Corporate and individual sponsors. For business, sport is an easy way to communicate. Sport has existed for years and is understood by almost everyone. Corporate sponsors are typically large organizations that wish to reach a mass target market and use sponsorship as a nontraditional technique to introduce their brand to new consumers. For local wealthy individuals, they sometimes are also interested in investing sport event.

Foundations. They are the easiest and most competitive sources of funding to identify. A foundation is a charitable trust or other tax-exempt, tax-deductible organization whose purpose is to distribute financial grants.

Venture capitalists. This individual or group of individuals specialize in funding small, start-up enterprises(註2). However it may be difficult to find venture capitalists who are willing to provide financial support for a one-time or hallmark sport event. In order to minimize their risk, the venture capitalists prefer to invest in those with excellent financial reports and prospects for long-term growth(註3).

Financial institution. They are indeed where the money is and an excellent source for sponsorship. As part of a sponsorship agreement, banks may provide a line of credit. Nations Bank, for example, is a sponsor of the 1996 Olympic Games in Atlanta and has arranged for a line of credit for the organizing committee based on expected revenue.

Public entities. This sector is another funding source that has become more prevalent. Local, regional and State governments may provide seed money, with or without restrictions(註4).

Others. It may include other sport organizations, your vendors (e.g. printer, insurance) and other related enterprises.

Reasons for Sport Event Sponsoring

Generally speaking, there are four most common reasons to support a sport event:

Brand awareness — to increase and maximize exposure or change perception;

Sales promotion — to increase and enhance sales volume;

Opportunities for consumer research — to reach specific or new target audiences;

Opportunities for sponsor's personnel or guests to have VIP access to sport event — to encourage and reward sales people and customers(註5).

What Benefits Can a Sponsor Expect to See

Sponsorship has become a complex process involving signage, hospitality, ticketing, merchandise, sampling, point-of-sale and in-store promotions, celebrity appearances, bounce-back coupons, video news releases, and other devices to help the sponsor maximize their sport event investment. All sponsors expect you to do your homework and to present not only a great idea but also a detailed marketing plan informing them the benefits they will receive.

In general, sport event marketers can promote to the prospects the following key benefits.

Title rights: Sponsor's name to appear in the title in the following manner: The XYZ Sport Event presented by ABC Sponsor;

Print advertising: Event program, event stationery, fliers, posters, T-shirts, tickets, media release with sponsor's name included;

Television and radio exposure (if applicable) and the right to use the event footage in the future;

On-site recognition during event: Banners, blimps, booths, and other signage;.

Pre-event promotions: Venue open-house, media day, autograph signing, athlete and/or coach press conference;

Promotions during event: Booth displays, product sampling, public service announcements, interactive experiences, sponsors name on athletes, and volunteer uniforms;

Entertainment opportunities: Box seats, reserved seats, sky suite, VIP parking passes, hospitality tent, catering, VIP reception, sport clinic, athlete personal appearances in hospitality area, transportation and hotel accommodations;

Relationship building between sponsor, spectators and charity;

Logo use in corporate advertisements and promotions;

Merchandise rights;

Direct mail lists;

Market research opportunities as approved by sport event manager;

A summary report detailing media exposure and results of any internal research(註6) (e.g. Sponsor recall or event public image);

Renewal option: right of first refusal to retain sponsorship(註7);

Marketing plan prepared by sport event account representative to assist sponsor in extending its sponsorship and merchandising of its product or service.

Packaging

The buzzword in sport event marketing today is packaging. World Cup Soccer tested this concept by incorporating television-advertising time into its corporate sponsors package. As more and more large-scale events seek sponsorship, smaller properties, for example, will need to make alliances with other sport properties. Summer prosperities will perhaps need to acquire a winter property so that you can go to a sponsor with an integrated package in the same way as the International Olympic Committee(註8).

It is advised that sport marketers find a medium and a supermarket sponsor, then will have the guaranteed reach and trade commitment that make selling cash sponsorship much easier.

Setting Sponsorship Level

There are many categories of sponsorship that can be sold. The generic levels of sport sponsorship are:

Title sponsor: The primary sponsor whose investment allows its name to be listed within the event title; for example, Pepsi Open Golf Tournament. All sponsorships are typically product category exclusive, which prohibits competing companies or product lines from also sponsoring the event(註9).

Presenting sponsor: mentioned after the name of the event, for example, The Rose Bowl, presented by AT&T. Not as valuable for the sponsor as title sponsorship, as most times the media in writing about the event will drop the name of the sponsor(註10).

Exclusive category sponsor: A sponsor whose cash, product and/or services investment is less than the title sponsor.

Single event or day sponsor: This sponsor has usually directed its sponsorship toward a specific category of the event program such as the torch run, award ceremonies, a stage where entertainment may be featured, opening, half, or closing ceremonies, one race (e.g. 100 meter dash) or one day of multi-day event.

Official sponsor: This sponsor may provide both financial and in-kind support through the donation of products or services crucial for the sport competition (e.g. balls, mats, gymnastic equipment, timing devices)

Media sponsor — print, radio, television, web site sponsors.

Co-sponsor — company that is part of an event with other sponsors.

Individual donors.

Others.

When determining sponsorship levels, you must first estimate the value by examining all data available to you, including television rating points, newspaper column inches, the value of cost per thousand attendees at the event, seeing a banner, or sampling a product(註11). According to Ukman of the International Events Group, "one of the primary factors in the determination of sponsorship fees is the cost of media in your market. The same property in Cleveland is not worth nearly as much as the same in Los Angeles. Then you look at the competitive marketplace." Is your sport event the only such event within 200 miles, or are there five others? Is your event a first-time event or is it established(註12)? What is the cost to sponsor other properties similar to yours? For example, if the event entitles the sponsors to on-site sales rights of soft drinks or hot-dogs, then it may be worth more to some sponsor in that category than to a bank(註13).

Warnings

When developing your sponsorship plan to attract prospective sponsors, marketers should bear in mind their motivations, and remember that sponsors are not banks and that sponsorship fees are more than charitable donations(註14). Marketers should treat sponsors as their most precious asset, maintain a client service attitude, and look ways to enhance the relationship. Here are three important warnings, which may get your sponsorship proposal rejected:

◆ Focus on benefits to you, not benefits to the sponsors;

◆ Focus on how much money you need, not the value to the sponsors;

◆ Present your proposal in an unorganized and hard-to-follow format. This type of proposal will leave the reader asking, "How good are these people anyway?" and "How do I justify spending this much money?"

Vocabulary 內文詞彙

mega	大型的，巨大的
hallmark	標誌，特點，特徵
funding	資金，款項，財源
meticulously	謹慎地，小心地
capitalize	為……提供資本
venture capitalist	風險投資商
public entity	公共實體

target market	目標市場
a charitable trust	慈善基金機構
exempt	免除，豁免
deductible	可扣除的，可減免的
prevalent	流行的，普遍的
vendor	商家
brand awareness	品牌知名度
signage	標誌，標識
point-of-sale promotion	銷售點（零售店）促銷活動
celebrity	名人，名流
bounce-back	回音，反響
footage	（影片的）連續鏡頭
banner	旗幟
blimp	軟式小型飛船
booth	展位，展台
pre-event promotion	事前、活動前促銷活動
open house	開放接待日，開放參觀日

media day	媒體宣傳日
press conference	新聞發布會
interactive	互動的
box seat	（運動場）正面看臺的座位，（戲院等的）包廂座
reserved seat	預留座位
sky suite	高空俯瞰套房
hospitality tent	社交活動室
logo	標識，商標
buzzword	行話
television-advertising time	電視廣告時間
title sponsor	冠名贊助商
presenting sponsor	指名贊助商
exclusive category sponsor	獨家贊助商
official sponsor	正式贊助商
in-kind	以貨代款的，實物的

Notes to the Text 內文註釋

1.Once you have prepared your plan, it is time to shop for prospects to invest in your sports event.

一旦你制定好商業計劃後就該著手物色潛在贊助商來對你的運動項目進行投資了。

2.This individual or group of individuals specialize in funding small, start-up enterprises.

這類個人或個人團體專門為新成立的小企業提供資金。

3.In order to minimize their risk, the venture capitalists prefer to invest in those with excellent financial reports and prospects for long-term growth.

為了使風險最小化，風險投資商一般傾向於投資那些財務狀況良好、具有長期發展潛力的體育活動。

4.Local, regional and state governments may provide seed money, with or without restrictions.

當地、地區或國家政府會提供一些種子基金，這些基金會附帶一些限制條件或者根本就沒有限制條件。seed money：用以吸收更多資金的種子基金。

5.Opportunities for sponsor's personnel or guests to have VIP access to sport event — to encourage and reward sales people and customers.

贊助商本人或者其客人可以作為貴賓參加活動——以此來激勵和獎勵銷售人員和客戶。

6.A summary report detailing media exposure and results of any internal research.

總結報告，內含詳細媒體報導情況以及所有內部調研結果。

7.Renewal option: right of first refusal to retain sponsorship.

續簽贊助優先權：擁有是否續簽贊助的優先取捨權力。

8.Summer prosperities will perhaps need to acquire a winter property so that you can go to a sponsor with an integrated package in the same way as the International Olympic Committee.

經營夏季體育活動的企業可能有必要和經營冬季體育活動的企業聯合起來，這樣就可以像國際奧委會那樣向贊助商推出一個綜合的整套產品。

9.All sponsorships are typically product category exclusive, which prohibits competing companies or product lines from also sponsoring the event.

所有贊助都是獨家產品贊助，它禁止競爭對手企業或同類產品對活動進行贊助。

10.as most times the media in writing about the event will drop the name of the sponsor：因為大多數時候，媒體在報導活動時會略去贊助商的名字。

11.including television rating points, newspaper column inches, the value of cost per thousand attendees at the event, seeing a banner, or sampling a product：這些資訊包括電視收視率、報紙專欄版面尺寸、每千名觀眾的成本價值、是否看到旗幟廣告、是否試購產品樣品。

12.Is your sport event the only such event within 200 miles, or are there five others? Is your event a first-time event or is it established?

你們舉辦的體育活動是方圓200英里內唯一的體育活動，還是另有5個其他的體育活動？這樣的體育活動是第一次舉辦，還是已經舉辦過多次？

13.if the event entitles the sponsors to on-site sales rights of soft drinks or hot-dogs, then it may be worth more to some sponsor in that category than to a bank：如果本次活動賦予贊助商在現場銷售軟飲料或熱狗的權利，那麼它對此類產品贊助商的吸引力就大於對銀行贊助商的吸引力。

14.and remember that sponsors are not banks and that sponsorship fees are more than charitable donations：並且要記住，贊助商不是銀行，贊助費也絕不是慈善捐款。

★★★★

Useful Words and Expressions 實用詞彙和表達方式

旅遊服務品質	service quality in tourism
旅遊服務規範	service specification in tourism
旅遊服務品質標準	standards of service quality in tourism
旅遊服務品質評定	evaluation of service quality in tourism
旅遊服務品質認證	validation of service quality in tourism
旅遊投訴	tourist complaint
旅遊投訴管理	handling of tourist complaint
旅遊安全管理	management of tourist safety
旅遊投訴理賠	settlement of tourist complaint
旅遊服務供方	service supplier in tourism

旅遊服務組織	service organization in tourism
旅遊服務企業	enterprise of service in tourism
旅遊定點企業	designated tourism enterprises
旅遊服務特性	characteristics of service in tourism
旅遊服務提供	service delivery in tourism

Exercises 練習題

Discussion Questions 思考題

1.What is sponsorship?

2.How do you understand the corporate sponsors of the sports event?

3.What benefits can a sport sponsor expect to see?

4.What are the differences between the title sponsor and presenting sponsor?

5.When making a sponsorship plan, what mistakes should a marketer try to avoid?

Sentence Translation 單句翻譯練習

1.在選擇營銷媒介和材料（media　and　material）時，大多數會議策劃者（meeting　planner）都會利用一種綜合的方法，將同一資訊做成不同版本（version），在不同的媒介中傳播。

2.旅遊廣告的目的是使用大眾傳播媒體向目標市場傳遞產品和服務資訊，並說服消費者購買產品。

3.節事營銷者（events marketer）透過對市場的深入調查能夠及時發現市場趨勢，對不斷變化的需求做出反應。

4.幾年前，橫幅（banner）廣告僅僅包括位於網頁（web page）上方的簡單的靜態（still）廣告，而現在由於新科技的出現，伴有影片和聲音的動態（moving）廣告有可能設計出來。

5.主辦方（host）最主要的責任就是要保證展會的客流量以滿足參展商（exhibitor）的要求，吸引他們以後繼續參加展會。

6.為了增加展會的客流量，主辦方可以邀請參展商發放獎品（prize）、樣品（sample）甚至風味小食品（local flavor）來吸引更多的人參觀自己的展臺。

7.在展覽、節日和營銷活動中可以經常使用「免費」一詞，因為它能吸引人們的注意力。

8.如果你想使街頭促銷活動（street promotion）充分引起公眾的注意，就選擇在市中心或其他人流眾多、交通發達的地方舉行活動。

Passage Translation 段落翻譯練習

Sport and special events parallel one another in numerous ways. Many people consider sport events to be a subset of special events and therefore share a number of things in common.

Professional and amateur sport requires rules to operate orderly and successfully. These rules may take the form of customs, traditions, protocol, or established player/team safety regulations. Rituals such as the singing of national anthems or the procession of athletes have become traditions; as such, their occurrence has become an unwritten rule in most sport special events.

The outcomes in both sport and special events are unpredictable. However, success is more likely with training, planning, and practice. Large corporate sponsors such as Coca-Cola and M&M Mars invest heavily in research to attain the greatest return on their investment. Coca-Cola's marketing strategy typically includes painting the town red and white with ads, billboards, umbrellas, and chairs while M&M Mars lights up the surrounding landscape with its product colors of orange, green, yellow, and brown. The planning takes years, not days, of careful preparation on signage placement; media buys; local, national, and international retail promotions; sales incentive contests; on-site hospitality; travel; accommodations; and ticketing to ensure success.

References 參考書目

1.Abbott, JeAnna(美), DeFranco Agnes(美), 王向寧.會展管理.北京：清華大學出版社，2004

2.Mason, Barry & Hazel Ezell. Marketing: Principles and Strategy. Texas: Business Publications, Inc., 1987

3.Bayne, Kim. The Internet Marketing Plan. New York: John Wiley & Sons, Inc., 2000

4.Boyd, Harper W Jr., Walker, Orville C.Jr., Larreche, Jean-claude.營銷管理（英文版）.大連：東北財經大學出版社，1998

5.Cateora, Philip R.International Marketing.McGraw-Hill Companies, Inc., 1996

6.Catherwood, Dwight W., Van Kirt Richard L.The Complete Guide to Special Event Management.New York: John Wiley & Sons.Inc., 1992

7.Chen, Po-Ju and Pizam, Abraham.Cross-Cultural Tourism Marketing, "Journal of Travel and Tourism Marketing", 01/01/2005

8.Coltman, Michael M.Tourism Marketing. New York: Van Nostrand Reinhold, 1989

9.Coltman, Michael M.Introduction to Travel and Tourism and International Approach.New York: Van Nostrand Reinhold, 1989

10.Foster, Douglas.Travel and Tourism Management.Macmillan Education Ltd, 1985

11.Graham, Stedman, Goldblatt, Joe Jeff, CSEP, Delpy, Lisa, PhD.The Ultimate Guide to Sport Event Management and Marketing.McGraw-Hill Companies, Inc., 1995

12.Herskovits, Melvin.Man and His Works. New York: Alfred A.Knopf, 1952

13.Hodgson, Adele.The Travel and Tourism Industry — Strategies for the Future.Pergamon Press, 1987

14.Holloway, J.Christopher.Marketing for Tourism.Prentice Hall, 2004

15.Honey, Martha.Ecotourism and Sustainable Development.Island Press, 1999

16.Kandampully, Jay.Services Management: The New Paradigm in Hospitality.Sydney: Pearson Education Australia, 2002

17.Kotler, Philip, Bowen, John, Makens, James.Marketing For Hospitality & Tourism.Prentice Hall, 1996

18.Leonard, H.Hoyle, Jr.CAE, CAP, Event Marketing. New York: John Wiley & Sons.Inc., 2002

19.Leones, Julie.A Guide to Designing and Conducting Visitor Surveys.http://ag.arizona.edu

20.Middleton, Victor T.C. & Clarke, Jackie.Marketing in Travel and Tourism, third edition.Elsevier Butterworth Heinemann, 2001

21.Mole, John.When in Rome.New York: Amacom, 1991

22.Morgan, Michael.Marketing for Leisure and Tourism.Prentice Hall, 1996

23.Morrison, Alstair M.Hospitality and Travel Marketing.Delmar Publishers Inc., 1989

24.Ricks, David A.Blunders in International Business.Cambridge, Massachusetts: Blackwell Publishers, 1994

25.Russ, Frederick A., Kirkpatrick, Charles A.Marketing.Little, Brown and Company, 1982

26.Seaton, A.V.Tourism the State of the Art.John Wiley & Sons Ltd., England, 1994

27.Skinner, Bruce E., and Rukavina, Vladimir.Event Sponsorship.New York: John Wiley & Sons.Inc., 2003

28.Swaroop, Aaditya.Experience Marketing: Changing the Conventional Definitions.PGP (2003-2005) .http://www.indiainfoline.com

29.Timothy, Dallen J.& Boyal, Stephen W..Heritage Tourism.Pearson Education Ltd., 2003

30.Vellas, Francois and Becherel, Lionel.The International Marketing of Travel and Tourism.Macmillan Press Ltd., 1999

31.Watt, David C.Leisure Tourism Events Management and Organization Manual.Longman, 1992

32.Watt, David C.Event Management in Leisure and Tourism.Addison Wesley Longman, 1998

33.William, Nickels.Marketing Principles (second edition). New Jersey: Prentice

Hall, Inc., 1982

34.Wilson, Ralph.Planning Your Internet Marketing Strategy.New York: John Wiley & ons, Inc., 2001

35."Zikmund & d" Amico.Marketing (second edition).New York: John Willey & Sons, Inc., 1986

36.Ohio Division of Travel and Tourism.Designing and Conducting a Survey

37.Learning Thru Leisure Consulting.Defining Tomorrow's Tourism Product: Packaging Experience.http://www.canadatourism.com

38.Aaditya Swaroop.Experience Marketing: Changing the Conventional Definitions.PGP (2003-2005). http://www.indiainfoline.com

39.Experiential Marketing.http://www.1000ventures.com

40.Experiential Marketing.http://www.brcweb.com

41.Experiential Marketing: How to get customers to Sense, Feel, Think, Act and Relate to Your Company and Brands.http://www.bizsum.com

42.http://gulliver.trb.org

43.阿德萊恩· 培恩，服務營銷，影印版，北京：中國人民大學出版社，1997

44.菲力普· 科特勒，阿姆斯特朗· 格里著，趙平，戴賢遠，曹俊喜譯，市場營銷原理，北京：清華大學出版社，1999

45.菲力普· 科特勒，營銷管理——分析、計劃、執行與控制，第九版，北京：清華大學出版社，2001

46.羅薩林‧ 馬斯特森，戴維‧ 匹克頓，營銷學導論，北京：北京大學出版社，2004

47.萊斯‧ 拉姆斯頓（英），旅遊市場營銷，大連：東北財經大學出版社，2006

48.勒‧ 盧姆斯頓，旅遊市場營銷，大連：東北財經大學出版社，2004

49.王向寧，會議和展覽會英語，北京：清華大學出版社，2005

50.向萍，旅遊英語，北京：高等教育出版社，1998

51.修月禎，旅遊英語選讀，北京：高等教育出版社，2000

國家圖書館出版品預行編目(CIP)資料

旅遊營銷英語 / 王向寧主編. -- 第一版.
-- 臺北市 : 崧博出版 : 崧燁文化發行, 2019.02

　面 ；　公分
POD版
ISBN 978-957-735-662-8(平裝)

1.英語 2.營銷管理 3.讀本

805.18　　　　108001811

書　名：旅遊營銷英語

作　者：王向寧主編

發行人：黃振庭

出版者：崧博出版事業有限公司

發行者：崧燁文化事業有限公司

E-mail：sonbookservice@gmail.com

粉絲頁　　　　　　網　址：

地　址：台北市中正區重慶南路一段六十一號八樓 815 室

8F.-815, No.61, Sec. 1, Chongqing S. Rd., Zhongzheng

Dist., Taipei City 100, Taiwan (R.O.C.)

電　話：(02)2370-3310 傳　真：(02) 2370-3210

總經銷：紅螞蟻圖書有限公司

地　址：台北市內湖區舊宗路二段 121 巷 19 號

電　話：02-2795-3656　　傳真：02-2795-4100　網址：

印　刷：京峯彩色印刷有限公司（京峰數位）

定價：800元

發行日期：2019 年 02 月第一版

◎ 本書以POD印製發行